The HOUR of the INNOCENTS

ROBERT PASTON

The HOUR of the INNO CENTS

A Tom Doherty
Associates Book
New York

THE HOUR OF THE INNOCENTS

Copyright © 2014 by Robert Paston

A Forge Book
Published by Tom Doherty Associates, LLC
175 Fifth Avenue
New York, NY 10010

www.tor-forge.com

Forge® is a registered trademark of Tom Doherty Associates, LLC.

Library of Congress Cataloging-in-Publication Data

Paston, Robert.
   The Hour of the Innocents / Robert Paston. —First Edition.
         p. cm.
   "A Tom Doherty Associates Book."
   ISBN 978-0-7653-2681-2 (hardcover)
   ISBN 978-1-4668-1540-7 (e-book)
   1. Rock groups—Fiction.   2. Nineteen sixties—Fiction.   I. Title.
   PS3616.A8656H68 2014
   813'.6—dc23

                                                                    2013025473

Forge books may be purchased for educational, business, or promotional use. For information on bulk purchases, please contact Macmillan Corporate and Premium Sales Department at 1-800-221-7945, extension 5442, or write specialmarkets@macmillan.com.

First Edition: May 2014

Printed in the United States of America

0   9   8   7   6   5   4   3   2   1

To my wife,
whose taste in music has
improved since high school;

to my brother,
who got all the musical talent;

and to my co-conspirators in Leather Witch:
It was punk rock a decade too soon.

ACKNOWLEDGMENTS

Special thanks to Bob Gleason, masterful editor and former steel worker, who "got it."

After-comers cannot guess the beauty been.

— GERARD MANLEY HOPKINS, "Binsey Poplars"

The
HOUR of the
INNOCENTS

ONE

The Army gave him a last fuck-you haircut on the way out. It made him look out of place even in the American Legion.

The vets who returned that year were different. I witnessed the change from the bandstand, week after week, from midnight on Saturday until three on Sunday morning. Their predecessors had come home from Nam, drained their GI savings to buy a Chevy Super Sport or a Plymouth Barracuda, and plunged into doomed marriages with high school sweethearts. Those former soldiers and Marines kept their hair as short as their tempers, got union cards through family connections, and shrugged off their years in uniform. When they came out to get drunk, the music was just background noise.

The Tet Offensive divided the past from the future. The vets who came home after that were as apt to buy a Harley as an Olds 442. They grew their hair—not hippie long, but defiant. Drugs arrived. And the new returnees asked us to play different songs. Instead of "Louie Louie," they wanted numbers from the Doors or the Stones or Cream. The fights that spilled outside onto the sidewalk continued, but these weren't the old collisions of tomcat pride. These fights were sullen. As if the vets were following orders they hated.

Matty Tomczik looked like a barroom brawler when he walked in.

He was defensive-lineman big, and that last military scalping had cut so close to his skull, you couldn't be sure of the color of his hair. With a wide Polish face and a fist-stopper nose, he came across as one more dumb-ass coalcracker unsure of what to do with his limbs in public. Later, I learned that what I read as oafishness was a shyness so deep, it crippled him around women.

Matty was surrounded by women that night. Angela, the wife of our bass player and front man, led Matty in with a pack of her giggling friends, beauticians and candy-stripe nurses who recently had discovered marijuana. Angela's long blond hair shone. A year before, when I first joined the band, she had worn a beehive and toreador pants. Now she had a San Francisco look, copied from magazines and complete with purple-lensed glasses she didn't need.

Working through the rote licks of "Light My Fire," I watched my enemy invade my world. The party's arrival at the side of the bar was a sloppy, happy explosion, with Angela posing for the crowd and waving to Frankie. Angela was the star of her own show and the perfect wife for Frankie, who'd shortened his last name, Starkovich, to Star for his stage persona.

The volume from our amplifiers reduced Angela's entrance with Matty to a pantomime: "Vestals Leading a Minotaur to the Sacrificial Altar." The song's roller-coaster organ riff kicked in one last time—Ray Manzarek's four bars of genius—and we wrapped up the song to spotty applause. Someone shouted, "Heavy, man!" But it hadn't been "heavy." It was plastic, the musical version of monkey-see, monkey-do. I hated playing other people's music note for note. But that was the price to be able to play at all.

I had fantasized about playing a number that would let me show off when Matty the Legend appeared, something that would let me go beyond aping parts from somebody else's record. I wanted to fire off a guitar solo that would shut him down from the start. I had pushed Frankie to announce "The Stumble," so I could riff on Peter Green's version from A Hard Road, but he blew me off with, "Later, man. That's not first-set stuff."

Now it was too late. The room's attention deserted us for the new arrivals. Angela and her gang got things going just by filtering through the crowd in search of a table. Attached or stag, the males were *interested*. With their paisley fabrics, beads, and scarves trailing over tight bell-bottom jeans, those girls promised sex that would soar beyond the typical backseat muggings of our world.

It was an illusion, of course. They were the same girls from Shenandoah and Frackville as ever, dressed up for a costume party. They were still as hard as anthracite.

Trapped under teased hair and with an extra blouse button undone for Saturday night, the other women in the room were less welcoming than their dates. Angela was a threat. And her girlfriends, judged by peers, were trashy sluts. It amazed me that Angela never got into a fight with another woman, given how she behaved when playing hippie. On the other hand, she still had a reputation from her years at Cardinal Brennan. She was all peace signs now, but Stosh, our drummer, claimed that Angela's preferred move in a catfight had been to grab just enough hair from the other girl's temple to rip out a patch of roots the size of a quarter.

She floated across the dance floor, towing Matty the Minotaur. His body seemed reluctant, and the expression on his face was dumb bewilderment. But his eyes were already fixed on my guitar.

I wouldn't have minded if he hadn't come home from Vietnam.

All right, okay," a preening Frankie told the microphone. Sweat had begun to darken his red hair and he braced his fists on his hips the way Mick Jagger would. When I auditioned for the band the year before, Frankie had still worn a ducktail. Now his hair inched below his collar, long enough to draw calls of, "Yo, faggot!" when he walked down a coal-town street.

"Ladeeez and gentlemen . . . ," Frankie went on, "we've got something special for you this evening . . . I mean something really special . . . just back from his all-expenses-paid vacation in Vietnam . . . on his first night home . . . our old guitarist from the days of yore, when the Destroyerz were known as the Famous Flames . . . Matty Tomczik."

I was seated in the audience by then, down in the thick of the cigarette smoke and beer stink. It pleased me when the response to Frankie's announcement didn't amount to much. The crowd didn't remember Matty.

" 'Purple Haze,' " somebody shouted from the bar. "Play some Hendrix, man."

I looked past the couples on the dance floor, most of them women facing other women. Matty silently tested the fret spacing on my Les Paul. His hands were the size of baseball gloves, with swollen-looking fingers, as if he had worked a lifetime in the mines. Hanging from his big shoulders, my guitar looked like a toy.

" '*Purple Haze,*' " the guy at the bar yelled again. He was one of those characters who were always around, small and scruffy, with a ragged mustache and wire-rims, one of the drunks who pretended to have drug connections. But I was grateful for his taste in music. I could never get the intro to "Purple Haze" just right when we played it, couldn't quite hear the odd combination of notes. Jimi Hendrix heard things others didn't and played things others couldn't. Matty had been away for two years, much of that time in Vietnam. He'd be stumped.

I *needed* Matty to disappoint his old friends, his schoolmates from up the line who had ducked the draft. It wasn't just that I was sick of hearing about what a great guitar player he was. I was scared. I had been with the Destroyerz for almost a year, the only replacement guitarist who worked out for them. We'd built a following. People even knew some of the songs I'd written myself and asked for one every so often. Now Matty was back, and although no one had said a word about it, I knew I was on my way out if he had any chops left.

I longed to smash their closed circle. The other members of the group were all older than me, in their early to mid twenties, and they shared that secretiveness, the inside-joke attitude, that people from the Hunkie towns north of the mountain used to exclude outsiders.

And I was from Pottsville, the county seat, which passed for civilization. To them, I was a born enemy, with a name that wasn't from Poland or parts east. After a year of playing gigs two or three nights a week, with practice sessions sandwiched in between, I was still shut out of every serious discussion among my three band-mates. I was just hired help. In a damned good band. A band that could go places, if Tooker got his act together on the keyboards. And I wanted to go places.

Up on the compact stage, Stosh leaned forward over his drum kit, combing the sweat from his mustache with his fingers and listening as Frankie conferred with Matty and Tooker away from the mikes. Frankie fingered a few bass notes, then stopped in the middle of a riff. I couldn't hear anything they said. Matty shrugged. Frankie leaned toward him, speaking, gesturing. Matty shrugged again and Frankie turned back to the microphone.

"All *right*! This one's for all you Hendrix fans out there. . . ."

Stosh laid down the tempo with his drumsticks and Matty took it away. He nailed the opening. As if he'd been playing Hendrix from the cradle.

Frankie edged his Fender bass up against the mike stand and shouted, *"Purple haze . . . all in my brain . . ."*

Matty curled the notes of the solo, hitting every microtone. He stood still, feet apart, eyes closed, head nodding just a few inches from the low ceiling. His fingers were dancing elephants. But they *danced*.

Matty shouted across the stage, and instead of returning to the vocal, Frankie and Stosh kept the bass and drums going, while Tooker—who'd been bluffing an organ part—dropped out. Matty just took off. Riffing wildly, beautifully, humiliatingly. Making his own music. Going to places that were Hendrix but weren't. As if Matty had merged with the wild man on the LPs.

Musicians are masters at rationalizing away a rival's talent, but Matty was too good. I sat there, alone at a side table, burning. His playing was brutal and melodic, dazzling, just pouring out of him. I could feel an electric change in the room. Even the serious drinkers knew something was happening. Every soul in that scuzzy, crowded Legion hall stopped and *listened*.

I hated it.

Matty didn't drag it out too long. At the perfect moment, he returned to the familiar riffs and Frankie howled the song to its conclusion, slapping his bass and rolling his shoulders, as dramatic as Matty was solemn.

The applause seemed almost as loud as the music had been.

It wasn't going to be one song and done, either. Matty meant to keep on playing. And I'd just go on sitting. I felt as if every other soul in the room knew that I was about to get the boot. All the hangers-on who wanted to talk about guitarists and groups with me, who begged me to get stoned with them, who wanted something from me they couldn't explain . . . they had Matty now. And Matty was one of their own.

After a round of dap-slaps onstage, heads came together for another conference about what to play next. Angela dropped into the chair beside mine, tossing her Indian scarf back over a shoulder. It was stifling in the room, but there wasn't one bead of sweat on her.

"He's good, ain't?" she said. "That Matty?" Smiling her all-purpose Angela smile. Beneath an embroidered black vest, a purple jersey gripped her breasts.

"Yeah," I said. Desperate to sound unfazed. "He's good."

Tooker hit a D on his organ and Matty tuned my guitar.

"And you're sitting here thinking he's better than you, ain't?"

"He's older," I said quickly.

"You think you'll ever be that good? You should hear him when he doesn't have a case of beer in him."

I opened my mouth to speak, then realized she was teasing me. Angela had a brilliant grasp of the weak points of her victims.

"*'Wipe Out!'*" somebody yelled. One of the old-timers, a shot-and-a-beer guy.

Angela leaned closer. She smelled of marijuana and Avon perfume. Up close, her features were one edge too sharp for beauty. A north-of-the-mountain girl trying to put it together, she was one of those blondes who look great from ten feet away.

"You didn't call Joyce. All week."

"We didn't hit it off."

"She thinks you did."

"We aren't a good match."

"You balled her."

I shrugged. "I'm not sure who balled who."

Her smile grew harder. "You always got to make out like you're so grown-up and hip. You're just a kid, Bark. And everybody knows it. What are you, one year out of high school? Playing in a band with the big boys. Like you're Eric Clapton or something. And you screw one of my best friends and don't even call her? I thought you rich kids were raised up to be gentlemen?"

"We're not rich."

I waited for her to say something mean about my father killing himself.

Instead, she told me, "I should pour this fucking beer over your head, you know that? For how you treated Joyce. She's not one of those college tramps of yours." Her inscrutable-Angela smile returned and she tapped a cigarette out of a flip-top box. "And stop looking at my tits." She lit up with a crimson Zippo, sucked in the smoke, blew it toward me, and said, "They're not my best feature, anyway."

Rather than dumping her beer over my head, she reached out and ruffled my hair, which was worse. "You're such a little snot," she told me. "Reading poetry to her and all. To *Joyce,* for Christ's sake. She couldn't understand half the words. You had her wondering if you were ever going to shut up." Stubbing out the cigarette she'd only begun to smoke, Angela rose. "She had a good time, even if you didn't. You'd better call her, before she tells her boyfriend."

Laughing, Frankie stepped back to the lead mike. "Okay, folks. Let's set the time machine for 1963!"

They really did play "Wipe Out," the ultimate un-hip surf-guitar tune, a staple from their old days together. Schuylkill County's answer to Keith Moon, Stosh hammered up the drum break. When they came back to the guitar line, Matty took off again, playing speed-freak riffs that took the main theme to places Coltrane might have found if he'd played electric guitar. Matty's baseball-glove fingers leapt out of each other's way as they bent the strings. He turned that barfly instrumental into a psychedelic march, playing lines so fast and crowded that it seemed he'd have to break off to catch up with himself. He snagged the guitar's volume nob with his little finger and cranked it up.

The crowd started to howl. Half of them were standing. I stood, too.

Five minutes earlier, I'd been anxious for him to hand my guitar back to me, to let me play out the set. Now I wanted him to keep going, at least until the next break. Even on my best night, I couldn't rival him. I couldn't come close. I'd never heard anyone who wasn't already famous play so well. I didn't want to follow him without an interval; fifteen minutes to let people forget.

He played the way I dreamed of playing.

When the applause died down, I shouted a request: " 'Goin' Home!' "

With Frankie showboating on the vocal and an extended solo from Matty, that one song would finish off the set.

Matty came down and took the chair that Angela had warmed. She was up on the stage with Frankie, talking to him as he toweled off.

"Thanks for letting me play your ax," Matty said. He spoke slowly, as if he found words hard to form.

"No big deal, man."

The guy who'd called for "Purple Haze" came up. Looking at Matty, he said, "Wow, man. Like that's all I can say, you know? *Wow.* That was some heavy shit. It was like Jimi was right in this room."

Matty looked down at the wet rings on the table.

"Welcome home, man," the intruder went on. "I been to Nam, too. FTA."

Matty nodded but didn't raise his eyes.

Stosh turned up with two bottles of beer and edged the fan aside. "Band talk," Stosh told him.

"That's cool. I'm cool with that. Just play more Hendrix, man." He walked away.

After handing Matty a Rolling Rock, Stosh sat down and tugged his shirt away from his chest: red satin, with mother-of-pearl buttons. "Cripes, it's hot," he said. Black hair clung to his neck and gleamed with sweat.

"They're too cheap to turn on the air conditioners," I said.

But Stosh was talking to Matty, not to me. "This is just June. Wait until August. You never played a hellhole like this. It gets like a locker room nobody cleans."

Matty swallowed some beer and turned to me. "Frankie says you write songs."

"Don't get him going on that subject," Stosh warned. "You'll never hear the end of it."

"Yeah, I've written some songs."

"I'd like to hear some."

Was he just trying to make me feel better? He had to know the score.

"I'll ask Frankie if we can play a couple next set," I told him.

"Bark, you don't learn *nothing*," Stosh said. He turned to Matty. "He's like a dog that won't learn." Stosh wiped his bandito mustache with the back of his hand and gave me a wise-up look. "You don't *ask* Frankie, Bark. You *tell* him. Or the shit never happens. Ever hear *me* ask Frankie for anything?"

Up on the stage, Angela's greeting scene with Frankie had turned into an argument. Stosh followed my eyes. "Never changes. It's always the same old story with them two." He grinned. "He needs to be more careful, though."

Angela stepped off the stage and marched for the door. You could see the school-hallway tough girl revive with each step, as if she'd tear off those love beads and shout curses.

"I better head this off," Stosh told Matty. "If she finds Tooker, they'll light up some smoke and he won't show for the set."

"Doesn't Marlene come to the gigs anymore?" Matty asked.

"Marlene? Not for years. Stays home with the kid." Stosh grimaced. "I wish to hell she *would* come and keep Tooker straight."

I was surprised when Matty didn't trail his old pal. Instead, we watched Stosh weave between the tables, fending off conversation traps, free drinks, and requests for songs. I figured that Matty wanted to talk some more, maybe to tell me himself that I was out. But he didn't say anything. He even seemed to have forgotten his beer. He stared at the stage. The jukebox played "(Sittin' on) The Dock of the Bay."

I had no way of knowing that Matty had spoken as many words as he did in a normal week.

Trying to make conversation, I asked, "So . . . what was it like in Nam?"

"Hot," he said.

TWO

No." I stopped playing and held up my right hand. "That's not how it goes."

The music petered out. Everybody was sweating and nobody was happy. But it was my song and I wanted Frankie to get it right.

"It's not 'she wasn't *that* special at all.' It goes 'she wasn't *so* special at all.'"

"What's the difference?" They all looked at me. Frankie had a stranglehold on his bass. Stosh panted behind his drum set, as wet as if he'd been hit with a bucket of water. Matty caressed the Stratocaster he'd just bought. Smelling blood, Angela and Joyce perked up from their swoon on the couch where the warehouse employees took their workday breaks.

Tooker had gotten the boot, not me. We were going to be an all-guitar band, with no keyboard player. When I got the call the day after Matty's return, I expected the worst. Frankie just reminded me that practice was at four. Tooker wasn't there when I arrived. I had no idea how the decision had been made, and Tooker's name had not been mentioned for the last two weeks.

I stepped up to my mike. I still felt insecure, but I was determined to get this right. "Just listen for a minute, okay? Listen to the way the line glides when you sing 'so.'"

Yeah, Cinderella married that handsome prince,
But her morning-after manners made him wince.
He soon found out that she wasn't so special at all,
Just another slut . . . who turned up at the ball.

We'd been rehearsing for almost three hours in the warehouse behind the printing operation Frankie's old man owned. It was miserable under the metal roof, but the warehouse was the only place where we could crank up our amps when we practiced. We'd begun by getting down "Jumpin' Jack Flash," which had just been released that week, then we worked through some standards to carry us through the remainder of the gigs the old band had booked. Finally, we had gotten to my new song, "Glass Slipper." It wasn't coming together.

When I finished singing, no one spoke. Matty tuned his high E string. He didn't seem interested in any lyrics—just the music—but I expected a smart-ass comeback from Frankie.

Stosh tapped his sticks on his snare rim, then said, "Well, *that* won't be our first Top Forty single."

"Just change 'slut' to 'loser' for AM radio."

"Okay, Shakespeare," Frankie told me. "'She wasn't *so* special at all.' Written from experience, no doubt."

Joyce sobbed massively and ran out of the building. Angela went after her.

"Hey, don't take the car," Frankie yelled.

Angela paused at the door and said, "Assholes."

"What's the matter?" Matty asked. It was the first time he'd said a word since helping each of us perfect our parts on the Stones song.

Stosh laughed. "Joyce robbed the cradle. She probably thinks the song's about her."

I was stunned. The possibility had never occurred to me. I was just trying to write with an edge, with swagger. The way my songwriting heroes did. The song wasn't about anybody.

"Bark reads them poems, you know that?" Frankie added.

Matty played a riff. Loud. It was the guitar intro to my new song. Matty had changed it, shifting the syncopation to make it punchier and adding two quick notes. He stopped, then played it again.

It infuriated me. That was *my* song, *my* riff.

Stosh came in on the drums, alive again. It worked better Matty's way. You could not listen to that guitar line and hold still. It was more of what I had wanted to write than what I came up with myself.

I picked up the changes and doubled Matty on the basic riff. The music *moved*.

Matty jumped the riff an octave higher, then tried a modal counterpoint. Frankie punched in the bass line and started to sing. Everything came together. It was one of those unexpected miracles that made all the frustrations and jealousies worth enduring, the reason we didn't knock each other's teeth out and go home.

We played straight through to the closing verse, with Frankie faking the lyrics he hadn't yet memorized. I had left a one-bar break for a drum fill in the middle of the last line. When we broke off the guitars and bass, we heard a car pulling out.

"Shit," Frankie said.

As I rolled up the microphone cords, I watched Matty put his new guitar away. It was a sunburst-finish Strat, nothing special, but he dried the fret board and body even more carefully than I wiped off my treasured Les Paul. He laid the instrument in its case as if soothing an infant in a crib.

Frankie and Stosh came back from loading speakers into our van. Frankie went to the water cooler, tapped a drink, and asked, "Who's going to Joey's party? I need a ride."

"You going to leave the van here?" Stosh asked.

"I'm not taking it to Joey's. Shit disappears."

Stosh shrugged. "I'm not staying late. I got work in the morning."

"A ride over's all I need. Angela'll be there with the car. Matty?"

"I need a shower."

Frankie laughed. "Soldier-boy needs a shower. Come on, man. Everybody wants to see you."

To my surprise, Matty turned to me. "Want to ride over with me? I'm just going to stop and get a shower."

"If Joyce—"

"She'll get over you," Frankie said. "Sweet Jesus. She's been fucked so many times her brains are fried. You can show Matty how to get to Joey's new place."

We finished loading the van in the last slanting sunlight. By the time Matty and I got on the road to St. Clair in his car, the air rushing in the windows had started to freshen. Since coming home, Matty had bought the Strat, two Fender Twin Reverb amplifiers, and a '62 Buick Skylark perfect for a drooling geezer who scratched his ass in public. Matty drove the back way, over a southern spur of the mountain. We passed between huge waste banks sprouting birches. Close by the roadside, a row of derelict company houses sank into the earth. The colliery behind them had been stripped to its skeleton.

"I need a favor," Matty said. He spoke slowly, as if reading from a scrap of paper in bad light.

"Sure, man. What?"

"We should change the name of the band. Can you come up with a new name?"

"Frankie and Stosh won't listen to me."

"I'll say it was my idea. If you just come up with the name."

"What's wrong with the Destroyerz?"

"We need a new name," Matty said. That ended the conversation.

Matty lived with his mother and father in a company house in St. Clair, a town shit on by history. The grid of streets on the valley floor was surrounded by silt banks and abandoned strip mines. The coal companies had gone, selling off the houses to families that had paid for them many times over in rent subtracted from a miner's pay. Those half-a-double shanties were the county's emblem, built by the thousands before the turn of the century, with indoor plumbing installed after the boys came home from World War II with change in their pockets.

I knew what the layout would be before I walked through Matty's front door: You went straight from the porch into a parlor furnished with a mock velvet sofa and chairs grouped around a console TV with the Virgin Mary on top. From the long wall, framed photos of the pope and JFK kept an eye on her. You continued through a dining room cluttered with knickknacks to the hard light of the kitchen, the family's ground zero. The table would be chipped at one corner from a refrigerator door swung wide on Saturday nights. Upstairs, two cramped bedrooms shared a bath. A sulfurous basement held a coal furnace and boxes of Christmas decorations stacked in a corner. Tuberculosis and ghosts lurked in the walls.

Matty's mother was a classic, her torso a sack of coal. Even at the end of June, a black cardigan warmed a flowered blouse buttoned to the neck. Mrs. Tomczik's graying hair was pinned to fit under a kerchief, and her cheeks had the suck that comes from discount dentures.

She stood in the kitchen, making a pot of halupkies. She said they weren't quite ready, then asked if we wanted to eat.

"Where's Pop?"

"He isn't come back."

"I'm going to get a shower and go out."

"You be careful, you hear me?"

Matty started to form a word, then changed his mind. He dashed up the steps, carrying his guitar case.

"Mrs. Tomczik? May I please have a glass of water?"

She turned from the stove. "I like that, when a boy has good manners." She could barely reach a glass from the cupboard. "I always taught my Matty good manners. Please and thank you. Yes, sir; no, sir. Father Stephens always said Matty was a perfect little gentleman."

The shower came on upstairs. Matty's mother fumbled around her kitchen with poor-health slowness. She handed over the glass of water—no ice—and really looked at me for the first time.

"Don't you get hot? With your hair hanging down like that? A boy with such nice manners shouldn't wear his hair like a girl."

"It's the style," I said. For lack of a better answer.

"My husband don't think it's right. I hope my Matty won't get ideas. My husband would go after him with the scissors."

I figured her husband would have to be an awfully big man to shear Matty, who looked as if he could put his fist through concrete.

"Matty's a grown man," I said. "He's been in the Army. In a war."

"But he had people to take care of him in the Army. Who's going to look after him now? I just don't want him getting in any trouble."

"You're looking after him. Aren't you?"

She almost spoke, then didn't. For a few seconds, she bore an uncanny resemblance to her son.

I drank my water. I could have downed several more glasses but felt odd about asking for a refill. Mrs. Tomczik turned back to her pot of cabbage rolls, adding tomato sauce from a Mason jar.

"Do you have any other children, Mrs. Tomczik?"

"Matty got one older sister."

I was struggling to make conversation. "Does she still live around here?"

"She's gone."

"Oh. I'm sorry."

"She's gone to New Jersey."

"Oh."

She turned toward me, wiping a big spoon with a dishcloth. "Tell me the truth now: Matty don't take drugs, does he? Yous don't give him no drugs, do yous?"

Matty came thumping down the stairs. His hair had grown out blond since he came home. A quick toweling hadn't quite dried it.

"Nobody gives me drugs, Mom." He bent and kissed her cheek.

"You be careful. Don't stay out too late."

The front door opened before we reached it. The man who came in had been tough when younger and still had a miner's forearms, but his belly was monstrously swollen now and his face looked as though it had been scoured with dry steel wool. Matty had four or five inches on him, but they both had the same pug nose.

"Pop," Matty said. He kept moving, veering around his father, who grabbed at his arm and missed.

"You *were* a bum. And you're *still* a bum," the older man said. "The Army didn't do nothing for you."

I accidentally met his eyes. They belonged to a really good hater. I smelled liquor.

"Aren't you going to introduce me to your girlfriend? Isn't that your girlfriend? I'm *talking* to you, boyo."

Matty ignored him. When the screen door clacked shut behind us, the red-faced man opened it again. "Bringing his queer friends around here," he announced to the world. "My son—"

Then he began to cough and couldn't stop.

Joey Schaeffer's new place was a shabby A-frame in the Lewistown Valley and, so far, one step ahead of any search warrants. The house hid in a tree line up a rutted road. A dead Volkswagen van sat in a fallow field, and the scent of manure rose from nearby farms.

A keg of beer sat in a tub of ice by the front door, but the party was inside. Joey wasn't big on décor, but he did have a terrific Fisher stereo system that only he was allowed to touch. Stoned, drunk, or both, women and girls danced on scuffed floorboards, with a few guys worming clumsily between them. Down a hallway, black lights turned an affectionate pair into ghouls. Most of the guests sat on cast-off sofas or cross-legged on the floor, rising now and then to share a hash pipe or joint outside—Joey's rules said "No drugs inside the house," a lesson he learned when his brother went to jail after spending an inheritance on lawyers. The other reason to go out to the backyard was to use the outhouse. The inside toilet had been clogged for days.

The guy who'd cried out for "Purple Haze" the night of Matty's homecoming coaxed me to share a bong with him up in the woods. I still couldn't recall his name. I told him I was already too wasted. It was a lie. I wasn't the least bit stoned, and I was even going easy on the beer. I had tried a lot of drugs, very fast, the year before, when the Summer of Love out in San Francisco turned into the Autumn of Dope across the country. At first, LSD was magic. Then it turned into black magic in the course of a trip with an unwashed girl from Philly. As for the lesser narcotics, pot or hash made music seem richer and more profound, but I didn't like the loss of control that came with them. I wasn't one of those musicians who function well when stoned. I took a few shallow tokes if pressed—enough to reassure people I wasn't a narc—then sat back and watched the show.

The Hendrix fan drifted off into the cigarette smoke. The Stones' *Aftermath* LP boomed on the stereo. At the first notes of "Under My Thumb," Angela materialized, blond hair decorating flesh bared by a scarlet tank top. She dropped onto the sofa beside me. Our shoulders touched.

"I am *soooo* stoned," she said.

"You're never that stoned when you say you are."

She thought about it. "Is that right?" she asked at last. With a giggle. I smelled her familiar scent of cheap perfume, pot, and woman. No one else smelled quite like her. "I guess you know all about me, Mr. Rich Genius?"

"I've told you: I'm not rich. We never were." It exasperated me when the subject came up. My mother was on the verge of losing her house, and my father's funeral bill had not been paid. "Frankie's old man has more money than we ever did."

"Frankie's fucking father . . ." She reached over, chose a strand of my hair, and stretched it between us. "You should come by the salon and let me trim you up."

Jagger sang, *"Under my thumb . . . is a Siamese . . . cat . . . of a girl . . ."*

Following my thoughts, Angela said, *"I'm* not under anybody's thumb."

"Where's Frankie?" I asked.

"Where do you think? Getting stoned out of his fucking mind on Joey's Oaxacan. If he keeps going in late, his old man's going to dock his pay, the tightwad bastard."

"When you leave, you need to take Joyce with you," I told her.

"I'm not responsible for Joyce."

Her tone told me they'd had a fight after leaving our rehearsal.

"That guy she's dancing with?" I said. "With the biker colors? He's with the Warlocks. Him and his buddy."

"I didn't come over here to talk about Joyce." Angela rearranged herself. Our shoulders parted, then came together again. Being a little stoned flattered her. It softened the tough-girl set of her mouth and eased the sharpness of her facial bones.

"What, then?"

"Matty. You think Matty's stupid. Don't you?"

"He's an incredible guitarist."

"But you think he's a dummy. Ain't?"

"I never said that."

"But you *think* it." She reached a hand across her breasts and ruffled my hair. "*I* know what's in that head of yours. We're more alike than you think. You and your house on Mahantongo Street."

"I don't live there anymore. We lived at the wrong end, anyway."

"You think you're better than us. *I* see it. Even if the rest of them can't figure it out. You look down on us."

I didn't have to respond. Frankie burst into the room again, laughing and pushing back his long red hair. All the girls and women looked his way. The range of females drawn to him always surprised me. But it was a great quality in a front man.

He glanced toward us, then edged in among the dancers, doing his onstage moves and lip-synching. No one else could have brought it off without looking like a fool.

"He's such a dickhead," Angela said.

"For the record, I don't think Matty's stupid."

"You're a liar." She leaned against me harder, so I could feel the bone beneath the flesh and smell her breath. "But I forgive you. You know why? Because you're just a funny kid. Most of the time you don't even know you're making it up."

"What's your point, Angela?"

"You know I dated Matty? Before Frankie. Not that we were serious or anything." She laughed. "Matty wouldn't do nothing the priest hadn't blessed in writing." She laughed again, with a bitter edge this time. "That wasn't a problem with Frankie."

"I can't picture you with Matty."

"Neither could Matty's mother. Look out for that one. She puts on her poor old babushka act, but she's a bitch." Angela rubbed against me, as if feeling a sudden chill. "You know Matty never skips mass on a Sunday morning? Never. I don't know if he's scared of God or of that old witch with her pinned-up hair."

"What about his father? I met him today."

"That prick. He's the reason Matty didn't go to college. Bet you didn't know that, Mr. Genius. Matty had a scholarship. To study mathematics. He was smarter than the teachers. But his old man shamed him into joining the Army."

"I thought he was drafted?"

"Matty wouldn't of ducked out like some people we know. But his old man made him join up."

"Why?"

"For Matty playing music. His old man wanted him to play football, he had his heart set on it. Matty was supposed to be this big football star. They even redshirted him in sixth grade. It was all his old man ever cared about. And Matty let him down. All Matty wanted all his life was to play music."

Joey put a Sam & Dave album on the turntable and notched up the volume. *"Hold on, I'm comin' . . ."* Meth was going around for the first time, getting people to dance at parties again. Frankie twisted and waved his arms in the center of the pack, facing one girl and then another. The only one he avoided was Joyce, who was still paired off with her biker.

Angela lit a cigarette. "Look at him," she said.

"How did Matty's father shame him into joining the Army?"

She smirked. "Ever hear of 'covering quarters'?"

I shook my head.

With a mocking laugh, Angela said, "No. You wouldn't of heard of it. I bet nobody in your family ever heard of it. Ask Stosh. Just don't ask Matty, okay?"

"Okay."

"Anyways, Matty got these two uncles." She sucked on her cigarette, then resumed speaking before all the smoke had left her lungs. "One's a Statie, a real crazy cop. That's Johnny, the youngest brother. He gets the final say in things, though. Except when the older brother, Tommy, puts one over on both of them. Ever heard of Tommy Tomczik and the Polka Masters?"

"No."

"They were big up our way. Anyhow, Tommy saw right off that Matty had talent—Matty started out playing the accordion, you know that? You should see the pictures, you'd freak out. This big Polack kid with a red accordion and a bright blue suit with the pants too short. 'Little Matty, the Wonderful Wizard of the Accordion.' But Matty wanted to play the guitar worse than anything and couldn't get no money to buy one—all the money from him playing with the polka band went straight to his old man, that was the deal to get Matty out of football. Well, this smart uncle, Tommy, notices Matty's real big for his age some ways, but everybody just sees him as a kid. So he's a ringer for covering quarters and nice Uncle Tommy tells him he can raise the money for a guitar, if he doesn't go blabbing to his parents or say anything at confession."

"What's 'covering quarters'?"

"Use your imagination. Or ask Stosh."

On the makeshift dance floor, Joyce hung her arms around the biker's neck. I caught her looking over at me. And at Angela.

"Anyways," Angela continued, "there's this gambling raid on a bar that's supposed to be closed for the night, it's like three A.M. or something. Matty's in the middle of the bust and he's, like, thirteen or fourteen. There's not just gambling charges, there's morals charges, too. Uncle Johnny, the State Trooper, gets his family's part hushed up quick, but he has to tell Matty's old man. Who's got something on the kid after that. Only he doesn't do nothing with it right away. He just holds it back and doesn't say nothing for years. And all the while Matty's terrified his mother's going to find out."

She cocked a knee on the sofa. "His old man doesn't even say nothing when Matty starts playing in rock-and-roll bands. He just waits until that scholarship comes in. Then he lays down the law: Either Matty joins the Army, or his old man tells his mother what he did." When she laughed, the sound was wrong. "Any other guy would've told his old man where to stick it. But Matty was *still* afraid of his mother finding out."

"How do you know all this?"

"From Frankie. They used to be best friends."

"I thought they still were."

She shook her head. "Not really. Something happened."

Joey put on Quicksilver Messenger Service and disappeared again. He was the deejay, master of ceremonies, and bulk dope vendor. I never saw him with a girl old enough to expect a cut of the profits.

Angela brought her face closer. "Don't look down on Matty, Bark. He's different. He's a good person."

Changing speeds, she gave me the full Angela smile and leaned against me hard. "You really do have the hots for me. Ain't?"

"You're Frankie's wife."

She laughed. "Like that makes a difference. You're *soooo* sweet sometimes."

She gave me a fallen-angel kiss on the cheek. Then she rose. She was just wasted enough for it to take two tries for her to get up from the sofa.

"I got to get Frankie out of here," she said. "He got work in the morning."

"Take Joyce with you." The biker was pawing her in the middle of the room. His friend sat watching them.

"Fuck Joyce," Angela said.

With "The Crystal Ship" on the sound system, Angela led Frankie toward the door, saying stoned good-byes. But Frankie broke off, pushing his wife's hand away. He stumbled over to where I sat. Leaning down over me, hand on the back of the sofa, he treated me to a blast of beer breath and stale smoke. He did not look good.

"Don't you let Angela get to you, all right? Don't let her get to you, when she does that flirting thing of hers. She don't mean nothing. The bitch just wants to make me jealous. I just wanted you to know that."

I shrugged. "We were just talking."

"She loves to talk. Don't she just? She did her first line of meth last week. Kept me awake all night with her yakking. Listen . . ." His face was soaked, and he smelled like a high school chemistry lab. "I just wanted to tell you . . . you're okay, you know that? You're okay, man. That song, the new one?" He shook his head. "You're a mean motherfucker, you know that? But it's good, you know? I just wanted to tell you . . . I really . . . like that song . . ." He smiled. Smiling wasn't Frankie's strong suit. He always tried to hide his teeth onstage. North-of-the-mountain dental care. "I just wanted you to know, all right?"

"Thanks. You'd better go, man."

"Don't worry about her. She just wants to drive to where we can pull over and screw. She likes things crazy."

I thought it more likely that they'd pull over for Frankie to puke. I'd never seen him so far gone. He generally kept his shit together. Tooker had been the one with the problem.

"You need a ride home, man?" Frankie asked.

"I thought you and Angela had plans?"

He closed his eyes and nodded. About to fall asleep and drop on top of me.

"Yeah . . . I forgot."

He woke himself up and showed me his crooked teeth again.

"Just another slut . . . ," he sang in my face, "who showed up at the ball . . ."

He staggered back to where his wife stood waiting.

The beer filtered through and I went out back to water the trees. I didn't intend to use the outhouse, which was vile.

Approaching the end of the yard, I heard someone behind me. It was Joyce's biker. And his pal. One in denim colors, the other in leathers. Goatees on hatchet faces in the moonlight.

"You little fuck," Joyce's friend said. "I hear you don't treat ladies with respect."

I held up my hand in a let's-talk gesture. The biker knocked it down and stepped in close. He jabbed me in the gut. I closed up like a scissors. Before I could recover, his friend said, "Mark him up good. The cunt."

I heard bone crack and the biker in front of me dropped hard to the ground. I saw Matty. He landed a haymaker in the middle of the other one's face, and I recognized the crunch of a broken nose. Mine had been broken in a bar fight the year before and the sound was unforgettable.

Both of the bikers lay on the ground, the first crumpled and motionless on his side, the other on his back like an overturned insect, covering his face with both hands and moaning. Seeping between his fingers, blood shone in the silver light. There had been no real fight.

"You okay?" Matty asked me.

"Yeah . . . ," I gasped. Still chasing breath. "Yeah . . . Shit."

"Want to head home?"

Matty didn't even look back to see if the bikers were coming after us. I thanked him, but he didn't respond.

When we got to his car, he said, "It all happens very fast. It's always very fast. If you're not fast, you're dead." I wasn't certain he was talking to me. Then he said, "Wait here."

"Where're you going?"

"Joyce."

He returned without her.

We drove toward Pottsville on the Tumbling Run road. The headlights drilled a tunnel through the forest.

Just short of the reservoir, Matty asked, "Did you think of anything?"

"Anything what?"

"A new name for the band. You were just sitting there all night. I thought maybe you were thinking about a name."

He seemed hopelessly naïve, believing that I could cook up a new name so quickly. On the other hand, he was right.

"How about the Killerz? With a 'z' on the end, the same as with the Destroyerz. We'd be saying that we're a different band, but there's continuity, too. For the people who are already fans."

"That's no good."

"Then how about something ironic?" I'd been setting him up for the name I truly wanted.

"What's the name?"

"The Innocents."

We stopped at the intersection with Route 61 and turned right.

"You think that's a good name?" he asked as we passed the car wash.

"Yeah. The critics would get the point."

"I'll talk to Frankie and Stosh. You don't mind me saying it's my idea?"

"No, man. Do what works."

"Want to go by the Coney for a dog?"

I was tired and not really hungry. But I said, "Sure."

In Pottsville, the stores that hadn't gone broke slept: Pomeroy's and Green's, the Sun-Ray and the Grace Shop. There wasn't a derelict left on the sidewalks.

"Those bikers were from the Warlocks," I said. "They're a Philly gang. Doesn't that worry you?"

Matty pondered the question for the length of a red light. "They're punks. Or they wouldn't have come after you together. They'll be too embarrassed to say what happened."

We parked by the Capitol Theatre and crossed the street to the all-night Coney Island. I figured we'd eat and leave, but Matty ordered a second chili dog and another glass of chocolate milk, then coffee. And he talked. In that slow, squeeze-out-the-words way of his, as if unwilling for the night to end. The knuckles of his right hand were bloody, but he said his fingers were fine.

"I'm going to work with Stosh for the summer," he said at one point. "Up his old man's bootleg hole. It's good money. When the band gets going right, I'm going to take accounting courses at the McCann School. On the GI Bill."

I almost said something about the math scholarship but caught myself. I wasn't sure how Matty would feel about me knowing.

"Everything's going to be all right," he said. "As long as I can play music." Shy, he looked away from me and toward the withering pies in the glass case. "Everything's going to be all right now. I just want to play music, that's all."

"Me, too." It was the truth. I loved music more than words could express. Only music could communicate what I felt, and one day it would. I was determined that it would. I'd practice, I'd learn, I'd improve. The hour would come when I would play the way I longed to play: as well as Matty did. *Better.* I dreamed of being famous, fantasizing about women and interviews. But that wasn't the heart of it. I loved music so nakedly that I could not have told anyone, even if the right words existed. One day, if I didn't give up, music would love me back. I was willing to sacrifice everything for that.

We talked about the groups we liked and about guitarists. We agreed that our band could be really good, that the ingredients were all there. We just had to want it badly enough, to work hard and not give up. Matty asked me how I'd learned to write songs, and I told him that they just came to me, that I couldn't explain it. I asked how he knew what to play without even thinking about it, and his answer was identical to mine. The night waitress finally stopped glaring at us and just looked out the window, waiting for a miracle.

THREE

I don't know which one of them started it, but by the second set Frankie and the go-go girl were flirting in front of the crowd. Half of the audience probably thought it was part of the act, while most of the rest didn't care. But things became flagrant even by Frankie's standards, and I worried about word getting back to Angela. We always covered for Frankie, but there were limits.

The stage at the Greek's was cramped, with an outlying platform on each side of the dance floor. The stands were for the go-go girls, who were a serious draw for the locals but a pain in the ass for us. The girls weren't strippers, but they were barely a half-step up, performing in skimpy bikinis and, sometimes, go-go boots. These weren't the scrubbed kids from the teen TV shows, but hard numbers out of Philly or Reading. They worked a circuit around eastern Pennsylvania, dancing two weeks in one club and then moving on. They were often bruised in unexpected places.

The music had to support the girls' routines, and we had a list of songs that usually worked, such as "Let's Spend the Night Together," "Sock It to Me, Baby," and a bubble-gum-meets-*Playboy* number from the Blues Magoos, "Take My Love and Shove It Up Your Heart." On weekends, with couples in the audience, we played two slow numbers per set, but only one, on the funky side, when the girls were the main attraction during the week.

The Greek's was the roughest club we played, in the toughest town in the coal region, Shamokin. The joint's real name—in neon—was "The Athena," but everybody in the business just called it the Greek's. Spiro, the owner, was known for his Mob connections, evidenced by his bouncers' freedom to beat drunks to a pulp without fear of the law. When you played Shamokin, you never knew if the night would end in a brawl or a mattress party.

That night was the last gig we played under contract as the Destroyerz. We planned to take a month off to polish new material and to work on more originals. Then, in September, we'd come back as the Innocents. Stosh and Frankie were already booking jobs, with Frankie the face of the corporation and Stosh as the accountant. I never knew a drummer who didn't handle the money.

So we all felt upbeat and loose, although there was an income gap ahead. We believed in the band and argued surprisingly little. But that night at the Greek's, Frankie was feeling *too* loose.

We played "Light My Fire," which had been off the charts for a year but remained the most requested song in the region. Matty did a stunning take on the organ part, punching on his fuzz tone and working his wah-wah pedal to make a sonic miracle. It didn't sound exactly like an organ—there was no way to get that fullness on a guitar—but Matty came eerily close.

Of the two dancers that night, one was overweight and cranky, with bleached hair, black roots, and a belly scar that looked like a centipede. When she danced, you just wanted to look the other way.

The second woman was another story. Compact and lean, with a helmet of black hair and a carnivore's eyes, she looked vicious, depraved, and alluring. Skipping the slut moves most girls repeated, she made dancing erotic through black magic. The eternal vixen, the siren from someplace dark, her name was Darlene, and she scared me.

Frankie was up for it, though. He stole moves from every singer who impressed him. At first the lifts were obvious, but over the weeks he somehow made them his own, becoming greater than the sum of the countless parts he pilfered. On a good night, he ruled the crowd. But Darlene conjured a buried side of him from back in the Famous Flames days, when the boys played stag parties at the Elks or the Odd Fellows. One of their popular numbers had been "I Love You So Much I Could Shit." The other tunes were less edifying. Now Frankie thrust out his crotch as Darlene waved her butt at him, licking her lips at the men around the front tables. When he sang, "Come on, baby, light my fire," it was all a bad act from a strip joint.

As we finished the song, Frankie stepped over to me.

"Hey, I'm going to sing 'Shake Your Moneymaker' tonight. All right?"

That was one of the few songs I got to sing. Except for the simplest harmony parts, I was restricted to one or two of my own songs and the occasional up-tempo blues number, "Look Over Yonders Wall," or "Got My Mojo Working." Frankie, Stosh, and Matty had all been choirboys. They could blend their voices on anything from the Byrds to Philly soul. I didn't fit.

Matty and I usually had a good time trading guitar licks on "Moneymaker," but that night the voltage was missing. We both kept glancing at Frankie and Darlene. It was embarrassing. The other go-go girl had gotten so angry, she barely moved.

The crowd loved it, though. Shamokin was that kind of town.

When the break came, Frankie jumped down to talk to Darlene. She was even smaller standing in front of him than she seemed on the platform. Her teeth were shockingly white. I wondered if they were dentures.

She smiled at Frankie, then traipsed off toward the door that led to the rooms upstairs. Officially, the Athena was a hotel, but I never knew anyone who stayed there beyond the dancers, who were the Greek's temporary property.

Frankie climbed back up on the stage. I had broken a B string and was kneeling to change it. The stage was tight and Stosh had to hand his floor tom over the cymbals so he could escape from behind the drum kit. Before anyone else could speak, Stosh looked at Frankie and said:

"Don't do it, man."

Frankie laughed.

After what he deemed a polite delay, Frankie walked around the bar, then disappeared through the door Darlene had exited.

"He better wear a rubber," Stosh said.

We were used to Frankie's appetites when Angela wasn't around, but we all sensed that this was not going to end well.

It didn't. The last set dragged, with Frankie faking energy he no longer had. He hammed up "When a Man Loves a Woman" so pathetically that we could have passed for a lounge act on the skids. The new string I'd put on wouldn't stay in tune. The crowd thinned. We did what we had to do and were glad to finish.

Our gear was almost all loaded in the van when Stosh went over to get our money from Spiro. The Greek handed him some folded bills. Stosh counted them.

He looked up. Surprised. And not pleasantly.

"The contract's for a hundred and sixty. This is only a hundred and twenty."

"When I booked yous, there was an organ player. Now there's no organ player. So I took out the organ player's pay."

"Spiro . . . hey . . . there's still four of us . . . we been playing this club for years. . . ."

The Greek's top bouncer stepped up beside his boss. Short and thick, with slit eyes, he looked faintly Oriental.

"Yeah, that's right," the Greek said. "One, two, three, four. I can count. And I hope to see the four of yous back on my stage sometime. In the meantime, tell Frankie not to bother the girls on my payroll. Hear me?"

Stosh heard him. I heard him. He spoke loudly enough for Frankie to hear him from the doorway to the street.

Crowded into the front of the van, we rode in silence all the way to Ashland. Then Stosh said, "That forty bucks was your cut, Frankie. No 'share and share alike' this time."

"She was worth it," Frankie said.

· · ·

I was sitting by the window fan in cutoffs, practicing scales, when a woman's footsteps clacked up the stairs outside. It was Angela, wrapped in a drugstore version of Hollywood sunglasses. She tapped on the screen door, shimmering in the light.

"Anybody home?" she said.

She knew I was home. She would have heard my playing, even though I wasn't plugged into an amplifier. Mrs. Dietrich, my landlady and downstairs neighbor, didn't mind girls but wouldn't tolerate noise. Her rules were fine with me, since it gave me an excuse to keep stoners from turning my rooms into a party pad. I wasn't big on humanity that year.

I rested the Les Paul against the lip of a chair and walked toward the figure gauzed by the screen door. When I opened it, Angela seemed startled, unusually diffident.

"It's my half holiday at the salon," she began stiffly, reciting a prepared speech, "and I needed something to do, I just felt like I had a lot of extra energy . . . I thought maybe your place could use a cleaning up. . . ."

I pushed the door wide, welcoming her. "I didn't know you knew where I was living."

"We dropped you off. After the block party. Remember?" She stood in the room's August torpor, taking off her sunglasses to scan my world.

"Have a seat."

"One of your girlfriends clean up after you or something?" She walked over to the kitchenette, peered into the sink, then recrossed the sitting room and prowled into the first of the two tiny bedrooms. My sheets were rumpled, but everything else was in order. Disappointed, she inspected the bath before returning to the main room, where the only mess was a litter of album covers on the floor by the stereo.

"Have a seat," I repeated.

"I can press shirts, if you need any done," she said. She glanced at the guitar. "I mean, I could be doing stuff while you practice, I don't want to bother you. Can I smoke in here?"

I got her an ashtray I kept under the sink. "Like a glass of wine?"

"I thought you people didn't drink until five? I read that somewhere."

"Five in the morning, maybe. People are all the same, Angela."

Head-shop earrings dangled chips of turquoise as she leaned into her lighter. "You don't believe that for a minute."

I opened a bottle of Yago sangria from the fridge and poured two tumblers.

Accepting her glass, she said, "I guess you know all about wines, ain't?"

I looked down at a strangely earnest face framed by pale hair lightened by the sun. She wore a peasant blouse with scarlet stitching. A small gold cross had escaped the neckline.

"You must be hot in those jeans," I said.

She laughed. "Well, that's a line, if ever I heard one."

It had been no more than a clumsy, unfiltered remark. I felt idiotic.

She got through her glass of sangria with north-of-the-mountain speed. Elbow on the arm of the chair, cigarette held high, she demanded, "Tell me about wine. Tell me how rich people drink."

The rich people I'd known before our country club membership lapsed drank highballs as fast as they could. As for wine, I only knew what I'd read in A Moveable Feast.

I poured her a refill. "Tell me before you come over next time and I'll get something really good for us to drink."

She considered the glass in her hand. "Isn't this good?"

"It's all right."

I put Filles de Kilimanjaro on the stereo, low enough to keep the neighbors calm. Angela studied the walls, the reprinted concert posters promoting San Francisco bands and two reproductions of paintings I thought I should like. Neither of us knew what to do next.

"Did you know Joyce moved to Philly with that guy?"

"Who?"

"That guy from the Warlocks."

I shrugged.

"She was always a little slutty," Angela said. She shifted her body, unsatisfied with the chair. Miles blew junkie slow. The electric piano flirted around his trumpet line.

"You really think the band's going to work out?" she asked. "That we'll all get out of here?"

"Sure. Yeah."

"Frankie thinks so. Frankie thinks you're the meal ticket. You and your songs. You and Matty."

"We all need each other."

"*You* don't need anybody. You could just leave and go anywhere you wanted. You're not stuck like the rest of us."

"That's not true."

Our Lady of the Sorrows, Angela shook her head. "He'll break your heart. You need to know that. Just when things get going really good, Frankie'll fuck it up. He fucks everything up."

She finished her second glass of wine and drew her knees together like a good Catholic schoolgirl. "Would you do something nice for me?"

"Depends on what it is."

"I'd like to see the inside of your house. Where you live."

"I live here."

"Please. I've never been inside a house like that. I'd just like to see what it's like. It'd be a trip."

"It's not that fancy. It's not even that big. You all have this crazy idea about my life."

"I know how big your house is. I've seen it. From the outside. It's the one that looks Spanish or Mexican or something."

"Built in the 1920s," I said. "When replacing terra-cotta roof tiles was considerably cheaper. It's the ugliest house on the street. It doesn't fit in."

"I think it's beautiful. I'd really like to see inside it. Just once."

It was Angela's lucky day. My mother had card club on Wednesday afternoons. Anyway, I wanted to fetch some books.

"You'll be disappointed. The furniture's old." North-of-the-mountain people liked shiny, new, and brightly colored things, the bolder the patterns, the better.

Angela offered to drive. She had a white Pontiac Firebird with a red interior. It was the family car by default, since Frankie's MG was usually in for repairs.

I insisted on taking my Corvair.

"I don't see why you want to live over here," Angela said, settling into the front seat of my rattletrap.

"Privacy," I said. But there was more to it than that. I didn't like to go home even for a visit. My mother, who was not old, had started drinking after my father's death. Or perhaps she just started drinking more. After a few months, old friends of my father's began to drop by in the middle of the day. Then there were men I didn't know.

As I drove across town, the air sucked through the windows was too dead to lift Angela's hair. Each red light drew a wave of sweat. Climbing Mahantongo Street, we passed the coal baron mansions and I parked on a middling block where an optimistic professional class had built their homes back in my grandfather's time.

I let us in the front door with my key. The house was stuffy and still. Angela examined the furnishings as if struggling to interpret a foreign language. In her world, wall-to-wall carpeting, not old rugs, signaled luxury. Timid at first, she soon began to touch things: cracked leather on chair arms, the silver frames presenting our edited history. Confronted with paintings, she found nothing to hold her interest and passed into the room that had been my father's study. It had not been dusted in weeks. Mrs. McClatchy no longer appeared, and only certain rooms earned my mother's attention.

Angela felt more comfortable in the kitchen. Appliances were appliances. She ignored the dirty dishes in the sink.

"Can we see upstairs?"

I looked at my watch. "Sure. I want to get some books, anyway."

"You have *more* books?"

I chose a cardboard box from the second pantry and we went upstairs. I let Angela roam while I foraged among the colored spines insulating my old bedroom. I had recently matured from reading Sartre to science fiction.

Angela rested her hand on my shoulder. I had not heard her approach.

"I'd love to have a bedroom like your mother's," she said. "It's like in a movie. Do you think she'd mind if I used the bathroom?"

"I'll meet you downstairs," I told her.

I dropped the box of books by the front door and went back to my father's study. People lied about him. The viciousness that followed his death had knocked the wind out of me. My father wasn't a thief. He was just a fool. And a weakling.

I heard the front door open. I met my mother in the living room, by the foot of the stairs.

"What are you doing here?" she asked.

"Just getting some of my books," I told her. I pointed at the box.

Upstairs, the toilet flushed.

"Who's that?"

"Just a friend. She came along with me."

My mother smelled of breath mints, which was never good.

Angela came down the stairs, half humming, half singing. She stopped on the fourth step from the bottom.

"Mom, this is Angela."

Angela looked like a deer caught in the headlights. She stumbled down the last few steps, brightening desperately, and said, "Mrs. Cross, you have such a beautiful home, I've never seen such a beautiful home . . . it's like, like, I don't know how to describe it, but it's got so much *class*, it's so, so . . ."

A blemish of white powder stood out under Angela's right nostril.

"I'm glad you like it, dear," my mother said. "Now, if you'll excuse me?"

Back in the car, Angela asked, "Did I do something wrong?"

"She's always like that. We're not getting along right now."

"Bummer. But your house is really classy."

"It's not my house. It may not be hers much longer."

I almost reached over and dusted under Angela's nose, then realized she'd be mortified.

I drove back to my rooms in Jalapa, a faded neighborhood in a fading town. I parked the car.

"Can I have another glass of wine?" Angela asked. "I need one."

I carried up the books, eyes at the level of Angela's ass. For the first time, I felt genuinely sorry for her in a way that didn't involve Frankie's antics. She *knew* there was more. She just didn't know what it was. Or that it was far from perfect.

My guitar and the stereo were still there. That was always a relief. It really was the rougher side of town.

Angela kicked off her sandals while I got the wine. I had left Miles on the turntable and she turned the music back on. When I came back from the kitchenette, her earrings and the gold cross lay by the stereo.

She drank her wine halfway to the bottom, then set down the glass. Looking at me, then turning slightly away, she said, "You were right. I really am too hot in these jeans."

She took them off.

Angela stood there for one perfect moment. Slender legs, slightly bowed, rose to light blue panties. The hot breeze from the fan fluttered her blouse. As her expression dissolved from boldness to doubt, I stepped against her.

She was lighter than I expected. I had set the mattress and box springs on the floor, to spare my landlady the drama. Angela and I dropped heavily, awkward for a moment, until our lips rejoined. Kissing someone you thought you knew is one of life's great shocks. Others are so different from what we expect.

Angela kissed brutally. Her lips and tongue craved too much. She held my head with both hands, pulling my hair toward her. Our teeth met. And she bit.

The rest of her body held still.

I pushed up her blouse. She wore no bra. I touched her. I tasted blood, unsure of whose it was.

She moaned the instant I escaped her lips. I slipped down, kissing her neck and shoulders. The salt on her flesh stung. My kisses left flecks of blood.

Her body remained tense, her responses abrupt and confusing. When I touched her through her panties, she almost convulsed.

She pushed me away.

"Please," she said. "No."

I broke the splendid contact of our flesh. Angela sat up hard and pulled down her blouse, drawing her knees against her.

"I can't," she said, shaking. "I'm sorry. I just can't."

I rested my hand against the small of her back, fingers touching cloth, palm on her flesh. My lack of anger surprised me. Perhaps I was relieved.

The music ended. The needle complained, waiting to be lifted.

Low on her back, she had a birthmark the size and shape of a peach pit. I grazed it with my thumb until I realized she was crying. I never connected Angela with tears.

"I wasn't being a cock teaser," she said. "*Please* believe that."

"I know," I told her. For once, I actually grasped what I claimed to understand. What had almost happened was something we both wanted and something neither of us wanted.

I took my hand away. Touching her, even in human solidarity, kept desire awkwardly alive.

"I wanted to fuck you so bad," she said, "and I just couldn't." She had stopped crying. "Would you get me my cigarettes? Please? My purse?"

I retrieved her bag and stood over her, staring down. The powder spot under her nose had been rubbed away. With her eyes pinked by tears and her arms locked over her knees, she looked like a punished kid.

"Angela?"

She raised her eyes.

"I've never seen you look more beautiful than you do right now."

She twisted up her mouth. "You're full of shit. My eyes are all red."
She was Angela-in-armor again. After lighting a cigarette, she let it
dangle from her lips as she went out to pull on her jeans.

I followed and watched her.

"I better go," she said while fussing with her earrings. "Thanks for
showing me your mom's house."

"You okay?"

"Yeah. I just got to go and make dinner for Frankie." But she didn't
move toward the door. She glanced around the room a last time, settling her attention on my books.

"Would you give me something to read? Something you think I'd
like? I'll give it back to you."

"Sure . . . what kind of stuff do you like to read?"

"I liked *Valley of the Dolls*."

I pulled out a paperback of *From the Terrace*. Her hometown,
Frackville, was in it under another name.

"It looks long," she said.

"It's a fast read. If you don't like it, I'll think of something else."

She accepted the book, still doubtful.

"Keep it," I told her.

In a surprise attack, she kissed me on the cheek—that electric
fallen-angel kiss of hers—and clutched the handle of the screen door.

I listened to her sandals on the steps.

When the sound of her car faded, I tried to pick up practicing where
I'd left off, repeating scales in alternate fingerings. But Angela left a
demanding ghost behind. I could smell her, taste her.

My mother phoned in the middle of the A-minor scale.

"Don't you *ever* bring a tramp like that into my house again."

Across the nation, cities were still smoldering. Vietnam led the evening news. Headlines warned of trouble at the upcoming convention
in Chicago.

We didn't care. The band delighted us. Maybe it was Matty, the previously missing chemical compound, but each of us played better and tighter, newly aware of what we brought to each song. The Destroyerz had been four musicians playing at the same time. The Innocents played *together*. Each burst of progress was a high. Except for occasional protest lyrics in the songs we covered, we had no politics.

We had music. Some practice sessions went better than others, but on the good nights, we startled ourselves. Each of us knew that this was something different.

One evening in the dog days of August, we fell into a jam that wouldn't stop. I couldn't play at Matty's level, but he never complained. He just let me take my solos in turn. And I played with a power I could never summon before. The music was alive, a wonderful roar, colossally greater than flesh, strings, and speakers.

It was past time to quit when we killed the jam. We still had to load our gear into the van so the warehouse could get back to business in the morning. But Frankie said, "Yo, hey. Let's do 'Angeline' one more time."

Stosh put down his milk bottle of Tang and started the beat before the rest of us were ready. The song had been aggressive as I'd written it, but as we worked out our individual parts it became an attack of merciless guitar riffs. The bass line pounded and Stosh thumped his drums as if he had murder in mind.

I kicked off the main guitar motif. Frankie entered with a plummeting bass line that hit bottom, then drove forward. Matty screamed in above us, completing a manic, metal world. Stosh machine-gunned with his sticks.

Cocking his head at the mike, Frankie sang:

Oh, Angeline . . . someday I will break out of this waking dream . . .
Angeline . . . science is the mother of the man machine . . .
Angeline . . . I love to watch your wires glow in ecstasy . . .
Oh, Angeline . . . mechanical perfection lying next to me . . .

Stosh came in on high harmony for the chorus:

But how much do you really feel?
Tell me if our love is real . . .
How much does the program mean?
Sweet Angeline . . .

Matty tormented his guitar, slashing the damned with razors, as we crossed an instrumental bridge. We tightened back into another verse and chorus, then it was my turn to solo. I'd worked out a sequence of riffs that climbed the frets until I was bending my B and high E strings halfway across the neck. Frankie swooped down on the microphone for the last verse. His voice was agonized and exactly right:

Angeline . . . they say the pain of love is just a memory . . .
Open up your vision screens and look at me, just look at me . . .
Angeline . . . maybe this is all a programmed memory . . .
Maybe I don't really feel this agony, that's killing me . . .

Instead of driving into a closing chorus, the music stopped as if struck off by an ax. With Matty quietly backing the vocal line on guitar, Frankie sang, almost whispering:

In the sequence of the body . . . I can feel the hand of God.

And that was it. We were drained. I wondered if we would ever play that song as perfectly again.

Frankie laughed. "I can't believe I'm singing a song about screwing a robot. Instead of 'Angeline,' I might as well just sing 'Angela.'"

FOUR

The evening was a disaster. Had Angela been a dog, her ears would have gone straight back when I walked into the practice session with Laura. She went through the motions of greeting someone new, all peace, love, and smiles, but her hostility filled the room like a stink. Angela's hackles had never gone up at any other girl I'd brought around.

And Laura and I had walked into an argument.

"What's this all about, Frankie?" Stosh demanded. "For real?"

"For fuck's sake. It's eight hundred bucks for four nights. That's a lot of bread, man. Plus free rooms."

"The Rocktop's a rip-off. Half the time, Mario doesn't pay up and the union won't do shit. It's the worst dive in the Poconos. You said that yourself, the last time."

"Mario never stiffed *us*. Look, it's four solid nights of work."

"What's wrong with the gig?" I asked.

Stosh turned to me. With his Tartar eyes, bandito mustache, and black hair brushing his shoulders, he looked like a Polish pirate.

"What's wrong is that I got us in as the opening act at the Farm Show Arena in Harrisburg that night. It's a big show."

"For union scale," Frankie said dismissively.

"But it could be a break," Stosh said. "Paul Revere and the Raiders are supposed to headline. We could blow them away."

The polarity in the band had reversed. Stosh was normally the one who put money first, with Frankie concerned about building our reputation.

"The arena's the better gig, Frankie," I said.

"You stay out of it," he told me. "Just write your songs."

Matty spoke up: "We all get a say. Him, too."

I thought Frankie was going to lash out at Matty, but he restrained himself. "Okay, what do *you* think? Four nights and two hundred apiece? Or charity work for one night?"

"Stosh is right," Matty said. "It's an opportunity."

I just didn't get the situation. Frankie knew better.

"I guess I screwed up, then," Frankie said. "'Cause I already signed the contract with Mario."

"You shouldn't of done that." Stosh walked away. "That is really the shits, Frankie."

"Argue later," Matty said. "We need to rehearse."

We tried to make things whole again through the music. But we didn't click. With our first paid jobs just over a week away, we didn't sound awful, but we didn't sound like the Innocents. It was not the introduction to the band that I had envisioned for Laura, either.

Impressed by Deep Purple's cover of "Hush," we'd hunted through older hits for songs we could supercharge ourselves. Matty arranged a medley of early Beatles tunes, recasting them as big-amp white soul. We began with "I Feel Fine," which Stosh howled in his coalcracker-goes-to-Memphis voice, then Frankie took over the lead vocal on "I've Just Seen a Face" as we layered harmonies over roughneck guitars.

The vital organs were all there, but the body refused to come to life.

After sitting politely on the sofa with Angela for a half hour, Laura offered me a smile and went outside with her book. Tenacious in our anger at one another, everyone with a musical instrument attacked Matty's arrangement. The medley rebuffed us.

Lighting another cigarette, Angela followed Laura outside. I hoped she wasn't going to start anything. I didn't want Frankie to pick up on what had gone down between Angela and me.

"Let's try something else," Stosh said, "and come back to this later."

"How about a break?" I asked.

Frankie immediately took off his bass. Stosh stuck his drumsticks into their metal quiver. Only Matty continued to work on his part.

The warehouse held the heat of the late-summer days, but the evenings had begun to darken and cool. I found Laura and Angela sitting on the loading dock, five feet apart, both of them reading in the dying light. Laura had *Les Liaisons dangereuses* in her hands. Angela was reading *From the Terrace*. Or pretending to. There was no hint of a conversation between them.

Frankie came up behind me and took in the scene.

"Now you got everybody reading," he told me.

"Not you, though," Angela said.

"I don't want to ruin my eyes." Pivoting toward me and lighting a cigarette, he said, "She's had her nose in that thing all week. Somebody at the salon gave it to her." He knelt beside Laura. "Excuse me, but we haven't been introduced right. I'm Frankie. The band doesn't always fight like that."

I felt the impulse to hit him. The irrationality of the evening was contagious.

"So, what are *you* reading?" Frankie asked her.

Laura closed the book and handed it to him. "It's about a hustler," she told him.

Frankie flipped through a few pages. The text was in French.

"You read this stuff? You and Bark are going to be perfect for each other."

Angela's profile would have cut steel.

We needed to get back to work. Frankie tossed his cigarette onto the gravel and told Laura, "Watch out for this guy. He's a real lady-killer."

"It's kind of you to warn me," Laura said.

Angela seethed. I would not have been too surprised to emerge at the end of our practice session and find her standing over Laura's corpse. I had been so exhilarated by the sudden advent of Laura in my life that I acted blindly. Bringing her to the rehearsal out of the blue had been a stupid move. I had hoped to impress her and had not given Angela a thought.

The second round of the rehearsal went better. With Stosh a nailed-down dynamo behind his drum kit and Matty standing still while his fingers raced, Frankie and I were developing our center-stage theatrics, playing off each other for an invisible crowd. As the darkness thickened, both women came back in, but neither seemed the least interested in the music. Laura tried to read through the noise. Angela smoked one cigarette after another. The Beatles medley came to life at last, then we worked on Steppenwolf's "Born to Be Wild," which perfectly fit the image we sought to project. When we turned to "Angeline," the performance was crisp, if not as thrilling as during our last session.

By the time we started packing up our gear, everybody had accepted Frankie's maneuver regarding the Rocktop gig in November, although his motivation remained baffling. And there was other business to discuss.

"Joey Schaeffer wants to do our sound," Stosh said.

"What's Joey know about doing sound?" Frankie asked. "Joey's a stoner."

"He's never as stoned as the people around him," I told them. Joey played at being a head, but he calculated the benefits and risks. He didn't make offers impulsively. "What's the deal, Stosh?"

"Joey'll buy his own PA system. Altec Lansing speakers, the works. We don't have to pay him a cent until the band gets going right. Frankie, you're always complaining we need more volume on the vocals."

"What's he want after that, a full cut?" Frankie asked. The role reversal of the earlier evening was playing out again. There were pieces to the puzzle that I didn't have.

"He knows better," Stosh said. "Joey just wants something to do, to hang out with us. He wants be in a band any way he can. And a monkey can learn to work a sound board."

"A monkey with a good ear," I said. "Joey has a good ear for music." When he wasn't in his party master guise, Joey and I listened to music he never played at his tribal gatherings, from Charlie Parker to Tim Buckley.

Joey also struck me as a canary in a coal mine: When he left somebody else's party suddenly, you knew it was time to go. Unlike his brother, Joey was a survivor.

"He want a contract or anything?" Frankie asked.

"He just wants to impress chicks. To strut his stuff."

"Joey really believes in the band," I said. "He told me. After the last rehearsal he came to. I think he just wants to touch the music any way he can."

Matty snapped the buckles shut on his guitar case and said, "If Joey Schaeffer does our sound, he doesn't sell dope at our gigs and he doesn't carry, either. He stays straight, until we're done playing. No second chances."

Frankie said, "Joey'll never go for that."

"Yes," I said. "He will."

Frankie looked at me. "Yeah, I forgot. You and Joey are fish from the same pond."

Joey and I didn't really share a background, except that we both grew up south of the mountain, where the coalcracker accent collided with Pennsylvania Dutch. He and his brother, who was doing federal time, came from a well-off Orwigsburg family, the honest-to-God trust fund set. The parents had burned to death in a car accident. Leaving the Wedgwood Restaurant's bar, they had pulled into the path of a tractor-trailer cresting the hill. Joey had promptly dropped out of college to enjoy his good fortune.

He could afford a sound system, even without his dope business. Dealing was just his way of being cool. Calling himself a "sound engineer" for an up-and-coming group would be a step up in coolness, the way Joey saw things.

"Just think it over," Stosh said. "We can let Joey know next week. We don't play no big halls till the end of the month, except for the Bloomsburg thing."

Laura showed more interest in our discussion than she had in the music. I felt as if we were being studied by an anthropologist.

Breaking down a mike stand, Frankie said, "How about those Jew kids in Chicago? They're getting more than they bargained for, ain't?"

Stosh snickered. "They think Chicago cops are tough, they ought to try Shenandoah after a football game."

"They're trying to change the country for the better," I said. "They're trying to end the war." I sounded insincere, and I was. With a bum knee from playing Midget League football, I was in no danger from the draft and could not have cared less about the protesters at the Democratic convention. But I felt I had to speak up in front of Laura.

"They don't care about the war," Matty said quietly. "They don't know anything about the war."

"Then what, exactly, is all that shit about?" Frankie asked.

"It's about them," Matty said.

Out in the parking lot, Matty followed me to my car. As I came back around from putting Laura inside, he said, "I wanted to ask you something."

I was impatient to be alone with Laura. To see if she thought she'd made the greatest mistake of her life that afternoon.

"I have to drive down to Philly on Saturday," Matty told me. "To visit a friend. I thought maybe you'd like to come along for the ride?"

"Can't. I'm giving guitar lessons until two."

He seemed genuinely disappointed. Then he said, "If I went down on Sunday, instead, would you want to ride along?"

"Sure. If Sunday works for you." It was our last free weekend before we started playing gigs again, and having known her for less than ten hours, I already hoped that I could spend it with Laura. Had anybody but Matty invited me, I would have turned them down. I was drawn to him in a way I could not explain.

"I'll come by your place," he said. "Nine too early?"

"No, man. Nine's great."

He walked off toward his car.

As soon as I got behind the wheel, I pulled Laura to me and kissed her. Her response was not what it had been a few hours before.

"Have you slept with that woman? Angela?"

"No. Almost. But no."

We drove. As we entered Pottsville, Laura canceled the silence.

"She's a vampire."

I met her in the Pottsville Library. Impossible to miss, she looked right through me. Her dark hair was pinned up against the heat and she held a sculptural stillness as she stared at an illustration in a book. She looked demure and effortlessly beautiful, instantly haunting, exquisite. I had never seen anything like her in the flesh, and I felt an unprecedented dread that she'd walk out the door and fade into the sunlight.

The late-summer air hung dense in the narrow hall, resisting the fans. I pulled the books I wanted as quickly as I could and took a chair just down the table, facing her. Given that every other reading table was free, my move was hardly subtle.

Her skin had just enough color to show that she didn't avoid the sun. Up close, her hair was a very dark brown, not black. Dampness shone on her neck.

I made an act of paging through a music text, pausing at opaque charts.

She was studying an art book of some kind. I could see colored forms, but nothing identifiable from where I sat. She refused to look up.

"Art history major?" I whispered when I could wait no longer.

"I don't have a major yet," she said. For the first time, I glimpsed her eyes. Ice blue, they made an unsettling contrast to her hair.

"What school?"

"Penn State."

"I meant the art. The book."

"The Pre-Raphaelites."

"Aubrey Beardsley," I said. His was the only name that leapt to mind. "Fey porn for rich gents."

The sculpture came alive. Her back straightened. Her blue eyes shot me.

"Beardsley wasn't a Pre-Raphaelite," she said. "Although there were obvious stylistic influences in play. He was certainly homosexual, though. Is that why you're familiar with his work?"

Before I could gather a reply, she turned her book toward me, raising it to share the illustration that so intrigued her. She had been studying the portrait of a woman whose face turned back over her shoulder. The model had angular features, pouting lips, clothes-rack shoulders, and a cascade of auburn hair. She was a dead ringer for Frankie.

"Dante Gabriel Rossetti painted her. He was in love with her."

I grasped a lifeline. "She wrote poetry, right?"

"That was his sister."

"It's not really my period."

"What *is* your period?"

"I go for manlier artists. Rembrandt . . . Caravaggio . . ."

She laughed so loud that the librarian froze in place.

"What's so funny?"

"Caravaggio was the most notorious homosexual in Rome. I guess they didn't put that in your book of pickup lines."

"I'm not really good on the Renaissance."

"Caravaggio was early Baroque. Mannerist, actually."

She thrust a small hand toward my books but couldn't quite reach them. I held up the music text so she could read the cover.

"Counterpoint? You must like Bach."

"Sure. I love Bach."

"What's your favorite cantata?"

This wasn't going the way it was supposed to go. I wasn't going to get away with answering "A Whiter Shade of Pale."

"Every one of Bach's cantatas has something special," I told her. "It depends on your mood." I found her more alarmingly beautiful with each new humiliation.

"What about Köchel 527?"

"Absolutely."

She didn't even bother to change her expression. "Don't you *ever* quit? Köchel 527 is Mozart. *Don Giovanni.* Which I'd think would be a favorite of yours. You play the guitar, right?"

"How'd you know?"

"The fingertips of your left hand. I dated a guitarist. Not for very long. What's the other book you have there, Mr. Clapton?"

On firm ground at last, I held it up for her to see. Dostoyevsky. *The Possessed.*

"Which translation?" she asked.

She caught up with me at the crosswalk. To my astonishment.

"I'm sorry for being such a bitch," she said. "You really were endearing."

No girl had ever called me "endearing" before.

"I was a horse's ass."

"Am I expected to argue the point?"

"You're the most beautiful woman who ever stood on this corner."

"Please. No more pickup lines. Truce?" She held out her hand. "Laura Saunders."

"Will Cross." I took her hand and, worried about holding it too long, let it go too quickly. "That wasn't a line."

"Beautiful or not, I'm hungry. And thirsty."

"There's a pizza place just down the block." I tried to remember how much cash I had in my pocket.

The two Italian guys behind the counter at Roma Pizza were befuddled. In their universe, no woman who looked like Laura would have anything to do with a male whose hair fell onto his shoulders.

"You seem to win new fans wherever you go," I said between bites.

"Italian men are hopeless."

"Like guitarists?"

"Rock musicians aren't exactly pillars of society. May I have that, if you're not going to finish it?"

I had intended to eat the rest of my slice, but I passed it over. The request was the first thing that didn't tally with my image of her playing tennis on a grass court and devastating prep school boys.

"I eat like a horse," she said, as if reading my mind.

"You said you're going to Penn State?"

"Schuylkill Campus. I must've committed a grievous sin in a previous life. It's where Penn State dumps third-raters."

"I go there," I said.

Her recovery skills were more agile than mine. "Then we can be third-raters together."

"I asked to go there. So I could keep playing in my band. My mother wanted me to go to Penn, like my father."

"I was accepted at Penn," she said. "The scholarship wouldn't reach, though."

"You don't strike me as a scholarship girl. More 'old money.'"

"You're not a very good judge of people. You and Caravaggio."

"Where are you from?"

"Doylestown."

"Not Main Line?"

"Doylestown. If you want the whole story, my mother's a schoolteacher and my father sells insurance. They're divorced. Penn State may not be Penn, but it's affordable. Unfortunately, the terms of *that* scholarship condemn me to Schuylkill Haven, Pennsylvania, for the first two years *and* to the local dormitory. I arrived yesterday and I'm still figuring out the bus schedules. End of saga."

I knew the dormitory well. It was in a converted Bureau of Mines building across the highway from the miniature campus, which previously had been the county home for the indigent. The girls had no trouble slipping in and out of the dormitory's first-floor windows after curfew.

"Like to walk back to my apartment for a glass of wine? I could show you some of Pottsville along the way."

"Would I find the corpses of your former wives behind locked doors?"

"Bartók," I said. *"Bluebeard's Castle."*

"Well, well! Don Juan's apprentice isn't *all* bluff."

"Look, I know I'm tripping all over myself. But I don't want you to walk away yet. I just don't want you to disappear."

"You really are endearing. Pop quiz. What's your favorite novel? Answer right now. Your fate depends on it."

"Fathers and Sons."

Her playfulness eased. "That's a good answer."

"What's your favorite?"

"Le Grand Meaulnes."

"Alain-Fournier."

"Have you read it?"

"No." I wasn't going to try bluffing her again.

"It's about the way love always disappoints those who believe in it most."

"Do you believe that?"

"I've never been in love. I wouldn't know." Catching me off guard, she reached across the table and seized my hand. "Are *you* going to disappoint me?"

"As long as it's not sangria," she said as I approached the refrigerator.

Pivoting toward the cabinet that protected the cereal and bread from all but the most intrepid mice, I pulled out a bottle of Bolla Valpolicella from the stash Frankie kept stocked for me. Not only wasn't I old enough to buy alcohol in the state store, I wasn't supposed to be playing in bars all night.

When I turned back toward her with the glasses, Laura was still on her feet, despite the heat and the walk.

"You should get rid of the Dalí print," she said, accepting the wine. "You're better than that. Why the Grünewald?"

"I have a Gothic sensibility."

"I'd say you were Georgian. More Joseph Andrews than Peter Abelard." She unpinned her hair and shook it out, then took up her wine again and turned on the concert posters. "I'm afraid I don't really care for your kind of music. Does that disappoint you much?"

"What don't you like about it?"

"It all sounds the same. And the lyrics are silly."

"Ever listen to Jefferson Airplane?"

"No."

"Or Bob Dylan, for that matter?" I revered Bob Dylan.

"I think he's pretentious and silly."

I took her glass from her, set it down, and kissed her.

She kissed me back.

I adored everything about her: her taste, her smell, the fragility that strengthened into wildness and collapsed in elated exhaustion. A first, infatuated coupling often provokes the illusion that no previous sex could ever have been its equal. I already understood that. Yet Laura was different in ways beyond my ken. I lay beside her, with my world upended. The stillness after the blaze of flesh evoked the hyperlucid interval in an LSD trip. All else before that afternoon had been clumsy, childish nonsense.

I opened my mouth to speak, to praise her. She laid her fingers over my lips.

"Don't say anything."

But she and I teemed with arrested words. Inevitably, some escaped.

She broke the impeccable silence. Clutching me tightly, as if suddenly terrified, she told me, "I never wanted anything in my life the way I wanted you."

"That wasn't my first impression."

She hugged me again, less fiercely. "I had to pretend a little."

For the first time in my nineteen years, I feared the passage of time. I did not want the afternoon to end. But the world is as it is. Eventually, I had to go to the bathroom.

"Excuse me," I said. "Just for a minute."

"As long as you come back."

As I rose from our damp sheets, I noticed blood.

"I didn't realize you had your period," I said.

"I don't."

FIVE

I couldn't see why Matty wanted me to ride along to Philly. Every attempt I made to start a conversation died. We skirted Reading, took the turnpike from Morgantown to King of Prussia, then rattled down the expressway. The boathouses and the art museum popped up across the river. All I got out of Matty was that Alvin Lee was a sloppy guitarist and we were going to Philly to check on a guy he knew. The clouds overhead wouldn't rain and Matty wouldn't talk. The radio was all Motown and corn syrup.

After we crossed the bridge, Matty turned away from John Wanamaker's and City Hall. I hadn't expected that. Despite my taste for playing big-amp blues, I was uncomfortable around spades. A previous, naïve trip to North Philly to hear B.B. King at the Uptown had convinced me that I wasn't welcome on their turf, while back in Pottsville, the number of blacks had almost reached the vanishing point. As King Coal died, kick-the-helpless politicians shut down the last struggling brothels on Minersville Street to make way for low-income housing, a boulevard to nowhere, and kickbacks my father shunned, sealing his fate.

During Minersville Street's heyday, Louis Armstrong and Pearl Bailey had played Pottsville, Packards and Cadillacs lined the curb outside of speakeasies, and everyone knew which local doctors had lucrative sidelines. Now our Negroes worked on garbage trucks and kept out of the way. I knew two by name, from Pottsville High. The angry one got a scholarship, the funny one dropped out. On the other hand, if any white boys were entitled to play the blues, it was the coalcracker kids from the patches north of the mountain, whose yonko families had been slaves to the Reading Company and the Lehigh Coal and Navigation. I was along for the ride, just as I was with Matty that cloudy day.

Columbia Avenue still had a smattering of bars and jazz clubs after the Philly riots, but the street looked like an old rummy with gaps in his teeth. The uproar hadn't been as fierce as in Detroit or Washington, but clusters of buildings had burned and shops wore plywood windows. Black Power graffiti covered blistered posters. Two white guys in a clanking Buick Skylark attracted attention.

Matty knew less about that part of Philly than I did. It soon showed. We got squirreled around south of Columbia and west of Broad.

"We're looking for North Bouvier Street. The 1500 block," he told me.

We might as well have been in Africa, with the tribal elders dolled up for church and all the young warriors hungry for a fight.

Matty got us to our destination, though. We parked and faced the mockery of sullen kids. Half my size, they spooked me. None of it fazed Matty.

He pressed the doorbell until convinced it didn't work, then he knocked. A lean kid down on the sidewalk asked, "You cops? You come to bust Crip Carley?"

Matty knocked again, then looked down from the stoop at the kid. To my surprise, the kid retreated instantly.

The door opened. A caricature peered out at us, a heavy woman got up in her Sunday best. Either she wore a wig or her hair had been done by Dow Chemical. She didn't say a word, but waited for one of us to speak.

"Mrs. Carley? Is Gerald home?"

"You police?"

"No, ma'am. I'm a friend of Gerald's."

"He don't sell no drugs, and he don't take no drugs, if that's what you're after."

"Yes, ma'am. If he's in, would you tell him Matthew Tomczik's here to see him? Please?"

It took the woman a moment to process the request. Then a high stone wall crumbled between us.

"That Sergeant Tomczik? The one Gerald went on writing me about?"

"Is he home?"

She turned and shouted. "Gerald! Gerald, you get out of that bed and come down here! Somebody here to see you." Judging me as superfluous, she turned back to Matty. "Sergeant, you talk to my boy. You tell him he got to stir himself up. They took his leg, but he still got a head on his shoulders. You tell him that for his mama, all right? And you come on in here now. Sunday dinner isn't fancy this week, but you're welcome."

The row house was the urban-slum version of the company houses back in Schuylkill County. The odor was strange, as if perfumed, but the only other difference was that the woman's house was scrubbed to perfect cleanliness, a condition rarely encountered north of the mountain. The furniture was equally bright, plush, and cheap-looking, although the picture of Jesus on the living room wall announced a darker Savior.

The footsteps on the stairs sounded like the approach of Long John Silver. When the small young man with the artificial leg had descended far enough to see who had come to call, he spoke the second most versatile word in the English language:

"Shit."

They hugged each other, a bear embracing a jockey. It was the most emotion I had seen Matty display.

When they broke apart, Matty's face became inscrutable again.

His Army buddy's expressions shifted constantly, as if he couldn't decide which mask fit best.

"Shit," he said again. "Shit, I can't *believe* this, man." His Afro looked as if it had been groomed with a flyswatter.

"You watch your mouth," his mother told him. "In this house."

"It's all right, Mama. Sarge here done heard worse."

"Well, you save your nasty language for the street out there. Not in my house." The woman seemed positively exhilarated by our presence. "You boys sit here and visit. I'm going to do my cooking and you all come when I call." She waddled off and left me to imagine the story of her life as Matty and his pal felt their way back toward each other.

"You got a gig yet, Doc?" Matty asked.

"Sure, Sarge. Sure. More than one."

"Don't call me 'Sarge.'"

Gerald Carley shielded his eyes, as if from a spotlight. "Man, I can't believe you're sitting here. Just sitting right here. *Sarge.* Sitting right here. Craziest motherfucker I ever known."

"I thought we could play some music. I've got my guitar out in the trunk."

Alarm pinched Gerald's face. "What're you driving?"

"A '62 Skylark."

Gerald laughed. It sounded like the "tee-hee-hee" of a comic book character. "That's all right. Nobody going to fuss with that car. People got pride."

"Got your sax back?"

"Yeah, I got it, man. And I'm going to pay you back, I'll make good on it. How's Nick Toomey, man? He got to be out now, too."

"He's dead. I wrote you."

Gerald shifted his artificial leg. He handled it like an enemy. "Yeah. I didn't read all the letters. When I first got back. That crazy fucker. Crazy asshole motherfucker." He shut the back of his right hand over his eye. "Stupid fucking honkie motherfucker."

"We all liked Nick."

"How about Everett? What about King Kong?"

"Home. He's okay."

Gerald wiped his left eye. "That dumb-ass nigger's *never* going to be okay. Born to carry a baseplate. Makes me ashamed to think of him, wish I was Chinese or something. He marry that big brown cow? Used to *scare* me with that woman's picture."

"I don't know. Probably."

"He'd be dumb enough to do it. But Nick, man. Nick was all right. The worthless motherfucker. He step on a mine or some shit? That asshole?"

"Blood poisoning."

"You're shitting me."

"He picked something up."

"Shit. What about Mote?"

"Down at Fort Benning. Last I heard."

"Lifer asshole." Gerald let down his chosen mask for a moment. His smooth, small face grew earnest. "Man, you still think about that shit all the time? Nam and all?"

"No," Matty insisted.

"Got a gig yourself, Sarge?"

"Yeah."

"Serious?"

"Bark here writes songs for us."

It was the first time I'd been acknowledged since Gerald came downstairs. I rose and reached out my hand. "Will Cross."

He barely touched my fingers. " 'Will Cross'? Like 'Will he cross the street?' " He tee-heed and put on an armored smile. "This his first trip to the zoo, Sarge? He wouldn't have lasted two weeks in Second Platoon." He shook his head. "Not even two days."

"You would've looked after him, Doc."

"Not a chance." He glanced at me. "He's a born FNG. You just have to look at him. And he'd stay a Fucking New Guy till they stuffed him in a body bag and loaded him in the belly of that Free- dom Bird. That, or they'd make him some dick officer."

"Mind if I use the latrine?"

Gerald pointed around the corner. "Not a honey wagon in sight. And paper on the roll."

Matty rose. From the low chair in which I sat, it seemed his head would scrape the ceiling. The house had not been built to accommodate Polack miners and their broods.

Just before Matty left the room, he turned back to Gerald and said, "He's not an FNG, Doc. That's all over."

I expected Gerald to ignore me in Matty's absence, but he only waited until he heard a door shut before asking, "That crazy motherfucker kill anybody yet?"

"Matty?"

"Yeah. Him. Sergeant T. Sergeant Shake-and-Bake. Who do you think I mean?"

"No. He hasn't killed anybody."

"Well, praise Jesus."

"He's a quiet guy. All he wants to do is play music."

Gerald laughed. *Tee-hee.* But the sound turned savage and the mirth was not supported by a smile. "He's the meanest motherfucker ever *walked,* man. You *never* seen anybody go to killing like that. He *loved* killing fucking dinks. And he was *good* at it. You never seen nothing like it. He *loved* that shit." Staring into his lap, Gerald shook his head. "Me, I hated it. I didn't want no part of whitey's war, didn't want to hurt nobody. So I raised my hand to be a pill pusher. And look what it got me. But Sergeant T, man, he ate that shit up like it was Rice fucking Krispies. And *he* comes back all in one piece, after all that crazy shit he done." Laughter shrank him. "Driving a Buick."

"You're pulling my leg, right?" The instant I spoke, I was sorry for my choice of words.

The aroma of frying seeped in from the kitchen.

Gerald looked at me. I'd never associated brown eyes with such coldness. "*Ask* him. You ask good old Sergeant T." He smiled, flashing yellowed teeth. "Ask him about the time he broke the lieutenant's jaw. You ask him about that." He snorted. "Honkie motherfuckers couldn't make up their minds whether to court-martial him or give him a medal."

A toilet flushed.

"What happened?"

"They gave the crazy fucker a Silver Star."

"Matty won a Silver Star?" I'd read enough *Sergeant Rock* comics and seen enough episodes of *Combat!* to know that a Silver Star mattered.

Gerald laughed. *Tee-hee.* "He didn't tell you that, man? John fucking Wayne didn't tell his homeboys?"

"No bullshit, okay? Matty really has a Silver Star?"

Footsteps approached.

"Shit, no. He got *two.*"

Mrs. Carley had to stretch to feed us, and the food wasn't southern cooking as described by Eudora Welty, but I was grateful enough to take it seriously when she thanked the Lord on our behalf. Eating was rarely at the top of Matty's priorities, although he became impulsively hungry at odd hours. The fried pork cutlets, lima beans, and mashed potatoes put something in my gut for the march ahead.

A laden twist of flypaper dangled above a loaf of bread. The iced tea was sweeter than Kool-Aid.

Our hostess gave Matty an enveloping hug when we left, nodding in my direction. With Gerald toting his saxophone case and teasing Matty about his choice of automobiles, we headed off to a Sunday afternoon jam session. Gerald was anxious to show off Matty's playing, remarking that "these cats never heard a white boy *play.*"

The venue was a blinds-down club where the cigarette butts from Saturday night still lay on the floor and stray glasses remained on tables. The music was as confused as the times. Old dudes with conk-job hair and shiny suits blew cool jazz, while younger musicians with beachball Afros and sunglasses pushed the jam toward electric funk. Blues wasn't on the menu. We sat and listened. Sitting through a full rotation of musicians seemed to be the dues you paid before approaching the stage with your ax.

Instead of reacting against the appearance of two white guys, the musicians and their all-male audience ignored us. It was our turn to be invisible.

Gerald stepped up to take his turn as an ancient drummer who worked with brushes gave way to a sticks man in an African smock. Gerald spoke to the new drummer, then to the dude playing the house piano. The jam moved into a phase that wanted to be electrified Coltrane but drifted between bursts of notes and awkward gaps. Meant to be impudent, the beat meandered. Given Matty's interest, I expected Gerald to be an impressive player, but every time he started to get going, he fell back on stock riffs. His breath control seemed off, too. The bass player was good—an old-fashioned walking man—but the drummer just wanted to break things.

As that round of music petered out, the old guy who'd been doing a Wes Montgomery imitation on the guitar unplugged and stepped offstage. Gerald motioned for Matty to come up. As he crossed the unswept dance floor with his Stratocaster, the audience of musicians moaned theatrically. One loud comment warned of "faggot noise."

Then Matty played. The small crowd's initial reaction was to lean forward and check their ears. The keyboard man began calling changes in key and rhythm, determined to stump Matty. But Matty followed every shift easily. When the trumpet player stepped over to challenge him with a call-and-response, Matty played back every Dizzy Gillespie swoop and curl perfectly. He did the same with Gerald and his sax, then with the piano man. By that time, the other musicians in the room were hooting encouragement, marveling at the talking dog, the white guy who had real chops.

The problems began when Matty took the lead. He dispensed ear-teasing lines and what-was-that? jazz chords so swiftly that I didn't recognize the musician who played with the Innocents. The chromatics were more complex than anything I'd ever heard him play. Nobody could repeat his riffs back to him. And the irony was that Matty never meant to show off. I understood that in my bones. When he played music, he just became oblivious. The demons in his fingers took control.

The jam session tradition calls for musicians to try to cut one another, to outshine rival players. But Matty wasn't out to cut anybody. He was just letting the music inside him escape. And he didn't know how to stop. He wasn't greedy. He scrupulously let the others take their turns at soloing. But each time his turn came back around, he humiliated the other players. He might as well have burned a cross on the corner.

Everybody in the room sensed the swelling tension. Everybody except Matty, who played with his eyes closed, having the time of his life.

The other musicians let the jam die. Gerald quickly took Matty by the arm. Time to go.

As he packed up his Strat, Matty finally came down from the clouds and sensed that something was off. He wanted to say good-bye to the cats. But nobody was interested. He didn't get a word out of them.

One player spoke to Gerald as we left, though.

"Junkie."

Out in the street, Matty turned with a question, but Gerald, who looked shattered, addressed me:

"You know how *crazy* this motherfucker is? You want to hear it? He goes to Bangkok on midtour R and R. You know, Pussy-town? Bang-Cock? Where every normal motherfucker rents him a girl for the week. And you know what this fool does? The great Sergeant T? Think he wants any slope pussy? Not him, man. Not Sergeant fucking T. He *pays* this singsong gook band to let him sit in on guitar for the week. Crazy motherfucker thought all the GIs were clapping and cheering for him when he's up there. They were *laughing* at him, man. 'Cause he's going to go back to Nam and get the shit blown out of him just like everybody else and he don't want no pussy. Just wants to borrow some cheap-ass Jap guitar won't even stay in tune. Man, that gook band *hated* him. Even the whores hated him. 'You number ten, GI.' *Everybody* laughed at him."

"Come on, Doc," Matty said. He tried to edge Gerald aside. Gently. "Let's talk, okay?"

"No more orders for me, Sarge. You crazy motherfucker. What're you going to tell me? 'Stop using and go to Sunday school for your free watermelon'? You crazy white motherfucker? Look what you left me with. Look at me, asshole. You should've let me die."

Matty reached to restore his grip on his comrade's arm. Gerald pulled away fiercely. "This isn't Nam, honkie. I don't need you. And you don't need me. What do you want, my other leg?"

"I don't want anything."

"You're a lying motherfucker. You want *everything*, man."

"Don't be like this, Doc."

"How should I be? 'Yes, Sergeant, no, Sergeant'? It's over, man. Go away."

"I'm sorry, Doc."

"Just fuck off, all right? You don't belong here. You don't need to come around here again. I'll send you your money back. I'll mail it to Asshole, USA."

He pegged off, lugging his saxophone case. Matty took one step after him, then stopped. We stood. Matty didn't know what to do, and I didn't know what to say.

After we'd been standing on the sidewalk for a few minutes, a black cat asked if we were looking to score.

We were already on the turnpike when Matty spoke.

"You should've heard him before. We'd come in from a month in the boonies and just play. But drugs got into him. Being a medic . . . it's a lot to take."

"What happened to his leg?"

"He tried to pull in this cracker kid. From Alabama. No. Mississippi. Corinth, Mississippi. That was it. New guy, cherry. We were spread out, working toward a *ville*. Kid took a nail. They used to shoot to wound a guy out in the open, usually in the leg, so the medic would come out to get him. They loved to kill medics, they knew it got to us. So they dropped this new kid in a minefield. Private First

Class Darryl F. Williams, from Corinth, Mississippi. Skinny kid. I'd just in-briefed him a couple of days before. Doc went out to get him and put his foot wrong. Doc was a short-timer, almost eleven months in-country. Lot of attitude. Officers hated him. But he was a good medic to the end. I saw him carry in guys twice his size."

Matty clicked on his turn signal. "We put out all the firepower we could and I got Doc back. He was crazy, screaming. Didn't want to leave his leg behind. Wanted me to find his leg. He needed a tourniquet fast. I was sure he was going to go into shock or bleed out. But he didn't. King Kong and Nick got him back to the company LZ and onto a medevac. But I couldn't let anybody else go out after the new kid. It was a decision I had to make, they left it to me. He was too far out there, no cover. We just waited while he bled to death. The gooks started yelling at us, telling us to come get him. In this gook English you never stop hearing in your head. They were laughing."

"He said you have two Silver Stars."

"That's not true."

"What *is* true?"

He turned on the headlights and drove into the dusk. "You can't say anything about this. One word, and I'm out of the band. And gone."

"All right."

"They gave me one Silver Star. And a Bronze Star before that. They wanted me to stay in the Army, to go to Officer Candidate School."

"Why didn't you?"

"I hated the Army. I just wanted to come home. And play music."

"What did you do? For the medals?"

"It doesn't matter."

"There was nothing in the papers."

"I cut a deal. With an NCO in Public Affairs. At brigade. He wanted a souvenir AK. He yanked the hometown press releases."

"Why didn't you want people to know?"

Matty thought about it, gathering words. "No man should be proud of what I did."

"He said you loved it."

"Doc never understood."

"He said you were good at it."

"That's different. That was an accident. Like having a good voice."

"Why did you do it, then?"

A shadow in the dying light, he shrugged. "You don't get a choice. It's not like in a book. I wanted to come home. And we couldn't both come home. Somebody had to die. The other guy, or me. I didn't want it to be me. It's nothing to be proud of. It's something to burn in hell for. Let's talk about something else."

But Matty was the one who hadn't finished talking. "I hated every single day I was there," he added. We slowed toward the tollbooth at Morgantown. "I didn't just count days, I counted the hours. I used to do the math in my head."

With the lights of Reading glowing on the horizon, I asked, "Matty? Why did you want me to come along today?"

"So I'd have to come back."

SIX

Angela stood on the landing, holding the paperback I had given her. It felt brutally early.

I pushed the screen door open.

"No. I just wanted to give you this." She held out the book.

"You didn't like it?"

"He only cares about people like you. And your new girl. He makes fun of people like me. People like me and Frankie. Like we're dirt."

"O'Hara didn't like anybody. Not even himself." I pushed my hair back off my eyebrow.

"You happy?" she asked. "With her?"

"We just met."

"But she's your kind. Isn't she? I hope you're happy. Somebody ought to be happy."

"Angela, it's just not the way you—"

"I'm a real person, you know that? I'm not just Frankie's wife. Or some hairdresser slut, like people think. I'm a person, all by myself. And I'm not just somebody to fuck."

"Keep your voice down. Please."

"You would've fucked me. You didn't care. Then you jumped right in bed with your little princess. I bet she drinks perfume so her shit won't stink."

"*Stop it.*"

She crumbled. Sniffing back the wetness in her nose, she said, "Do you know what it's like? To always be on the outside looking in? Wondering when life's going to start? *Real* life? Do you know what that's like?"

She looked as though she hadn't slept. I was tempted to ask her what drug she was on. But that would have rekindled the scene.

"Just come inside. I'm still half-asleep, okay? Let me get a shirt on. I'll make a pot of coffee."

"No. We'd both do something stupid." She began to cry full force. "I'm better than you think I am. I'm better than you know."

We both heard footsteps on the stairs and looked down.

It was Stosh. In his work clothes.

"I was just giving him back his book. It stinks," Angela declared.

Stosh came up beside her. He didn't look the least bit perturbed at finding his best friend's wife in tears at another man's apartment door.

Wiping her face with the back of her hand and sniffling, Angela said, "I got to get to work now."

Stosh watched her go. She threw herself into her car and slammed the door. Grinning, he nodded at the book in my hand.

"That the one somebody at the salon gave her?"

"Stosh . . ."

He was wonderfully amused. "Got any coffee in this dump of yours?"

"Listen . . . nothing happened."

He waved it all away. "Don't worry about it. Everybody knows Angela got a thing for you. We're taking bets on when she's going to beat the living daylights out of that new girl of yours."

I led him into the apartment. He had coal dirt on his boots.

"Who's everybody?"

He laughed. "Even Matty's probably figured it out by now. He's the one to look out for, by the way. I just mind my own business."

"What about Frankie?"

"Frankie isn't worried. He knows Angela. He thinks it's funny. Keeps Angela's mind off what he's up to. He knows she won't give you any. Even if she wants to. Nice Ukrainian girl like Angela won't cheat on her husband for the first five years, no matter what. After that, though, it's 'Katie, bar the door.' You going to make coffee, or not? I got work."

"You going to quit? When the band gets going?" I lit the burner and set the tin pot over the flame.

Stosh snorted. "Think I want to stay down a coal hole all my life? I'm, what, twenty-three? End of every shift, I spend ten minutes blowing black snot in my handkerchief. It's a decent living, though."

"Bootleg holes are dangerous. I worry about you."

"Naw. You don't worry about me. You worry about the band."

The first coffee scent was as beautiful as Julie Christie. Matty and I had stayed up late, playing our guitars without amplifiers. He tried to teach me a few of the progressions he played in Philly, but they made no sense, I couldn't put them in a logical tonal order. I taught guitar a couple of days a week at the local music store and gave a handful of in-home lessons, while studying privately myself with an old jazzman who'd played with the Dorseys and Goodman until the bottle got him. I practiced three hours a day: scales, chorded scales, alternate fingerings. But what Matty played didn't conform to anything I'd studied.

"Sugar? Milk?"

"Black. Thanks. Listen, this thing with Frankie?"

"I'm not going to have anything to do with Angela."

"No, the Joey Schaeffer thing. With the sound system. You're for it, right?"

"Joey's going to surprise everybody. In a good way. He's smarter than he lets on. And he has a good ear. He's just looking for something to do, something hip."

"I need you to stay solid on this, though. I'll take care of Matty. But the three of us have to be solid, if Frankie kicks."

"What's Frankie's problem, anyway? He wants to play that dive in the Poconos. He doesn't want Joey doing sound for us . . ."

"I still can't figure out what's up with the Rocktop gig. But he doesn't like Joey because he made a pass at Angela. At one of his parties."

"Joey makes passes at everybody. Female dogs get out of his way. Anyway, you said Frankie didn't worry about anybody hitting on Angela."

"I said he doesn't worry about *you*."

"But he worries about Joey?"

"Angela likes her dope. Joey's got dope."

I shook my head. "Joey wants to be part of a band a lot more than he wants Angela. Or anybody else. Besides, he goes for the fifteen-gets-you-twenty types."

"I need you to talk to Joey, okay? When you get him alone somewheres. Read him the riot act. You're his pal, he'll take it seriously from you."

"I'm not exactly Joey's closest friend."

"You know what I mean. He needs to know this is serious. No messing with Angela. Because of Frankie. And no selling dope from behind the sound board. Because of Matty. Matty's death on that shit."

"I think it has something to do with Vietnam," I said.

"Yeah, well, whatever it is . . . make sure Joey has his shit one hundred percent together, okay? Hey, I almost forgot to tell you: Guess where we're playing just before Halloween?"

"The Fillmore?"

"Lancelot's Lair. Down south of Allentown. The place you always wanted to play so bad. We're opening for this New York band that's got a record deal."

"Terrific. Great. Want a refill?"

"Naw, I'd be pissing down the shaft, and I hate to do that. Pissing hunched over like that, then working in it." He rose to leave, moving briskly all of a sudden. "Just talk to Joey, okay?"

"You got it. Hey? Stosh?"

He paused by the door. "Yeah?"

"What's 'covering quarters' all about?"

His grin grew as wide as his lips could stretch. "Who's been telling you about Matty? Angela?"

I ate two blueberry Pop-Tarts, ran a half hour of scales, worked on Clapton's guitar part for "White Room," then put *Music from Big Pink* on the stereo while I took a shower. I faced a full day, including two classes, psych and medieval history, at the Penn State branch campus down in Schuylkill Haven, two go-to-the-home guitar lessons, and an evening band rehearsal. And Laura.

I had never been so infatuated, never known anyone like her. I was vain enough not to question my appeal to her but couldn't fathom what she was doing at the local campus. Or at Penn State, period. It was a prole school, and she wasn't a prole. I couldn't believe she hadn't gotten a full scholarship to Penn. Or to Princeton. Or Yale. But I was glad of it.

That Monday was the first day of the semester, when the freshmen sniff one another and the sophomore males sniff the freshman girls. The branch campus held its captives for only two years, then released them to University Park. It was my second year of disinterested attendance. Now and then I considered dropping out, but there was a vestige of pride involved. Although I had been on the outs with my mother for over a year, I lacked the will to disappoint her further. It was bad enough that I hadn't gone to a serious school. Being a Penn State dropout would have let her write me off forever. Besides, standards were so low at the branch campus that I could miss a week of classes if the band went on the road and still pass.

I parked the Corvair at the end of the lot and crossed to the tiny compound: A single macadam walk connected two buildings that for decades had sheltered the bedridden indigent and aged syphilitics shunned by their families. I expected to see Laura at any moment, yearned to see her.

She wasn't there. The weather was good, the students were dull, and the instructors were apprehensive. Heavy-legged girls from north of the mountain wore short skirts, kissing the desk chairs with the backs of their thighs and strolling around showing welts. Chalk screeched and earnest young associate profs, thin as saltine crackers, passed out mimeographed pages on which the purple ink had run like blood from Charles Martel and Karl Jaspers. A year earlier, the ROTC kids had harassed me over my hair, which had not been very long. Now my hair fell over my shoulders and they were newly subdued, unsure whether to be proud or embarrassed by the uniforms they were obligated to wear on the first day of class.

Neither Merovingians nor the diagrammed subconscious held my attention. I wanted Laura. But Laura had disappeared.

I was too proud and too cautious to ask any of the sophomore dorm girls I knew if they had seen her. Jewish girls from Northeast Philly—ed. majors every one—or moon-faced Micks from Nanticoke and Scranton, they knew enough about me to warn her off.

Over lunch, I sat in the basement cafeteria and ate a corned-beef sandwich from a vending machine. Still no Laura. A few students asked about the new band. I told them where we were booked in the coming weeks. A number of the freshman girls were noteworthy. But all were minor leaguers compared with Laura.

It occurred to me that I had better read Petrarch.

I checked the library, damning myself for not hitting it earlier. It was Laura's natural place of refuge. But the only student in the room was a kid with black plastic glasses paging through *Popular Mechanics*. I would have driven over to the dorm across the highway but didn't want Laura to think I was chasing her.

Was she avoiding me? I tried to be nonchalant but couldn't. I felt that I'd tear down massive walls to get at her.

I had to leave to give the two guitar lessons of the day, the first to a woman in Orwigsburg who had decided in middle age that she wanted to be Joan Baez or Judy Collins, the other to a housewife from Cressona who hoped to lead sing-alongs in her church. The latter flirted like a Tennessee Williams vamp and smelled of too much modesty in the shower, but I could charge more for in-home lessons and didn't have to give the music store a cut.

After two hours of driving, tuning cheap guitars, and the Mel Bay *Primer*, I returned for a last search of the campus. Except for a few dawdlers—boys with nowhere else to go and plain girls lurking with questions for bachelor instructors—the students were gone for the day. The cafeteria and library were empty.

I gobbled a couple of fifteen-cent burgers at Wixson's on 61—the cheapest and maybe the worst meal in the county—stopped to grab my guitar, then headed north. I had an hour and a half until our practice session, but I wanted to make a stop.

I drove over the ridge to St. Clair, then up the long grade to Frackville. The Hair Affair salon sat next to a flower shop that lived off funerals.

Angela was finishing up a customer. My appearance surprised her, but she took her time, drawing out the final snips and applications of hair spray. The room smelled of perms and pizza. A plump employee huddled with the receptionist. They snickered at me, and I thought I heard the name "Joyce."

Thrusting a tip into her bell-bottom jeans, Angela came over at last. She looked worn, fierce, and handsome.

"I just wanted to tell you," I whispered, "that you don't have to worry about Stosh."

Her eyes sparked. "Like I give a shit about Stosh."

"He didn't think anything was going on. It's all right."

"Nothing *was* going on. Don't be so afraid all the time."

So much for chivalric gestures, I thought. I shrugged and turned to leave.

"Come on," she said. "Sit down. Let me trim off some of those split ends."

She levered the chair down to the right height, draped a cloth around me—pulling the neck too tight—then adjusted the angle of my head with her fingertips. Her touch shot white-light voltage.

"What are you so wired up about?" she asked. "You weren't really worried about Stosh running to Frankie, were you?"

"No."

She began to caress my temples. "Close your eyes. Girls would kill to have your hair, you know that?"

The scalp massage was disarming. I didn't want it to stop. For the first time all day, I just let myself be in the moment.

Angela snipped at flyaway hairs. Her comb found an abundance of tiny knots.

"You can't just brush your hair," she said. "You got to comb it, too. I told you that last time. Want me to make it just a little shorter? Shape it a little more?"

"No. Thanks."

"All right. I just need to get this little bit. . . ."

She cut the flesh under my ear with her scissors. My yelp had barely faded when I found my hand wet and crimson. I was bleeding like a deer hung up to drain.

"Josette," Angela called with no special excitement in her voice, "get the first-aid kit. And the peroxide." Meeting my eyes in the mirror, she sighed like the lead in a high school play and said, "I'm so clumsy sometimes."

We went through the drill of cleaning the cut, then applying Band-Aids that wouldn't stick. My shirt looked as though I'd dumped a jar of spaghetti sauce over myself. But the wound began to clot. I'd have to rush home to change before our rehearsal, though.

Angela walked me out.

"No charge today," she told me.

Out of earshot of the others, I said, "You did that on purpose."

She smiled at me. Her Angela smile.

"I'd never do anything to hurt you," she said.

Joey Schaeffer was waiting for us at the warehouse where we held our practice sessions. Never lacking self-confidence, he had already bought not only the promised sound system, complete with new microphones, but a white Ford van to haul it in. He had also brought along a roadie, a guy who had followed the Destroyerz around and who drifted through Joey's parties. I had never been able to remember his name, which turned out to be Pete.

"I thought you guys might want to try this out before you made a decision," Joey said.

There was no powwow, no debate. Frankie was all for letting Joey do our sound, after all. I suspected him of tossing in a chip that had never mattered to him, playing it in return for the rest of us accepting the Poconos gig he'd booked for November—why remained a mystery.

Anyway, we were all friends again, high at the thought of our first gig. We were playing a welcome dance for the college kids up in Bloomsburg on Wednesday. It wasn't the hippest campus in Pennsylvania, but any campus was better than another coal-town bar. And the colleges were dumb enough to pay well.

It was impossible to get the full effect of the new sound system in the warehouse, but it was obviously far better than our old Fender columns. Once Joey got the feedback under control, you could hear every word of the vocals. Joey had done some homework.

On a break, Frankie presented us with the song lists he'd worked out for the sets on Wednesday. When we argued for shifting numbers around, he agreed immediately. Each set included three of my originals sandwiched between five to seven covers.

The practice went so well that I forgot about Laura for a while.

We soared. There truly is magic in the world. It astonished me that we had come so far so fast. The Destroyerz had been a top bar band. But I saw now that we hadn't been nearly as good as my vanity insisted at the time. In less than three months, we'd coalesced into a group that sounded professional. With Matty as the catalyst.

Matty the Killer. I already disbelieved most of what I'd heard on the trip to Philly.

· · ·

On my way back to Pottsville, I almost skipped my turn off 61 in order to head for the dorm down in Schuylkill Haven. But I would have gotten there just at the end of visiting hours. And I had my pride. I was determined not to run after Laura and make an ass of myself. If she wasn't interested, she could piss off. I stopped for gas, got a 5th Avenue bar from the old guy working the register, then drove home aching with thoughts of her.

Laura was sitting at the top of the steps, by my door.

"I was looking for you all day," she said.

SEVEN

It was Frankie's night. I had been so enchanted and daunted by Matty's guitar work, I'd forgotten that most listeners judge a group by its lead singer. The heads dug the guitar aces, but the straights just wanted to hear their songs well sung. And Bloomsburg was a straight school, mustering only a few forlorn girls dressed as hippies and half as many boys with shaggy hair. The rest of the crowd could have been held over from 1963. Change was in the air, but most of the students were unsure about the odor.

Frankie was in his glory, though, veering between his peace-and-love persona and teasing sexual swagger. Plain girls anxious to dream and pretty ones tempted to dare gathered closer to the stage as the night progressed. The new sound system amplified the power of Frankie's voice, as well as Stosh's blues howls and the three-part harmonies. We opened with "Jumpin' Jack Flash," went right into "Born to Be Wild," and never looked back. Matty played razor-blade guitar that made Keith Richards sound like Granny at teatime, Stosh sweated through his vengeance-is-mine drum parts, and I layered in the middle. But we were all just props for Frankie. Shirtless under a fringed suede vest, with muscles and a narrow waist above striped hip-hugger jeans, he worked the decisive female half of the audience. Red hair whipping and sweat flying, he laid on new moves stolen from the lead singer of the Other Side, a Minersville group that put on a brilliant stage show. If Angela had not come up that night—leading in a constabulary force of her girlfriends—Frankie would have had his pick of the room.

Laura had come along, too. For me, not for the music. In the short time we'd been together, no album I had put on the turntable could convince her that rock was worth a listen. She replied to the Grateful Dead with a recording of Ravel's String Quartet in F Major brought from her dorm room.

I played with her in mind, anyway. Yearning to break through to her, to excite her. Hoping she would catch at least a light case of the contagion infecting the crowd.

We really were on that first night out. The last month of playing just for one another and a few drifting visitors had made us hungry for the buzz you can get only from a crowd. And that audience was with us from the start. It was intoxicating.

Some of the impact came from Joey's new sound system, of course. The dance had been moved to a field house, where the bass and drums boomed, muddying the music with echoes. Fortunately for us, Joey and Pete had driven up early. When we arrived to set up our gear, Joey was ready to test the volume levels and balance to minimize the mush effect at the back of the hall. Still, every other factor just allowed Frankie to become the focal point of the hundreds gathered to dance or meet somebody.

Seated on a half-extended set of bleachers, Laura listened dutifully, as if to a dubious lesson. A guy who looked like a probationer on the sociology faculty hit on her but strolled off disappointed. Angela and her hair-dryer harem hung out by the sound board with Joey and Pete, forever judging the competition. Otherwise, every girl who wasn't dancing with a partner was Frankie's property.

He rolled his hips and shoulders, then drew back his red hair with both hands, letting his bass hang off his hips like the world's longest phallus.

"All right, all *right*," he said. "Now . . . something brand-new . . . one we wrote ourselves just last week . . . a heavy heartbreak trip . . ."

It was always a song that "we" wrote, never one I wrote.

"Hideaway" kicked off with a throbbing bass line in E minor. Matty did a high Robin Trower entry on the guitar, strings moaning. Stosh came in, punching up the jagged, move-move rhythm. I colored in the sonic gaps with second-guitar riffs and chords, strut-stepping across the stage toward Frankie.

He closed his eyes, brushed the mike with his lips, and made a girl-you-make-me-suffer face that rose beyond handsome to sublime. He began to sing in a wailing blue voice of seduction:

Hideaway . . . Hideaway . . .
Someday we won't . . . have to hide away . . .

Can't call you up, I can't . . . send you flowers,
We meet in stolen moments . . . we love in stolen hours . . .

Can't stop this train, though we . . . both been tryin' . . .
We love so hard that it's . . . next of kin to dyin'

Hideaway . . .

It was one of those songs simple and rhythmic enough to appeal on the first hearing. Frankie made tragic theater of it. I wouldn't have been too shocked if a coed had crawled onstage to give him a blow job. Between verses, Matty played a solo of molten glass.

At the end, we received the most applause any iteration of the band had gotten for an original song. And that was from straight kids whose highest aspiration was to return to their high schools as teachers.

I couldn't wait to play for serious rock fans.

Frankie wiped himself down with a towel, as histrionic as James Brown, slipping into his white-spade mode.

"All right, all right, all *right*! Grab the one you been looking over, fellas. 'Cause here we go now, here we go with 'A Change Is Gonna Come.' Make it happen now . . . hold her heartbeat close . . . let her *know* what you're feeling. . . ."

I noted that the prick was looking at Laura.

It was after one in the morning when we got back to Frankie and Angela's house in Frackville. A workday loomed, but a party was required. Frankie had stashed a half-dozen bottles of Asti Spumante in the fridge, and a cooler of beer sat on the kitchen floor. Joey supplied a brick of Red Leb the size of a Hershey Bar. There were no limits on dope after the gig was over, and even I took a couple more hits than usual. Laura shunned the little bronze pipe and Joey's proffered match, though. On the stereo, Steve Winwood's voice insisted that "heaven is in your mind."

A number of locals had driven up for the band's debut and they'd gotten the word about the party. In addition to Angela's girlfriends with their switchblade eyes, a couple of musicians from another band showed up, dragging in their emotional support, including an infamous strawberry blonde who was rumored, alternately, to be frigid, a dyke, or a secret nymphomaniac. She latched on to Stosh, who generally preferred a dollar in his pocket to a woman in his bed. Like Matty, Stosh still lived at home in his twenties.

"You guys were good . . . really heavy . . . ," a guitarist from Schuylkill Haven admitted grudgingly. "You heard the Steam Machine play 'Chest Fever' yet? Blew me away."

"I saw those kids in Hunger playing the Moose. Just god-awful. Doing all this Velvet Underground shit. Bass player looks like he's twelve. Plays his ass off, though, I'll give him that. . . ."

"I hear Life's getting rid of their horn section."

"I heard they're quitting."

"The Other Side's putting out a single."

"They getting paid for it?"

I didn't want to listen to any more musicians' gossip. Nor did I want to sit in on the acoustic jam upstairs in Frankie's den, a dungeon of Day-Glo posters, black lights, and lint from outer space. I just wanted to be on a mattress with Laura. But she'd been cornered by Angela. Who, to my astonishment, was making Laura laugh.

Matty dropped onto the sofa beside me, bottle of beer in one paw. "You okay, man?"

"Yeah. Just tired. Hash knocks me out."

"It was good. You know that? They liked your songs."

"*Our* songs," I said.

"No. They're yours. Don't mind Frankie."

"The crowd loved him. I don't think I really got it until tonight. How charismatic he can be, I mean."

Matty yawned. "I start at the McCann School tomorrow."

"Accounting. Right?"

Matty nodded. "Think I'll head home."

He raised his bottle of Yuengling, then lowered it again without drinking. He didn't move for the door. We listened to Frankie scatting blues upstairs. The guitarist from Haven was trying to play slide guitar but didn't understand open tunings.

Laura eased away from Angela, smiling still. But she wore a social smile now, the kind my mother wielded.

She edged in between me and Matty, forcing us to give her little rump space on the sofa. "*You* both should be very happy," she said gaily. "Everybody loved you." She turned to Matty. "I thought you were very good. I could tell that much."

"That's a major compliment," I told him. "Laura's not impressed by the kind of music we make."

"That's not true," she said. "I never said I wasn't impressed. I just said I don't like it."

"What don't you like about it?" Matty asked. Reticent around women, he sounded genuinely curious.

I saw Stosh slip out the front door with the strawberry blonde.

"It's . . . it's too disorderly," Laura told him. "There's no discipline . . . no rigor. It's all just energy, uncontrolled. There's something anarchic about it. Nihilistic."

"That's the point," I said. "It's a revival of the Futurist philosophy of creative destruction."

"The Futurists were fascists. I concede the point, though. There *is* something fascist about your music. That album you played . . . the Jefferson Airplane . . . half the songs sound like marches for masses headed off a cliff."

"It's existential."

"No," Laura said, "it's not. It's self-indulgent. It's talent in the service of ego, not in the service of art."

"All art emerges from the ego. Caravaggio . . . our favorite faggot . . ."

"You're stoned. You even smell stoned. Your music may move people, delude them even. But it isn't *art*."

"But it's fun," I said.

"That's dishonest. You believe it's more than that. You take it seriously. I know you do. You can't not take things seriously. I knew that about you the moment I saw you. All your laissez-faire posturing is nonsense. You think you're going to change the world. But you don't know how hard the world is to change."

"Do you?"

Laura twisted around to face Matty. Framed against him, she looked like the prim mistress of the manor interrogating a peasant giant.

"What do *you* think?" Laura asked. "I think you love music, you really do. But do you think it matters in the great scheme of things? I'm not trying to be insulting. I just want to know if you believe your music makes a difference?"

"It makes a difference to me," Matty said.

Driving down the Frackville grade toward St. Clair at four A.M., Pete wrecked Joey's van. Pete was so stoned that he walked away undamaged, immunized from harm by a vaccination of hashish and beer. But the Ford was finished.

The next day, Joey bought a new van. It made me wonder how big his trust fund really was.

" ' 'Tis true, 'tis day; what though it be? O wilt thou therefore rise from me?' "

"Rise and shine, Cleopatra. Places to go and things to do."

"That wasn't Shakespeare, it was Donne," Laura said.

"And it's after nine. You have classes."

She drew me back toward her warm white breasts. " 'An age in *his* embraces passed, would seem a winter's day . . .' "

"That's not an accurate quotation. And it's not winter. And the citation of poetry is the enemy of sincere emotion."

"Who said that?"

"I did. I just made it up."

"Please make love to me again. I want to feel you in me. I love it so much."

Later, as the hour burned out, she clutched me like a refugee unwilling to give up a last bundle of possessions.

"I wish we could just stay like this. Forever."

"We'd get bedsores."

"Don't be so prosaic. Please. When you can be so romantic."

I was calculating how I would fit my three hours of practice into the form of the day.

"All right. We'll stay here forever. But no books. You'll be bored to death by lunchtime. Let me get us some coffee."

"Don't go. Not yet. Five minutes."

The darkened eyes of sleeplessness only enriched her beauty. I realized there and then that I lacked the poetry within to describe her adequately. Maybe that's what made me want to rise. The gorgeous collision of our bodies only left me feeling outclassed by something intangible. I drew out the physical until she was pained and raw, but the Laura that mattered most had not been penetrated.

I wondered if she made me feel the way Angela felt about me.

"Coffee," I said. "*Now.* Let me up."

"The brute takes what he wishes and departs."

In the doorway, I turned to look at her again. I almost said, "I love you." I ached to say it. But I was afraid she'd laugh and tell me it was far too soon to know. She wanted romance, even possession, but I wasn't sure how Laura felt about love.

"How many sugars?" I asked.

The sun was out again and the Schuylkill River ran bright pink, its daily color determined by the dye works. The gorge that funneled the highway remained a heavy, end-of-season green, waiting indifferently for autumn.

"May I see you tonight?"

"I'm unavoidable. But I really do have to study first. And I can't study while you practice."

We passed the painted Indian head on the mountainside.

"I'll pick you up afterward. I'll be parked down the road. Same place. At ten thirty."

"Do you love me for myself alone? And not my yellow hair?"

"You don't have yellow hair."

Curled against the passenger door, she smiled. "I've always been glad of that, actually. It seems so common."

"Speaking of blondes . . . you seemed pretty tight with Angela last night. You told me she was a vampire."

"She is. But maybe she's not as bloodthirsty as I thought. I don't know. I don't want to be a snot. And she really was nice to me, she tried to make me feel welcome. Although she did give me the third degree."

"About me?"

"Is there no end to male vanity? No. About me. Anyway, I've decided I won't be petty. I think my initial reaction to her was nine parts jealousy, one part insight."

"Trust the insight."

"I'm not going to let her intimidate me."

"That's different."

"You really didn't sleep with her, did you?"

"No."

"Please don't."

"I won't."

"Promise me that. Just that one thing."

"I promise."

"You'd break my heart," she said.

After enduring a stumbling lecture delivered from disarranged notes on the legacy of late Roman political forms among the Franks, I left the campus and the Carolingians, stopped by the Acme for a bag of groceries, dropped them off at my apartment, then drove to the house on Mahantongo Street.

I parked down on Norwegian, out of sight, and walked up the alley to the carriage house. It needed a coat of paint. I let myself in the side door with my key.

I didn't turn on the light. The unwashed windows let enough sun filter in to define the interior. It smelled of oil and of exhaust fumes absorbed into the wood since the Harding administration. Between the workbench and my father's car, there was barely room to open the driver's-side door. I didn't bother. I just stood there.

It always surprised me, when I came back, to find the car still there. It was a Chrysler Imperial, the last automobile my father bought and a source of friction in the failing household. My mother considered its purchase a faux pas. She called the Chrysler a "Jew car." Her family had driven Cadillacs since the 1920s, including the second-to-last Caddy to roll off the assembly line—body by Fisher—at the start of World War II and one of the first to roll off when production resumed again in a different world. My father had no money sense, and the Chrysler had been an amateur's attempt to save a few bucks. He should have tightened his belt at a different notch.

I leaned back against the workbench. At which my father had never worked. He had been educated above the ability to use his hands effectively.

I was not ready to look. I just stood there. A doomed fly looped below the exposed beams.

Why didn't my mother just sell the car? It was ugly. She hated it. And she needed the money. She still had her big-finned Cadillac, aging but proper.

At last, I turned about. Gripping the lip of the workbench with my eyes shut. Then I forced myself to open them.

I could no longer tell if any bloodstains remained. Mrs. McClatchy had scrubbed them away, even before the police gave their permission. But sometimes I imagined that blood reappeared on the surface of the wood. Like the handprint of the Molly in the jail, whitewashed for ninety years but ineradicable.

No attempt had been made to fill in the gouges where the cops pried out the bullet. The splintered wood still looked naked, pale and shamed, against the darker tone of the studs and the wall.

I hated to cry. I had sworn that no one would ever see me cry.

"You cocksucker!" I shouted. "You worthless, weakling, coward bastard. You coward, coward, coward, coward, *coward* . . ." I came to the end of words and howled for a minute.

When I opened my eyes, the light in the bay had changed.

My mother stood in the doorway.

"It doesn't help," she said. And she walked away.

EIGHT

We had no interest in Buzzy Ritter's party. Matty didn't know him, and I had been on the outs with Buzzy since March, when his attempt to acquire me as one of his acolytes ended in mutual disappointment, acid-trip hangovers, shots from a deer rifle, and a final, repugnant vignette with two girls at his farmhouse. Reputed to have the highest IQ ever recorded in his Dutch-country high school, Buzzy had dropped out of Columbia. After drifting to the West Coast and then Colorado, he came home to be a god or, at least, an avatar. In short order, Buzzy had taught me enough about casual evil to awaken a dormant Puritan streak in my character.

I had shunned him for six months. But the stars in the heavens are tyrants.

Matty came over to my apartment after late mass, bringing two hoagies as an offering. The first October rain had come overnight, but the sun burned through by noon and a wet world gleamed. It was the sort of day that tugs you outside. I would have liked to spend it with Laura, but she had gone home to visit her mother.

I had offered her a ride to Doylestown, but she'd insisted on taking the bus, turning a ninety-minute drive into a four-hour journey. She'd told me that her mother was sternly conservative and would need to be prepared for my debut. Entrusted with her own key—something no other girl had ever received from me—she'd promised to come straight to the apartment when she got back late Sunday night.

Matty and I sat in my living room, with me playing an acoustic guitar and Matty's volume low as we worked on an extended song to fit the musical fashion for profundity. Our progress was slow. I worked best alone, while Matty, who dazzled me with his cascading improvisations, could not write a singable melody to save his life. His attempts at producing lyrics were even more inept. When I came up with a verse or chorus, though, he could forge marvelous bridges and haunting interludes. It gave me great satisfaction to be able to do something Matty could not, to take the lead for a change. Instead of closing the gap between my guitar skills and his invincible talent, all of my fervent practicing only left me further behind. Jealousy ebbed and flowed.

Our intended masterpiece had the working title "America: Speed Limit 90." But we were just trading licks, waiting for inspiration, when Joey Schaeffer showed up.

"What's happening?" he asked. He had begun to grow a beard, which was coming in full and black. "Working on the symphony again?"

"There's half a hoagie in the fridge, if you're hungry," I told him.

Joey picked up the new *Esquire*. The two dead Kennedys and Martin Luther King had been gimmicked onto the cover, their cutout figures imposed on a field of white crosses. It was a disappointing issue. Joey quickly tossed it back atop the latest issue of *Crawdaddy!*

"Listen," he said. "You guys need to go to Buzzy's party."

"Buzzy's an asshole," I said.

Matty had nothing to say.

"Yeah, he can be an asshole," Joey admitted. He concentrated on me. "But he knows he blew it with you, man. He wants to make amends, you know? He specifically asked me to get you to come."

"I don't do skid row orgies without running water."

"It's just a regular party."

"Come on, Joey. Why does it matter to you?"

"Buzzy and I go back, man. He helped my brother out. For what it was worth. Anyway, he just called me up and asked me if I could get you and some other guys from the band to come over. He's a groupie at heart. Know what I mean?" He switched his effort to Matty. "Tooker's new band is playing at the party. It's just some dumb-Dutch hicks from Tremont and Pine Grove, kind of a downer, but Tooker really wants you to hear what he's doing. He's still bummed out, you know? He wants to show you he landed on his feet."

"There's no electricity out at the farm," I said.

"They rented a generator. Look, Buzzy's really sorry for being such a shit," Joey told me. "And Tooker's just trying to salvage a little pride. You really ought to go. It's like, you know, noblesse oblige."

"Buzzy still telling everybody I'm a narc?"

"He stopped that shit months ago. You were supposed to be his only anointed son, you know? You were a major defeat in Buzzy's war on reality."

"And I was supposed to be Frodo, so he could be Gandalf. All his Tolkien crap got really sick. If anything, Buzzy's a two-bit Dark Lord. And his Shire's got bad karma."

"He's over all that, too."

Buzzy's farmhouse was haunted by the walking dead. He surrounded himself with strays who more or less did his bidding. Buzzy controlled the dope and, thus, his tribe. It embarrassed me, infuriated me, that I had believed we were cosmic brothers, with Buzzy the elder. Our relationship had played out right after my father's death.

"If you need company," I said, "go get Frankie. He never met a party he didn't like."

"I already asked him. He's stuck taking Angela to the movies. She's got her ass up about something. And Stosh still feels funny about Tooker."

Matty spoke up. "Tooker had no discipline. His playing wasn't good enough."

His tone was a revelation. Belatedly, I grasped that it hadn't been

Frankie or Stosh who fired Tooker from the band, but Matty. It gave me a passing chill to think that Matty could come home from Nam, listen to us for a few songs, and make a decision to give an old pal the boot. It didn't square with the image I had of him being content with the universe as long as he could play music.

"Shit, why not?" I said. "Come on, Matty. It's too nice to stay inside."

I still didn't want to have anything to do with Buzzy. But I wanted to see Matty and Tooker together. I wondered what else I'd been missing.

Matty shrugged. "I guess it wouldn't hurt."

Buzzy's farmhouse sat in a glen at the end of a road so rutted, you had to take it at five miles per hour. That feature had been crucial to Buzzy's selection of the property, since it meant that any police raid would offer plenty of warning, unless the cops were willing to come over the hills on foot and work down through the woods. Otherwise, the property offered only fields so barren that the Pennsylvania Dutch had abandoned them, a collapsing barn full of black snakes, and a house watered only by a hand pump in the kitchen and another in the yard. The site was lush and madly overgrown, colored now by autumn.

Joey crawled along the farm track, cursing every time a deep hole punished his Shelby Cobra. Joey wasn't an obvious materialist, but there were two things he would have defended with his life: his Fisher stereo system and that growling black Mustang.

I sat bunched up in the back, with Matty barely contained by the bucket seat in front of me.

"I should've unloaded the van and brought it," Joey said. "This is going to tear out my exhaust."

We had the windows up to keep out the combination of mud and dust, so we didn't hear the band until we got close. Forewarned of our approach by the Mustang's growl, Buzzy waited in the field where everybody parked, a sovereign condescending to meet the foreign ambassadors at the edge of his kingdom.

He grinned, beaver-toothed, and shook my hand. He had enormous hands. The greasy fringe of hair on his forehead didn't quite cover a thick array of blackheads.

In the background, an amateur band blundered through "In-A-Gadda-Da-Vida," an endless number destined to replace "Wipe Out" as the favorite song of rubes aching to be hip. The noise from the generator was almost as loud as the music.

Leading us up toward the house through damp grass, Buzzy said, "I hear the new band's great. The Innocence, right?"

"The Innocents."

"Yeah, right. I hear nothing but good things about you, some heavy shit. You hear Arthur Brown yet? *That* is serious music. . . ." He adjusted his path to walk closer beside me. Our sleeves brushed. "You and I ought to make a fresh start. Let bygones be bygones. Things got crazy."

"Still got your deer rifle?"

He grinned. The Beaver of Evil. "New Remington twelve-gauge, too. I've been cleaning the snakes out of the barn."

I was tempted to make a comment about the snakes in his head. But there was no point. We were there. And I was the chimp who had agreed to come. Just bring on the memories of nausea and degradation.

Yet, something else lingered down deep. At his best, Buzzy could be charismatic, almost hypnotic. I had been impressed by his ability to quote philosophers germanely, until I discovered that he read philosophy only in search of quotes. He reminded me of Bazarov in *Fathers and Sons*, rich with indefinite talents and bound for a pointless end. One talent Buzzy didn't have was musical ability. During our mutual infatuation, he had asked me to give him guitar lessons, but he'd never practiced seriously. He expected things to just come to him and resented it when they didn't.

Tooker noted our arrival and nodded. The band was awful, not even in tune. After applause from three or four stoners for the Iron Butterfly number, they launched into an off-key version of "Incense and Peppermints," psychedelia packaged by corporate America.

Buzzy had parties and Parties. This was a Party, with perhaps fifty visitors wandering around, a few of them tripping their brains out. Males outnumbered females four to one, and the girls looked in need of shampoo and penicillin. I did my best to avoid a would-be guitar player from Schuylkill Haven who wrote sappy songs and ate too much LSD. He wore an orange paisley shirt with a Russian collar. It made him look like a reject from *The Mod Squad*. I wondered if he was my replacement in King Buzzy's court.

Several guests were drug connections with whom Buzzy had dealt during my tenure. A few were truly bad hombres, including two black dudes from Harrisburg with an overweight blonde in tow. Otherwise, the usual Buzzy crew was there, shiftless guys in their twenties who hung out at the farm for weeks when their homes became untenable. In the past, society would have classed them as bums. Now they had been promoted to hippie status, representatives of the counterculture.

Old Bronc was there, too. He'd been busted for holding up a gas station but must have gotten out on bail while awaiting trial. Deep into his forties, Bronc wanted to be Neal Cassady, although he didn't know who Neal Cassady was. He claimed to be a former rodeo rider and did have bowed, busted-up legs. He said he knew Ramblin' Jack Elliott and played a few chords on an old Kalamazoo, braying cowboy tunes. He was always willing to do the manual labor around the farm, rolling up his sleeves to reveal jailbird tattoos, and he acted as Buzzy's collector when drug debts were overdue. He was unfailingly polite to me, jocular and humble. I hated to be within a mile of him.

Beer in hand, I strolled over to talk to Tooker while the band was on break. At three in the afternoon, he was stoned and drunk.

"You sound great, man," I lied. As all musicians do.

"It's coming along. You know how it is."

"Glad it's working out for you. Listen—"

"Don't say nothing. I know it wasn't your fault. I know that, man. Screw them. Anyway, this is a better gig for me, you know?"

"That's cool."

"What's eating Matty? What's he got to be such a shit about?"

"What did he do?"

"Rick—our guitar player, Rick—asked him if he wanted to jam with us. And Matty blew him off, just walked away. What's wrong with him?"

"Nothing I know of. He seems normal to me."

"Yeah. Well, you didn't know him before. He's, like, spaced out or something. I think Nam made him crazy, that's what I think."

"Matty's not crazy."

"You didn't know him. You didn't know him, man. He was different." He drained his bottle of beer. "Know what I think? I don't think he ever got over Angela. That's what I think."

"Come on, Tooker. That was back in high school."

He looked at me oddly. With something newly alert in his bleary eyes. "That's, like, when it started."

"Angela told me she and Matty dated in high school, but it didn't come to much."

Tooker guffawed. Drunk and splashing spit. He had the same north-of-the-mountain teeth as Frankie.

"Oh, man . . . that's rich. She told you that? Don't you know enough not to believe a thing Angela says? 'High school.' Yeah, and then some. They were hot and heavy for years, until Matty's old lady made him dump her. Then she goes with Frankie on the rebound, but she can't get over Matty. I mean, what the fuck? Didn't you pick up on *any* of this, man? Anyways, Frankie asks her to marry him, he's head over heels in love with her, always was. But Angela just wants Matty and she's holding out. Then Matty's old man pulls that Army thing on him. Angela fucked his brains out, trying to get pregnant, trying to keep Matty from enlisting. But he went and did it, anyway. She only married Frankie for revenge."

"Is any of that true?"

"What have I got to lose? They fucked me over good, ain't? Some pals. . . ."

"Nobody told me any of that."

"They never will. If I wasn't drunk, I probably wouldn't. You don't belong, man. Don't you see that?" He smirked. "*I* belonged. And look where it got me. Nobody says nothing, anyway. They don't even talk to each other. They just fuck up each other's lives and pretend like nothing happened."

Tooker was unsteady, grabbing for an invisible railing. One of the other musicians came over to get him. It was time for them to play again.

"Hey, man," Tooker said. "You. Bark. *You* want to jam with us?"

"Sure," I said. "Later."

The generator belched back to life and the noise resumed.

Joey partied with a pair of gypsy bikers, forming a clique that shut out the general shabbiness. Probably talking business, I figured. Everything to do with the farm seemed decayed. Not decadent, though. "Decadent" was too classy a word. Buzzy's whole scene seemed pathetic now. And I had to admit it had always been like that.

I found Matty alone behind the house, nursing a beer by the dried-up well that Buzzy claimed led down to a realm of demons. Buzzy loved to goof on stoned kids, playing with their heads until he owned them.

"These people are jackals," Matty said when I came up.

"I'm sorry. I don't know why I agreed to come."

"Joey knows how to get what he wants. You know these people, though?"

"I'm not proud of it."

He looked at me with judgment in his eyes. "Do you . . . believe in good and evil? Like in the Bible?"

"Yeah. Yes."

"This place is evil."

"I'll grab Joey and see if I can get him to leave."

"Let him be," Matty said. "Joey's different. None of this touches him. He just glides over it. I've known people like that."

"You want to stay, then?"

"No. I'm going to walk."

"It's a long way."

"I can hitch a ride, once I get to the hardball."

"The Dutchies won't pick you up."

"Then I'll walk until somebody does."

"I'll go with you. This place gives me the creeps these days."

We started back toward the house and the dirt road out of the glen. One of Buzzy's original cast intercepted us. His pupils were dilated to the size of black dimes.

"Hey, Will . . . hey, far out, man . . . Frodo's back . . ."

"We're just leaving, Mike."

"Oh, man . . . you try the new shit Buzzy's got? It's, like, some seriously heavy Mex. *Super* heavy. It's laced with *some*thing, man, it's got to be . . . it's some heavy shit . . ."

"Enjoy it," I said.

"You can't go yet, man. Remember Janie? Janie Duerffler? You remember Janie. She's upstairs, pulling a train. You ought to go up, man, check it out, say hi. Or, like, say 'High,' you know?" He giggled.

"That was never my thing," I said, more for Matty's ears than for Mike's.

I remembered Janie all right. She was about fourteen. Maybe fifteen now. Buzzy had pulled her in from the gas station in downtown Pine Grove, where she hung out. She had been in awe of him and his Corvette, a scrawny child pretending to be tough, desperately in need of attention. From that first night, she did whatever Buzzy told her to do, whenever he told her to do it. Everybody thought it was funny.

Had we moved five minutes sooner, everything would have been all right. But we didn't.

We were headed over to let Joey know we were leaving when the screams began. The sound didn't come from some tripping chick surprised by a snake from the barn. These were real screams, as naked as a blade.

They came from the house.

Matty moved before anyone else could dial the right channel. He was bewilderingly fast, slipping through the doorway with the too-quick-for-the-eye smoothness of one of the barn snakes.

I followed him. As if I had no choice, as if Matty had to be followed. Maybe that was how things were in Vietnam.

He had already gotten up the stairs before I reached their bottom. Frozen in astonishment, half a dozen stoners sat around the desolate interior, watching a movie unfold.

Shouting. More screaming. Matty's voice. Bronc's.

The action was in the bedroom reserved as a crash pad, where two vile mattresses lay side by side on the floor. Bronc stood by the bed with his pants around his ankles and his hard-on withering. Bone white and pathetic, Janie cowered against a wall. Her left eye was bruised and swelling.

"Get him away, get him away," she begged. "I don't want him doing it to me."

A shotgun leaned in the far corner.

"Get out," Matty told Bronc. "Now."

"And who the fuck are you?" Bronc said. "Mind your own business. We're just having a little fun."

Bawling her eyes out, Janie cried, "Get him away from me . . . please, get him away. . . ."

Matty lowered his voice. The way a rattlesnake coils. Bronc didn't read the signal.

"Pull up your pants and get out," Matty said.

"You want to screw her, get in line. Now beat it, before I throw you down the stairs."

Janie tried to cover herself with a sheet trapped beneath her rump. I had never touched her. It truly had not been my thing. And I had been mocked for it, the butt of jokes among Buzzy's retinue. Now, looking at her, all blotches and protruding bones, it seemed a miracle that she ever attracted anyone. Or that anyone ever wanted sex at all.

Conditioned by useful violence, Bronc dove for the shotgun. Pants still around his ankles, he twisted around on the floor and brought the double barrels up at Matty.

Janie shrieked.

Matty knocked the twin muzzles aside. A massive blast tore the ceiling, pulling down chunks of plaster and drawing billows of dust. Before Bronc could realign the gun, Matty tore it out of his hands and landed, knees down, on top of him.

He began punching Bronc in the face. With stunning force. Blood burst from human meat, spattering the wall. Janie screamed as if scalded.

Even in that tumult, Matty punched only with his right hand, his picking hand, while holding Bronc down with his left—the hand that really mattered to a guitarist.

Bronc stopped cursing or trying to fight back. Matty had pulped his face. It flashed through my mind that he was going to kill him.

"Matty! *Matty!* Jesus Christ. Stop, man. *Stop it!*"

Matty put a big fist into Bronc's mouth with such force that I expected it to go down his throat.

I broke out of my physical trance and stumbled across the mattresses, grabbing Matty by the shoulder.

He came up at me. His eyes were mad. He braked his fist just inches from my face. Dust swirled like the smoke of battle.

Matty grunted, then gasped. I recalled how, on that first night, he had put me in mind of a Minotaur.

He pushed me aside. Not too hard, but firmly enough to make it clear I had better get out of the way.

In the corner, Bronc mewed and wept.

"Put your clothes on," Matty told the girl. Without looking at her. "Get out of here."

She listened, moved, hurried.

Matty picked up the shotgun. Putting his right foot on Bronc's chest to level him out, he thrust the barrels into the bloody crevice that had been a mouth.

"You want to play with guns?" he asked Bronc.

His finger was taut on the trigger.

"*Do you?*"

Weeping, Bronc shook his head as best he could. His shrunken dick shot piss.

"I can't *hear* you," Matty said. "I asked you if you want to play with guns?"

Things had plunged beyond justice to a level of brutality, of rapturous cruelty, I had never witnessed in any coal-town fight. Matty jammed the barrels deeper into the broken mouth, making it impossible for Bronc to answer him. The room stank of cordite and rancid sex. Bronc's piss trickled to nothing. The old dust from the ceiling slowly thinned.

The air went out of Matty. His posture softened. He tossed the shotgun on the bed and lifted his foot off Bronc's chest.

"You're a lucky man," Matty told him. "Next time, you listen when you hear the word *no*." He gave Bronc a tap with his foot that was almost friendly, then turned to me and shrugged.

"Let's get out of this pit," he said.

We left Bronc sobbing, soaked with blood and piss.

Buzzy waited at the foot of the stairs. Matty tensed again. I thought he would pin Buzzy against the wall. Instead, he just tried to brush past.

"It was just a misunderstanding, man," Buzzy told him, taking him by the arm. "Janie gets funny sometimes. It wasn't anything. Really."

"That was rape."

Buzzy grinned, beaver-toothed, still clutching Matty's bicep. "You can't rape Janie, man. I mean, she's screwed half the county. And probably most of her relatives."

Matty broke his nose.

As we emerged from the house, I saw Joey trot for his car. The bastard was going to abandon us. To protect his goddamned Mustang. Or just his own ass.

The music had stopped, but the generator throbbed on. The tribes had gathered in front of the house. Digging on the excitement.

"What a trip, man," Mike the Minion said. "Anybody dead?"

"Come on," I said to Matty. "Let's just go." I wanted to take him by the arm, but I was afraid to touch him. His soul was someplace else. No longer crazed, his eyes just looked exhausted.

Before we could push through the mob, a mad growl rose behind us.

Matty turned. Fast.

Bronc had managed to get up off the floor and make it down the stairs. He stood in the doorway. Holding the shotgun.

His face was a Halloween mask slathered with ketchup. One eye had already swollen shut, but the other gave him enough visibility to identify us. He lifted the twin muzzles toward Matty and stepped out into the yard.

He wanted to speak, to gloat at last. But his broken mouth wouldn't let him.

Amid gasps and a few brief screams, everyone else moved back. I knew that I should try to intercede, to step between Bronc and Matty. But I was afraid.

Edging back, I said, "Don't do it, Bronc. Don't do it, man. It's murder, it isn't worth it."

Bronc made an animal noise. He wasn't going to take his eyes off Matty for an instant.

Buzzy came out, holding a filthy dishrag to his nose with one hand and the deer rifle in the other.

"Shoot the sonofabitch," he told Bronc.

Bronc raised the shotgun another inch, finger on the trigger. But he hesitated. Buzzy contented himself with carrying the rifle but made no move to use it. Never one to do his own dirty work, he just stepped up beside Bronc.

"Blow his dick off," Buzzy ordered.

Joey hadn't driven off, after all. He sidled up to Buzzy and Bronc with a friendly Joey smile upon his face. I didn't know if he meant to make peace or simply to switch sides.

I misjudged him. As soon as he got in position, Joey produced a snub-nosed revolver and rammed it up under Buzzy's chin. So hard that it cocked Buzzy's head back.

"Drop the rifle," Joey said. "And tell Jesse James he better put down the shotgun."

Bronc glanced back over his shoulder. It was all the time Matty needed.

The shotgun went off again. A girl screamed, folding up and falling, shot in the foot. Before she hit the ground, Bronc went down himself. In possession of the shotgun again, Matty smashed the butt into Bronc's jaw. Bronc should have been dead, but he was tough meat.

He was finished, though.

Matty collected the deer rifle from the ground at Buzzy's feet.

"Let him go," he told Joey. "He's a coward." He took the two weapons, crossed the yard, and dropped them down the old well. No one got in his way.

We drove back down the road on golden leaves.

"I guess the party wasn't a good idea," Joey said.

NINE

The hoagie's remains were soggy from sitting in the fridge. I ate alone, in silence. After I finished, I stayed at the kitchen table, staring at the swirls in the Formica. When the phone rang, I leapt up, hoping it was Laura at the Trailways terminal.

My mother's voice was no substitute.

The conversation was muddled at first, which told me the call was serious. On mundane matters, my mother came straight to the point. Now I sensed her struggling against dignity grown frail.

At last, she said, "Will, this is difficult for me. I've made mistakes . . . since your father died. I won't make any excuses. But it's going to be different now."

For my mother, this amounted to emotional nudity. Yet she sounded sober. Serious, but not maudlin. My mother was not into maudlin.

My anger remained. It made me reluctant to speak.

"I thought," she continued, "that you might come home for dinner on Wednesday. I'll make a roast. We could talk things over."

"The band has a job on Wednesday. In Wilkes-Barre."

"Are you free on Thursday?"

"Mom . . . listen . . ."

"I just feel that we should talk. Try not to hold too much against me."

"It's not that. That wasn't what I meant. I was just going to ask if I could bring someone along."

"Not that woman? The one who—"

"No. Not her. Someone else."

"Do I know this girl?"

"No."

"What's her name?"

"Laura. Laura Saunders."

"She's not a Pottsville girl."

"No."

"Where did you meet her?"

"She goes to the Penn State campus. Down in Haven."

The eternal Swarthmore grad, my mother hesitated. Confronted with the equivalent of a Negro foundling on the doorstep.

"She's very intelligent," I said. "You and she can talk about Flaubert."

"Why would we want to talk about Flaubert? Was that meant to be sarcastic? Do you know her family? How long have you known her?"

I counted. "Five weeks. A little more."

"That's not very long."

"We're not at the altar yet. And, really, she chews with her mouth closed."

"Don't be smart."

"Don't give me the third degree, then."

"Are you serious about this girl?"

"I like her."

"That's evident. I just thought . . . perhaps you and I should sit down together and have a conversation. About our family situation. To clear the air."

"I thought it might be good to have her there," I said. "As a referee."

"That's unfair of you."

"I meant we'd both have to be on our best behavior."

"I've stopped drinking, if that's what you mean. There. Does it make you happy to hear me say that? All right, bring her. If it means so much to you."

"She's a nice girl, Mom."

"Won't that be a change? All right. Thursday, seven?"

"Seven."

"Do you know, Will . . . that this is the first time you've ever asked to bring a girl home to dinner?"

I drove to the bus terminal, impatient to see Laura. When she stepped down to the sidewalk, tired yet bright, I hugged her shamelessly.

She pushed me back a few inches, making a face.

"You smell like a shooting gallery. And your breath stinks of onions." Then she smiled. "Nonetheless, I have decided that I love you."

To the chagrin of an old woman lurking on a bench, I lifted Laura in my arms and carried her to the Corvair. There are no sterner arbiters of morals than the aging poor.

Upon reaching the apartment, our routine was to paw off each other's clothes as soon as we got inside, making it as close to the bedroom as we could before collapsing in a tangle. Even if we were apart for only one night, Laura made love as if, at any moment, she might be prevented from doing so ever again. No girl in my past had ever taken to sex with such audacity. Her urgency could be almost masculine until she felt me inside her. She broke the rules.

That night, I needed things to be different for a little while. Inside the door, I kissed her but then asked her to sit on the sofa. I took a chair facing her.

"I just need to look at the miracle of you for a minute," I told her.

She mulled that over. "Well, I've never *been* a miracle before . . . but I suppose I can live with the responsibilities." She drew in her eyebrows. "You must have had an interesting day. Did an old girlfriend show up? With a gun? And a bag of onions?"

"Laura . . . I want to apologize about something. A while ago, you said you wished we could stay in bed forever and hide from the world, just be with each other. Remember? I made a joke about it, I was an ass." I looked at her, at this beautiful, earnest, ravishing human being who had descended from unknown heights into my life. "I wanted you to know that I understand. I wish we could just lock the door and never come out of the bedroom, just hold each other forever."

"We'd get bedsores," she said.

Before any clothes flew off, heavy footsteps climbed the stairs. Matty called my name and knocked on the door.

I let him in. He looked distraught. Or as much so as his chunk-of-wood face allowed. He glanced at Laura, jarred by her presence. I don't know what he had expected. I wasn't living in a monastery.

"What's up, man?" I asked.

He nodded to Laura, then focused on me.

"I had some trouble at home. I need to let things calm down. I'm sorry for intruding. I just thought . . . maybe I could stay in that back bedroom of yours? Just for a night or two."

"Sure. Of course. What happened?"

He sat down, heavily, in the chair I had occupied while trying to reach Laura.

"I did something stupid," he said. "I don't know what else I could've done, though."

"Would you like some coffee?" Laura asked. I sensed it was a means to leave us alone. Symbolically, at least. The kitchenette was only a few feet away.

Matty shrugged and said, "Thanks." It was unclear whether that meant yes or no, but Laura got up and disappeared from his view.

"I have this uncle," Matty told me. "Uncle Johnny. He's a state cop. He's always been a bully. Thinks he runs the whole family. Tough guy, started out as a prison guard. Anyways, he and my old man are there when I get home. With my mother crying her eyes out. Johnny and my pop were drunk. They thought they were going to give me a haircut."

Even after three and a half months home, Matty's hair was hardly the pride of Haight-Ashbury.

"I decked him. Uncle Johnny. I told him to knock it off. But he wouldn't listen. He grabbed my hair and tried to use the scissors. I put him out. I didn't beat him up or anything. Just put him out cold. One punch, that was all." He grimaced, but with more sorrow than disgust. "My old man ran halfway up the stairs. Scared of me. My mother was afraid I killed Johnny."

"You sure you didn't?"

He tested his right hand. The knuckles were a mess. Matty had been through a busy day.

"He'll be all right. He'll be angry, he's used to everybody backing down and taking everything he dishes out. But he'll be all right."

I thought of Bronc, of his face like a Jersey tomato struck with a baseball bat. When Matty showed up at the door, my first thought had been that the police were after him. But Buzzy would never go to the police. And Bronc certainly wouldn't. As for the girl who caught part of a shotgun blast in her foot, they would have concocted some story by the time they reached the emergency room. Given the refreshments at Buzzy's party, she probably wouldn't remember what actually happened.

When I failed to speak, Matty repeated his request: "I'm sorry to ask, to barge in like this. But do you mind if I bunk here? Just for a day or two?"

"Stay as long as you like. Until things calm down."

"I'll find a place," he said. "I don't need much. But I can't stay at home anymore. There'd just be more trouble."

"Just stay as long as you like," I repeated insincerely. Nothing against Matty, but I valued my privacy with Laura. With other girls I hadn't given a damn, but I didn't want any other man listening to our love-making.

"I'm sorry to intrude." He glanced toward the kitchen. Laura was stretching to reach the coffee mugs in the cupboard. "Just black for me, please."

Laura smiled through the archway. I could tell she wasn't happy, but I didn't sense the depth of her mood until Matty went down to his car to fetch his guitar and a bag of clothes.

Hugging me in his absence, she said, "Please . . . take me back to the dorm."

"It'll be all right," I said. "We don't have to do anything. We'll be quiet."

"It's not that."

"What is it, then?"

"He scares me."

In two days, Matty was gone. He rented a room on Market Street, just above Garfield Square. Before he left, he took the old sheets from his bed and washed them at the Laundromat. No trace of his presence remained behind, not one cigarette butt or a single blond hair in the bathroom. Maybe that was a Vietnam habit, too.

I was glad when he left, although he had been no trouble. It wasn't only that I longed to be together—noisily—with Laura. I also needed privacy to write, to work through the embarrassing, faltering melodies and stupid rhymes that drag on until, out of nowhere, the magic returns. I was having unprecedented difficulty, at least when I tried to write a song for Laura. I could not produce anything worthy of her. In the past, I had been able to knock out songs for new girlfriends within a day of meeting them . . . although I was not above recycling songs in which the descriptions of the flesh and its circumstances were not overly specific. But every effort I made to capture Laura in words and music came to nothing. I could write about imaginary women with ease. Once I even caught myself cobbling together a song that reeked of Angela. But I wasn't going to be this Laura's Petrarch with a guitar.

With Laura herself, life seemed all passion and wonder. That Tuesday, waiting out Matty, we skipped a campus rally to raise money for Czechoslovak refugees and drove south through the perishing autumn under a bright, cold sun. On a back road, on impulse, I pulled over by a field of cornstalks. Without a word, as if she already knew what was to come and welcomed it, Laura followed me into the field until, barely out of sight of the road, I laid her down in a rasping world. She wore a short brown corduroy skirt, which I pushed up around her waist.

She didn't come along for the gig in Wilkes-Barre. Our music still did not move her and, to my amusement, she took studying for each minor quiz as seriously as a final exam at med school. She was utterly brilliant and surprisingly lacking in confidence. Unwilling to be convinced that she could get A's without opening a book, she was the most earnest human being I had ever met. Except, perhaps, for my father.

It was just as well that she skipped Wilkes-Barre. That night felt like a setback. Nothing dreadful happened, but not much good did, either. Frankie, who had put off replacing his old Vox amp, blew a speaker during the first set. And for the first time, Matty just went through the motions, his mind elsewhere. Out-of-sync strobes from an amateur light show fought against the beat. The kids in the crowd were all right, and the two guys who booked the hall had no complaints, but the spark just had not been there. We were just another band, and it alarmed me. For the first time, I wondered if it was possible that we might fail.

By the next morning, my confidence was back. Every band had off nights, and every musician knew it. Matty had been through a crazy patch—Buzzy had phoned me, worried that Matty was going to report a rape to the police—but he loved to play so much that I was confident he would be over it by the weekend gigs. And Frankie broke down and shelled out for a new amplifier, a heavy-duty Ampeg.

Even the dinner with my mother went well. She and Laura chattered about French literature, leaving me behind. And Laura looked radiant. I had been jarred when I picked her up. Her tumbling hair, which I loved, had been shorn away. Angela had driven down to the dorm, taken her back to Frackville, and treated her to a styling. My dismay lasted only a moment, though. Against what I would have expected, Angela had done amazing work, framing Laura's perfect bones with a cut that fell somewhere between Edie Sedgwick and a Carnaby Street Ava Gardner. The new hairstyle made Laura look impossibly glamorous, as if she must take for granted the silver place settings my mother had laid out. I could not wait to drive her back to the apartment.

It seemed that Angela had made her peace with Laura and me. I was glad of it. And a little disappointed, too.

On Friday afternoon, as I was changing clothes for a gig in Reading, my mother called again. After minimal pleasantries, she got to the point.

"Will . . . there's something wrong with that girl."

"Oh, Jesus, Mom . . ."

"I can't put my finger on it, but there's something seriously wrong with her. Call it a mother's instinct. For want of anything more definite."

"You never like any girl I'm with."

"That's not true. I didn't say I didn't like her. I do. She's charming. And very bright. Well brought up, whoever her people may be. But something isn't right about her."

"Well, she's right for me," I said. Letting my frustration show.

"I hope so," my mother said. "Please be careful."

TEN

My mother had an insidious way of sowing doubt. Despite my-self, I scrutinized Laura's minor actions in between our bouts of fuck-and-talk. Unless I counted a woeful inability to cook, I could find nothing wrong with Laura Saunders at all. On the contrary, I could not imagine how things could be more right.

The cooking incident veered between touching and hilarious. Laura even burned coffee, but one day after class, she sneaked up on the bus, stopped at the Acme to buy the ingredients listed on a recipe for quiche Lorraine, and had already turned the kitchenette into an apocalyptic landscape by the time I came home. She took me to task for having an incomplete set of measuring cups. I had never seen any-one expend such concentration near a stove or fight so hard to mask wrath at inanimate objects. Laura combined ingredients with minute care, only to discard them and start again. I had to turn off the stereo so she could concentrate. Dinnertime passed and the evening marched on toward the hour of a society supper. At last, she produced some-thing faintly resembling a casserole. Or a quiche as refined by Picasso. The top was scorched in patches the color of coal dirt.

"We can't eat this," she said, tears bursting from her eyes as we sat at the table.

I was glad that *she* said it.

"Maybe you shouldn't have tried something so hard?" I said, hoping to comfort her.

Laura leapt to her feet, eyes hating me and the universe. It was jarring, unlike her.

"What do *you* know about what's hard? What do you know about anything?"

She locked herself in the bathroom for an hour. When she came back out, she had gotten over things. I made us Campbell's soup and toast, then we went into the bedroom, where all things could be repaired.

Stymied in my attempts to produce the song Laura deserved, I read to her from the poems Petrarch wrote to his Laura. I had gotten the book from Penn State, on an interlibrary loan. It took a month. Petrarch was, to say the least, unfashionable. Nor were many of the poems appropriate to us. But I selected those that might apply and read them aloud in the fortress of our bedroom:

> *I bless the spot, the day, the very moment*
> *when my eyes, finding you, did dare to lift,*
> *and I say, "Soul of mine, be humbly grateful*
> *that fortune honored you with such a gift."*

"He must be better in the original Italian," Laura said, nuzzling closer. "Don't you think he was lucky, though? That she died? He never had to be disillusioned."

"I'm not sure *she* felt very lucky. Dying of the Black Plague."

"But the poems aren't about her. Not really. They're about him, don't you think? I suppose all love poems are really about the poet."

"You don't believe he felt the lightning bolt? When he first saw Laura?"

She rubbed against me. Seeking warmth, not sex. "He was probably *looking* for the lightning bolt. She just happened to be standing there. On that bridge. She was convenient."

"I felt a lightning bolt. When I first saw you," I told her.

"Are you sure you weren't looking for one yourself?"

"You said—I'll never forget what you said—you told me that, when you saw me, you'd never wanted anything else so much."

"That's different. Women know what they want. When they finally see it. Men just want what they see."

"Cleverness precludes depth. According to Aristotle."

"Aristotle was a menace. Look at all the damage he did."

"And Petrarch?"

"He was a fool," she said. "A lucky fool. He fooled himself and made a great success of it. I mean, don't you think he chose to venerate a married woman on purpose? Because he knew he couldn't have her? That way, he wouldn't have to be disappointed, if the sex turned out to be a mess. Or if she smelled or had bad breath. For all we know, she might have been as stupid as a washerwoman. Where does he say a word about her intelligence? His Laura's not a real person. She's just an object, an empty vessel filled with his own visions. The Black Death did him a favor. He could mourn her forever, without risking anything. There's something perverted about poets, don't you think?"

"I thought you loved poetry?"

She thought about that, then said, "Maybe I'm perverted, too."

I slept with another girl. The Saturday before Halloween, we played Lancelot's Lair outside of Quakertown. It was one of the best rock clubs in eastern Pennsylvania, with a serious audience. We opened for a New York band, Humanity, that had an album coming out the following week.

We blew them away. It was costume night and the audience was giddy over itself before we played a note. A black-lit crowd of gypsies, pirates, tarts, cavaliers, space aliens, and freaks with head-shop wardrobes *wanted* to be excited, to go on a rave, as if playing dress-up released them from their usual constraints. They fed us energy as we tuned our instruments.

We kicked off with "Angeline." The song's cascades of guitar riffs grabbed the room. After that, we roared through a set of all-original material: "Hideaway," "Glass Slipper," "America: Speed Limit 90," and a half-dozen others. A girl dressed as a sultry witch planted herself in front of my side of the stage and never moved from the spot. She was a dead ringer for Grace Slick of the Jefferson Airplane.

Energized, I danced over to Frankie with jagged steps and we played off each other, keeping the visuals lively while Matty soloed in the background. The two of us had a preening contest, singing into the same mike, call-and-response, for the "Garbage Landscape" section of "America: Speed Limit 90." We faked a fencing match with our instruments, never quite letting the necks touch. During his drum solo, Stosh went so wild he knocked over a cymbal—which further electrified the crowd. Perhaps they longed for destruction.

When we sliced off the last, mad, cacophonous ending, the crowd roared. We didn't even get offstage before it was clear that we had to play an encore.

Frankie knew how to read an audience better than any front man who wasn't already a headliner. Instead of calling for another original, he gathered us in by Stosh's drum kit and said, " 'Bristol Stomp.' "

The choice took me aback. The old Dovells' doo-wop number was something we did as a gag in coal-town bars to get the beehive-hairdo holdouts dancing. Then I grasped what Frankie was up to: It was all about the beat, the rhythm, now. "Bristol Stomp" had a get-dirty beat that we powered up into a sexual war dance. Nobody could hold still after two bars. Lyrics and sophistication were irrelevant. The crowd needed music for a tribal ritual.

Frankie's instincts were dead-on. The audience wasn't as cool and hip as it believed itself to be. Everybody ached to be part of the show, to bounce around like idiots and yell, Communards at the let's-fuck barricades.

With the mob wonderfully raucous, Frankie repositioned his bass across his hips, strode to the lead mike, and cried, *"Time for a party!"*

Stosh counted us off. And the room exploded. Even Grace Slick's kid sister turned from the stage to dance with a big, plain girlfriend.

Frankie, Stosh, and Matty had grown up on doo-wop, last-date, wreck-the-car, feel-her-up-at-the-malt-shop harmonies. The music was louder and far more polished now, but vocally, they reverted to their Famous Flames days. Frankie's long red hair could have been a ducktail.

We *owned* that room. Matty inserted a solo that took hot-rod guitar riffs on a space odyssey, making the dancers sweat and wave their arms: Happy, stoned on volume, they gave up the sense of self to be part of the beast. It was the anarchist's version of Hitler's Nuremberg rallies.

We tightened back to a last round of harmonies. Stosh tossed his internal metronome and notched up the beat. The hall had grown physically hot and a girl fainted, startling her fellow dancers. Had we called for that mob to kill, it might have done so.

The sensation wasn't frightening. It was thrilling.

As we wrapped up, the crowd—a great, conglomerate monster— howled and cheered and stamped hundreds of feet. It wanted *more*.

The club manager, a pseudohipster with a Skip Spence mustache, rushed onstage to shoo us off. We were spoiling the plan. Humanity, the New York outfit, was supposed to star that evening. But any musician in that room understood that if the headline group fell one inch short of brilliant, they were going to flop.

Frankie's face shone, high on the adulation pulsing from the crowd. Stosh was soaked with sweat. Only Matty seemed unmoved, although I knew he would have played all night.

"Great set, guys, great set," the manager told us, unsure of what he was witnessing. He couldn't think beyond the printed program. Yet he sensed the danger in losing the crowd.

He decided that the size of the type on the advertising posters confirmed the importance the mob would assign to each band. Descending into the audience—to a couple of boos—he waved to the elevated booth that controlled the stage lights.

Lancelot's Lair had two facing stages, allowing different bands to follow each other promptly, without shifting equipment. The lights dropped on our side of the room and the spots came up on Humanity's gleaming equipment. Their drummer was already onstage, but the rest of the band was missing.

The manager forced his way through the crowd, then climbed up on the main stage. After positioning himself behind the center microphone, he waved his arms for quiet.

"Got to move on," he said, "keep on truckin', cowboys and Indians . . . because, you know, we have something really phenomenal for you tonight . . . a Halloween treat, and this is no trick . . . I'm talking about candy for your ears, people. . . . Here they are, straight from New York, the stars of tomorrow, with their brand-new album . . . let's hear it for Humanity!"

The crowd gave the still invisible band a decent round of applause. But they clearly felt that their party had been spoiled.

There are few things more gratifying to a musician than seeing the band that follows his own fall flat. Humanity went facedown in a ditch.

At first, the group's members delayed coming out of the dressing room, letting the club manager stand there, stumped, with only the drummer to prove that Humanity existed. We understood what was happening: The other musicians wanted to put some space between the sets, to let the audience forget and relax their loyalties.

When they did come out, they made mistakes that doomed them. After we had whipped the crowd into a dancing, partying frenzy, they started off their set with a phony cerebral number, limp-dicked Vanilla Fudge, built around sustained organ chords that were meant to signal profundity. It was all architecture and no beat, the kind of number that might work on an album but would leave a fired-up audience unmoved. And their bass player was stoned. He kept missing his entries and exits, flubbing the count in ways a drummer can't cover. They must have thought the hicks in Quakertown would be thrilled with any tidbits tossed from a hot Manhattan band. They were wrong.

I didn't have to find Grace Slick's kid sister. She found me. Her witch's hat was gone and she had combed her long hair. She asked me if I wanted to go out in the parking lot and get high.

I was as high as I needed to be from the fervor of the crowd. But smoking a joint or a few crumbs of hash was the social ritual that had replaced the shared ice-cream sodas of yesteryear. And I had an overload of energy that needed an outlet.

Perhaps I was miffed that Laura had gone home again—a ritual repeated every second weekend—instead of coming along on a night I'd told her could be important. Maybe it was frustration that the love songs I longed to write refused to be summoned. It could have been that I was scared of what I felt for her, too. My fantasy of a rock musician's life involved a procession of ruthless conquests amid groupies of starlet beauty—like those who sometimes appeared in *Rolling Stone*. Instead of feasting on legions of girls and women, I thought about Laura constantly, daydreaming about her while I gave guitar lessons to kids who only wanted to pick their noses. I wanted her all of the time, as if she were a drug that had taken me captive. It made me feel cheated.

I went to the closet that served as the B-team dressing room and got my suede Ike jacket. I felt furtive, although I faced no danger from wagging tongues. No one in the band was going to report me. We had a code. And Angela was home in bed with a cold. I was free to do as I wished.

A struck match jeweled the eyes of a pale-faced girl. As she sucked in the first smoke, a seed popped. The sparking joint lit her face. For one can't-forget moment, she became Mary Magdalene, as painted by an old master. Leaning against an Oldsmobile at the back of a gravel lot.

She passed me the joint. I went through the motions.

"That was incredible," she said.

"What kind is it?"

"I meant your band. Man, you were just incredible. Heavy songs.

I really got into you, into your music. I guess you could tell." She shivered. Theatrically. "It's cold out here."

I folded her in my arms. It was a small shock: the different height, the strange scent, a foreign texture of hair against my cheek. I took the joint, squeezed out the fire, and kissed her.

It was my first encounter with a woman who wore a garter belt without panties.

We were booked into a local motel. Instead, I went back with Joan to her apartment. Frankie had joined the party as a date for her roommate, a big girl startled and pleased by his attention. He had failed to find a better deal for the night. Joey and Pete packed up our gear for us.

Frankie was glad to be off his leash. The only liquor the girls had in stock was a bottle of crème de menthe. Frankie drank it over ice cubes, glass after glass, as we passed a hash pipe around their living room. He sprawled on a beanbag chair, with the roommate clinging to him. Her sweater had been teased off of her and she sat, heavily, in a white bra. Frankie reached down to unzip her jeans.

"Let's go in your bedroom," I told Joan.

She took me by the hand.

Her witch's costume fell away, but her spell remained unbroken. By the light of candles that spiced the air, her pale flesh and dark hair seemed the stuff of pentagrams. Her nakedness felt aggressive, faintly threatening, and more enchanting for it. Lean and confident, she was not afraid to ask for what she wanted.

After striving for an hour to impress each other, we lay on her bed, her face upon my chest. I stroked her tumbled hair. Appetite and wonder still trumped guilt. On the other side of the wall, her roommate wailed encouragement to Frankie, who just grunted.

"I don't like your singer," Joan said. Music to my ears.

"Most women do."

"I doubt it. He's just the kind of guy who convinces them they like him. I know his type." She mewed a laugh. "You're something else, though. You look like Mr. Innocent onstage. Your band's name fits. You, at least. And the big guy, the other guitar player."

She touched me with long fingers. When I kissed her, she tasted of the two of us.

"I don't want this to be a one-night stand," she said. "But if it's going to be, I want my money's worth."

I hoped to feel more of a traitor than I did. The guttering candles cast demons onto the walls. Witchery. I already knew that Joan could not compete with Laura in a single way that mattered. But I didn't care. I was already calculating how to see her again.

Joan was on top of me when Frankie barged into the room, tugging her roommate behind him. They both were naked.

"Hey . . . we thought it would be cool to change partners for a while . . . party time, folks. . . ."

Joan made no effort to cover herself or get off of me. She only paused to glare at Frankie and say, "Get the fuck out of here."

My determination to see Joan again faded less than a mile from her apartment. I was sick, literally nauseated, at what I had done. Our mandatory morning sex had been perfunctory, cold, a trial of weary bodies. I felt as though I had cheated right in front of Laura and made her watch.

With the smell of another woman still on me, I realized that I loved Laura irrevocably. I told myself it was foolish, that we were kids, that it wouldn't last, that a world of women waited to be devoured. It made no difference. I felt the love that poets claimed to know.

Hung over, Frankie stank. I drove, longing to brush my teeth and shower. Headed home, we stopped at a diner for breakfast.

Over scrapple and eggs, Frankie said, "If you ever screw Angela, I'll kill you."

ELEVEN

This time, it was Frankie at my door. At four in the morning. Hammering and shouting for Angela.

I caught a curl of hairs in my zipper as I rushed from the bedroom. Switching on the light above the tiny porch, I opened the door. Frankie stood in the drizzle, wearing a child-molester raincoat and a Phillies cap.

Before I could speak, he said, "Tell Angela to get out here. Right now."

"She's not here. For fuck's sake. Why would she be here?"

"I know she's here. Tell her I said to get her ass out here."

"She's not *here*, Frankie. Come in and see for yourself. Just let me make sure Laura's got the covers up. And stop yelling, for God's sake."

He stepped inside, watering the floor. The wetness on his face was not all rain.

"Do you know where she is? If you know, tell me."

"Why should I know where your wife is?" I turned on a stronger lamp. "Jesus Christ. It's barely four o'clock."

Frankie sat down. Without taking off his raincoat. "She didn't come home. Angela always comes home. Even when she's out late, she always comes home. I thought maybe she'd be here."

"Why would she be here?"

He tried to make a joke and become Frankie Star again. "There's no accounting for tastes."

"Well, she's not here. I haven't seen her in over a week. And I haven't heard from her. Did you try Joey's?"

He stiffened. "Why would she be at Joey's?"

"It was just a thought. Joey's parties can go all night."

"Is he having a party?"

"I have no idea, man. I told you, it was just a thought. What about Stosh?"

"He wouldn't know anything."

"Matty?"

The look in his eyes sharpened. "She knows better."

"You must've called her girlfriends?"

"Those sluts. You can't let them know anything. Unless you want the world to know it."

"Look, Frankie . . . you're sitting here soaking wet . . . and she's probably home now."

"She's not. I just called from the pay phone outside Town and Country."

Imagining the band's disintegration over bullshit, I took things back to the basic proposition, the one that concerned me. "Frankie . . . come on, man. You've got to get any ideas out of your head about me and Angela. There's nothing between us. And there never was. I'm in love with Laura."

I read the skepticism on his face. He was replaying our recent adventures in Quakertown.

"I know what you're thinking," I continued. "But I mean it. I really am in love with her. You're getting snakes in your head over nothing."

He pondered the universe. "Yeah . . . yeah, I know, I know. I just get wound up. She does that to me. Hey, what I said? In the diner last week? That was stupid. I was just pissed, you know? About how things went down that night. I know Angela loves me. But there's something going on. I don't know. Maybe it's just the speed. She's doing too goddamned much of it. I wish I could get her to knock it off. It's just the worst shit for her. It's got her jumping out of her skin, the least little thing sets her off."

"Can't you get her to throttle back? Maybe you should get her to start coming to all the gigs again. You could keep an eye on her."

"I don't want her coming to all the gigs. Don't say nothing to her about that, okay?"

I nodded. Okay.

"The other night," he said, "I tried to talk to her. I really wanted to sit down and talk. I mean, her meth thing is starting to cost real money. She sneaks it, but I know. And I *tried* to talk to her. She just went screaming nuts, broke every plate in the kitchen. Those dishes were a wedding present from my mother—what am I supposed to tell her when she comes over to the house? Then Angela takes off out the door, snoot in the air and dishes all over the floor. Dragging her ass over to St. Mike's again. She's over there all the time now. If she isn't popping pills or snorting lines, she's praying to the Virgin Mary. If I didn't think the priest was a fruit, I'd think he and Angela had something going on." He shook his wet head. "Maybe your people are right. Maybe we're all nuts, ain't? Screwball Matty running to confession every time he breaks a guitar string. Like the baby Jesus gives a shit. And now Angela acting like Bernadette of Lourdes on crank. Next thing, it'll be Stosh signing up for the seminary. . . ."

"I don't quite see Stosh as a priest."

"You don't know Stosh, either. Anyway, Angela's not even a real Catholic. I mean, she is, but she isn't. She's a Uke, not a Polack. Her maiden name's Yushenko. Her people think they're real Catholics, but you should hear Father Wajda go off on that subject, once he's been at the Four Roses. I mean, if she was Lithuanian, it'd be different." He looked at me. "What're you? Besides Protestant?"

"Episcopalian. But I stopped going."

Frankie smirked. "The ones with the money. I should've known."

"I never pictured Angela as religious."

"On Sunday mornings she is. Her and crazy Matty. It's okay, though. It keeps her from doing anything really stupid."

"Doing too much meth is pretty stupid. Couldn't you talk to her priest? Get him to talk to her?"

Frankie waved his right hand, dismissing the notion. "Father Kalashko can't stand me. I told you, it's a mixed marriage. We're Polish, her crowd's Ukrainian. Cossack shits. They're not even the good Ukrainians."

Swimming back to shore, he eyed my new guitar. Music was our life preserver.

I had not put the guitar back in the case the night before, leaving it on the guitar stand by the stereo. I had bought a Rickenbacker twelve-string, fire-engine red with a white pick guard. I liked the jingle-jangle sound the Byrds had on their early albums and thought the chime effect of the twelve-string might work on harder rock numbers, filling in the texture of songs like "Angeline." The Rickenbacker wasn't going to replace my Les Paul, only supplement it and add to the band's identity.

"Feel like playing some music?" Frankie asked.

"Jesus, Frankie. It's, what, five in the morning? And Laura's sleeping."

"I wasn't thinking. It's been a crazy night."

"Why don't you go home? She's probably there. Use the phone, if you want. She just might not be answering. Maybe she's pissed that *you're* not home, you know?"

Eventually, I got him back on the road. Bleary, I headed back into the bedroom, stripped off my jeans, and lowered myself into bed beside Laura.

As my head hit the pillow, she clicked on the bedside lamp and braced herself on an elbow.

"What was *that* all about?" she asked.

"Frankie thought Angela was here."

"Why would she be here?"

"That's what I asked Frankie. I don't know. They're going through a bad patch."

Laura hesitated before she spoke again. I could tell she was choosing her words with particular care. "Don't get involved. Please, Will."

"I have no intention of getting involved."

"She's dangerous."

"I thought you were best buddies now?"

"No. We're not. I'm civil to her. Because it's sensible to be civil. For your sake, your band. And I pity her. Married to that ass and stuck in Frackville. It's the most depressing town I've ever seen."

"You need to see more of the county. Frackville's a jewel."

"You're changing the subject. What I meant to say is that people like her are only nice to people like us when they want something. Or when they need something."

"'People like us'?"

"You know what I mean."

"She's still a vampire, then? Despite the knockout job she did on your hair?"

"Vampires start by trying to gain your confidence. In literature, they're very seductive."

With her hair gently rumpled, Laura looked awfully seductive herself.

"Turn out the light," I said. "And come to Daddy." I held out my arms.

She shot from the bed, pale as a vampire's dying victim. With her back pressed against the cold wall, she said, "Don't *ever* say that to me."

Joan, the girl from Quakertown, phoned that afternoon. She must have gotten my number from directory assistance.

"Hello, Mr. Innocent," she said.

Fortunately, Laura was down at the campus.

"I forget, is it Samantha or Glenda?"

"Which witch would you prefer?"

"I really liked the costume." I was stalling.

"It's hanging in the closet. I can put it back on anytime you want. Feel like taking a drive?"

"Can't. We have a practice session. I'd never make it back."

"Like a visitor, then? I could fly up on my broomstick."

"Listen . . . Joan . . . I owe you an apology . . . I should've told you . . ."

She laughed. Knowingly.

"You're married. Aren't you?" She paused for one breath. "High school sweetheart?"

"Yes," I lied.

She didn't speak. But she didn't hang up.

"I'm sorry . . ."

"Oh, shut up." She laughed again. The sound was not as fierce as I had expected. "Men are *never* sorry for what they do. They're only sorry when they get caught doing it. I should've known. No guy's as sweet as you were if he isn't cheating. Tell you what, Mr. Innocent Married Man. Call me sometime when you're not married." She laughed a last time, still without evident spite. "I guess I got my money's worth, anyway."

I expected her to hang up, but she didn't.

"Another thing: Tell that dick lead singer of yours to stop calling me. It isn't going to happen."

Later that week, I picked up Laura after a rehearsal, but my mind was on a new song that had sparked in my head as I drove. When we got to the apartment, I told her I needed a couple of minutes with the twelve-string. God only knows where songs come from, but the hook riff, one verse, and a bridge had appeared fully formed in my head. I sat down and played the guitar line, then shifted to chords as I sang:

Black Jane unlucky . . . Black Jane unlucky . . .
Black Jane unlucky . . . lucky girl . . .

Gipsy downtown read it in her cards,
Said that she could see us in her ball . . .
Witches whispered: I've been in your stars,
Janie, you get me—or you don't get no man at all . . .

I needed to lock in the melody. It was almost there. But the bridge wanted a tryout, too. I shifted from the home chord to the fourth:

You were such . . . a good girl for so long,
You half believed that you could fool the world.
Then I kissed you . . . and damn to right or wrong . . .
You knew with that first kiss that you were just that kind of
*   girl . . .*

Laura yawned. The drama of it was worthy of Bette Davis.

I stopped playing.

"It's humbling," she told me. "Here I am, ready, willing, and anxious to go to bed with you . . . and you'd rather play your guitar."

"Oh, come on. I just didn't want to lose this."

"I'm jealous, though. How can I not be? If you think about it, you spend a lot more of your waking hours holding a guitar than you do holding me."

"Well, you're not here. You're either at class, or you're studying. Though God knows what you're studying for. Partially housebroken chimpanzees could ace the exams down there."

That only annoyed her more. "You don't take things seriously."

"That's not true. I take *you* seriously. I love you. And I take music seriously."

"I wonder if you don't love your music more, though? I mean, if you had to choose between us?"

"That's not fair. And it's not a rational proposition."

"I don't want you to be rational. I want you to be passionate. About me. The way you are about music."

"I'm not?"

"Not tonight."

"And last night?"

"Last night's gone. It's always tonight that matters. For us. Not last night. Not tomorrow night."

"That sounds like a line from a French film."

"It isn't. It's the truth. Nothing exists but right now. We don't know what tomorrow will bring."

"I thought you were reading Kierkegaard. That sounds more like Kerouac jerking off." I put down the guitar. "All right. If nothing exists but right now, let's not waste any more time."

She knew she had been unfair. She made it up to me.

"You're on the Pill, right?" I had never thought to ask her.

"No. But I'm careful about counting the days."

My mother wore her old Chanel suit, an extravagance committed for her by my father back when Jackie Kennedy ruled the fashion roost and our family finances held promise. Her lawyer, Barry Levenger, had the documents ready for our signatures in his office, which smelled of cigarettes and furniture polish. There was a small trust fund in my name. My father had specified that the money could not be touched until I turned twenty-one. My mother's lawyer, a family acquaintance whom I did not like, had found a way to break the trust, as long as I was willing to sign it away. I didn't mind. The $31,000 in the fund would keep my mother in her house for another year or two. And I didn't want anything from my father. Besides, I was confident that the Innocents would be making serious money soon.

Leaving the Thompson Building on that sharp November day, my mother pulled on her gloves—black kid—and asked, "How's Laura?"

"Why ask, if you don't care?"

"But I do care. Of course I care. I'm your mother. And you're enamored of the girl."

"I'm in love with her."

My mother gave up her attempt at social niceties. "You're just like your father. You need a woman who's flawed."

· · ·

Does any mother like to see her son with a woman who might be her equal? To be fair, I don't think my mother ever realized how lonely I had been. It wasn't the only-child nonsense from the quizzes in Psych 101. I had always drawn people who wanted to make friends— if not always the friends I wanted to make. In Little League and Midget League football, then after a screwed-up knee confirmed my vocation with the guitar, I always had people around me. But I never had anyone I could talk to about the things that started to matter. Elsewhere, people talked about books and music and films in a wonderfully sophisticated manner, their lives a constant exchange of profound views about existence, I was sure. And all I had were the fading streets of Pottsville.

In high school, I subscribed to *Evergreen Review* and mail-order books from Grove Press—not just the gents' porn, but books by authors whose very names were portents: Gombrowicz, Robbe-Grillet, Duras, Goytisolo. I did not enjoy a single one of their novels, but I dutifully read them through to the last page. I spent a great deal of painfully husbanded money on those books before I belatedly began to suspect that the problem might lie with the authors and not just with me. I had no guide. My mother had read, but she read no longer, and her remembered tastes dead-ended at Proust. My high school English teachers were sincere, but their horizons barely reached Steinbeck. After I saved up to buy the boxed recordings of Maria Callas singing *Carmen,* the music teacher told me she couldn't sing. She adored Kirsten Flagstad.

Laura was the woman of my dreams. Brilliant, beautiful, decorous in public, and lascivious in private, she was the smartest human being of any age or sex that I had ever met. She'd read everything, memorizing half of it. When she got beyond her quick-draw cleverness, her judgments possessed an integrity that marked them as her own. I never caught her repeating a critic's view—a sin of which I often had been guilty. If that made her eccentric, or flawed, or whatever it was my mother believed she detected, then I was flawed, too.

I did have a sense of irony. Without one, you couldn't survive with the north-of-the-mountain crowd. I long had mocked myself for "living in the someday me," instead of draining everything from the moment, as rock musicians were supposed to do. With Laura, someday had arrived.

She was the only girl or woman I had ever dreaded losing.

A good day ended badly. It began well, with a call from Stosh that I almost missed. I had been listening, with headphones, to the new Steve Miller Band album right up to the minute I had to dash out the door to drive down to class: "Quicksilver Girl" was the greatest American love song ever written to a hooker.

Stosh, who could be almost as stoic as Matty offstage, sounded as wired as a kid on Christmas morning. Word of our gig at Lancelot's Lair had circulated. Fast. The Electric Factory in Philly wanted us to open on a Wednesday night just before Christmas, just six weeks away. A no-frills hall near the city's heart, the Electric Factory was the most important showcase for new bands in Pennsylvania.

The dream was coming true.

"There's no national name on the bill," Stosh told me, "but they've got two breakout Philly bands playing."

"Sounds like it could draw talent scouts."

"You read my mind."

"That's great, man. Really."

"Word's getting around. I'm getting calls for dates we already got booked."

That reminded me of something: "I just wish we didn't have Frankie's Rocktop bullshit next week."

Stosh agreed. "We should've done the Harrisburg arena. That could've been a break, too."

"Ever figure out what Frankie was thinking?"

"I'm still stumped. But the Pit of the Poconos it is. For four nights, anyway."

"Well, we've got Lehigh this Saturday. That should be good. If they got the word out, we'll pull in the Lancelot's Lair crowd. Hey, I have to get on the road. Classes."

"Big Man on Campus," Stosh said. His sneering had grown more good-natured over the months.

"How's Red, by the way?"

"Great, man, she's just great. Good things come to the guy who waits, you know?"

Days of dull rain had given way to Indian summer. With copper-colored leaves sweeping over the walks, the campus looked almost like a college catalog. The ROTC cadets were drilling as I walked from the parking lot. Hoping Vietnam would be over before they graduated, I figured. To the extent we bothered thinking about it, we expected Nixon to nuke North Vietnam the day after his inauguration.

My spirits were soaring, despite the state of the world. Who really cared, anyway? Music mattered more than any election.

Passing a pair of unplucked girls in duffel coats, I recited to myself, " 'Practice your beauty, blue girls, before it fail. . . .' "

That day, few women lacked a trace of beauty.

After a sleeping-pill lecture on the schism between the churches of Rome and Byzantium, I strolled over to the office of the young instructor responsible for my psych class. Dr. Kessler was popular, since he graded in the spirit of the gentler Christian saints, redeeming the most wretched. He never had trouble filling up his classroom, whether for his Introduction to Psychology courses or for the sociology sessions that filled out his galley-slave schedule. Since I would miss two classes during the Poconos gig, I needed to get the readings and any additional coursework in advance. I was scrupulous about going through the motions, less so about the work. The poor guy always acted surprised when a student took him seriously.

Frail, earnest, and virginal, he invited me to sit down.

Before I could speak, a colleague of his leaned in around the door frame.

"John, you have a call on my line."

Kessler didn't even merit his own office phone. He apologized for the interruption and told me he'd be right back.

I stood up and looked outside. At least they gave him a window. A marvelous gust swept between the buildings. Talking to a boy on a bench, a girl brushed a golden leaf from lofting brown hair. Every minute spent indoors was wasted.

Turning away, I noticed a paper misaligned halfway down a stack of midterms. It bore a circled red F with an exclamation point.

Nobody got an F in one of his classes. It was physically impossible in a Newtonian universe.

I listened for footsteps and heard none. I couldn't resist looking to see who was stupid enough to fail one of his courses. I reached across the desk and peeled back the papers above the one graded a failure.

Filled out in a child's scrawl, the paper showed a carnage of red ink. The name at the upper-left corner was "Laura Saunders."

That Saturday, Matty and I drove down to Allentown a few hours early for the Lehigh gig. He wanted to stop at a music store that carried Ernie Ball strings, and I was due for a visit to a nearby head shop, just up the street from Hess's, that carried hard-to-find albums issued by minor labels. Most of the music was disappointing, but the shop had introduced me to Pearls Before Swine and H. P. Lovecraft. The latter's version of "Wayfaring Stranger" updated Christianity to the fascist era.

The salesman in the music store knew Matty and convinced him to try out a Gibson L-5 that had just come in. While Matty conjured the ghosts of Charlie Christian and Django Reinhardt, I wandered down the block to the head shop. It was one of those days when I couldn't bear to listen to him, when the ease with which he played out-of-thin-air wonders chipped at my confidence. I still dreamed that, eventually,

I'd break the code and play as well as he did. I practiced until I had to soak my fingers in hot water. But the dream was growing harder to sustain.

You could smell the incense out on the sidewalk. I climbed the stairs to the shop.

Joan stood leafing through a rack of record albums. She smiled when she saw me. It struck me for the first time that she had old-fashioned posture. As my mother did. Joan was no Swarthmore girl, of course. Not even a Smithie. But, straight and lean, she had a model's lines and a courtesan's charm.

"You bastard," she said. Still smiling.

"I never thought I'd run into you here." It was an idiotic thing to say.

Mistress of the situation, she laughed. "You probably never thought you'd run into me anywhere. Girls are just supposed to disappear, right? Like disposable diapers?"

"No . . . I'm glad to see you. I mean it. Really."

"You're a terrible liar. Like your line about being married. Or did you forget your wedding ring again?"

I looked down at my hand. It was a stupid thing to do.

"It's your other hand. If you were married for five minutes, you'd know that much. Will . . . it's all right. You're not going to catch me peeking in your window. Okay? But please tell me one thing honestly. Just for my peace of mind. You're in love with somebody, aren't you?"

"Yes."

"And I was just a test to see if she was really magic? Was that it?"

"There was a lot more to it."

She had a wistful smile that deserved to be photographed. "I wish I'd meet just one man who wasn't predictable."

"It *was* more than that. Honestly. I looked down from the stage and saw you—"

"And I was bewitching. I know. Please don't worry. I'm not mad. Disappointed. But not mad. I got what I wanted when I wanted it.

Two sides to every story. Okay?" Her smile bloomed again. "You're so sweet. You didn't even realize you didn't have to lie."

"I never intended to lie to you. That's the truth. Things just happened."

"Didn't you think I might have the least bit of curiosity?" Bemused by the human race, she shook her head. "Well, you got away with it this time. The Wicked Witch won't haunt you and your Snow White."

I didn't know how to end the situation, but Joan did. She stepped against me and kissed me full on the mouth, wet and delicious.

"Call me sometime when you're not in love," she told me.

She walked out, passing Matty by the front counter.

I made a show of inspecting the ranks of albums, then bought one that I didn't really want.

On the way to the parking lot, Matty said, "That was the girl from Lancelot's Lair. Wasn't it?"

"Yeah. I didn't expect to run into her."

We walked a few more steps.

"Don't try to be Frankie," Matty told me. "You're not him. You wouldn't want to be him."

"I never wanted to be Frankie," I said. That was one ambition I truly had never felt.

Matty wasn't listening. He was thinking and talking.

"If you love someone," he said, "and they love you, don't mess it up."

The next week, before we drove up to the Poconos, I wrote a song for Laura.

TWELVE

That Wednesday afternoon, I crammed my two guitar cases, a small suitcase, and a clutch of clothes on hangers into the Corvair. Heading for the Rocktop Club in the eastern Poconos and four nights of playing for drunks. My attitude didn't improve when, one street from my apartment, a state police car pulled up behind me.

Any male with long hair in Schuylkill County in 1968 was paranoid around cops. I was clean and my car was clean, but it got my attention when the Statie turned left at the intersection with 61 and followed me over the ridge to St. Clair. He didn't turn on his bubblegum machine, though. And I stayed under the speed limit.

The cop closed up behind me at every red light in St. Clair. Then he trailed me up the Frackville grade and onto the newly opened stretch of interstate. Whenever I checked the rearview mirror, he was there, a couple of car lengths back.

I told myself that I had nothing to worry about—then wondered if I did. Had something come out of the mess at Buzzy's farm back in October? Was Joey still dealing on the sly, tainting me and the band by association? Every girl in my life was over eighteen . . . although that wasn't a major concern in the county, where things started early and people just closed their eyes.

I kept my speed down, didn't pass anyone, and took great care not to swerve.

On a lonely stretch of ridge between ravaged coal valleys, the Statie finally turned on his siren and lights.

I pulled over.

He got out of the car: a big guy, all shoulders and chest. I fished my paperwork out of the dashboard pocket and rolled down the window.

With a slab of face and temples all but shaved below his cap, he looked like Mussolini after a bodybuilding course. His name tag read "Tomczik," but I didn't need to see it. The family resemblance to Matty was unmistakable. Would life sculpt Matty into a monster, too?

"License, registration, and proof of insurance."

I handed him the documents.

"Put your hands on the steering wheel and keep them there."

I did as told.

"William Barker Cross," he said, "the Third. From behind, I thought you were a girl."

"What was the problem, Officer?"

"Don't get smart with me. You know what the problem was."

I had no idea.

"Do you know how fast you were going?"

"Just under the speed limit."

"Go ahead. See what being a smart-ass gets you. I clocked you going ninety-four miles an hour."

I caught myself on the verge of saying that the Corvair wouldn't do eighty going downhill. He knew that. This was his way of getting back at Matty. I knew that. I would've liked to ask him what it felt like when his nephew coldcocked him. But he had all the power and I had none.

"I thought I was going under the speed limit," I said. As respectfully as I could.

"You think the limit's a hundred miles an hour?" He drew out his ticket pad. "You're going to lose your license for this. For six months."

"Officer, I—"

"You don't want to talk back to me. When I'm letting you off easy. After you ran a red light back in St. Clair. And passed illegally."

"No, Officer. I don't want to talk back to you."

He snorted and wrote. "You won't hear nothing until the spring. Docket's always backed up. But don't think you been forgotten, when you don't hear for a while. We don't forget. You're going to get to walk on your own two legs for a while. So you can learn to obey the traffic laws." He cocked his head and smiled down at me. "I wonder if I should check your car for drugs?"

He didn't. He just tore off the ticket and handed it to me. "It's your lucky day, Mr. Cross. You could've lost your license for an entire year. I'm giving you a break. You drive carefully from now on."

Things got worse. So much worse that I didn't say a word about the ticket to Matty or anyone else. I decided I'd talk to my mother's lawyer about it. I didn't like him, but he could tell me how much it would cost to get the citation pulled. He'd couch the number in terms of legal fees, but just about anything short of murder in front of a mass audience could be fixed in the county. I just wasn't sure if I would have the money.

We hadn't even finished setting up our gear on the stage when we learned the reason Frankie booked the gig. Darlene, the go-go Cleopatra last seen at the Greek's in Shamokin, was dancing at the Rocktop all that week. She looked even harder, meaner, and sexier than before, all taut wires under hard-rubber flesh.

"You sonofabitch," Stosh said to Frankie. "You shit-eating sonofabitch."

"Hey," Frankie said. To Stosh and to all of us. "I had no idea she'd be here."

I thought Matty was going to knock him down. Instead, Matty took his guitar to his motel room across the parking lot. We didn't see him again until it was almost time for our first number.

Our performance that evening wasn't our best. Frankie, whose first private encounter with Darlene may not have been all that he'd hoped, toned down his sex-show antics. He still seemed better suited to the old Famous Flames, though. Or to some scuzzy lounge at the Jersey shore. The rest of us kept it professional, but there were few hints of the group that had electrified the crowd at Lancelot's Lair—or even of the band that had the frat boys freaking out down at Lehigh.

Frankie and Darlene disappeared during the first break, but not the second. Stosh smirked and remarked, "She's probably more than even Frankie can handle."

The owner, whom nobody liked, was content, though. The band played its sets, took requests, and kept the dancers happy. We could have been any one of over a dozen groups on the circuit.

We had an agreement that we could rehearse in the afternoons while the club was closed, but Frankie didn't show up for the first session. It reignited the anger everyone felt. Even Joey, who cultivated a laid-back image behind the sound board, clearly had the ass. Pete, his sidekick, sat there shaking his head, taking off his wire-rim glasses, and putting them back on again. Frankie had broken a trust: You didn't blow off a rehearsal.

We needed to work, too. Things were coming together so well for us, moving so fast, that we had to prepare to cut a demo tape to peddle to record companies. There was no block of open time in our schedule until after New Year's, but we all had agreed to book studio time in January. The first step was just to hear ourselves on tape and find out what didn't work. Live performances could thrill a crowd, while the same band or song might not transfer well to an album. We were confident, though. Our only disagreement lay in the choice of studios. Matty and I were all for booking a Philly studio with full-time engineers and a track record, but Stosh and Frankie wanted to save money by going with an evenings-only studio in Reading the first time out.

After discarding some of my older stuff, we had fourteen solid original songs, which the others felt would be plenty. But I was determined to get us up to eighteen or even twenty originals. I wanted us to have a choice of what went on an eventual album, with no filler songs. Too many groups had gotten one big chance, only to blow it. Everything I'd read about the business led me to believe that at least one song out of three would flop when the tape started rolling. I was determined to get it right. Matty was my ally.

Without Frankie, there were limits to what we could rehearse. If anything, his absence highlighted his indispensability. He wasn't only an incandescent front man, he was a rock-solid bass player whose years of working with Stosh had given the two of them a connection just short of telepathy.

But Frankie was off with Darlene the Devil, his little carnivore with her too-white teeth and black-lacquer helmet of hair. I had hoped we could start work on an arrangement of the song I'd just written for Laura—I wanted to surprise her—but it needed Frankie, with his tenor switch turned on. The number had a sweeping melody line set to powerful, chiming chord changes. A blend of ballad and rave up, it was different from anything I'd written before . . . or from anything I'd ever heard.

And it truly was for Laura, although I wasn't certain she'd get it until I told her so. Songwriting is a form of conjuring, and her name wasn't one of the magic words. Unless it was inserted in the body of a line, as in the old tears-for-teens song "Tell Laura I Love Her," the name didn't sing well. It couldn't open a line strongly and couldn't close one at all. So, although the song expressed my feelings for Laura, the name of the woman in the lyrics was Carlotta.

That afternoon session clearly wasn't the right time to introduce a new song, though. Stosh was so furious at Frankie, so harsh in his criticism, that Matty finally told him, "Forget it. Let it go. Unless you want the band to fold. There's nothing any of us can do about it now."

Thursday night, we plodded through three more sets.

On Friday, I tried to talk to Frankie. No one else would. On a break from his adventures with Darlene, he joined me for a lunchtime ride down the mountain to a diner off the main road. I missed Laura and worried about her now. I would have driven back to see her the previous afternoon, had I known the rehearsal would come to nothing. But I kept my resentment in check. I didn't want the group to come apart, and the current problem had multiple angles to it.

Frankie's table manners were as bad as his teeth. When he got to his second cheeseburger, I decided to do my guidance counselor best.

"You know, Frankie . . . if Angela decides to drive up here one of these nights, it's not going to take her fifteen seconds to figure out what's going on."

With beef-and-bread mush filling his mouth, he told me, "Don't worry about Angela. She hates this place. She won't come near it."

"Or if any of her friends show up."

"They hate it, too."

"Come on, man. Darlene's trouble from ground zero. You have to see that."

"Well, if she is, she's the kind of trouble I like. Hey, give me a break, huh? I can still see that Joan bitch riding up and down on your dick. Tell me you weren't having a good time."

"That was different. I made a mistake."

"Well, you sure looked like you were enjoying your mistake. Man, she looked *hot*. Maybe you should make mistakes more often?" He laughed, then put on his know-it-all smile. "I'll bet you get tired of that brainy pussy all the time, just yak-yakking away. Know what I think? I think you really like them dumb and dirty." He laughed again. "Takes one to know one, don't it, Bark?"

"I asked you to knock off calling me 'Bark.'"

He grinned. You weren't going to see those teeth on an album cover. Not even if they were brushed. "Okay. 'Wilbur.'"

"It's not 'Wilbur.' And you know it. It's 'William.' 'Will' to my friends. If you'd like to try being one."

He went into a Mr. Ed imitation: "*'Wil-l-l-l-bur-r-r.'*"

The waitress, who did not appear to be a happy woman, glanced toward us: two assholes who looked as if they'd stiff her on the tip. Beyond the plate-glass window, snow flurries teased the gray landscape.

"Look, Frankie . . . just last week you were telling me how much you love Angela."

"That was last week," he said, taking another bite of cheeseburger.

The flurries turned into the first snow of the season, early and unwelcome. By the time darkness fell, the roads were bad. I wasn't surprised at how empty the club remained, but that anyone showed up at all. We played to a dozen people at four or five tables, with a few regulars at the bar slobbering over Darlene.

She seemed to have cooled on Frankie, who had shown up on time for the Friday afternoon rehearsal. He still faded into the darkness with her after the last set, though. The rest of us sat around in the room Joey shared with Pete, drinking Wild Turkey and messing around on unamplified guitars with Johnny Carson mugging in the background. We let Pete sit in on harmonica. He was teaching himself to play blues harp and not making great progress. I didn't mind him jamming with us after hours, though. His desire to play music was so earnest that I felt sorry for him. Perhaps I recognized a cosmic connection. Matty didn't seem to mind, either. He just played right past him.

I had always blown off Pete in the past, back when he trailed our band like a needy dog. Lately, though, I had registered him as a person. He didn't ask for much, just to be around the band and do whatever odd jobs needed doing. Physically the smallest of us, he was always there to lift the heaviest speaker cabinets and amps. With his bushy mustache, wire-rims, and thin hair down over his shoulders, he looked like a caricature of a hippie weakling. But he worked tirelessly and he was easily our biggest fan. He knew every lyric by heart.

Recently, we'd started giving Joey a cut of 12 percent. It didn't begin to pay for the sound system or the van. Joey passed most of it on to Pete. Everyone wanted to be around a band, to share in the power and the glory, hoping the radiance would rub off on close associates.

Johnny and Doc gave way to Tyrone Power on *The Late Late*

Show. Joey dozed off behind his thick black beard. The rest of us were too tired to play any pranks on him.

Around two in the morning, we all perked up one last time. Stumbling outside, we had a snowball fight under a sky blown clear and star-burned. Then we went our separate ways to bed, feeling drunk and fraternal, facing a hungry morning until a plow made it up the mountain.

A few rooms down from mine, Frankie and Darlene were having a fight.

By Saturday—our last night at the Rocktop—the road had been cleared and the room was packed. Word on the band had gotten out, and a number of under-twenty-one heads were turned away. The size of the crowd not only got us back into our all-conquering groove, but meant we were less likely to have an argument with Mario, the club's owner, who loved to trot out excuses why he shouldn't have to pay the amount specified in any given contract. It was clear that we were hot and he'd want us back. We didn't intend to tell him that he was never going to see or hear us again once we got off his mountain.

Frankie became a serious front man again. As far as Darlene was concerned, he was of less interest than a dead mouse in a neighbor's basement. When she danced, she ignored all of us, playing to the barflies. On our breaks, Frankie flirted with a table of older women, the thirtyish kind who wore fake pearls, worked as secretaries, and screwed the boss. If he meant to make Darlene jealous, it didn't work. She was just putting in the hours until she could go.

I had never seen a woman who looked so vicious, in every sense of the word. If Frankie had been a fool, he'd also been brave.

By the end of the night, we all were relieved that the episode was behind us. Mario paid up without quibbling, and Darlene disappeared, leaving Frankie behind with most of his body parts intact. No one intended to stay overnight, despite the free rooms. The road shone with patches of ice, thanks to the plummeting temperature, and the parking lot slush jumped over the tops of our shoes as we loaded our gear, but we were determined to make it home that night, even if it meant driving fifteen miles per hour. We had four vehicles for the six of us and planned to convoy, at least until we reached the interstate.

Stosh and Pete were off fetching their bags from their rooms. Frankie and I stood in the cold behind my Corvair, wishing for coffee and watching as Joey and Matty checked that our gear had been loaded properly in the van. We had rearranged the packing plan to shift weight forward so the vehicle wouldn't fishtail on an icy patch. Beside me, Frankie shivered and said, "If we ever make it big, I'm moving to Florida."

Near the front door of the club, a car backed out. Late boozers, I figured, glad they were headed down the hill ahead of us and not behind us.

Instead of turning down the drive, the car, a dark Lincoln, circled the lot and stopped in front of us.

Two men got out. The driver remained behind the wheel.

"You. Romeo," one of the men said to Frankie. "Get in the car." He spoke with a hard Philly accent.

"Fuck off," Frankie told him. But his voice did not sound assured.

Matty turned from the van. The man who had remained silent drew a gun, warning Matty off. The thugs knew what they were doing. They kept trouble at a safe distance.

"Come on, Romeo," the other man said, producing a small automatic of his own. "We just want to educate you a little. About the laws of personal property, which you don't fucking understand."

Glancing over to be certain that Matty was safely at bay, the speaker strode over to Frankie, took his arm, and pressed the pistol's muzzle against his temple.

"We're just going to have a talk. Nothing for anybody to worry about. Now get in the car."

"Don't," Matty commanded.

The thug who had been silent spoke to Matty: "Move one more inch, and you'll never move again."

"Don't get in the car," Matty said.

"Shut your fucking trap," the gunman holding Frankie told Matty. "Stay out of this. Unless you want your lady-killer pal to have an even worse time of it."

He jerked Frankie toward the Lincoln. Frankie went along, as slowly as his kidnapper would let him.

Once he had Frankie on the floor behind the front seat, his captor got in, lowered the window, and trained his pistol on Matty. The thug who'd been covering Matty got in the far side, behind the driver.

The car tore off.

Red taillights disappeared behind black shrubs.

"What are we going to do?" Joey asked.

"Shut up," Matty said. He didn't move one muscle.

I tried to get through to him: "We have to—"

He twisted toward me. Furious. "*Shut up! Listen!*"

In the mountaintop silence, the only sound was that of the Lincoln speeding down the hill.

"Just listen," Matty whispered.

A few motel rooms down, Stosh emerged with his ancient suitcase.

Matty held up his hand: *Stop! Silence!*

The car descended forever. Forever was about three minutes. Then it stopped.

Matty turned to Joey. "You have your pistol in the van? Tell me the truth."

"Yeah."

"Give it to me. *Move!*"

He turned to me. "You—drive. Do what I say the instant I say it."

Joey produced the revolver. Matty checked the cylinders.

"Need more rounds?" Joey asked, already moving back toward the truck.

"No," Matty said.

I got behind the wheel of the Corvair. It wasn't going to catch the Lincoln in a car chase. But I grasped that Matty expected to find Frankie near the bottom of the mountain.

Bewildered, Stosh asked what was going on.

"Later," Matty said.

"It's Frankie," Joey told Stosh. "He's in deep shit."

Compressing himself to squeeze into my car, Matty said, "The rest of you stay here. Until you hear the horn."

"Be careful, man," Joey said. It sounded silly.

"Turn off the headlights," Matty snapped at me. "Just parking lights."

As soon as we cleared the lot and turned down the mountain, Matty told me to cut the engine and coast.

"Your brakes all right?"

"Yeah."

"They noisy?"

"I never noticed."

"Just watch the road. When I tell you to stop, you stop. And stay in the car. If you hear a shot, you drive off as fast as you can, whichever way the car's pointing. And don't stop. You won't be able to help me, if there's trouble."

"I couldn't just—"

"Shut up. Watch the road." He rolled down his window and leaned toward the night. Listening.

It was the most terrifying driving I'd ever done. We needed to gather speed to manage the intermittent upward grades. The tires sought out every patch of ice. Without the traction the drivetrain provided, steering was difficult. If I oversteered, I didn't trust the guardrails to stop us from plunging into the trees.

It seemed like a roller-coaster ride for the damned.

"Turn on the engine," Matty said abruptly. "Go!"

"What—"

"They're moving again. Turn on your engine. Let's go."

Firing up the ignition, I almost veered into the side of the mountain. But the engine pressed the tires to the road thereafter. I picked up speed.

"Turn on the headlights."

I did.

A few seconds later, we saw the naked body by the roadside. I stopped.

"Keep going," Matty said. "Stop just past him. We don't want to be in the headlights."

I drove another ten yards and pulled over.

"Flashlight?"

"Under the dash."

"Keep the engine running. Crank up the heater."

Matty leapt out, tearing off his coat.

I looked back. The body was in my blind spot.

Matty came up on the driver's side. I rolled down my window as fast as I could.

"You have a blanket in the trunk? Or anything else?"

"No." Then I thought. "There's my dirty clothes. In my suitcase."

"They wouldn't fit. Get out and help me. It's all right. They're gone."

Frankie lay on Matty's jacket, eyes closed, clutching himself between the legs, quivering. There was no blood. His face was unmarked.

Matty pulled off his shoes, took off his jeans, and knelt, bare-legged, to put the jeans on Frankie.

Frankie wouldn't let us pry his legs apart. He was conscious in some form, although he kept his eyes shut tight. Moaning and weeping, he didn't form any words.

"They went for his kidneys and his nuts," Matty told me as he bullied the jeans up Frankie's legs. "Help me. Turn him over the other way. I don't think any bones are broken. Maybe some cracked ribs, I don't know. There may be internal bleeding, though."

"I thought they were going to kill him."

"He wasn't worth killing." Pushing Frankie's hands away and zipping up the fly of the jeans, Matty added, "She isn't worth killing anybody over. Everybody has their value. She was worth a beating, not a murder. The local VC were like that. They knew just how far to go. We never figured it out." He shook his head. "He won't have a mark on him, once the bruises heal. I don't know how bad his balls or kidneys will be. The medics will have to figure that out. Help me get him into the jacket."

At the wrong touch, Frankie howled.

As Matty pulled his shoes back on over wet socks, he couldn't resist telling Frankie, "You're lucky."

We got him into the passenger's side of the Corvair. The rest of the car was crammed with my guitars and luggage.

"He'll make it to Hazleton. You can get there in a little over an hour. We need to get him away from here. You know where the Hazleton hospital is?"

"Yeah. Yes."

"Tell them he was in a fight and you found him afterwards. Nothing else. Get going. And beep the horn three times."

I hit the horn. "What about you?"

Bare-legged between his boxer shorts and shoes, holding a pistol in one hand and my flashlight in the other, Matty looked ridiculous and dangerous.

"Joey'll be down in a couple of minutes. Or Stosh. Hit the horn again as you're leaving. Don't speed and don't stop. Even if Frankie asks you to. If he pukes, clean it up later. If you see their Lincoln, keep going."

"What about Angela? Should I call her?"

"I'll take care of Angela," he said.

THIRTEEN

I made it back to the hospital on Sunday evening, just in time to see Angela march out. Wearing a murderous look, she abandoned Frankie's room and clacked past without seeing me. A nurse stepped out of her way.

Stosh and his girlfriend, Red O'Malley, had come upstairs with me. Red followed Angela back toward the elevator.

"I wouldn't be surprised," Stosh said, "if Angela gives it to him worse than his Mob buddies."

"She's got a right to be pissed."

Stosh shrugged as we approached the nurses' station. "I didn't say she didn't. I'd just never want to be on Angela's bad side."

I had delivered Frankie to the emergency room just after three in the morning but had not gotten out of the hospital until almost seven. The local cops wanted to talk to me. I told them they'd have to talk to Frankie, that I hadn't seen anything that happened.

"Probably drug business," one cop, a sergeant, said to his subordinate. "He probably got what he had coming."

By the time I reached home, it was daylight. I showered, set the alarm, and crashed. I was due at my mother's house at two for Sunday dinner. Without Laura. She had gone home for all of Thanksgiving break.

After the meal and a civil conversation, I stopped back at the apartment to scribble down notes for a song idea the Rocktop gig had given me: "Working as a dancer in a bar . . . watched her half-lit body through a beer glass that reflected both our lives . . . dusky barroom lights . . . wonder where she'll rest her head tonight." Then I filled up with gas and drove back to Hazleton. "Hey Jude" was still on the radio, after almost two months. I hoped that one day we'd have a hit that big.

I expected to find Frankie dozing, with tubes needled into his veins. Instead, he was wide awake and unconstrained. He grinned when Stosh and I walked in.

"I'm okay," he declared. "I'm going to be okay. I woke up with a hard-on you wouldn't believe."

"What about your kidneys?"

Frankie moved his shoulders, then winced. "Who cares? The parts that matter are going to pass state inspection."

"What did the doctors say?"

"They're running tests. I'm pissing some blood. But at least I'm pissing."

"Listen, Frankie," Stosh said. "You want me to cancel the gigs for this week?"

We had four scheduled, beginning on Thanksgiving night: two at clubs, one at a college, and another at a no-booze, kiddie disco right there in Hazleton.

"Don't cancel anything. I'm okay."

"Hey, we're not going to roll you onstage in a wheelchair," I put in. "We can cancel a job or two."

He grew irritated. "I said I don't want you to cancel *anything*. I'll be out of here in a couple days. Guaranteed. We'll just miss a couple rehearsals."

"You going to be at your best?" I asked.

He smiled. "When haven't I been? Aw, go on. You're all worried about nothing."

I wished that I had a photograph of him laying naked in the slush and quivering in agony. To give him another view of himself.

"They got you on painkillers?"

"Darvons whenever I want them. Just ring for the nurse with the ass wider than the door. I could get used to this treatment." His expression shifted. "Either of you see Matty? You talk to him?"

We shook our heads, almost in unison.

"He didn't come up."

"He's probably tired," I said.

"You're tired. And you're here."

"Frankie, you sound like a kid. You're not the only creature on God's green earth, man."

"It's the Darvon. Gotta love 'em."

Footsteps stopped at the door: Frankie's parents. His father did not look happy. His mother just seemed worried. The change in the atmosphere made it clear that Stosh and I were unwelcome.

"Hey, you come up tomorrow, bring me a chocolate malt, all right?" Frankie told me.

Red sat waiting on one of the vinyl chairs by the nurses' station. "I thought you might want some time for boy-talk," she said.

"His old man and old lady showed up," Stosh told her. "That was them went down the hall."

Red nodded. "The nurse was on them about the Blue Cross paperwork."

I had grown allergic to the new stretch of interstate between Hazleton and Frackville, so I said I was driving home the old way, down through Tamaqua. Stosh and Red followed me and we stopped for greaseburgers at the Five Points Diner by the Tamaqua railroad crossing.

Pouring a cascade of sugar into his coffee, Stosh asked his girl, "So . . . what was Angela so mad about? You find out?"

"Everything," Red told him.

· · ·

The front door of my apartment was unlocked. I knew I had secured it when I left. Given the neighborhood, I felt a constant concern for my guitars and the stereo. I had my departure routine down.

I switched on the light in the main room. Nothing. Both guitars were there. The stereo slept.

But the quiet wasn't right. I had the uncanny feeling that some other living thing was present. Beyond a mouse or two. And I smelled a cigarette's ghost.

Matty's uncle, the Statie, crossed my mind. Was he lurking to bust me for a crime he'd set up, some drug thing? He could've done that more easily up on the highway.

I clicked on the kitchenette light. Nothing had been touched.

Were Frankie's tormentors of the night before waiting for me? That made no sense, either.

I strode toward my bedroom, determined not to be afraid of spooks.

When I turned on the light, I found Angela, propped up on my pillows, with the sheet and blanket pulled up above her breasts. Her golden hair spread over bare skin.

She smiled at me.

"How'd you get in here?" I demanded.

She lifted her slender shoulders and dropped them again. "Your landlady. I told her it was your birthday and I had a surprise for you. She's seen me around enough."

"It's not my birthday."

She refreshed her smile. "Maybe you should celebrate, anyway?"

Before I could tell her to get out, she kicked the covers down around her ankles and cocked a bare leg.

"I'll bet she never let you do that to her," Angela said.

Chastened by black coffee, I sat at the kitchenette table in gray light, practicing scales on the Les Paul. The gulf between my mind and my fingers widened as I waited for Angela to wake up. After we had exhausted every possibility between us, she had taken a couple of barbs to come down and sleep.

A naked ghost crossed the hall, disappearing into the bathroom. I had been surprised at her thinness, the feeling of fragile bones. It wasn't the way I thought of her or remembered her from our summer encounter.

The toilet flushed and the shower came on.

I felt sick. First it had been Joan. Now it was Angela, an immeasurably worse betrayal. And not just of Laura. Didn't I have any self-control, any discipline, at all? Didn't I mean a single word I said, one promise I made? Suddenly, forcing myself to practice three hours each day no longer sufficed as a badge of moral rigor.

Was I just a weakling? And a coward? Like my father?

Angela came out with her hair still wet. It lay heavily on the yoke of my father's monogrammed robe. The hem dragged on the floor. When she kicked it aside, red toenails flashed.

"You look like you didn't get much sleep," she said playfully. Putting on her Angela smile like makeup. Her complexion had roughened over the months, I had felt it under my lips. I blamed that on the speed and whatever else she was shoving down her throat. Angela had always had perfect skin, even under the paint she wore when I first joined the Destroyerz.

I felt sullen. But I didn't have it in me to be rude. Maybe that was yet another weakness. I carried the guitar to its stand by the stereo and returned to the kitchenette.

"Coffee?"

"With milk, if you got any. No sugar." She took a seat sat the table, facing the chair I had occupied.

I served her and sat down again.

She compressed her smile. "You're not as good as Frankie, you know that? Just like you're not as good as Matty on the guitar."

"I didn't know I was being graded."

"I bet you were grading me. How did I do?"

"A-plus," I told her. Honestly. Bitterly.

"You'd be better if you didn't get so ashamed of what you want. Everybody wants stuff they're not supposed to." She looked at me, seeking my eyes. "I knew. Didn't I?"

"I'm sorry I was a disappointment."

"I didn't say you were disappointing," she told me. "Just that you're not as good as Frankie. So tell me something. What really happened to that sonofabitch? It was all about some woman, wasn't it? Some cunt?"

"I didn't see him getting beat up."

She smirked. "Nobody saw anything. Nobody ever does. Fucking Frankie. Why do you all cover for him all the time? He'd screw any of you over for a ham sandwich. He'd fuck your precious Laura on a street corner in broad daylight, don't think he wouldn't."

"She wouldn't, though."

"You sure?"

"Yes."

Her smile broadened. "Yeah. I think you're right. I really do. I guess that's the least of your problems with Her Highness."

"What's that supposed to mean?"

"Can I have some more coffee? No, that's wrong, ain't? *May* I have more coffee?" She shifted her butt on the wooden chair. "Are you as sore as I am?"

I poured what remained in the pot. "Leave Laura out of this, okay?"

"I can't," Angela said. "I care about you too much. Somebody needs to protect you." She took a long sip of the coffee. It must have been scalding. "Couple weeks ago? When I didn't come home that night? When Frankie was shitting his pants? Want to know where I was?"

"It sounds like you're going to tell me."

"I am. Because I care about you. And I want to protect you. Before she really hurts you."

"Where were you?"

"I drove down to Doylestown. Where she told me she's from."

"And?" I tried to maintain an appearance of cool. But the atmosphere had turned ominous.

"How old do you think she is? Your little sweetheart?"

I shrugged. "Eighteen, probably. She's just out of high school. So . . . probably eighteen. She's an Aquarius, so she'll turn nineteen in a couple of months."

Angela grinned in triumph. "She's eighteen, all right. Try almost twenty-one. She got nearly two years on you."

"How do you know that? How would you know anything?"

"Like I'm stupid? You always think everybody else is dumber than you. Jeez, you and Frankie are two peas in a pod. Like I told you. I took a ride down to Doylestown. And I went to the library and checked the high school yearbooks. Your precious angel didn't just graduate, Will." Angela reached her hand across the table and laid it over mine, comforting me in advance. "She's class of '66, not '68. And you know where she's been all this time? You have any idea?"

I withdrew my hand and sat up straight. I felt the sort of fascination that keeps you in a reptile house when all of your instincts want you to move on.

"You got the least idea where she was?"

"No."

Angela sat back, enclosing her coffee mug in slender hands. She drank again and held on to the mug.

"The funny farm. The loony bin. The nuthouse. Your Laura. They had her locked up in some fancy place down by Philly."

"You're lying."

"Ask her yourself."

"You couldn't know that. How could you know that?"

She lit the room, coldly, with another conquering smile. "You want to know anything goes on in a town, you go to a hair salon. Josette from up the Hair Affair went to beauty school in Allentown with this girl from Doylestown. She put me in touch." Her smile tightened. She enjoyed playing with me. A Siamese cat of a girl. "Want to know *why* she had to be locked up in the booby hatch?"

"No."

"Yes, you do. I know you do. I'm telling you all this for your own good, Will. To protect you."

"I don't want to know."

"Her father tried to screw her. The night before her high school graduation. He didn't get it in her, though. He's a drunk, you know that? She got away and locked herself in the bathroom. Your little angel swallowed everything in the medicine cabinet. They say she was weird before that, but I guess that was the last straw. Gives you the creeps to think about it. Ain't?"

"You're the lowest bitch on the face of the earth," I said.

The charge didn't faze her. "Go ahead. Call me names. You'll get over it. Then you'll see I did all this for you. To protect you." As she leaned toward me, I smelled coffee breath and more. "She took advantage of you. She lied to you, your little Laura. Look what she's done to you, Will. You look like a fool."

"You're fucked up. You and your meth. No, that's not right. You were fucked up before you got into speed."

She looked at me, her smile a crooked line. "And you think you want me to go now. Ain't?"

She stood up and opened my father's robe.

That morning, I learned that Angela loved to be hurt.

FOURTEEN

I believed her. My father's death and its aftermath had taught me that while cruel people lie, brilliantly cruel people wield the truth. And Angela's story made sense. After she left my apartment, I thought, wryly, of one of the last exchanges Laura and I had before I left for the Rocktop gig and she went home for Thanksgiving. I asked her if I couldn't sneak down to see her for at least one afternoon. She told me: "I don't want to chance it. Really, my mother's been a bit odd ever since her divorce."

The unmasking of Laura's recent past didn't make me angry at her. I understood the desperate urge to lie. It made me mad at Angela, though. Is there anything crueler than spoiling the dream two lovers agree to share? Is our happiness so unbearable to others? I seethed at my mother as well, for being right when I saw nothing amiss. Her bull's-eye hit reduced me to childhood status, just when I was struggling to be a man. As for Laura, I only loved her more. I tacked to the other extreme, seeing her as a tragic figure now, not a superior being who might escape me. Pity amplified my love: A romantic imagination is insidious. I longed to hold her, to clutch her and protect her, but would not see her until a gig the following Sunday, when she had promised to meet me at Franklin & Marshall.

A mirror in a woman's guise, Angela left me shattered. My appetites were stronger than my heart. A rock guitarist was supposed to be a sexual buccaneer, if not an outright pirate, reveling in flesh taken captive and then thrown overboard with a laugh. I had relished the role in my fantasies but found I lacked the ferocity required. I could not resist temptation, but I could not revel in it, either. Betrayals have consequences, and I feared them. I hurled myself into sex, then felt remorse at my lack of loyalty. Twice, I had betrayed Laura without hesitation. Even if mad and dishonest, she deserved better. There was nothing to me, no rigor. I had no character.

I resolved to care nobly for Laura. Yet, while I never fantasized about Angela, I imagined fresh grapplings with Joan, who seemed so gorgeously normal.

When Angela had gone, I stripped the mattress, bagging the sheets and my father's robe for a trip to the Laundromat. I cleaned the bedroom and bathroom so thoroughly that Mrs. McClatchy would have found no fault. An earring of Angela's had been tucked in where the box spring met the floor. It struck me that she had left it there on purpose.

"Angela wants to know if you'd like to come up the house for Thanksgiving," Frankie said, "since Laura's not around to keep you company."

"Can't. I promised my mother I'd spend Thanksgiving with her. But thanks."

It was a relief to have an excuse that Angela couldn't expose as a fraud. I imagined the proposed dinner with her and Frankie turning into a nightmare of curses and violence.

Angela had not hinted about our encounter, and she didn't seem to have told anyone else what she knew about Laura. Frankie was released from the hospital on Tuesday afternoon. On Wednesday, the band got together for a strategy session and laid-back rehearsal with the convalescent. Everything seemed normal.

We compromised on the demo. We would book an initial block of time at the cheap studio in Reading. After fine-tuning the songs based on what the tape revealed, we'd book the Philly studio for the real demo. As for work, offers continued to come in, but we agreed to hold some key dates open a while longer, until we saw how the pre-Christmas gig at the Electric Factory went. Hardly four days after Frankie's beating and a crisis that threatened to finish off the band, we were all in good spirits and confident. Stosh told us he was quitting his uncle's mining operation, and I had already turned over my guitar students at the music store.

Frankie was still hurting, though, and popping prescription downers. We didn't try any demanding rock-out numbers, but worked on a goof arrangement of "Winter Wonderland" for the holiday season. Frankie hammed it up like Robert Goulet on mescaline. I cracked up the guys with rewritten lyrics for "I'll Be Home for Christmas." The new first line was "I'll be stoned for Christmas." It went downhill from there. The novelty numbers were for the bars and the college crowd. We wouldn't perform them at any serious gigs. After more clowning around, I finally got the chance to introduce the song I'd written for Laura. I ran through it with my guitar turned down and no mike.

Carlotta, just knowing you're out there keeps me alive . . .
I know how you're trying, it saves me from all compromise . . .
And the way that I love is something no words can describe . . .
Carlotta, I'm lost in the thought of your wide-open eyes.

Carlotta, I know you've the soul of a traveler, too.
It's that and these ribbons of starlight that bind me to you . . .
When the moonlight runs wild and illumines the landscape
*   with blue,*
The roads in the farthest of countries remind me of you.

After the chorus, there was another double verse, chorus, bridge, double verse, chorus, and wrap-up. I thought it had some great lines, such as "The lips of our lovers leave kisses and scars on the years." When I finished, I waited for everyone's approval.

After a stretch of embarrassed silence, Frankie said, "It's too wordy. It doesn't rock."

I looked at Stosh, who just shrugged.

I turned to Matty.

"Frankie's right," he said. "For once. It's all about words, not the music. It doesn't . . . I don't know . . ."

"It doesn't grab you and shake your ass," Frankie told me. "It's not like your other stuff. You write some heavy shit, man." He did two light karate chops on one of Stosh's cymbals. "Stick to the beat, man. Keep it rockin'."

Stosh smiled. "It reminds me of that folk crap I caught you listening to. Donovan or whoever the shit it was."

"Tim Buckley."

Twice before, the band had rejected heartfelt suggestions of mine, although not songs I had written. The first time had been when I thought we should do a Dylan medley, while the second occasion had come just after the release of the Love album *Forever Changes*, which I thought was a masterpiece. That time, too, Frankie said that the song I wanted to cull was too wordy and didn't rock.

"Okay, forget it," I told them. "Here's another one I just finished. It's kind of country-rock, like the last Byrds album. But harder. Buffalo Springfield with edge. Just let me run through it."

I played a Keith-Richards-goes-C&W lead-in, straight C major. Then I sang:

She told me that her name was Sally Reno,
Working as a dancer in a bar,
And she had this crazy notion . . .
That faith was all it took to be a star.

I spent a little while with Sally Reno . . .
Her loving made me shake my head and smile,

But I kept a space between us,
'Cause even heaven wears out after while.

I closed my eyes and did a guitar run leading into the chorus.

Well, here's to Sally Reno: She always kept the faith,
And that's more than I could do in Sally's place.
Yeah, I remember Sally in that dusky barroom light . . .
I wonder where she'll rest her head tonight . . .

The song went on for several more verses, with no bridge. Matty began to play Nashville-on-acid riffs around the melody. Near the end, Stosh tapped along on the snare drum with his fingertips.

As soon as I finished, Stosh said, "I like that. I don't hear a dance beat, but I like it."

Matty nodded.

Finally, Frankie said, "Yeah. Heavy song, man. Good album stuff. But you can sing that one yourself."

I almost phoned Joan that night. Instead, I stayed up late, practicing without an amplifier and calling myself an asshole. On Thanksgiving morning, I worked for three hours with the amp turned on, keeping the volume low. I was trying to hone my sound, to train myself to manipulate the Les Paul's tone and volume knobs more skillfully. Matty could do it without thinking or looking, curling his little finger around the control appropriate to the instant, at any point in a song. I wasn't quick or sure enough to do that and had always relied on setting the controls on my guitar at the start of a number, then just shifting between pickups with the toggle switch or, at most, turning up the volume knob for a solo.

As much as I practiced—sometimes I managed five hours a day—I seemed to have reached a plateau. As part of the ensemble, I fit in fine. But my lead turns lagged Matty's by a discouraging distance.

Whenever I thought of my collision with Angela, my only satisfaction was that I had gotten something Matty wanted and couldn't have.

I passed a polite and desolate afternoon with my mother and my father's ghost. The food was richer in memories than flavor. My mother and I had reached a tacit agreement not to speak of Laura. I was doubly glad. After Angela's Sherlock Holmes revelations, I was afraid I'd blow up if my mother so much as mentioned Laura's name.

I could have endured Matty or even Frankie being right about Laura, had they questioned our relationship. But I couldn't bear it from my mother.

We were both relieved when the hour came for me to drive down to Lebanon for a club job. My mother and I had reached a point where we hoped to rebuild our relationship but didn't know how. My father had been our binding mechanism. He was the one who knew how to laugh and take others along for the ride.

The club had a go-go dancer, but Frankie didn't even look at her. He was still a little drugged out, but he performed solidly enough. The band was tight. The days off seemed to have helped us, not hurt us. The kiddie gig on Friday was a hoot. By Saturday, Frankie was post-Darvon and we rocked a club in Scranton well past the official closing time. On Sunday, we headed south again, to Franklin & Marshall, a university sufficiently expensive to have a vibrant drug culture.

Laura showed up, as promised. I had no idea how she had gotten to Lancaster, but her ice-blue eyes looked clear and untroubled. Her face seemed charged with joy at our reunion.

"I wish we were in your apartment," she said.

But we weren't. It was time to play, and she went over to the bleachers to sit with Angela and Red, who opened a space for her between the two of them.

The job went well. Everyone was in the best of spirits. Stosh had killed an eight-point buck out bow hunting and he said he was going to have a party for everybody as soon as the meat came back from the butcher dressing it.

On Monday morning, I asked Laura to marry me.

She said, "No." Then she smiled and laughed, before crying and telling me, "I wonder if you'll ever know how terribly much I love you?"

Stosh held his venison party on the Sunday afternoon before the Electric Factory show. Red had a place of her own, one half of a double in Mahanoy City, and she hosted. Stosh wasn't quite living with her, but the two of them behaved as if they had been together, happily, for years.

We took the back way over the mountain. A dirty sky hung low over gaping strip mines, and naked birches climbed enormous waste banks. Runoff flowed orange by the roadside, scouring beer cans and broken bottles. "Keep Out" signs and rusty chains marked the edges of company property. No friend to man, a wild dog chased the car. The road's surface had buckled, and fault lines in the macadam grabbed my tires. Our landscape had been raped for over a century, then abandoned. Laura said, "I don't know how people can live here."

Inside Red's house, the human magic warmed us. Everyone was in high spirits, and a rough coal-town comradeship took us in thrall. Methed up or not, Angela appointed herself as Red's kitchen maid, rushing about with heaping plates and allowing Red to maintain her mild aloofness. Joey and Pete had both shown up with dates, all of them stoned to giggles except Joey. For once, his girl of the moment looked as if she might be at least eighteen. Pete's date was a Dutchie gal twice his size who went straight for the food.

Red had put up a real Christmas tree, even though artificial trees were in vogue north of the mountain—Angela and Frankie had a big aluminum tree with dime-store balls, but Red's tree was straight from my childhood. The evergreen scent evoked memories the instant the door opened. The next aroma, floating above the cooked-meat smell, was the fragrance of boilo heating on the stove. Boilo was the holiday beverage of choice north of the mountain, the Hunky reply to eggnog. You began with bootleg white lightning, then stirred in honey, cloves, cinnamon, perhaps a bit of peppermint or nutmeg . . . every family guarded its secret recipe. Fools—which meant most of us—knocked it back in shots. It was like swallowing hot cough syrup that ferried tiny hand grenades straight to your brain.

In addition to the deer roasts and venison meatballs, there were rings of kielbasa with condiment dishes of horseradish or ketchup straight from the bottle, big bowls of pierogies—some deep-fried, others boiled to be eaten with sour cream—and lima beans cooked with bacon, a few other vegetables that interested no one, pumpkin pie squirted with Cool Whip, and paper plates laden with Christmas cookies painted in tooth-killing icing. Between pots of boilo, we drank beer or coffee and laughed. I could not recall a time when we all seemed happier.

Red had an old console stereo—a Magnavox—and the background music alternated between Rosemary Clooney or Nat King Cole singing Christmas songs and an inscrutable selection of pop albums that gave no hint of Red's own personality. Then Frankie discovered a hidden Monkees album, which resulted in a round of teasing and urgent cries to put it on the turntable. Everyone sang along until, after three or four songs, a consensus arose that we had heard enough. Thereafter, we strummed guitars and sang. Matty could play anything by ear and he accompanied us as we howled carols and holiday songs. I learned that Laura had a lovely alto voice. Midway through "Silent Night," the other voices began dropping off, one by one, as she continued to sing to Matty's soft chording. Laura knew the words to every verse.

The party didn't run late. Perhaps we all sensed that a day so perfect shouldn't be pressed too far. By nine that night, Laura and I were back in my apartment, nestled close on the sofa. We had a bit too much alcohol in us, but that, too, was part of the blessing of the day. The lamps were off and only the strand of lights on my Christmas tree lit the room. The small tree was a Scotch pine, my father's favorite.

We were happy. No matter what had gone before or what might come after, that night we felt the happiness in each other, as if happi-

THE HOUR OF THE INNOCENTS ・・・ 173

ness were as palpable as a breast or a beating heart. A jazz piano album of Christmas standards—purchased at a discount store—played softly. There was no need to say a single word. All that we lacked was a fireplace. My mother's house had a handsome tiled fireplace, but the hearth had been cold for years.

"I'm so happy," Laura said, breaking the spell. We couldn't help ourselves, we had to talk.

"Me, too. Everybody was happy today. Even Angela."

"She does seem to be a terribly sad person," Laura said. "I'd hate to have her life. With Frankie. And everything else. Matty's in love with her, isn't he?"

"Yes."

"He needs a girl. I wish I knew the right girl for him. He deserves somebody nice. Somebody nicer than her."

The stereo played "Silver Bells."

"Well, at least Stosh found somebody," I said. "He and Red seem perfect for each other. I just hope marriage doesn't take the edge off his drumming."

Laura tensed. Just slightly. She drew a few inches away from me.

"They're getting married?" she asked.

"They haven't *said* anything, I didn't mean that. But I'll be surprised if they don't."

She looked down at me. The lights on the Christmas tree shone in her eyes.

"I guess that would make sense," she said at last. "If they both plan to stay around here. Marriage would be a good cover for both of them."

"What are you talking about?"

She looked at me again. Bewildered by a foreign alphabet and deciphering me as best she could.

"Don't tell me you don't know," she said. "You don't have to pretend with me."

"Know what?"

"That Stosh is a homosexual."

It was my turn to pull away and sit up.

"That's not true. That's absolutely nuts. He's a coal miner, for God's sake."

"You don't think there are homosexual coal miners?"

"Laura . . . Stosh isn't queer. Come on."

She shook her head in disbelief at my naïveté. "You mean to tell me you've known this guy for years and you haven't figured out he's a boy's boy? The guy who never met a satin shirt he didn't like? Your friend who never had a girl until Red?"

"Well, he's got one now, doesn't he?"

"My God," Laura said. "You really have no idea. Do you? Red's a lesbian. You didn't pick up on that? That's why they get along so well. They give each other . . . protective coloration, I suppose you'd call it."

"What makes you think Red's a dyke?" I recalled the old rumors about her.

Again, Laura had to pause over a decision before answering me.

"Well, if I hadn't already figured it out for myself, I suppose it would've been clear enough when she followed me into a stall in the girls' bathroom at Franklin and Marshall. She had her tongue halfway down my throat and her hand in my pants before I could push her away."

"What did you do?"

"I bit her tongue. She's really an aggressive bull dyke type. I mean, we get along okay. But you have to be clear with her. Then it's all right, she's just one of the girls."

"Does Angela know?"

"Of course. I don't think Angela misses much. She was waiting there when we came out of the restroom. Red's terrified of her, I can tell you that. She'd do anything to keep Angela's mouth shut. And I mean anything."

"I really had no idea. About Stosh. I just had no idea. I'm still not sure I believe it."

"You people really do lead a sheltered life up here," Laura told me.

"Jesus," I said, sinking back into the sofa. "Poor Stosh."

"Why? Maybe he's happy. Who knows? I'll bet he's happier than Angela, anyway. She may be the unhappiest person I've ever met."

"She was pretty happy today."

"She was so doped up she forgot to flush the toilet."

"So . . . what was it like? Kissing Red?"

Laura laughed, happy again. "Don't be an ass." She kissed me.

We fit our bodies back together and didn't move until long after the stereo's needle reached the dead zone in the center of the record.

We are not fair. We mean to be, but we are never fair. Even as I held her close, I couldn't stop wondering who else might have shoved a hand down Laura's pants.

Don't blame the snake. It was the human beings who spoiled Eden.

FIFTEEN

Framed by snow flurries, my visitor looked like an undercover narc: hair timidly shaggy, jeans pressed, leather jacket too new, complexion too healthy.

"Will Cross?"

I nodded. Was he going to read me my rights?

"Sorry to bother you. I'm trying to link up with Matthew Tomczik. His mother sent me to his friend Stanley. He told me Matt might be here."

It took me a blink to remember that Stosh's legal name was Stanley.

"Matty's not here," I told him, with the Blues Project on the stereo behind me. "He went to Philly."

"When do you expect him back?"

The guy's stiffness reeked of cop or some other form of officialdom. He was trying to kill the taint, but it wouldn't die.

"Look, I don't know who you are. Or why you're here asking me questions about Matty."

Wounded eyes, downcast face. As if he had blundered badly in a foreign language.

"Sorry. I wasn't thinking." He held out his hand. "Larry Masters.

I'm a friend of Matt's. Or maybe I should just say 'acquaintance.' We served together in Vietnam. I've been traveling around, visiting a few of the guys, and I wanted to look him up."

His demeanor had broken and changed. Awkwardly earnest, he became a bareheaded pilgrim on a winter journey.

There was room at the inn. And the innkeeper had questions.

"Come on in," I said. "I'm not sure why he went to Philly, but he'll be back by evening. We have a songwriting session."

My visitor stepped inside, wiping his nose with a well-pressed, whiter-than-snow handkerchief. He brightened. "He's playing music, then? Everything worked out? Does he have a band?"

Al Kooper wailed through "Wake Me, Shake Me." I lowered the volume.

"Groovy music," my guest commented.

If any serious human being had ever used the word *groovy*, it had been at least two years earlier. But there was something so earnest about Larry Masters that I couldn't bring myself to be a smart-ass.

"I was going to make myself a sandwich," I told him. "Want one?"

"That'd be great. If I'm not imposing."

In the warmth, he began to shiver.

"Take the chair by the radiator," I said.

He smiled. "I'm still not used to the cold. I guess you can tell. That's a nice Christmas tree."

Wary of being suspected of sentimentality, I just shrugged and lit the stove, then pulled a ring of Dutchie sausage from the refrigerator. As I sliced the meat for frying, I said, "I met another one of Matty's buddies. Couple of months back. Little spade dude. Doc Something-or-other."

"Doc Carley."

"Yeah."

"Old Doc. I tried to get him a Silver Star." He snorted. "Battalion wouldn't even approve an ARCOM. Sergeant Major just hated him."

"Redneck?"

"No. Sergeant Major Jefferson's a Negro. But old school. He'd just go nuts whenever Doc pulled one of his Black Power stunts. Terrific field soldier, though. Doc, I mean. Braver than I ever was."

"I hear Matty was pretty brave."

Flipping the meat in the frying pan, I heard my visitor shift in his chair behind me. "I'll bet he never told you that himself."

"No. Doc mentioned it. Coffee? A beer?"

He thought about it. "I'd better stick with coffee. Too early in the day."

"Matty won a bunch of medals, though. Right?" The record was over. I slipped past my visitor to turn off the stereo. I wanted to hear every word he had to say.

"Sergeant Tomczik . . . he seemed like one of the heroes in the *Iliad*. He was just . . . I don't know, different from the rest of us. An old-fashioned warrior."

"Not Achilles, I take it?"

"No. Hector. The reluctant one. Who does it anyway."

"Hector dies. Matty didn't."

"I'm still amazed at that. Given the risks he took. I mean, he did things you wouldn't believe, that other soldiers couldn't believe. You'd be watching it happen, and you wouldn't believe he was doing it. There really was something mythic about him, the 'mighty warrior' of yore." He smiled. For the first time. Faintly. "His guitar could've been a lyre. Maybe I came here to see if he's really real."

"He's real. Ketchup on your sandwich?"

"I guess you don't have Louisiana Hot Sauce?"

I'd never heard of it. "I have mustard."

"Ketchup's fine. I was just asking."

I set our plates on the kitchenette table and Larry Masters joined me.

"So . . . what did you do? In the Army?"

He paused again. "I was Matt's company commander."

"That means you're a captain, right?"

"Was. Past tense."

I looked at his faintly shaggy hair, which yearned to be cool and failed.

"You got out?"

Another hesitation. "No. I was forced out. I wanted to court-martial a general's son." A spectral smile came and went. "My mistake. So the Army gave me the boot."

"You wouldn't have quit, anyway? With the war?"

He waited until he had finished chewing and swallowed before answering. His table manners would have pleased my mother. "No. I wouldn't have quit."

"You liked the Army?"

Uncomfortable, he rolled his shoulders. A fringe of hair shifted to reveal an ear missing a third of its shell. "It doesn't really matter. Since the Army decided it didn't like me. Thanks for the sandwich, by the way."

"Want another one?"

Feeling his way in a world that had moved impossibly fast in his absence, my visitor began to answer but hesitated again. A former officer and a combat veteran, he feared being impolite in a cheap apartment in Pottsville, Pennsylvania. Stranger in a strange land. I didn't think much of military types—it wasn't cool to do so—but I couldn't help feeling sorry for the guy.

The world didn't always make sense in that year of lost souls.

"Well, I'm going to make another sandwich for myself. It's just as easy to make two."

"That'd be great," he said. "Thanks."

"So . . . ," I began as I went back to slicing sausage, "what did Matty do to get his medals?"

Buck Sergeant Matthew F. Tomczik told his squad to stay put, then made his way up through the jungle, stepping over weary men resting on their rucksacks. He found the new platoon leader and his platoon sergeant crouched at the edge of a trail. With his PRC-25's antenna folded over, a sweat-soaked radio humper knelt behind the command group. As Tomczik approached, the commo kid shot him a "Please, get us out of here!" look.

The radio squawked with calls for help.

Across a low ridge, the sounds of the firefight continued: wild bursts of shooting, with abrupt lulls. Victor Charles had waited until First Platoon was out of the range fan of its supporting 105s before springing an ambush. And this one was serious. Most combat actions were over in five minutes or less, with the VC pulling off before the grunts could get organized and call in fires. This fight gave no sign that the gooks were quitting.

The new lieutenant ignored Tomczik, something his predecessor would not have done. Instead, the taut young man—who looked like the quarterback on a prep school team—thrust his map at the platoon sergeant.

Sergeant First Class Campbell was an alkie E-7 hanging on for twenty.

"We're going right up that trail," the lieutenant said. "I realize there's an element of risk. But First Platoon needs help fast."

The platoon sergeant fingered his stubbly chin. His eyes weren't fully engaged. "I don't know, sir. That's asking to get hit. I really don't know if we should do that."

"We can't just let First Platoon be overrun. Listen to that." Lieutenant Gibbons gestured toward the radio and the distant gunfire. Mortar rounds tubed and popped. Not friendlies. "There's no air, it's all up north. There's no time to waste."

"I'm just not sure, sir," the platoon sergeant repeated.

"Sir?" Tomczik said. "We can't go up that trail. That's what they want us to do."

"Why aren't you with your men, Sergeant Tomczik?"

"I just thought—"

"You need to observe the chain of command. The Army isn't a democracy."

Tomczik glanced at the platoon sergeant, who wasn't going to be of any help. The radio man looked sick.

"Sir," Tomczik tried again, "this isn't about First Platoon. It's us. We're being set up. First Platoon's just the bait. They *want* us to go up that trail. They're waiting for us."

The lieutenant's expression shifted between irritation and doubt. Then he said, "I don't need tactics instruction from you, Sergeant. Go back to your men. And get ready to move out. Our fellow soldiers are dying—do you understand that? And I'm not about to abandon one of my classmates."

Arriving to replace a lieutenant who'd been shot through the face, Gibbons had let his men know that he'd been eleventh in his class at West Point and first in his class at Ranger School. He counted on his peers to spread the word about his father.

Tomczik stood up to his full height, something he rarely did in the boonies. "Sir, if we go up that road, you're going to lose half this platoon. If we're lucky."

"Sergeant Tomczik, I want to see you in the presence of the company commander when we go back in. The era of insubordination is over in this platoon."

Matty looked at the platoon sergeant a last time: Nothing.

"Yes, sir," Matty said.

"And another thing," Lieutenant Gibbons said. "Since you seem to be our resident expert on tactics, your squad can take point." He nodded toward the firefight. "We've wasted too much time already. I want your squad on the move in two mikes. And I expect you to move out sharply."

"Yes, sir."

As Tomczik hustled back toward his men, the line doggies in the other squads grasped from his look that nothing good waited in their future. Soldiers edged farther out of his way than necessary. The short-timers checked their rifles and made themselves small.

Reaching his squad, Tomczik said, "Let's go. *Now.* Christensen, you've got point. We're lead squad. Double the interval. We're moving up an open trail."

The groans, complaints, and curses were instantaneous.

"That cocksucker el-tee's brain-dead," a rifleman said.

Tomczik ignored him and turned to the platoon medic, who liked to move with his squad. "Doc, tuck in with Sergeant Rodriguez for this stretch. We're going to get hit. And we're going to need you."

"Somebody needs to frag the fucking el-tee, before he gets us all killed," another soldier commented.

Tomczik turned on him. There were sharp limits to the bitching he'd tolerate. "Hammond, I ever hear you say that again, you'll be in Long Binh until they turn out the lights. Move out, Third Squad."

He hated every step. Moving too fast, in the open, along a track that amounted to a shooting gallery. Watching the bush, he counted his paces, trying to judge when they'd step beyond the range of their fire support. The VC knew too much. They always knew too much. Today, they'd known that Charlie Company's platoons would be moving separately and going deep. He wished he understood how the enemy could know so much, while his side knew so little.

"Maintain your intervals," he called softly. "Pass it on." They had to be out of the 105 mm fan now. On their own, high and lonesome. With the crest of the ridge ahead and the firefight sputtering beyond.

The close-in quiet was too quiet. Behind Tomczik, the radio broke squelch, rasped, and spoke of casualties in a tiny, frantic voice.

The humidity weighed the men down like wet sand in the heat. The insides of Tomczik's thighs had been rubbed raw for days. But misery became just another fact of life. It was unavoidable. Unlike stupid decisions.

Word came up the line. Lieutenant Gibbons wanted him to pick up the pace. He nodded as if in acknowledgment but let Christensen do his thing. Walking point sucked badly enough without some butterbar lighting a fire under you. Let Christensen worry about the VC, mines, and booby traps. That was enough for any man.

Tomczik understood that each enlisted man in the column was

praying that this wouldn't be his day to get hit, that by some miracle
he'd make it through what was coming. The dense bush on either side
of the trail should have been their ally, but now it was an enemy. They
should have hacked their way through the jungle, no matter how long
it took. Now they were moving over naked earth that begged each
man to put his foot down in the wrong place.

He ached to let the music play in his head. To flee into it. To hide.
But he couldn't. The platoon had become his burden. It wasn't supposed to be that way. But it was.

Maybe the el-tee would be all right, given time. But his education
was about to turn expensive for other men. Tomczik hated it, and
accepted it.

A devil inside his head tried to lure him to recompute the days and
hours until he could get on a Freedom Bird for home. But he needed
to concentrate, to stay aware. To see what others might miss.

With the harness inside his helmet soaked and gripping his skull,
the magic switch clicked. In an instant, he developed the vast aware-
ness he couldn't explain. Every detail of the world became more pre-
cise, each color more intense, each faint sound louder.

The sounds of the firefight had stopped.

"Break right! Into the bush!" he yelled.

A soldier behind him stepped on a mine. The VC let loose with
everything they had. Soldiers crumpled.

Right flank. Charge. Follow me!

The wounded screamed.

He tore a grenade from the side of an ammo pouch, yanking the
pin as he ran. He hurled the little green ball directly to his front before hitting the ground, rolling under the blast, and coming up firing.

"Let's go, let's go. *Charge through them.*"

He shot his way through a machine-gun position his grenade had
crippled, then he wheeled left and collided with a VC rising from the
earth to fight. Tomczik caught him under the chin with the point of his
rifle butt, pulled back the weapon, and shot him. He knelt and shot two
more men from behind.

Instinctively, he turned. Just in time to put a burst into a man lifting a rifle.

After ejecting his empty magazine, he slapped in a full one and scanned for his own men. He could hear them firing, the crisper notes of the M-16 rounds arguing with the rattle of Chinese AKs. But no one on his side was giving orders. The only American voices were either screaming curses or crying out for Doc.

Tomczik began to work down behind the ambush line. He stayed low to avoid friendly fire, but leaves and stalks fell around him. Fixing on the heavy bark of a machine gun, he tossed another grenade, pitching it with all his strength to drive it through the greenery.

In the wake of the blast, he heard noises behind him and rolled over, weapon ready.

Two of his men.

He sent them hand signals: *Quiet. You on my left, you on my right. Follow me.*

Crawling, he led them back through the game-of-chance bullets piercing the undergrowth. Just in front of his hands, a snake shot out of his line of vision. He kept going. Listening. Judging. Magnificently alive.

He understood what the two men with him were thinking: Where's he taking us?

He knew, but he didn't know.

Then he *knew*.

Tomczik stopped. With the odor of fish sauce teasing his nostrils. Struggling to keep up, his two soldiers could just see him through the stinking mess of greenery.

More hand signals: *On my command, up and charge. Follow me.*

He gave them a short ration of seconds to ready themselves, but not enough time to think. Then he flagged his hand at them and rose. Firing.

In a half-dozen strides, they were leaping down into the VC command post. Hastily concealed, the position was little more than a big foxhole. In a howling, writhing crush of humanity, Tomczik emptied his magazine, killing men so intimately that their blood splashed back on his face. Dodging bayonets, he knocked down men with his rifle, ripping the jagged sight across their eyes and hammering skulls and spinal columns. The plastic stock broke like an old man's bone. Fighting at last with his fists, he broke an officer's neck. Looking into his eyes as they rolled back.

It was over. Scarpetti sat bleeding, a stunned look on his face. Byron shook his head at the carnage they had wrought.

Tomczik picked up his rifle, but it was truly broken. Then he spotted the bugle, the poor-man's radio.

He picked it up and blew it for all it was worth. He'd fooled with another musician's trumpet in a polka band years before, but he couldn't really play. It didn't matter: The worse the sounds, the better.

He lowered the instrument and told Byron, "Get ready. They don't know what's going on, but they'll be coming this way. Scarp, can you get up and fight?"

The wounded soldier nodded but failed to move. His eyes telegraphed uselessness.

Tomczik took up Scarpetti's M-16, loaded a fresh mag, then quickly gathered up two AKs and rammed full magazines into them. He laid the enemy weapons at the ready, then leaned over the edge of the hole beside Byron and said, "You've got everybody on the right. Short bursts."

That was when the real killing began.

"I never saw him so much as flustered," Larry Masters told me. A ghost smile visited his mouth and disappeared. "Except one time. We were moving as a company. It was a battalion-level operation, three solid weeks in the boonies. One night, we had to hunker down in this network of rice paddies. It was just a shitty place. Literally. But we didn't get hit that night, so that was a plus. In the morning, we're waiting for battalion to give us the order to move out and I see Matt squatting to take a dump—nothing happened in private out in the bush.

Well, he hollered like he'd stepped barefoot on a dozen cobras. Only time I ever knew him to lose discipline. It shocked everybody. He had leeches on his dick and his balls. All swollen with blood. They excrete this chemical that numbs you, so you don't realize they're on you until you actually see them."

My visitor laughed. The sound was almost healthy, as if the bomb of memory had been disarmed. "And Matt's hung like a horse—I'm sure you've noticed." My visitor grinned. "He used to make the colored guys nervous, I swear. So this went down as one of the company's memorable moments. Matt calmed down and burned off the little bastards with a cigarette. And he wasn't the only one. Half the company had them on their legs or all over their backs, even on their faces. We had to medevac an E-4 who had them up his ass. Hey, don't tell Matt I told you about that, okay?"

"You the guy who wanted him to be an officer?"

"No. No, that was the battalion commander. The brigade commander, too. Matt was a legend by the time he was halfway through his tour. I would've given him a good write-up, if he'd wanted to go to OCS. But he didn't. I thought he made the right decision, to tell you the truth."

"Because he wouldn't have made a good officer?"

My guest shook his head. "You don't really know who'll make a good officer. Until the bullets start flying. Matt probably would've been a solid junior officer out in the field. Garrison might've been another story. He really wasn't interested in all the eternal-Army stuff. And he wouldn't have been one of the ring-knockers, the West Pointers, or the wannabes. I wasn't in a position to say anything, but I was glad when he told Colonel Everett he just wanted to do his time and get out. Old Everett was pissed, though. I think that was one more strike against me—as his company commander, I was supposed to persuade him."

"But you didn't try?"

"No."

"Like a beer? It's just the local swill."

"It's late enough, I suppose."

"*Why* didn't you try to persuade him?"

Larry Masters, ex-captain, thought about the question. "It just didn't feel right to me. I mean, here's this phenomenal soldier, born to fight. But he didn't care about it. He didn't *value* it. He was just chained to the bench and rowing his oar until his sentence was up. Matt just happened to row better than anybody else. But he didn't want to spend his life in the galley. Anyway, his heart was in his music. A fool could tell that much."

"You've heard him play?"

He nodded. "Plenty of times. When we came in from the field. He had this cheap PX guitar that looked like it'd been through a half-dozen firefights. And a tiny amplifier. Supply sergeant used to haul it around for him when we redeployed. And Doc had this kiddie saxophone. One of the other colored men would play bongos or beat out the rhythm. The soldiers used to crowd into the hooch to listen, or gather outside it. Before he was killed, I used to send Sergeant Campbell around to disperse the audience." He snorted. "I hated to do it, since I liked to sneak out to listen to them myself. But one mortar round could've taken out half a platoon, if I let them bunch up."

He scratched his disfigured ear, unthinking, elsewhere. "I do remember one night, though . . . one night in particular. It was a really heavy kind of dark. Monsoon season. Air thick as a swamp. We'd come in from two weeks in the boonies that afternoon, and I'd just had a come-to-Jesus session with the battalion commander: 'You numma ten, GI.' I felt unjustly persecuted and generally pissed at the world." He sighed. "I just meant to stick my head in their hooch and tell them to knock it off, that it was late. But I found myself sitting . . . just sitting . . . in this little niche of sandbags out in the darkness. Listening. To Matt. There we were, all of us moldy and miserable, jungle-rot lepers with the permanent shits, down at the ringworm round-up. In the middle of a war that made less sense every day. And I'm sitting there listening to the most beautiful music I've ever heard." He repositioned his backside in his chair. "Anyway, it seemed that way to me."

His face tried on a series of expressions, but none of them fit. "The truth is . . . I don't know if you'll understand this . . . the truth is that I was sitting there and crying like a kid. I just started to cry. Listening to that music. Crying, where nobody could see me. I mean, it was a lonely place. People all around you, all the time, every minute. But Nam was just the loneliest place in the world."

He forced lightness into his tone. "I guess that sounds silly to you. But speaking of lonely . . . is Matt getting married? To his girl? I forgot to ask."

"No. He's not getting married."

The ex-captain frowned. "Did something happen? Is something wrong?"

"No. But he isn't getting married."

"I thought he had a girl. One he was serious about." He drank the last of his beer. "I probably misunderstood. I only had a couple of what you might call personal conversations with him. You have to keep your distance. As a commander. The men have to think you have some kind of magic. Even though you don't. And, to tell you the truth, Matt wasn't the most approachable human being I've ever met. The younger soldiers were just in awe of him. They called him 'Sergeant Fury.' He hated it." The ex-captain laughed a quick bark. "I guess we were all young. Some of them were just kids, really. It just seems different over there. I just remember asking Matt if he had a girl back home. I guess I misunderstood the answer."

"No problem." I fetched him another beer. "So . . . if Matty got a Bronze Star for that ambush stuff, what'd he have to do to get a Silver Star?"

Larry Masters looked down at the floor. "That involved Lieutenant Gibbons, too."

The remainder of the platoon lay behind a paddy dike, weapons ready and watching as Sergeant Rodriguez's squad approached the hamlet. Rodriguez was down to seven men, including himself. Since

Lieutenant Gibbons had taken over, the platoon had suffered a 45 percent casualty rate. All of the men were aware of the scuttlebutt that Captain Masters had tried to relieve the el-tee, but the CO's superiors had been unwilling to risk the wrath of the lieutenant's three-star old man back in the Pentagon.

Sergeant Tomczik hated what he saw: seven men moving across a broad, brown paddy at noon. Begging to be taken out by a single machine gun. Had it been his decision, he would have enveloped the hamlet, then cleared it from the rear, with a single squad positioned for covering fire. The lieutenant had done the opposite, holding the bulk of the platoon near himself and sending in a squad too weak to defend itself. Lieutenant Gibbons always liked to keep at least two squads near the command group.

Rodriguez tried to move his men in bounding overwatch. But there was no cover. So the soldiers just took turns kneeling in the mud while their buddies slogged forward. The sun hit so hard that an M-60 barrel could burn your hand before it fired a shot.

It was more than two hundred meters to the cluster of hooches. Too far for accurate supporting fire from the rest of the platoon, if the squad got into close combat. Nothing about the movement made tactical sense. And Rodriguez knew it. He hadn't wanted to go. But Lieutenant Gibbons had given him his standard song and dance about cowardice and a court-martial.

Tomczik always kept an eye on the lieutenant now. And one thing *had* changed: Gibbons was no longer so quick to make a decision. The new problem was that he avoided decisions, only to make bad ones too late. His moods were unpredictable. One day, he'd try to ingratiate himself with his subordinates. The next morning, he'd be stiff and dismissive. In the beginning, Tomczik had wanted his platoon leader to be less demonstrably aggressive, less obvious about his pursuit of medals at his men's expense. Now the el-tee was, if anything, too timid, obviously avoiding contact with the enemy. The short-timers were content with that, but to Tomczik excessive caution was as likely to get men killed as swaggering brashness.

It was like music. There were times to let it rock and times to hush things down. And you had to sense the difference.

Tomczik brushed a posse of ants from the stock of his rifle and swept a small population from his chest. Shifting a couple of feet to his left, he kept his focus on the advancing squad. They were just entering the hamlet. The place looked deserted. But you could never trust appearances.

"Fucking ants," Specialist Byron said. "They're all over the place."

"Shut up," Tomczik whispered. Then he added, "DeLong, I want the sixty ready to stop anything coming over that dike behind the hooches."

"Got it, Sarge. Ain't nobody coming in that way."

But they didn't have to come over and in. The VC were already inside the hamlet. They waited until Sergeant Rodriguez ordered his men to start clearing the hooches. Then they began firing out of their spider holes.

Every soldier in the squad fell. Some writhed upon the ground. Others lay dead-meat still. In seconds, the VC had pulled back into their hides. There was nothing to shoot at. Except the platoon's own wounded.

Down one squad, the platoon would have to work its way around the hamlet and come in from behind, after all. Although the VC would have the rear dike covered, just as Tomczik had wanted it kept clear. It was going to be a mess.

No, it already was a mess.

In the hamlet, two pairs of men in black pajamas darted from separate hooches. Each team grabbed a wounded American, then used him as a shield as they pulled their captive inside.

"Shit," Doc Carley said. "Motherfuckers." He pulled a Lucky from the ration packet stuck in his helmet band. But he made no move to light the bent cigarette.

Corporal Halversen scrambled up the dike and dropped flat beside Tomczik. "Sarge, we got a problem."

"We've got plenty of problems."

"There's a pack of dinks, must be fifty or sixty—"

"VC, or NVA?" Since Tet, they'd been seeing more North Vietnamese regulars in their sector."

"No, naw. Gook civilians. They must be from the *ville*. They're all back there in a gully. Jones and Babitch are keeping an eye on them."

"Does the lieutenant know?"

"Sergeant Riker went to tell him. But he thought you should know, too."

At that moment, the lieutenant and Sergeant Riker dropped behind the dike, headed rearward. Tomczik sensed the world slipping out of balance.

"Corporal Garrity. You've got the squad. Keep an eye on the *ville*. You see any VC movement, send a man to get me, ricky-tick."

It was just great. American wounded taken prisoner. And the platoon leader and two squad leaders headed away from the firing line. Tomczik hoped the new platoon sergeant would rise to the occasion, but he had his doubts. In the ten months he'd spent in-country, he'd seen the quality of the 11B senior noncoms plummet. The good ones just got killed and the Army replaced them with homesteaders from Camp Swampy.

Before Tomczik could move, they heard the first screams. From the hamlet.

"Motherfuckers."

"Shut up," Tomczik said. The VC were trying to lure them in. They knew Americans couldn't resist trying to save their comrades. The gooks were tougher. They'd let anybody die. For their cause.

The only cause the Americans had was one another.

Tomczik had seen enough recovered bodies to know that torture didn't have to be refined to do the job.

"Nobody moves," he said. "Hold in place. Watch the *ville*. Nobody fires without a clear target. Halversen, show me where the dinks are holed up."

Two American voices were screaming now. The sounds carried wonderfully in the afternoon calm, so dehumanized that no one could identify the victims. Every man's instinct was to charge across the open paddy without wasting another minute. But Tomczik went after the lieutenant first.

The Vietnamese had hidden themselves in a gully between a line of trees and the jungle. As if they'd left their homes quickly, unsure of where to go. They sat crammed together. Staring up at the Americans. Shaking. Some tried to smile. None spoke.

The lieutenant looked at Tomczik in alarm. "You should be back with your men."

"Yes, sir. I just thought you might need help."

"Sergeant Riker's with me. And these men. Go back to your squad. We just have to take care of this."

"Sir . . . we've got to move out. The VC—"

"Then help." The lieutenant's eyes looked past him. Gibbons turned to the soldiers standing guard over the Vietnamese. "They're all VC. Anybody can see that. I want them all killed."

A private with "FTA" inked on his helmet band lifted his rifle. But he didn't fire.

Sergeant Riker said, "Sir . . . them's civilians . . . just kids and all . . ."

"*They're VC.* Kill them." He looked at the two junior enlisted men. "I ordered you to fire."

"Nobody fires," Tomczik said.

The lieutenant turned a maddened face toward him, then wheeled about and lifted his own rifle. Before anyone could reach him, he had emptied a magazine into the crowd.

As Gibbons lowered the weapon to reload, Tomczik leapt up beside him and tore the M-16 from the lieutenant's hands. The shrieks and wails from the gully sounded as he had always imagined lamentations in the Bible stories.

He broke the lieutenant's jaw, knocking him cold. Gibbons fell on his back and slipped a few feet down the gully's bank. Nobody moved to help him. The other soldiers stared at Tomczik.

"Nobody fires again," he said. "Not one round. I don't care if they have an artillery battery hidden down there. *Nobody fires*. Got that? And pick up the lieutenant."

He didn't wait for a response, but took off back toward the line of soldiers behind the dike. Instead of heading directly to his own squad, he trotted, sweat-soaked, up to the platoon sergeant's position. Sergeant First Class DesFresnes was a former drill, straight from Benning. He looked overwhelmed, paralyzed. Shiny boots and midnight barracks inspections didn't help anymore.

Tomczik went to ground beside him. "We need medevacs. At least two. The el-tee went nuts. He shot up a bunch of civilians. I don't know how many were hit."

"Battalion won't green-light any dust-offs for gooks," DesFresnes said. "There's a brigade sweep going on. We got more to worry about."

Tomczik brought his face close to the senior NCO's. "Just try. Tell them the general's little boy needs a dust-off. Somebody broke his jaw."

"What—"

"And give me some smoke." He reached down and tugged a canister from DesFresnes's web gear. "I'm going to take care of this."

Tomczik hustled off toward his men. As he passed down the line, he tapped the shoulders of his two best shots. "Keep your eyes on the hooches, not on me. Fire at any muzzle flashes."

"Where you—"

With no further preparations, Tomczik dropped over the far side of the dike and moved toward the American screams as fast as the paddy mud let him.

They wouldn't fire at him. Not until he came close. Very close. He understood them. They'd been having a ghostly conversation for months. And now he understood them. But they wouldn't understand what he was doing: A single American splashing across an exposed rice paddy had to be a trick. They'd let him get close. He was sure of it. They just had to let him get close.

He knew the odds were better than good that he was going to die. But it didn't matter; abstract knowledge was irrelevant. It wasn't that he cared nothing for his life. Life had never seemed more brilliant than in those minutes spent wading across the paddies. It was only that he no longer belonged to the common world, he was operating in a hidden universe behind the one others knew. It was as strange as those time-bending stretches when he played so well that commonplace things dissolved.

Just as he knew the notes to play, he knew what to do now, invading the souls of the men he was going to kill and who meant to kill him. Men who could see him clearly. Juiced, he waited for the flash from a muzzle, the crack of a shot. If he would even hear it. He and his opponents were engaged fatally now. There was no chance that all would remain alive.

He felt the eyes of his own kind on his back, while the eyes of his mortal enemies watched him approach. He didn't duck, or cringe, or move evasively, but came straight on through the paddies. Aware that the last ten meters before he reached dry land formed the kill zone he had to pass through safely. He hoped his enemies would not understand that, that they'd want his carcass close enough to drag off.

"Let them be confident," he prayed. "Let them wait. Let them be sure of themselves. Just let them wait."

He needed them to be greedy for another wounded prisoner, to distrust what they saw, to fear a trap, snipers, anything.

Judging his ground, he plodded on, avoiding any spurt of speed that might provoke a nervous shooter. He tried to etch the hamlet's layout, the buildings and the distances, into his brain. Seeking to register every slight depression, every fold of the ground.

The world had gone remarkably silent. Even the insects had paused in curiosity.

A knee-high mud bank rose five meters away. The ground beyond was dry.

What did they expect him to do? He listened to their minds as he closed the distance. They'd expect him to drop behind the little embankment, to catch his breath after the plod through the mud, to get his bearings. An impatient enemy would shoot him first.

In a burst of movement, he leapt onto dry ground, hurling himself to the left and tucking his body into a dusty swale. Gunfire chased him, hunted him. But they couldn't fire low enough from their positions.

He pulled the smoke grenade from his harness and lobbed it behind himself, between the village clearing and the paddy. It hissed out a purple cloud, "Goofy Grape" in fire-support lingo. As the smoke spread, the VC fired into it, expecting him to use it as concealment. Instead, he ran the other way, through clear daylight, diving behind a hooch.

Rounds punched through primitive walls. One shooter was close. Tomczik low-crawled along, as fast as he could, until he ran out of cover. He closed his eyes just for a pair of seconds, to listen to the report of the enemy weapons. Trying to get a fix on their positions.

The screams of the prisoners had stopped. He hoped his actions hadn't led the VC to cut their throats.

He hurled a frag grenade and dropped low again before sprinting through the dissipated blast and the excited dust. Emerging into the clear, he kept running. Until he reached the rear rank of the hooches.

He heard cheers in the distance. From his own kind. But the purple haze by the paddy's edge obscured the view back toward his comrades.

No bullets pursued him. That told him two things. First, the VC had known which way the Americans were coming earlier in the day and probably even knew which platoon it was, who was leading them. So they'd gotten lazy and failed to dig firing positions that would let them fight in any direction. He was behind them now.

The second thing was that there weren't so many of them. A dozen at most, probably fewer. Just an ambush team meant to kill and pull off before becoming decisively engaged.

It was his turn now. He began hunting human beings.

He went dead still. Time had become his friend, not theirs. And they knew it. He listened. For what seemed a very long time but was only moments. He heard nothing but the howling beyond the smoke. Like crazy Rebel yells.

A doomed man's sandal found a kernel of grain on the floor of a hooch. At the crack, Tomczik fired a full burst through the thatch and bamboo.

A creature cried out, stunned at the disarrangement of its body. Tomczik ran. Bullets bit the air around him again. Auto bursts, sloppy fire. He couldn't spot the shooter. Behind him. Somewhere.

He crashed through a bamboo door, weapon ready, and found nothing.

The faintest movement caught his eye. A hatch in the floor, closing the last millimeter.

He looked around for blood, for evidence of a captive American. And found none.

Pulling his last grenade from an ammo pouch, he primed it.

A black-clad figure appeared in the doorway. The man appeared confused by what he saw. That gave Tomczik just enough time to raise his M-16 one-handed and put a burst into the other man's torso.

He couldn't see a grip or notch to open the hatch in the floor. So he just set the grenade over the frail wood, released the lever, and hurled himself out into the dust.

After the blast, he dashed back inside, with thatch already burning above him and moans from the compartment under the floor. He emptied a full magazine through the splinters, trying to find human flesh through the smoke and underground gloom. The moaning stopped.

He reloaded. Counting how many full mags he had left: two.

He scrambled outside to work down the line of hooches from the rear. Two black-clad figures climbed the dike a dozen feet away. Fleeing.

Tomczik killed one and wounded the other. One shot for each. Sparing his ammunition now.

In the hooch the two men had evacuated, he found PFC Milton Weinberg, with the skin peeled from his chest and slight muscles unveiled. To save their bullets, the VC had crushed his skull.

Tomczik registered that the firing had ceased. The shouts, the wild hollering, had come closer. He scuttled out the backside of the hooch and low-crawled to where he had a view over the paddy.

The smoke had thinned to nothing. A dozen GIs splashed through the last stretch of water and mud. Yelling like kids unleashed to break anything they wanted.

Farther back, the rest of the platoon was strung out all the way to the dike. His men had come after him. The others had followed. Had the VC held in place and kept their machine gun ready, it would've been a massacre.

Tomczik waited until his soldiers reached dry earth and began to spread out tactically. It was strange to watch them from the enemy's perspective. One after another, they began to call his name.

He shouted back. Telling them to go to ground, to do things the right way. In case there were any stay-behinds.

Going through the hooches, they found Sergeant Rodriguez's corpse as well. With his cock and balls cut off and stuffed in his mouth. There were seven bodies to recover, the entire squad.

It had all been for nothing.

"I wrote him up for a Distinguished Service Cross," my visitor told me, "but the brigade commander felt DSCs should only be for officers. The battalion commander agreed with him, of course. And then there was the business with Lieutenant Gibbons. A Silver Star didn't call as much attention to what happened as a DSC would've."

"What happened to him? The general's kid?"

Larry Masters was on his fourth beer, while I still nursed my second. Beyond the window, the mid-December darkness thickened. I had missed my hours of practice but didn't care.

"I wanted to court-martial him. But nobody in the chain of command wanted any part of that." He twisted his mouth. "Know what they told me? 'Only four Vietnamese died. Forget it.' I mean, I'm no softie. I didn't have a problem with killing the enemy. And I could accept that sometimes civilians got caught in the middle of things, that mistakes were made. But when a U.S. Army officer goes berserk and orders his men to fire on a pack of terrified noncombatants, something's just plain wrong. Whether it's four dead, or four thousand." He slapped down another empty bottle. "Plenty of bad things happened. Not because we wanted them to. It's not the way people say. You don't go out looking to hurt innocent people. You even start off thinking you're protecting them. But it's a war. And bad things happen. No matter how hard you try. That lieutenant was off the reservation, though. What he did was . . . unforgivable."

"But he got away with it?"

"No. Not exactly. I did manage to get him a field-grade letter of reprimand and gave him an efficiency report that were both career enders. I figured his daddy could get the letter yanked from his file, but not the OER. They asked me to soften it, but I just couldn't do it. What that sonofabitch did, what he tried to do, ran against everything I'd been taught, everything I believed in as an officer."

He sat back and softened his posture. "Anyway, they fixed his jaw, got it all wired up, let his promotion to first lieutenant go through, and reassigned him to MACV as some one-star's aide-in-waiting. Not all of his old man's friends could help him in the end, though. First Lieutenant Stephen Forsythe Gibbons wound up beating the hell out of a prostitute in a room at the Caravelle Hotel. Oh, he might've gotten away with bloodying up a dink hooker. But not with doing it at the Caravelle. That got the ambassador's attention. So Dad's pals sent the little shit home with a Purple Heart. For his broken jaw."

Masters sighed. "I got my walking papers not long after that. The revenge of the Green Machine. 'Unfit for service.'" He chuckled, but the sound wasn't happy. "I'm not sure exactly what I *am* fit for, to tell you the truth."

"What do you plan to do?"

"I don't really know. My wife divorced me while I was in Nam. There weren't any kids, so I can go anywhere I want. I'm just not sure where I want to go."

"Well, you don't want to stay around here. We're all clawing tooth and nail to get out."

"I just stopped by to see Matt. I'm actually on my way to New York. My wife's father liked me better than she did. He may have a job for me." His eyebrows tightened toward each other. "You don't think he'll mind, do you? That I came to visit? I know some guys just want to put Nam behind them."

I took the question seriously. "I'd say Matty's of two minds about all that stuff. I mean, that's how it strikes me. But I really don't know. He was glad enough to see Doc, we drove down to Philly to see him. Although that was another story."

"How *is* Doc?"

"He's a junkie. Or the next best thing."

My guest frowned at his beer bottle. "Some people can't deal with what they go through. Only they don't know it until afterward."

"Look, I'm going to make a box of macaroni and cheese for dinner. You're welcome to share it. Although it's not going to make you faint with pleasure."

"Better than C-rats."

"Help yourself to another beer."

"I should go pick up a couple of six-packs. I'm drinking you out of house and home."

Matty rapped on the door. I hadn't heard him on the stairs, which was odd. But I knew his knock the way you know a girl's footsteps.

I flicked on the outside light. Matty stood there in a dark suit, without an overcoat. I let him in.

The sight of his former company commander startled him. He came partway to attention, then froze.

Larry Masters held out his hand.

Slowly, Matty took it. And he held it.

"Hope you don't mind me dropping by. . . ."

"No, sir. No. Not at all."

"No more 'sir' stuff. That's over and done with. It's just 'Larry' now. I got out myself, by the way."

"I never thought you'd leave the Army."

"Long story. For another time. It's good to see you, Matt." My visitor summoned his best smile of the day. "You look like a hippie or something. That hair."

Matty ran his fingers over his scalp, the way women do if a man or a mirror unsettles them. He looked a little freaked out. In a black suit that didn't fit properly, with a white shirt and black tie, he could have passed for a down south preacher in a Depression-era movie.

"You look like you've been to a funeral," I said when I could get a word in.

"I was," Matty said. He looked at the ex-captain. "Doc's."

SIXTEEN

Compared with the guys in the Philly bands, we looked like thugs masquerading as hippies. With suburban teeth, amphetamine waists, and managed hair, they resembled the musicians in photo shoots for *Rolling Stone*. Even their roadies looked more polished than we did.

I had gone to plenty of concerts at the Electric Factory, a reclaimed industrial building in center city, and should have had better sense than to expect behind-the-scenes magic. We squeezed into a corner of one of the dressing rooms as the Philly bands partied with select camp followers. A fat joint went around in the management's absence, but only Frankie took a token puff when it got to us. For the Philly bands, this was an easy gig, with their fans taking advantage of off-night prices. For us, it was a death match.

The Factory was the premier place in Philly for name acts not yet able to fill the Spectrum, as well as for local bands hoping to break out. Of all the halls we had played, this was the one where the odds were best that a talent scout or producer would be in the audience. For the first time since Matty walked into the Legion, I got the inside shakes.

The Philly boys weren't rude. Just condescending. They pretended to treat us as equals but made it clear that they didn't take us seriously.

If the Factory's booker had heard about our performance at Lancelot's Lair, these guys had not. Or they didn't believe what they'd heard. We were yokels in the big city, booked in error or as a joke.

A guitarist in a buckskin jacket and Stephen Stills cowboy hat gave Matty the nickname "Dumbo." Picking country runs on a big Gretsch, the dude giggled, all in stoner fun. The name caught on among the musicians and hangers-on.

Matty smiled and didn't say a word. But I'd come to know him well enough to sniff an odor of fury. When he beat the crap out of Bronc and broke Buzzy's nose, those actions had sprung from an inspired rage, from adrenaline rapture. The vibes he radiated now were cold and more frightening.

Matty could take a ribbing. His north-of-the-mountain crowd could be merciless teasers. But Larry Masters had come down with us—he was taking the morning train up to Manhattan—and Matty was embarrassed. I suppose we're forever doomed to yearn to impress those who once held power over us.

Matty's routine was to warm up without an amplifier before we went onstage, running through shaman riffs to witch out the demons. Now he only tuned his guitar, bending over its body to hear through the ruckus, then laid it in its case. I understood. He wasn't going to tip his hand, wasn't about to alert them that we were serious players. Let them pass around another joint or two. Let them get can't-tune-my-B-string stoned before we ambushed them.

Matty was hunting human beings again.

The atmosphere worsened when Angela came with her girlfriends. A carload of beauticians and factory girls, they'd driven down after work, speeding-ticket fast. In Schuylkill County, their getups passed for fabulously hip. In Philly, they were rubes. The local girlfriends and groupies rolled their eyes behind the backs of women grown men fought over back home.

The toilet we shared was disgusting.

. . .

If many of our gigs had belonged to Frankie, that night was Matty's. We kicked off our set with "Angeline." My nerves disappeared as Stosh counted off the tempo. We tore into the song.

When Matty's solo came around, the notes exploded from his amp. For anyone with musical sense, it was breathtaking. Had you only seen his fingers fly over the Stratocaster's neck, you might have thought he was scalding his fingertips, unable to find a place where they could settle. His playing excited Frankie and me into jagged antics. On the drum fill, Stosh went nuts. By the time we jackhammered into the final verse, you could hear the audience shouting over the music's roar.

I glimpsed Joan, who had made her way to the front of the crowd. I was glad, almost thrilled, to see her. I ached to impress someone, to have someone close by who could *be* impressed. If only for a forty-minute set.

She smiled up at me.

Matty didn't wait for the applause to die. As I swapped the Rickenbacker for the Les Paul, he stepped out of his safety zone by the amps and strode up to Frankie.

"I want to play 'Bad Boy.' Now, not later."

Frankie shrugged. It was the first time Matty had ever interfered with the order of a set. As the audience calmed, Matty turned to me.

"If you don't mind," he said, "I'd like to play both solos myself. Just this once." He added, "Please, Will."

Coming from Matty, the word *please* embarrassed me.

I nodded. Sure. Do it.

Matty couldn't write a song to save his life, but he had cooked up a dazzling guitar instrumental. Usually, I took the first solo, then he followed.

Matty surprised us all again. Breaking his tradition of onstage silence, he pushed up to Frankie's mike and announced, "We call this number 'Message from Dumbo.'"

I never heard a guitar played so savagely. Hendrix and Pete Townshend smashed their axes doing their Theatre of Cruelty acts. Matty revered musical instruments and wouldn't have harmed a kazoo. But the sound of his playing made me think of living beings suffering through torture. In another first, he took center stage, huge and still except for his flying left hand, with his eyes closed and his face worshipping the rafters, blond hair falling straight onto his shoulders. Colored lights floated over him.

He ran out the number twice as long as usual, taking it to places no other guitarist was going to rival that night. If ever. He played so well it grew vicious, purposely humiliating the idiots who had written him off as a lummox.

He tweaked his volume knob with his little finger, going even louder. A machine-gun cascade of notes cut invisible flesh.

The Electric Factory was the home of cool, where the cosmically hip sat cross-legged on the floor and judged bands harshly. Matty had them standing up and howling.

As he played that long solo, I understood at last: The exploits his former company commander had recounted were identical, in spirit if not in kind, to Matty's guitar assaults. He really was a killer. And the crowd loved it.

We all made perfunctory nods to the notion that our music was about peace. And love, of course. But it never was. It was raw aggression. I don't mean only the music of the Innocents, but all of it, from the pop outbursts of the British bands to the flower power pretensions of West Coast groups. It was all about domination, the many hues of anger, outright rage. It wasn't even about sex: That was a sideline. We sang hymns to death in countless, gorgeous voices.

Jim Morrison saw through the lie. And the glimpsed revelation devoured him.

The crowd became the now familiar beast of many heads, a creature that consumed each individual. It felt the urge to fight and fuck at the same time, but all the monster's clumsy members could do was clap and yell.

We swaggered into "Hideaway." I looked down and found Joan's eyes. Amid the emotional turmoil and mighty noise, she looked wonderfully sane and separate. I wasn't going to sleep with her. Not that night. I fought the impulse, even as I relished the possibility. I had committed myself to Laura, who was back in her dorm room, studying doggedly, sparring with devils I could not begin to imagine. It was my *duty* to be loyal to her, to stick by her.

I was too young to understand that duty is love's assassin.

Matty's efficient fury was contagious. We didn't just put our hearts into that set, we invested our souls. By the end, we were brined with sweat, as though the looming holiday were the Fourth of July, not Christmas. For all the heady nights we'd had as a band, we had never played with such passion or with such a lack of mercy. But there was no sloppiness, not one out-of-place note. We hit each beat on the microsecond, with the precision that stabs below the listener's consciousness. We were disciplined *and* savage, filling that hall with a thrilling sense of danger. The music was every bit as barbaric and insidious as our worried elders feared.

I suppose we became Matty's new squad on that stage. High on the crowd's frenzy, we wrapped it up with "Glass Slipper," unplugged our guitars, and walked off amid an uproar. Had Matty said, "Follow me!" we would have marched straight through that crowd, stormed into the dressing rooms, and clubbed the shit out of those skinny suburban kids who had held their noses when the hicks showed up.

But Matty's mission was over. He had no rounds left. As we left the stage, I glimpsed his drained-of-blood face.

The now familiar pattern repeated itself. Cupid, the second band on the bill, delayed coming out. The audience felt the old urge to touch the music, to become part of us, and we fielded cries of "Great set!" and "Heavy shit, man," or "You blew me away, brother, you blew me the fuck away, you know?" Strangers wanted to shake hands, to touch a shoulder.

Startled, I spotted Joyce and her biker boyfriend from the Warlocks. But they were yucking it up with Angela, who looked as slender as a wraith in profile. All the bad blood had drained away. Everybody longed to be cool with the band.

I hunted for Joan, who had faded into the crowd. I just wanted to be polite, to thank her for coming. To maintain the connection. Just to stand smell-it close for a few minutes. I wasn't going to spend the night with her in Quakertown. No matter how badly I wanted to. But I didn't want to let her go too quickly.

She came out of the corridor that led to the ladies' room and headed straight for me. As if I wore a neon sign with her name on it.

She smiled: Grace Slick on the cover of *Surrealistic Pillow.*

"You were *bad,* man. I mean, you guys were *evil.*"

Joan understood a lot of things.

"I guess that's a compliment."

She laid a flame-shaped hand upon my sleeve. "Oh, come off it. You know you were great."

I had believed that she drew me because she was sane. But kindness was Joan's real attraction. Beyond the splendid sex and cynic's veneer, she was *kind.* Without calculation.

"Joan, I just—"

A sleek dude stepped between us. Hair long, but not too long. Gold-rimmed glasses, trimmed mustache, clear skin. He wore a leather jacket that looked as if native servants had saddle-soaped it for months. I pegged him for late twenties or early thirties.

"If I'm not intruding, I'd like a word," he said.

The sunshine girl of sex, Joan smiled. "You know how to reach me, when you want to," she said, then headed straight for the exit.

Mr. Cool held out his hand. He looked West Coast, or maybe Manhattan. Those were worlds I knew only from magazines and books, so I couldn't read all the signals. But he didn't look Philly.

"Milt Ehrlich," he said. "Eclecta Records."

I shook his hand. He gave me a business card. In the bad light, I could just make out his name, the logo of the label, and "Artists and Repertoire."

In the background, Cupid's musicians were finally taking the stage, plugging in and screwing around with their tuning.

My new acquaintance followed my eyes.

"I didn't come down from New York for those clowns," he said. "The closing act was the draw. Mind if we go in the dressing room and talk?"

I didn't mind.

As we crossed the hall, I saw Larry Masters leaning against a vertical beam, alone. Of all the different kinds of alone you can be, he looked the worst. I suppose the whole scene seemed a lurid bacchanal to him, a mockery of what he'd been through, of his recent whys and wherefores. Or maybe he had understood more about Matty's playing than he could bear.

Milt Ehrlich and I sat down in the smaller dressing room, which had been abandoned. The stink from the nearby toilet trumped a ghost of pot.

"You're the songwriter," he said. "Am I right?"

"How'd you know?"

"You look like the songwriter." He smiled a big-city smile. "Frankly, you wouldn't be in that band if you weren't. You're not bad, but they're better." He interlaced his fingers and pulled them apart again. "Your lead guitar player's got the best chops I've heard in a long time. And the singer, the guy on bass, has great stage presence." His eyes drilled harder. "You're not signed to anybody?"

"No."

"I'm glad. Your songs are good, by the way. They grab the ear and stick with you. Good arrangements. A producer could work with that material. How many originals on your playlist?"

"Seventeen," I said immediately. "We're working on two more."

"Same quality as what you played tonight?"

I shrugged. "To the extent I can judge."

"It really was a powerful set, one serious trip. And I almost didn't make the scene in time to catch it, I was waiting on a call from the coast." His eyes gleamed behind his glasses. "I don't think you made yourselves any friends in the other groups on the bill, though. Where are you boys from?"

"Pottsville." It was the only town of ours that I thought he might know.

"Pottstown?"

"No. Pottsville. Up the line, in coal country. Schuylkill County."

He nodded. "Oh, yeah. I've driven through there. Never felt the urge to stop."

"I wouldn't recommend stopping."

"Tough place?"

"Tough place."

"And you're hungry. All of you. Right? I mean, you've got an edge—I wouldn't want to meet your guitar player in a dark alley. Or the drummer, for that matter. You're not exactly living off Daddy's checkbook, are you?"

"No."

"Cut a demo yet?"

"We're going into the studio soon. In January."

"Send it to me. The address is on the card. Call me and let me know it's coming so it doesn't end up in a stack somewhere." He reached into the pocket of that flawless leather jacket and drew out a gold-trimmed pen. "Give me the card back for a second. Or never mind." He pulled out another card, wrote a word on the back, and handed it to me.

The word was "cacophony."

"It's a code," he told me. "Say it when you call. It tells my secretary to put you through, that you're not bullshit. If I'm not in, she'll take a message and make sure it gets to me. So . . . just curious now . . . what would you think about signing with Eclecta? I don't mean we're there yet. Far from it. I need to hear a tape, see you a few more times, run it all by Mac Steinman and a producer or two before we get to serious talking. But how do you *feel* about the label?"

I tried to be cool, to keep my excitement under reasonable control. Eclecta was the in label, known for the best sound engineering and production in the business. A few of its bets had gone huge in the past few years, elevating the label from hipster obscurity to wide cult status. Eclecta was the label serious groups aspired to be on.

"It's a good label," I said. "Good sound quality. Good bands."

"And we don't cook the books, by the way. Ask anybody who's signed with us. We don't pay as much up front, I'll tell you that right now, but our groups actually get their royalty checks." He grinned. "And *don't* tell me it's all about the music, not the money. Even if you believe it. Get an album out, and see if you're not checking the mailbox every single day. Happens to every group that walks into a studio."

"It's all about the music," I said.

He answered with a slow, knowing nod. "The songwriters always say that. It's always the songwriters who're pure as Orphan Annie. Then they go to court over their publishing rights, fighting for every last penny. But look, Will. Do your demo. And don't rush it, I can't sell anybody up in New York on a rush job. Take your time, get it right. *Then* send it to me." He rolled back in his chair, as if nursing a bad spine. "I take it you haven't even been talking to other labels, to anybody else?"

"No."

"Well, if they approach you, talk to them all you want. But don't sign anything. Not until you've had a chance to do your homework. Based on this one hearing, I think the Innocents would be a good fit with Eclecta. Frankly, we just signed a political-activist band from Detroit that isn't a quarter as good. So give me a chance to make the case. To you and to my people. Once we've got a solid demo." He glanced toward the door. "Speaking of the business end . . . that guy who had your lead singer cornered?"

"I didn't see him."

"Well, take my word for it. Your pal was talking to Danny Luegner. He's in the management game. Thinks he's a producer, too. But he's strictly Mummers Parade. Philly, not Manhattan." Milt Ehrlich's facial muscles tightened. "I'm not into put-downs, not my thing. Negativity's a bummer. But—and I'm telling you this for your own good—don't sign anything Danny Luegner puts in front of you. Nothing, never. Danny isn't Santa Claus. Nobody in the game wants to deal with him, outside of some Mob clubs and one-hit-wonder labels with zombie engineers. Eclecta won't have anything to do with him, I can promise you that. Not under any circumstances. Mac hates him, and Mac doesn't hate many people, he's very Zen. Danny Luegner's the original scumbag. If he ever gets your name on a contract, he'll tie you up in knots for the rest of your life. And it won't be about the music for Danny, I'm ashamed to call him a landsman."

He pulled out a silver case and offered me a thin black cigarette. I shook my head. He lit up. "I wouldn't give him my piss to drink if he was dying of thirst in the desert. Don't lose my card, all right? Your band has a future, Will. I've heard enough bands to know. Just keep your shit together."

Then he was gone.

When I went back out into the hall, Cupid was wrapping up its set. It had not been their night. The applause faded quickly.

Angela appeared beside me. We both looked at the stage. Reviving an old habit, she leaned her shoulder against my upper arm.

"You were fantastic," she said.

"Matty was great."

"Matty was beyond great. But the whole band was fantastic. You know how you looked? I mean, you yourself?"

"No. How did I look?"

"You looked like you always wanted to look. For once. Mr. Rock Star. For real. So who was that guy you went off with?"

"He's from a record company."

She pulled away. "Well, go find Frankie and tell him. Some little fucking Jew has him cornered. Does that mean you'll get a recording contract?"

"Maybe. We've got to do the demo. It's complicated."

"Figure it out, okay?" She grew pensive. Uncharacteristically so. "I need you to figure it out, Will."

A cast of light revealed her worsening skin.

"I'll do my best," I told her.

Angela cackled. "You really were great, you know that? The rock star under the fancy lights. With the girls all lined up. It's a shame Little Miss Genius wasn't here, ain't?"

She reached up and gave me the last fallen-angel kiss I would ever receive from her. Even her lips felt too thin.

We stopped for coffee at the Howard Johnson's on the turnpike. Adorned with Santa caps, the waitresses working the night shift just wanted the pain to stop.

Crammed into two booths, we were simultaneously weary and buzzed, aglow with vanity and wreathed in cigarette smoke: the band, Joey and Pete, plus Angela and her tribe of Catholic school girls who'd decided they didn't want to become nuns after all. I drank black coffee and ate a brownie.

"This guy's talking serious money," Frankie said. "I mean, he's ready to go."

I swallowed. Too fast. "I told you what the guy from Eclecta said. Nobody in the business—nobody serious—will deal with that guy. Danny Luegner's notorious."

"All I know is he says he can deliver. I'm all for giving him a chance. Anyway, how do you know that guy was really from Eclecta? He could've been some phony trying to come off as a big deal, some plastic fuck."

I pulled out the business card again.

"He could've had that printed up," Frankie declared. "Anyway, those Jews are always trying to give it to each other up the ass. I wouldn't trust any of them without a signed contract."

"Yeah, and how many Jews do you know?" Angela asked from the adjoining booth.

"You stay out of this. Listen, this Luegner guy wants to sit down and talk turkey."

"How do you know *he's* not a phony?" I asked.

"He manages Cupid. That's why he was there tonight."

"Yeah, *they're* really going places."

"They weren't so bad."

"They weren't so good, either," I said.

"They weren't," Matty agreed. Stosh did a drumroll on the table-top.

A sour-faced waitress poured another round of coffee. "You know, I can't tell the boys from the girls anymore," she said. She'd already given up on her tip.

"You probably never could," Angela told her.

"You, you're a little hussy, if ever I saw one," the waitress said. "With that bleach-blond hair." She slumped off.

"You're a hussy, Angela," Frankie said. "You hear that? With bleached hair."

"And you never noticed? Yeah, that's me. Mrs. Franklin T. Starkovich. I guess I should pull my pants down and show her."

"Look," I said, "the first thing we need to do is to get in the studio and cut the demo. And we need to do it right. I mean, this is it, this could be our break. We've got a guy at Eclecta Records interested, for God's sake. That's what we always wanted."

"That's what *you* always wanted," Frankie said. He chuckled. "I'm holding out for Reprise. Me and Frank Sinatra. I could dig that." He started singing "Strangers in the Night." Making a show of eyeing up the waitress, who was wiping the counter and chewing her lip.

"Give her a break," I said. Waitresses, the beaten-down ones, conjured my father. He was always a good tipper, even when times were hard. He told me never to stiff the little guy. He never understood that he was a little guy himself.

"Get her phone number," Stosh said, knocking off a flam with his index fingers. "Bark wants her phone number."

"You shut up," Angela told him. "Red needs to put some manners on you. Will's trying to tell you something."

Frankie's expression shifted. Then he smiled again. "When Angela was little, she always wanted a hamster. She got Bark instead."

"Let's just do the demo tape, all right?" I said. "Then we can talk managers and record deals. Meanwhile, we've got all the work we can handle."

"We'll have more after tonight," Stosh agreed.

Matty yawned. When he stretched, his arms became a wingspan.

"We need to do the demo tape," he said. "Right after the holidays. Then we'll see."

And that was that.

"Ask that old bitch for separate checks," Frankie said. "Just to piss her off."

As we crowded out past the locked-up gift shop, I told them, "I'll be right back." It was a kid's gesture, but I went back inside and laid a buck on the table by the pennies they'd left as a mockery of a tip. I apologized to the waitress for our behavior. She was too tired to be interested.

One of Angela's friends waited for me outside by a newspaper box. She asked if she could ride home with me.

I told her no.

SEVENTEEN

I finished re-stringing my Les Paul, then pulled on a coat and went out to get the mail. I received one card, but it was the best of the season.

"Happy Halloween" had been crossed out and "Merry Christmas" penned in underneath. The image was of a grinning witch on a broomstick, flying across a huge orange moon.

Joan was cool. She didn't sign it or show a return address: nothing to give a jealous girlfriend evidence.

I needed the boost. It was Christmas Eve. I tried to put a good face on it but felt about as lonely as the old not-quite-bums in the Davis Hotel lobby. The impulse to dial Joan's number hit me powerfully, but I mastered myself. Despite a growing disenchantment that I could not admit, I was determined to be Laura's white knight. Angela's revelations hadn't released me, they'd sentenced me.

Anyway, Joan would have Christmas plans. The family thing, at least. Calling her only to be put off seemed a worse prospect than not calling her at all.

I didn't know what to do about, or for, Laura. I tried to love her nobly, but her final exams confounded my best intentions. She studied obsessively, treating me as an annoyance, almost an enemy. There were nights when I felt like a mere bedroom appliance. Laura fucked with grim determination, ever less interested in pleasing me. Off the mattress, she became abusive, deriding my music. She challenged me to drop the guitar and "write seriously." But to me, rock verged on the sacred. We, the music makers, were the apostles of a new art form. Laura was scornful.

I did write a short story. To please her. And to show her that I could. She read it in my presence and grew livid.

"You plagiarized that," she said. Peering at me past eyelid battlements. "You copied that, you stole it."

I hadn't. I was furious.

"From who? Where? Tell me."

"I don't know," she told me. "I haven't read everything in the world."

"Then how do you know I copied it?"

She put on an expression that sought to be knowing and superior but just looked miffed and bitchy.

"I know," she said.

But she didn't know. And I was incensed when, in an odd way, I should have been complimented. But I had been up against the charge before. In tenth grade, I wrote a melodramatic poem of a dozen quatrains for an English class and a teacher I admired. Called to the principal's office, I found the teacher waiting with an accusation of plagiarism. Prefiguring Laura, he could not say from whom or where I'd lifted it, but he thought the poem too good for student work.

The poem was entirely mine. Seething and self-righteous, I stood up for myself. Lacking evidence, the teacher soon backed down— disappointing the principal, who saw me as pure trouble. The irony was that the poem was utterly wretched. By the time I began to grow my hair, the thought that I had written such mush mortified me.

After dismissing my story—just before she went home for Christmas break—Laura demanded a major bedroom performance. I did my best. For the first time in my life, I found making love a chore.

Between sex and sleep, Laura clung to me terribly, a cartoon character grasping a branch at the cliff's edge. In the morning, she told me she didn't think I should waste my time trying to write.

And yet, she was piercingly beautiful. My sense of her physical being had been the product not of infatuation, but of judgment. Her profile belonged to an Edith Wharton heroine.

For Christmas, I gave her an emerald-and-gold French scarf. She admired it politely, wore it around the apartment, and then forgot it when she left for the bus station. She gave me a paperback of Flaubert's *Sentimental Education*, unwrapped, commenting that it was better when read in French.

Devils chased her.

My mother was gone for the holidays, too, but that was a relief. Our relationship had been improving, but I was plagued by the memory of the Christmas before, when our dinner together in the old house had pantomimed a Eugene O'Neill play. This year, she'd been invited to Florida by a Swarthmore chum. Palm Beach sounded like a suck-ass place to me, but I got the sense that my mother was going to be introduced to an eligible bachelor.

Before she left, I gave her a French scarf, too. I had a bit of money coming in at last and had made an expedition to Hess's in Allentown, where she'd patronized the store's exclusive French Shop before our finances turned sour. I was still a sucker for the animated Christmas tableaux in the department store windows and I treated myself to a holiday lunch, alone, in Hess's downstairs restaurant, where the wall murals neutered Diego Rivera's Mexico. I remembered how it all had delighted my father.

My mother gave me a two-pound box of Mootz chocolates, our one local delicacy, and a pair of engraved silver cuff links that had been my father's. I did not possess a single double-cuffed shirt in those days, but my mother knew what I wanted.

As the afternoon sank toward holiness and darkness, I practiced until I couldn't bear to hear myself any longer. I hadn't been abandoned entirely, but I was counting down the hours until it was time to rejoin humanity. Red and Stosh had invited me to spend the evening with them, then bunk over and stay on for Christmas dinner. The north-of-the-mountain tradition meant getting drunk before midnight mass, crowding into church—there was no ID check for non-Catholics—then getting drunker afterward until you passed out or daylight reached the manger. After a few hours of sleep, there would be black coffee and an exchange of gifts, followed by the long preparations for dinner.

I put on an Andy Williams Christmas album borrowed from my mother's house. I would have been disgraced had any friends seen the record in my possession. But I wanted to hear the carols, to sit by my tree and remember. Nostalgia is never more powerful than in the young.

When the phone rang in the fading light, I rushed to turn off the stereo before picking up.

It was Red.

"Will, have you heard anything from Angela?" She sounded distraught.

"No. Nothing. I was just sitting here listening to Paul Butterfield."

"What about Frankie? He call you or anything?"

"No. Has something happened?" My first thought was of a car accident. My second was of Angela and drugs.

"You need to go up to the house. To see if Angela's okay."

"What's going on?"

"Go up and check on her, okay?"

"What the fuck, huh?"

"*Please*, Will. She needs somebody to see if she's all right."

"What about you? You're closer."

"I can't get mixed up in this."

"But I can? Where's Stosh?"

"Out trying to find Frankie. Before something happens. With Matty."

"Would you just tell me what's going on?"

"I can't. Not over the phone. I'll tell you later. Please just drive up there. She might . . . I don't know, she might do something dumb, you know?"

"No, I don't know. Did she and Frankie have a fight? Did he hurt her?"

"Yes. I mean, I don't know if he hit her or anything. But she's out of control."

"How do you know that?"

"She called me."

"And?"

"Will, please. Stosh and me, we can't get any more mixed up in this. You have to do this. *Please.* She trusts you. I think you're the only one of us she trusts."

"What about Matty?"

After a killing pause, Red said, "He's crazy."

There was no response to my knock. I stood on the front porch. The paint was scabbed. Beside me, three plastic choirboys waited to be plugged in for the evening. The house remained dark.

On every side, Christmas lights trimmed half-a-double facades. Tiny lawns that longed for snow hosted glowing Santas, reindeer teams, and a gang of broom-armed snowmen. But the street was hushed with the start-drinking-early silence.

Holding my ear to the door, I heard Angela weeping.

Coming up the Frackville grade, I'd spun out on black ice, just missing the guardrail and the drop into the creek. The Corvair wasn't meant for coal-region weather, and the studs on my tires might as well have been skates. So my nerves were already stretched.

The door was unlocked. Frankie and Angela locked up only when leaving or doing dope.

I could make out Angela's form, but not her features. She sat on the stairs, bawling. I felt for the light switch. When the bulb came on, she hid behind her knees. With her limbs gathered in, she looked childlike.

The artificial Christmas tree had keeled over. Its silver branches lay on shards of broken ornaments. Unopened gifts had been hurled about and their wrapping paper kicked in.

"Angela . . . it's me." It was a stupid thing to say.

She looked up. I had never seen such misery on a face. In the wake of my father's death, my mother's face hardened.

As if her tears had burned off flesh, Angela's face seemed a skull. Her hair looked thinner, too. Even after the weight she'd lost on meth and her skin's coarsening, she had always kept a vestige of allure. That Christmas Eve, she looked like a creature found in a concentration camp.

"Go away," she said. In a broken voice.

"What's the matter? What can I do?"

Burying her face again, she wept on. Her pain seemed so naked and unguarded that I could not fit it to the woman I knew. She cried as if she had been hollowed out.

I sat down beside her and put an arm over her shoulders.

She uncoiled, sweeping me away. For a dreadful instant, our eyes met.

"*Don't touch me.* I never want another man to touch me."

I retreated as far away as the stairwell let me.

"Angela . . . please . . . what can I do?"

She turned on me. "You're all the same. You bastards. Every one of you. You're dirty, lying bastards." She would not meet my eyes again. "You always cover up for him. Even you. *Even you,*" she repeated.

"What's Frankie done? What's the matter?"

She slapped at me. Striking my torso open-handed. Then she closed her fists and continued hitting me.

"I told you to get *away* from me. . . ."

I stood and abandoned the staircase. "All right, I'm sorry. If I've done anything to you, I'm sorry. Call me, if you need anything."

"*Don't go,*" she said. "I don't want you to go, I didn't mean that." She balled herself up and leaned against the banister. Howling again, a tormented animal.

I wanted to touch her, to pet her. To show a basic human solidarity. But I was afraid of igniting another tantrum.

"Should I make you some coffee? Angela? Would you like me to get you anything?"

"No. Please. Just stay here. I don't want anything." Sobbing on, she sounded like an asthmatic struggling for breath.

I sat on the stairs again, below her. She touched my hair, but her hand retreated instantly.

"If you don't want to talk, that's okay," I said. "I can just sit here."

She tried to muster herself. "Please, Will . . . don't make any of this into one of your songs. Please don't write a song about this. *Please* don't."

"Angela, I'd never do anything like that. For God's sake."

"But you *do*. You always do." She sniffed back the wet in her nose. "You change little things, but I know. I always know. Please don't write a song about this. I'd just die. Promise me you won't."

"I promise. I don't have any idea what's going on, anyway."

"But promise me."

"I already did."

"Tell me again."

"I promise I won't write a song about anything that has to do with whatever's going on. All right?"

"You have to mean it, though. I'm so ashamed."

"I mean it. Okay?"

She bumped her backside down the stairs until we sat side by side. When she clutched my bicep, I felt finger bones through my sweater.

"We're all going to get out of here, ain't? The band's going to make a record and we're all going to get out of here. Tell me."

"I hope so."

"Tell me it's going to happen. That you won't let them leave me behind. Don't let them leave me here. I'll do anything you want . . . anything, anytime . . ."

There was nothing left that I wanted from her. Skeletal fingers chewed into my arm.

"You don't have to do anything for me. We're *all* going to get out of here."

"Don't let Frankie fuck it up, Will. I'm sorry for all the bad things

I ever said to you. I'm sorry for everything I ever did wrong, for being mean. I never meant to be bad. I'll make it up, I swear I'll make it all up to you."

"Angela, you don't owe me anything. Come on now."

She renewed her grip. "Tell Frankie I forgive him. If you see him. Tell him it's all right, that it's going to be all right. Tell him I forgive him."

"For what?"

She drew away, but more slowly this time. "Just tell him. He'll know." She began to cry again. When she balled her fists, she beat her knees, not me.

"If you'd just tell me what's wrong," I said.

She clutched herself and wept. "I feel so dirty. It makes me feel so dirty. Don't ask me anything else. It's all right. You can go. Please go. You should go now. Merry Christmas."

I stood up. "Are you sure you're all right?"

She raised her face and looked at me as if I were the greatest fool in history.

"If you must know, he gave her the clap," Red told me. "She just found out today." We were drinking eggnog laced with Irish whiskey. "There. Now you know. Does that make you happy?"

It didn't make me happy. It made me feel sick.

"I'll bet it was that dancer bitch," Stosh said.

The same thought had struck me. But Frankie had gone through a couple of strays after the Poconos gig. It could have been any one of them. Or Frankie might have shared the love with his one-night stands, Typhoid Mary with a dick.

"Does Matty know?" I asked.

"Yeah."

"Angela told him?"

Red looked horrified. "God, no. She'd never tell him anything like that." Red downed her eggnog like a highball. "I'm sure by now she's sorry she told me. But she was just freaking out, you should've heard her."

"Then how does Matty know?"

"Frankie called him."

"What?"

Red shook her head. Stosh told me, "Listen, Bark . . . Will . . . those guys got something crazy going between them. It was there before Matty went to Nam, and he brought it back with him. And there's nothing any of us can do about it. We all just have to live with it."

"You mean the jealousy thing? Over Angela?"

Red grimaced and rolled her eyes. "If that was all. I, for one, don't think Angela matters anymore. Not much, anyway. She's just a bone at the dogfight. I mean, look at her, Will. Have you seen her arms since she started hitting up? Even when she's covered up, I'm embarrassed to be seen in the street with her. She looks like a junkie."

The truth was that junkies rarely looked that bad that fast. In the myth of our time, heroin was the destroyer of worlds, but the embrace of meth took women down faster than smack.

"Frankie hasn't made things easy on her," I said.

"Like she's made things easy on him?" Red practically spit out the words. It was not the response I expected. "I'd be looking around for other women, too."

I almost said something I would have regretted. Instead, I turned to Stosh. "So . . . I'm trying to get this straight . . . Frankie calls Matty to tell him he gave his wife the clap. What's he, a dog marking his spot? I mean, this is sick."

"Yeah, it's a bummer. But it's not like it's the syph," Stosh said. "That rots your brain."

I didn't know what to say. I didn't know these people. After almost two years of playing together, of virtually living together, I had no idea what they were all about.

"So Matty's out looking for Frankie now?"

"No, no. I found him. He's okay. He's just waiting around to take his old lady to midnight mass, once the old man's passed out. Don't worry about Matty, he'll be all right."

"You don't think he's going to beat the hell out of Frankie? Or kill him, for that matter?"

"Why should he? You don't none of you understand Matty like I do."

Red tried to help me out. "Look, Will . . . Frankie's driving Angela away. That's what Matty wants, isn't it? Matty's smarter than you think. A lot smarter. He knows how to get what he wants."

"So Matty's happy watching Angela turn into a walking skeleton? And he's thrilled that her husband gave her a dose? What's he going to do, marry her corpse?"

Stosh tried making a joke to lighten things up. "Well, at least the meth'll keep the corpse jumping, ain't?"

I held out my empty glass. "May I have another, please? Double shot of whiskey this time?"

We were on our third round together, and the two of them had been drinking before my arrival. As Red took the glass from my hand, our fingertips touched and she asked, "Will . . . was there ever anything going between you two? Anything serious, I mean? Did you have some big crush on Angela for a while?"

Stosh laughed and held up his empty glass as well.

"The only person Bark ever had a crush on," he said, "was himself."

St. Pat's was packed for midnight mass, and the smell of mothballs fought the reek of alcohol breath. With restless young people ranged around the back of the church and stuffing the vestibule, the priest's words were audible only in snatches, like a singer with a faulty mike cord. The statues with their bleeding hearts were awful, but the music buoyed me.

One constant over the years was that the band never accepted bookings for Christmas Eve or Christmas Day. Even at their lowest, they were too Catholic for that. Anyway, the best-paying jobs kicked in just afterward, and even the worst group in the state made a killing on New Year's Eve.

Beginning on St. Stephen's Day, we were booked solid through Greek Christmas. And now I had to hope that the band wouldn't fall apart, thanks to Frankie's cock.

The older people in the pews struggled to maintain an air of piety, but midnight mass was a party for everyone else. Where I stood with Red and Stosh, a huddle of teenagers grew impatient with the service. Some were falling-down drunk, but none dared leave. My own faith asked the soul's commitment, but Catholicism insisted only that folks show up.

Those around me whispered and squirmed until I felt alone in my need to pray. I wasn't exactly the archbishop of Canterbury in those days, but I submissively asked Christ's mercy upon us. I prayed for grace to descend upon Angela, upon Laura and my mother, upon Joan and Red, upon all of us. I prayed for us all to be happy. But my heartfelt plea was for the band's success.

EIGHTEEN

The stars seemed misaligned. Our holiday gigs had gone well enough, with the tension between Frankie and Matty only adding fuel to the musical fire, but New Year's Day brought more than dry-mouthed headaches. Tooker, our old keyboard player, had been killed in an early-morning car wreck, riding shotgun in Buzzy Ritter's Corvette. Tooker went through the windshield. Buzzy was in the hospital, expected to recover, a cosmic injustice. Still resolutely unaware of much that was going on, the local cops merely charged Buzzy with drunken driving. Word on the street was that he and Tooker had been tripping their brains out on LSD laced with speed, in addition to draining a bottle of Lord Calvert whiskey.

Angela lost her job at the salon. She did not go quietly. I heard about it thirdhand, through Red, so I didn't know if Angela had become too unreliable or if it had to do with her fading appearance. She no longer seemed much of an advertisement for a beauty parlor.

Drugs baffled me. Some people could do them in daunting amounts with impunity, while others became entrapped almost as fast as addicts in cheap films. One caste of musicians could play high, but another could not. A notorious heavy user might remain in robust health, while a different body chemistry turned his girlfriend into a leper from

Ben-Hur. Some druggies got wasted and forgot to wash or work, while others, sardonic and entertained, made a profit. Fewer women fell into a drug trap, but those who did fell harder than the men. I found no moral lesson in any of it, only a stern reminder of life's unfairness: The wages of sin were death, but only for some of us.

An overheard remark made me suspect that Frankie had started dealing serious dope. If true, it made no sense. We had money coming in from the band, and anyway, Frankie could put in time at his father's printing business whenever he felt short. Old Man Starkovich was doing fine, and Frankie, an only son with two fawning sisters, was set up for life. If music failed us, he still would inherit a business.

I decided he might be dealing to skim enough meth to keep Angela supplied. Or maybe it was greed, the one sin that didn't afflict me. I just didn't want him to get popped and wreck the band. At least he seemed discreet. I struggled to put his antics out of my mind.

On a Tuesday evening in January, we went into the low-budget studio in Reading to cut a trial demo. The time and effort were wasted. Claiming to be a four-track affair, the control booth displayed only a crude two-track machine barely adequate to record the radio commercials that were the studio's bread and butter. The engineer cared nothing for music, the studio lacked sound baffles to isolate our instruments, and the first playback had a sound quality that would have embarrassed a metal shop. The engineer, a German immigrant, complained about the *"Dreckwetter"* outside, then threatened "consequences" when we canceled the second evening we had booked.

I destroyed the master tape so no one would ever hear it.

I also managed to move up our first date at the reputable studio in Philly, although Frankie still had doubts about the cost. He'd been having phone conversations with Danny Luegner, the manager who wanted to sign us, and Frankie was on his high horse about "real" record companies paying for demos if they were interested in a band.

In one of my rare outbursts, I told Frankie that if nothing came of it, I'd pay his share of the demo's costs myself. Losing my temper never made me smarter.

Laura was the unexpected bright spot.

"I'm so glad you like it," she told me.

"I do," I said. "I really do."

The belated Christmas gift was a guitar strap in soft brown leather. I'd never seen one finer.

Laura kissed me so tenderly, I barely knew her lips. "I'm sorry I was such a beast. It's really unforgivable. I was just so frantic. You don't know how important it is to me to maintain a perfect 4.0." She stepped back, penitent. The winter light darkened her eyes. "That's no excuse, of course. None whatsoever. And you were so endearing all the while, so kind. I really don't deserve you."

Which man does not find sudden kindness suspect? I couldn't decide whether she had been prescribed a new medication, had cast off a burdensome boyfriend back home, had murdered her mother, or felt genuine remorse.

She wasn't finished. Her talk assumed the quality of rehearsed speech.

"The worst of it is how *monstrous* I was about that story you wrote. You did it for me, and I lashed out at you. It was so unfair. I do believe I was jealous, to be frank. I've always wanted to write well. And there you go dropping a splendid short story in my lap, something you just scribbled out, when I was struggling to get through my English final. I do think intellectual jealousy's more insidious than sexual jealousy. Don't you?"

I wasn't so sure. And I didn't want to find out.

"I'll have to go to hear you play now. To see if you're wearing your new strap. Did I mention that I want you to meet my mother? Not just yet, I don't mean. I've been laying the groundwork, though. She's so frightfully conservative. In the social sense. If only she sees past your hair, she'll be impressed by your intellect. And you *can* be charming. Do you have a jacket and tie you could wear? If worse came to worst?"

Even after we tumbled onto the mattress, she seemed to remember that I was a human being. Fucking became making love again. The only thing that didn't change was the fierce, wordless way she would cling as we waited for sleep. Laura wasn't physically strong, but once, in the dead of night, I awoke in a grip so tight that I could not move.

"I wouldn't fuck her with *your* dick," Joey Schaeffer said. Paging through a back issue of *Rolling Stone*, he had paused at a photo of Yoko Ono. "Man, what does the guy *see* in her?"

I shrugged. I didn't get it, either.

"We should've just killed all the Japs at the end of World War Two, you know?" Joey added.

"Peace, man."

Joey laughed. "Piece of ass. But not that one, brother. Makes my nuts shrivel up, just looking at her."

I rose to flip the record. We sat in my apartment, on a day as bleak as a coal bank, listening to *The Hangman's Beautiful Daughter*. Joey appreciated the Incredible String Band, the north-of-the-mountain guys didn't. "The Minotaur's Song" always made me think of Matty.

I cued the tone arm. "Listen to how they shift the time signature and the meter of the lyrics. It's Tennyson on acid."

"They're crazy fuckers, you know?" Joey leaned closer to the radiator.

"The Incredibles? Or the Japs?"

"No, no . . ." He wobbled his head from one side to another, as if reluctant to wake up from a swoon. "I meant the guys in the band. The other guys. Sometimes I think they're from a different planet than you and me."

"They are," I said.

We had shared a joint of Acapulco Gold, then eaten a bag of Oreos between us. Joey was mellow, but I was just annoyed. I should have been practicing. I had more work to do for the recording session in Philly, I needed to nail down the last solos we usually just improvised.

But Joey was a con's con. And I liked him. He got the jokes my band-mates didn't understand. He had talked me into the joint "for old times' sake." Joey never liked to smoke alone.

"Stoned again," I said. Raising my hands in false supplication.

"You're not stoned, man," Joey said. He cocked his head and inspected me. "I don't think I've ever seen you truly stoned in your life. I mean, not *stoned* stoned. It's like you're always standing back and watching everything."

"I thought that was your gig? Leaning back and digging on the fourteen-year-olds?"

He cackled. "It's different when I do it. I'm just having a good time. You, it's like . . . I don't know, it's like you're always judging everybody, like you've got everybody in a police lineup. Even dropping acid, you were like that." He scratched under his beard. "I been reading about the French Revolution. I mean, that was some heavy shit that went down, they didn't fool around. None of that pansy crap, revolution between semesters and Daddy goes your bail. And I can't make up my mind whether you're Danton, or Robespierre pretending to be Danton, or what. I mean, think about it . . . who *would* you send to the guillotine?"

"Carol Burnett."

"No, I'm serious."

"Whoever gave Angela her first snort of meth," I said.

"See? You been thinking about it all this time. It's like all the while I was reading, the deep waves were flowing into *your* brain." He pondered the universe. The music ran out again. "Heap bad karma for Frankie, but heads must roll. Who's next? I need to start a list."

"I always thought you were the one who turned Angela on to meth?"

Joey was startled. "Me? Man, speed's the *last* thing I ever would've laid on Angela. I mean, some free smoke, sure. I used to think she was pretty hot. Maybe some Quaaludes, if things ever got that far. But she needed shit to smooth her out, not crank her up. I mean, look at her now."

I nodded. Ready to get back to the music. But Joey wouldn't let it go.

"You'd really send Frankie to the guillotine, though?"

I shrugged. "Figuratively speaking. The long-suffering people of France have submitted a list of righteous complaints against Citizen Starkovich."

Joey laughed. "No, man. No 'figurative' shit. Lay off the word games for a minute. We're talking the real thing, the big blade. Chop-chop. Who'd be second?"

"How much did you smoke before you got here?"

"Don't be so uptight. We're off today, remember? No school. So who else is on the secret list? Who gets the ax?"

"Come on, Joey. I'm not some kind of monster. *Sailor*, okay?"

"Yeah, play Steve, man. I'll bet he's a monster, too. We're *all* monsters, all of us. Like all those crowds cheering and yelling and getting high on blood when the heads got chopped off—know what that made me think of when I was reading about it? A rock concert, man." He giggled. "I'm telling you, brother: Everybody's got a monster inside, *everybody*. Some are bigger, some are smaller, some are better-looking, but the bogeyman's always in there. Just waiting for the right moment to pop out from under the bed. And you, man . . . you're, like, this nice, well-mannered monster. People think it's safe to pet you. Except that it's not. And once they stick their fingers between the bars, it's too late. People think they're using you, getting over on you. But all the while it's you using them, just eating them up."

"Thank you, Dr. Freud. I think I'll ask Dr. Jung for a second opinion."

"That's why you and me get along, you know that? You do this Mr. Sincere act with people who don't know you, that's your thing. I play dumb-Joey-with-his-brains-fried, always good for a toke and a joke, that's my thing. And we both let on that we're in for the duration. But we always know when to stop, when it's one tab or one toke too many. That's the real difference between us and them, man. We're monsters, too, but we're not the monsters who fall off the top of the skyscraper. We hang around for the sequel. We're survivors."

"Danton and Robespierre didn't survive."

"Then you're like that other guy, the one who always conned everybody."

"Talleyrand?"

"No, no. The spy guy. Is that Boz or Steve singing?"

"Boz. You make it sound like I'm the biggest prick going."

Joey shook his head. "Naw. *Way* too much competition. You're okay, man. You mean well. Sort of. I didn't mean to bum you out. It's just, like, with the name of the band, for instance. All of them think *you're* Mr. Innocent. They have no idea. None whatsoever. Poor Angela, for Christ's sake . . ."

"What about Angela?"

The phone rang. I cut off Steve Miller's voice, if not his head.

"Will Cross? Milt Ehrlich, Eclecta Records. Remember?"

"Sure."

"Just checking in. How's everything? How's the band?"

"Good. Busy."

"Done that demo yet?"

"We're going into the studio tomorrow. Down in Philly."

"Good, that's good to hear. When you've laid down some tracks you think are righteous, get the tape to me. As we discussed."

"Absolutely."

"I have to tell you, Will . . . your music stuck with me. That's the first test. Plenty of good bands out there, technically speaking. But the music has to stick with you, and most of it doesn't. Yours does."

"I'm glad to hear that."

"How booked up are you, by the way?"

"Our schedule's pretty packed. The weekends, anyway."

"If I could get you a weeknight gig here in New York, could you make it?"

"If the roads are okay. Sure."

"Check your schedule for me. For, say, the next two months. Mail it to me, all right? I want a few people from Eclecta to hear you. And I want to hear you again myself, the sooner the better. I'll see if I can't find a spot on some bill for you, it could be short notice. Now, I'm going be honest with you, Will. Sometimes I hear a band the second time and wonder what I was thinking. I dug what you were laying down in Philly, but that was in Philly. I need to take your temperature in front of a tougher audience."

"We won't disappoint you."

"Any other labels approach you, by the way? Since we talked?"

"No. Just that Danny Luegner guy. He's been talking to Frankie, our lead singer. We're scheduled to meet with him tomorrow night, after our recording session."

After a pause, Milt Ehrlich told me, again, "Just don't sign anything. The guy's a snake. I'll tell you exactly what he's going to do, he pulls the same shtick every time. He's going to offer to set you boys up with a couple of good-money club gigs. Without taking his commission, to show goodwill and so forth. And that's fine, if you want to spend the rest of your life playing Mafia joints in Jersey. But the guy can't deliver a serious recording contract, or any decent concert venues. Which is what you want, right? He's the original bad trip, that guy. Danny's famous for breaking up bands, picking out the people he sees as walking dollar signs and dumping the rest. That's one thing Danny Luegner actually *is* good at, splitting people up." He sighed. "Let me know where you are, if you're going to be on the road more than a day or two. Leave a number with my secretary, she's cool."

And that was it.

"Who was that?" Joey asked.

"The guy from Eclecta Records."

"Man, wouldn't that be a trip? If it worked out?"

"Yeah."

"You should be happy."

"I am happy."

Joey shook his head. "You're Robespierre. Definitely Robespierre."

"I'm just worried about Frankie. The shit he pulls."

Joey snorted. "Well, I'm more worried about Matty. And you should be, too. That business with the cop, his uncle or whatever he is. I mean, none of us need that right now."

There had been another confrontation between Matty and his uncle John. They hadn't come to blows this time. Instead, his uncle had drawn his service revolver and ordered Matty to leave his parents' house. According to Stosh, who'd been there, Matty had just turned his back and walked away. With his mother wailing, "Don't shoot him, Johnny, don't shoot my boy. . . ." Stosh made it sound funny.

"Matty can handle it," I said.

Matty had to handle two of my guitar parts. I felt humiliated. Overall, the recording session went well. The engineers were surprised that we played with such precision, that we needed so few takes to nail a song. The raw-mix playbacks sounded as good as any of us could have hoped. Most of my parts were just fine, but I stumbled during two intricate sequences, one in which Matty and I played superfast runs that harmonized with each other and another in which we traded speed-freak riffs. When I'd played live, my performance had never been a problem on either number. The studio was another world, though, isolating each slight error, each minor imperfection and missed note. You could hear that I wasn't hitting right on the money with Matty, that I lagged and, at the crucial moments, just blew it.

I insisted on doing the overdubs myself but only became more flustered with each failed take. Frankie made no secret of his impatience as the hands on the studio clock drew bucks from his pocket. At last, Matty pulled me aside.

"You're trying too hard, man. It's okay. Everybody has off nights. Let me do it this time, so we can get back in the groove and get out of here."

With the tape rolling again, he played my parts perfectly on the first take.

We still got four songs in the can in five hours, although the mix-down would be extra. One of the engineers congratulated us on being the least stoned band he'd recorded in months. Both of the engineers seemed to get off on our music and said they looked forward to our next session. Given how much they heard—and endured—it struck me as a good sign. I just wished that I hadn't been the only member of the band to fuck up.

When we left the studio, everyone else was skying on the quality of the tracks we had laid down, but I remained frustrated. I didn't want to sit down with Danny Luegner, our would-be manager, either.

We were going to be his guests, and he had reserved a table for five at Bookbinder's, pointedly leaving out Joey and Pete, who'd come down to the studio with us. My parents had always dismissed the sea-food house as a place for tourists who didn't know any better, but it was a perfect choice to impress guests from north of the mountain. At Luegner's insistence, each of my band-mates started with a jumbo shrimp cocktail, to be followed by whole lobsters. I ordered chowder and crab cakes.

Barrel-chested and runty, with curly hair, Luegner could have played Pan in a Steve Reeves movie. With all of the shrimp devoured, he piped in my direction.

"Frankie tells me you've been talking to Eclecta Records."

I nodded.

"Who's been talking to you? Milt Ehrlich?"

"Yes."

Luegner caressed his mustache. "Milt's all right. Small potatoes, but he means well. A little desperate." He looked around the table. "Wouldn't you boys rather sign with a major label?"

"Eclecta's a major label," I said. "It's got great prestige."

"You can't eat prestige." He chuckled. "Oh, I know it's got this for-the-artists reputation. Don't believe it for a minute. I know Mac Steinman, the one-man band up there, and he's a skinflint when it comes to advances."

"But they pay royalties honestly."

"Are you sure about that? I could tell you stories that might make you think otherwise, my friend. You—" He grabbed a waiter by the sleeve. "Take mine away, too, clean this up. Listen, Will . . . Eclecta got lucky with a couple of bands. But they're all small-timers, they think small. And from what I'm hearing, the label could very well fold. Then where would you be? Tied up in a dead-letter contract, and nobody else wants to touch you. No"—he looked around the table again—"you boys need to be on a major label. Like Capitol, say. Wouldn't you like to be on the same label as the Beatles? And the Beach Boys?"

"Who do you know at Capitol?" I asked.

Luegner smiled. Pan in his lair. "You boys take care of the music, I'll take care of the management side." His smile warmed, growing friendlier, more indulgent, and his eyes moved from my face to Frankie's, then to Stosh's, and back to Frankie's. "Now, I understand. Don't think I don't. It's the most natural thing in the world for young Mr. Cross here to be anxious to sign a recording contract. After all, he's the one who benefits almost immediately. You can cheat musicians on royalties all day long, but you've got to pay the songwriter." He shook his head. "I've seen groups where the songwriter's driving a Ferrari and everybody else in the band's still eating canned soup. It's all about the royalties and the publishing rights, that's where the money is."

I had never discussed any of that with the other guys.

"As far as I'm concerned," I told Luegner and everyone else, "we can divide up the songwriting royalties evenly. I don't care about that. It's a group effort, anyway."

Luegner waved the offer away. "No, no, we couldn't do that. This is about fairness. You write the songs, you get the royalties. That's the way it works. But, as your manager, it would be my job to look out for the interests of the entire band. And I wouldn't want to see you rush into anything you'd live to regret."

The main course arrived. The lobsters were presented with a flourish and fanfare that would have delighted the soul of any first-time visitor from Punxsutawney.

"I ain't wearing no bib," Stosh told the waiter. "Get away from me."

"You boys"—Luegner picked up again—"you've got real talent. And that's the truth. I knew that much before you were done with your first song. The sky's the limit, if you play your cards right. But I want you to think hard about the future. Most groups don't." He smirked, letting us all in on a secret. "Most managers don't, either. They're content to play checkers. But you've got to play chess in this business, you've got to think several moves ahead." He turned to me again. "Now you, Will. Your ability to write songs, that's a gift. But I want you to do something for me, something for everybody here at this table. Forget the gimmicks for a little while. All this psychedelic music, acid rock or hard rock, whatever you want to call it . . . all the hair down to the waist and the craziness . . . it's already dying. A couple of years from now—maybe just one year—nobody's going to want to hear songs about screwing robots or sexed-up versions of fairy tales. Or strippers, for God's sake. People are going to want what they've always wanted: moon, June, true love, and heartache. Take my word for it, I've been in this business a long time. All that mountain-of-amplifiers stuff's on its last legs. So—just as a test, now—I want you to write a couple of real love songs for Frankie here to sing. I want you to think about the group, not just about what's in that brainy head of yours, all right?"

"I always think about the group. I write for the group."

"But let's just see what you can do for Frankie, all right? I mean, he's your meal ticket, isn't he? Of course, Matthew's a superb guitarist. And Stosh could find work as a session man any time he wanted it, I could put him into any studio in Manhattan. But your average listener . . . that person identifies with the voice, that's all that he or she really hears. And I want you all to be thinking in terms of careers, not just one album that nobody buys and nobody ever hears. This can't just be about somebody's ego. Where do you want to be *ten* years from now? I mean, you take Frankie here. He could be another Tom Jones."

I laughed out loud.

No one else did. Of course, they were busy wrestling their lobsters to a gruesome standoff.

"Don't you have faith in Frankie's talent?" Luegner asked me.

"Frankie's a great front man. In a great band."

"But that's my point, Will. Frankie's willing to sacrifice a starring role, to submerge his talent in the group . . . for the benefit of the rest of you. He could be a solo artist any time he chose." Luegner smiled. "Maybe trim his hair a little bit. But he could have a thirty-year career. Longer. Do you really think the kind of music you play is going to last that long?"

"It's doing okay right now." I didn't know how to respond effectively. I saw what he was doing, the way he was cutting me out of the pack, making me the scapegoat. He and Frankie must have been having some long and interesting talks. But I just couldn't muster the words to fight back. And I was still reeling from being the weak link in the studio.

"I've seen musical fashions come and go, Will," Luegner told me. "They just come and go. Only the strong survive. Now, maybe all of this is just a hobby for you—I understand you're in college, is that right? But for your friends here . . . this could be a lifelong career, they're at a turning point. I need you to think of them."

"Your lobster's getting cold," I said.

He waved that away, too. "You boys are more important to me than food. Matthew, I see you're already finished. May I offer you one of my tails? I'm really not hungry, to tell you the truth. I'm in here so often I get tired of it."

"Why are you interested in us at all, if you just want to change us?" I demanded.

"Who said anything about changing you? You've got a great band. I can't wait for your first album, Will. I'd love to have another gold record on my office wall. But I want that album to be the first of many. On a reputable label. I want all of you to be thinking three, four, five albums from now. You want to write your college-boy lyrics now, that's fine. That's the Zeitgeist, I understand that. Same with the music, those hammers-of-hell songs of yours. In the longer term, though, Frankie's voice is much too good for that. Your fellow musicians here are too good for that. They could do anything they wanted. I don't want the material to obscure their talent."

"What do you want to make us into? Gary Puckett and the Union Gap?" I turned to my right. "Frankie? Is that what you want? Or do you want to be another Robert Goulet?"

"There's no need to get argumentative," Luegner told me. "Nobody here said anything about Robert Goulet. And, to tell you the truth, Frankie's voice is better than Goulet's, if you want my opinion. Just give it a little training. You boys like a little dessert? Some coffee for the long drive home? I hate to admit it, but sweets have always been my personal weakness. Listen to me now. Let me tell you what I'm going to do. As a demonstration of how much I believe in you, in *all* of you. As a show of good faith, I'm going to set up some real-money gigs for you, say, a few good club dates. That's where the money is, anyway—do you know how much a house band can make in a week in Vegas? Not that we're talking Vegas just yet. And another thing: I'm not going to take a commission, not for these goodwill gigs. I don't want you to sign anything, either—I wouldn't even let you. I need to show you what I can do for you. No pie-in-the-sky recording contract promises. All that will come in time. Let me start by putting a little serious money in your pockets."

"That's exactly what Milt Ehrlich said you'd pull," I told him.

He beamed. "See? The man knows me. He knows I get results. Everybody knows Danny Luegner. Now, if you boys think your stomachs are up to it, I highly recommend the cheesecake."

NINETEEN

Matty finished chewing the bite of hot dog and said, "Don't turn this into a contest between you and Frankie, Will. He'd break up the band before he'd let you win."

I stopped my cheeseburger halfway to my mouth. "It's Luegner who's trying to drive in a wedge, not me. He wants me out. I mean, that's pretty clear. *He's* the one who wants to break up the band."

"Look, I don't like the guy, either." Matty took a drink of chocolate milk. He was the only grown man I knew who touched the stuff. "And Stosh doesn't think much of him, I can tell you that. But he's got a hook in Frankie, he knows what Frankie wants to hear. But you can't talk to Frankie, Will. You've got to let him figure things out on his own."

"And if he doesn't figure them out? In time?"

"We just have to wait. And hope, I guess. Let's see what your contact from Eclecta comes up with. Frankie can be flattered, but he can't be suckered completely. A firm record deal would trump a couple of club dates. But you have to lay off him for now. Just play along, all right? You attack Luegner and Frankie takes it as a personal attack. And don't expect us to gang up on him. The band doesn't work that way. You going to finish your fries?"

I was ill at ease with all of it. With the sudden emergence of Danny Luegner as a factor in our lives. With Matty's insistence that we meet at the Coney Island, not at my apartment, as if we had to talk on neutral ground. And slush had soaked through my boots on the walk downtown, leaving my socks sopping.

"So . . . what am I supposed to do? Just watch while Luegner tears the band apart?"

"Let him put up, or shut up. I told you." Matty glanced at the waitress, who had been a fixture behind the counter for as long as I could remember. Recently, she had dyed her hair blond. Thirty years too late.

"He'll come through with those club gigs he promised. The guy from Eclecta warned me. It's his standard setup."

"Listen to me, Will. I mean it. I want you to listen to me for once. Never let an enemy know you're nervous. Never show fear. You can act as though you know you're going to win, or like you don't care who wins. But never let on that you think there's a chance you could lose." He shook his head. "I used to daydream about Coney Island dogs in Nam. But they're really not that good, to tell you the truth. Fries are okay, though."

"Matty? What do *you* want out of all this? Really?"

"To play music. To play good music."

"And? I mean, you must want more than that?"

He considered the question. I still could not square the big, slow character across the table from me with the superman who had served in Vietnam. Or even with the music that burst out when he held a guitar. Unlike me, he never even seemed to practice seriously. He just played.

"I want," he said, "people to leave me alone. That's it, I guess. To play music. And be left alone."

"But don't you want to be on albums? Like we always talked about? To have your playing recorded? So it won't just be lost? Don't you want more people to hear you?"

He shrugged. "I suppose. Sure. That would be great." But he was still pondering the basic question. His face grew somber. "We don't all want the same things, Will. As long as there's enough overlap, like in the band, things are okay." He pushed his empty plate away. "I never know how to say things so they come out completely right, I wish I had your way with words. I mean, take Frankie and this Lueg-ner guy. Everybody can see that Frankie's being selfish, that he's being a jerk. But look at you and me. We're selfish, too. I don't know, maybe I'm the most selfish of all of us. In his way, I guess Frankie's just more honest about it."

"And Stosh?"

"Stosh isn't selfish. Not like you and me and Frankie. Don't mix up greed and selfishness. They're not the same. He's mostly afraid."

"You mean because—"

Matty raised a hand. Like a priest about to give a blessing. Or a warning.

"We don't need to say some things out loud. What I mean is that he's afraid of being left out. He always was, as long as I've known him. He wants to be accepted, to be part of something other people think is important. Frankie wants people to adore him, for every girl on earth to fall in love with him. But Stosh just wants people to like him, to let him be one of the guys."

"You really don't care if people like you. Do you?"

"I like it when people like the music I play."

"But you don't care if they like *you*. Do you?" I felt that I had grasped something important, although I had only seen what had been there, in plain sight, from the start.

"I want people to not bother me. I told you."

"But you risked your life for other people. In Nam."

"That was my job."

"That's not a real answer."

He shrugged. "Maybe I care what happens to people. To some people. I just don't care if they like me. I don't want them to hate me or anything, I don't mean that. I just want everybody to leave me alone. Doesn't that make sense to you?"

"You cared about Doc. Didn't you want him to like you?"

"Doc had a gift. I cared about his gift. And I was responsible for him."

"What about Angela, then? Don't you care what she thinks of you?"

He went utterly still for a pair of seconds. Then he told me, "That's my business. There are things nobody else would understand."

"Don't you ever want to just *talk*? To a friend?"

"No."

"You care what happens to Angela. I know you do." Anger surged within me, abrupt and unreasonable. "How in the name of Christ can you let her fall apart? How can all of you just let her fall apart like that? While we all just watch, like it's some kind of horror movie? How can Frankie do it?"

"She's Frankie's wife."

"That's no answer."

Matty looked at me as if I were a new recruit who hadn't learned a thing. "She's Frankie's wife. He'd let her die before he'd give her up."

"And you'd let her die, too?"

"Angela won't die."

"Matty, look at her. She looks like a hag."

"She doesn't look like a hag."

"Then what would you call it?"

"She looks tired."

"She's *killing* herself. For God's sake."

He pulled up the drawbridge. "It's none of your business, Will. It doesn't concern you and you need to shut your mouth now. I don't care what might have happened or what didn't happen. But you're not part of this, you're an outsider." He looked down at the mess on the table, then met my eyes with an expression cleansed by force of will. "Just forget it. Go home and write a song. That Luegner guy was wrong, you know. The things you write will last."

"Don't shut me out. *Please*, Matty. . . ."

He tried to smile but failed. "There's nothing more to say about it," he told me. "Words only make things worse."

· · ·

I didn't go home to write a song. My mother had extended her stay in Palm Beach, a hint of courtship. Every few days, I had to check on her house, to make sure the furnace was still running and the pipes were okay. From the Coney Island, I walked down to the Necho Allen Hotel and turned up Mahantongo Street. When a woman slipped in the slush in front of the Reading Company offices, I rushed to help her. She regarded my long hair with dread, as if I would seize the opportunity to inject her with a lethal dose of heroin. Sleet pricked my face. I wished I had worn a hat.

By the time I reached my mother's house, my hair was heavy and my peacoat sodden. With my boots pulled off, my socks squished on the wood floors and the carpets, leaving a trail. I turned up the heat and showered in my father's bathroom, with the water heater knocking so badly that I could hear it two floors from the basement. Then I foraged for dry clothes among my father's wardrobe, something I had never done before.

In each of the drawers, the underwear, socks, handkerchiefs, sweaters, and folded shirts had gone undisturbed for two years. The items I selected fit jarringly well.

I laid my jeans over a radiator to dry, then went downstairs in pajamas and a heavy cardigan. The furnace growled, reminding me to top off the coal hopper—which I should have done before taking a shower. But I wasn't ready to do any chores just yet. I prowled into my father's study, opened the drapes to admit the gray light, and sat behind his desk. The dust was readily visible, as if I had entered a tomb.

It was a day of firsts. Wearing my father's clothing, I opened the middle drawer of his desk. Then I went through each of the other drawers. As if I might find answers to questions yet unformed.

Behind the blue box with his Purple Heart from Aachen, he had stashed a copy of The Young Lions. Unable to fathom why he would have hidden the novel, I took it out.

Polaroid photos hid between the pages.

244 · · · ROBERT PASTON

We think we know ourselves, our lovers, our parents. But we know nothing. All we have are the finger paintings we make of them in fantastic, inaccurate colors to suit ourselves.

I slammed the book shut. Then I opened it again.

Milt Ehrlich called with stunningly good news. He had gotten us on the bottom of a bill at the Fillmore East in Manhattan in early February. A weeknight concert, with up-and-coming groups but no big names, it was an ideal showcase for our music. And going onstage at the Fillmore East was more than just a step toward the dream—it *was* the dream.

"I cashed in a lot of chips to make this happen," he told me, "and everybody who matters is going to be there. Don't let me down."

We played Lancelot's Lair again, as the headline band this time. Despite bad roads, a serious following showed up. From the first song of our first set, the surge of energy between us and the audience was powerful enough to blow out a transformer. We introduced two new originals we intended to record during our next studio session, a slow, bluesy number, "My Name Is Darkness," and a pedal-to-the-floor rocker, "Knife Point." Both songs let Frankie run through minidramas behind the mike stand and showcased Matty's ability to astound mere mortals. Trying to drive home that it was all about the band as a whole for me, I declined to take solos in either song and just filled in the architecture with underscoring riffs or accented the rhythm with jagged chords.

Musically, it may have been the best night we'd had until then. Onstage, everything was magic. On the solos I still merited, I played as well as I had ever done. Matty and I got into a scorching exchange of licks in the middle of "Hideaway." The crowd was our prisoner.

But there was a price for the emotional intensity. At the end of that first set, I felt so drained that I was almost sick. As if the audience had been drawing my blood, sucking out all my juice. Half in a trance, I meandered back to the tiny dressing room to change my soaking shirt. I couldn't snap back to reality, couldn't clear the psychic fumes from my head.

Stosh came in while I was changing.

"Jeez, we played the fuck out of things. Ain't?"

"It was a good set."

"Shit, it was more than good. It was great. You were on fire, man."

"Everybody was."

"The new songs went down good. I really like that one, 'Knife Point.'" He played a drum break on the wall with his palms.

Frankie came in. The room was little more than a closet and three was a crowd. "Get to know your buddy," he said as he rubbed past me. High school locker-room crap.

"Christ, I wish Angela wasn't here," he said. "Why'd she have to come along tonight, of all nights?"

She had been coming to almost every gig of late. She didn't seem to have much else to do. According to Red, Angela's doctor had given her a clean bill of health after a couple of shots, but her mental well-being was another matter. She behaved erratically and had started public fights with Frankie while our band was on break at two club gigs. That didn't win us friends among the owners.

I couldn't understand how she and Frankie could remain together. After the Christmas Eve trauma, I had expected Angela to move out or give Frankie his walking papers. Instead, they went on living together. When I tried to puzzle it out with Red, she just laughed and said, "What do you think the priest told her to do?"

Frankie pulled off his shirt, treating Stosh and me to a whiff of his armpits. As he bent to his gym bag to choose another stage rag, he told me, "That Joan cunt's out there waiting for you."

That snapped me back to full consciousness. My only disappointment of the evening had been that I hadn't spotted Joan in the crowd. Despite my neglect of her, I had expected her to show up in front of the stage, just as she had on the night we'd first met. My vanity was boundless.

She stood by the water fountain in the foyer. Waiting. When she saw me, she smiled. But her look was newly diffident.

"You make me feel like a groupie," she said. "Just standing here waiting for the big star to come out." She cocked her head and her hair gathered on one shoulder. "I guess I am a groupie, when you think about it."

"I wouldn't say so."

"You wouldn't know. Would you? I've tried everything, smoke signals, telepathy." She sighed playfully, almost the wry girl I valued. "But you never send roses."

"Joan . . ." Back in the hall, the band condemned to fill in between our sets kicked off "Season of the Witch." The coincidence seemed too perfect.

"Come on. I'm teasing you," she assured me. "Want to go outside for a couple of minutes? Just to talk?"

"Let me grab my coat."

"I could keep you warm," she said, choosing from her repertoire of good-humored smiles. "But I suppose that would be against the rules."

I wasn't in love with Joan. I knew that much. But I lacked a name for the form of attraction I felt toward her. It wasn't just lust, although that was certainly in the package. For years, my appetites had outrun my emotions. Catching up confused me.

She drew me toward her the way a lighted window draws a traveler.

"I didn't think you were going to show up," I said.

We walked between the rows of cars. Ice glinted.

"I almost didn't. When I started out, the road was so bad."

"I'm glad you made it. I'm glad to see you."

"And that, along with a quarter, will buy me a pack of Tastykakes."

We got into her car, a no-nonsense Delta 88 Olds. She turned on the engine for heat.

"Well, here we are," she said.

"Here we are."

"I guess it would spoil the fun to tell you that I'm in love with you," she said. "But I'm not having much fun, anyway. And *don't* tell me

THE HOUR OF THE INNOCENTS ・・・ 247

any lies. Please. I know you're not in love with me. Although I'm not ruling out all future possibility of it."

"I can't explain what I feel."

"Then don't. Don't fuck me up even worse." She lowered her chin toward her chest. Dark hair curtained her off. "Doesn't love suck, though? I mean, I hardly know you, you were a one-night stand. And here I am, twenty-six years old, and I think about you like I'm hoping against hope you'll ask me to the prom and bring me a corsage." Throwing her head back, she closed her hands on the steering wheel. But we weren't going anywhere. "I just want you to tell me one thing, all right? Just one thing, and don't lie about it."

"Sure. All right."

"You *like* me. Don't you? I mean, you genuinely, honest and truly, like me, right? If it wasn't for your other girl . . ."

"I really like you. I wish I had a better word for it."

To my wonder, a tear fled her eye. The neon sign on the club's roof tinged it pink.

I shifted toward her, to take her in my arms. She fended me off, gently, with both hands.

"Please don't. I couldn't handle it, all right?" She looked at me. But as she turned, her features were lost in shadow. "*Why* do we love the people we love? Why the fuck do we do it? Do you have any fucking idea?"

"No."

I felt incompetent. And stupid. I had assumed that Joan saw me as a desirable good time, but little more. I had judged her as tough enough to handle herself.

"I know what you're feeling," she told me. "I really do. I'm not totally stupid about guys." She looked away again. "I hope she's worth it, Will. I really do. I hope, whoever she is, she's worth what I'm going through." She shook her head. "You're a decent guy. Underneath it all. Behind all the strutting and posing and shit. That's the trouble, you know? It's such a worthless goddamned lie that it's better to fall in love with a decent guy. They're always taken before you get there. It's easier to be in love with some low-life shithead." She sniffed. "At least you know where you stand."

"I'm a fool."

"Yeah. That, too. Listen, I'm going to go home. I just can't do it, I can't go back in there and watch you. I'm not going to do it."

"All right."

"And you're not even going to try to persuade me? What on earth have I done to myself?" She granted me another good Joan smile, pale in the gloom. "'It's all right, Ma, I'm only bleeding.'"

I wanted to reach her, to tell her to give me a little more time and maybe things would work out. But I didn't think I could make the words sound anything but utterly selfish and piggish.

As I got out of the car, I scrounged up a tribute I could say and mean.

"Joan? Okay, I'm not in love with you. But I love how you *are*. I mean it."

"All the boys love it when they make girls cry," she told me.

Angela cornered me as soon as I passed the ticket booth.

"I've seen that one before," she told me. "She tries to make herself look like Grace Slick."

"She's not Grace Slick."

"She give you a blow job? Out in the parking lot?"

"Angela. Jesus. Give me a break."

"His sweet little girlfriend isn't with him, so he's off like a rocket. Getting blow jobs in the parking lot from any slut he can pick up."

"Stop it. What's the matter with you? Nobody gave anybody a blow job. And she's not a slut. Knock it off."

Compared with the lithe conversation stopper I'd had a crush on eight or nine months before, she looked almost unrecognizable. Her damaged skin stretched taut over her skull and her clothes draped loosely over missing flesh. Angela had never been voluptuous, but now she was positively emaciated. She looked sick. With her hair dull and thin, only her eyes remained furiously alive.

"Come out in the parking lot with *me*," she said. "I'll give you a blow job you won't forget. If that's what you want."

I drew back. But I kept my voice down. There was already too much interest in us. And I didn't want Frankie popping up and going nuts.

"I don't want anything. I'm trying to play it straight, all right?"

She tried to make herself appear seductive. Posing. The effect was pathetic, even comical.

"Just come out in the parking lot," she said, "and we'll see what happens." She reached for my wrist. "I remember everything you like."

I pulled away. "No. I'm not going out in the parking lot with you. Get a grip on yourself. You're Frankie's wife, for God's sake."

It was the wrong thing to say. I never knew what to say to any of them.

"Yeah, like *that* bothered you before." Angela glared at me. With hatred in her face. "You think you're too good for me. Don't you? All high and fucking mighty. You think you're too good for me. What, do you think something's wrong with me? Do you? Is that it?"

The truth was that I did think something was wrong with her. Everything about her had grown wretched.

I was afraid she'd start shouting. Instead, she closed the distance between us and looked up into my face with viper's eyes. "I know what the problem is," she said. "Don't think I don't know, you faggot. You cover it up so good, but you're a fucking queer. You faggot. You should get together with somebody else we both know, ain't?"

I turned my back and walked away.

"*Faggot*," she called after me.

That was on a Saturday night. By Sunday evening, Laura had come back from her biweekly journey home and she lay beside me on our mattress, with Tim Hardin singing quietly on the stereo in the other room. His voice was drenched with sorrow, and his songs mourned loves that failed.

Things had gone ever better between Laura and me. Her new kindness had not faded and she even seemed less terrified of exams. If she really had been locked away—and I could not doubt it—she probably had faced no end of painful "reentry procedures," as the astronauts put it. Perhaps things just took time.

She had come along to several of our band's performances and told me that it might not be entirely impossible to acquire a taste for our kind of music. At times, she almost seemed proud of me. And she got along well enough with everyone else. Angela treated her with brusque acceptance, while Red kept her mitts to herself.

With her head and that cushion of thick dark hair resting on my shoulder, Laura moved so that our flesh touched all along our bodies. Then she laid her arm across me, as if barring a door. We smelled of sex and sweat.

"It must be lovely," she said, "to be you."

"It doesn't always seem that way to me."

"I mean, everything's so easy for you. You write your songs, and the lyrics just come to you. And the way you wrote that story for me. You just sat down and did it. I wish I could be more like you."

"No, you don't." Again, it struck me how little we ever know about one another. My life was a constant fight to become the musician I longed to be, a war against music's forbidding complexity, against the recalcitrance of my fingers, against the ear inside the brain that could not hear the things that Matty heard. The songs, the lyrics, were insignificant compared with the ability to *play*.

"I don't mean I'd want to be like you in *every* way," she said. "Obviously, that wouldn't do us any good. But I wish I had your . . . your facility. Do you know the dictionary meaning of the word?"

"Yes."

"That's what I want. Your facility. I've hated being jealous of you. I think, really, that's the reason I did what I did."

"What did you do?"

She tilted her face up toward me, letting me see her paleness across my cheekbone. The altered posture pressed her breasts against me.

"Shall I tell you? I wasn't going to. I'd decided not to. But I don't like having secrets."

"You don't have to tell me anything you don't want to."

I feared some revelation about her madness, some admission that would tether me to her unmercifully. It was better to go on pretending I didn't know.

"You don't keep secrets from me, do you?" She laid a hand under her chin, the better to meet my eyes in the near darkness.

"Generally, no."

"You don't sleep with other women, for instance? When I'm not around?"

"Of course not."

"Well, I'm going to tell you. What I did was wrong, and I know it. I'm penitent, you see."

"Laura, you don't have to tell me anything." Whatever it was, I didn't want to hear it. I wanted her to shut up and go to sleep. Or to start making love again.

"When I was home . . . over Christmas break . . . I slept with some-one else. Please don't be mad. It was just one time. And I didn't really sleep with him, that's only an expression. We just had sex. It was awful, just pathetic. I felt sick afterward. It made me appreciate you even more."

"Why?"

"Because you're so much better. In every way."

"No. Why did you do it? Why did you fuck somebody else?"

"Please don't get angry. You and I are more grown-up than that. Aren't we? It was a mistake, I made a mistake. I'm so sorry, Will. I re-ally am. I had to get it off my conscience."

"But why did you do it?"

"I think I was jealous of you. That everything's so easy for you. I think that was really at the heart of it, that's what I was trying to explain earlier. And I'd known this guy for a long time, he's a doctor. I just ran into him. Out of the blue. To tell you the truth, I was surprised when he came on to me. I was, I don't know, in emotional disarray. But, down inside, I suppose I wanted to hurt you. Have I?"

I didn't know. Certainly, she had hurt my pride. But the news also came as something of a relief. She had handed me an excuse, if ever I needed one.

"Well, it's not good for my rock-star ego," I said. Speaking a line written for me by a stranger.

She paused for a moment—a long moment—then ran her hand over my body.

"Have you decided to forgive me?" she asked.

TWENTY

The profs at the local campus had forgiven all they could. I turned in clever papers, written easily, and had no trouble with exams designed to move the cattle down the trail, but even the most indulgent junior instructor expected me to appear in the classroom now and then. Consumed by the band's possibilities, I had been absent for weeks at a time, relying on plain, friendly girls to pass on the assignments and hand in my papers for me—I was an exploiter of the toiling masses, just ashamed enough to believe I was still decent at heart. Now I found I had to pay my dues.

That's how I met Angela in Chekhov. I had run out of choice courses at the campus and signed up for Drama from Marlowe to Miller with an assistant prof notorious for Freudian insights and laying his hands on the kneecaps of male students. One of the meager readings was *Three Sisters*.

And there she was, with better table manners and renamed "Masha." Perhaps no one else in the world would have made the connection, but it struck me by the end of the first act. An attractive woman, married young and unhappily, trapped in a provincial town, longing to escape, and, meanwhile, grasping at what slight pleasure she finds.

It wasn't hard to picture Masha hitting up with speed, given the chance.

Reading the play, then writing a silly paper arguing that the baron deserved to die, I finished with a renewed sympathy for the real woman poisoning herself with drugs and laying waste to every relationship she had. Perhaps nothing could ever fully content her, but Angela longed to give the world a try. And, I reminded myself, she had kept one crucial faith with me, never telling others about Laura's problems.

As for Laura, she wearied me, although I was too stubborn to admit it. Her calculated kindnesses annoyed me, and her conversation, which had seemed so wonderfully sophisticated, struck me now as gratingly pretentious. I thought of Joan when Laura and I made love but lacked the courage to make the fantasy real. Laura's history let me frame my cowardice as virtue, inertia as loyalty. As for that pathetic infidelity of hers—I pictured a doctor taking unfair advantage—it insulted my pride but moved me less than it should have. The brilliant girl had become a tiresome bore.

I hoped some painless event would take her from me. As she grew ever gentler, my temper flared. I had to read *The Glass Menagerie* for class and hated it. In lieu of making up a quiz I'd missed, I did an extra paper, insisting that the daughter was the villainess.

One snow-slowed day, I told Laura to wash her cunt.

Things were better in Florida. My mother called to tell me she had accepted a marriage proposal. She had met the guy for the first time over Christmas and her haste seemed embarrassing in a woman her age, but marriage was a better bet than moping in the old house and fighting the tug of the liquor cabinet.

She sounded excited, almost girlish, and forgot to ask me how my life was going. I congratulated her, more or less sincerely. She didn't ask me to attend the wedding, which would be in Darien, Connecticut, in the spring.

· · ·

Matty broke his uncle John's nose outside of a bar in St. Clair.

We know. We deny it to ourselves. But we know.

The studio lights had been turned down to create a smoky dusk. Behind the glass of the control booth, a green glow lit the face of the engineer. Frankie crushed out his cigarette and centered himself behind the lead mike, waiting for word through his headphones that the tape was rolling for the last vocal lay-down. The rest of us sat amid the jungle of amplifiers, drums, and cables, waiting for the instrumental track to come through the speakers mounted high in the corners. Except for the hard red EXIT light, everything in the world seemed to have softened.

Our collective mood was as fine as it could have been. The second session had begun with us listening to the mix-down of the earlier recordings. Since we all agreed he had the best ear, Matty had worked with the engineers after the first round. We sensed that he would be fair, that the volume level he approved for each instrument and voice would be right for the song in question, if not for the ego involved. The results were exhilarating. Played back, those first four songs sounded better than we had any right to hope.

We had booked an eight-hour block for our return visit and everything went smoothly. I nailed each of my parts this time and we laid down four more songs so quickly that we had time left over to work on the final mixes. Miraculously, there was no antagonism. Frankie even preempted my single criticism. For the one slow number on the demo, we had chosen a brand-new song of mine, "The Road to Heaven (Joey's Song)." Frankie had recorded it with what we called his "pretty-boy voice" on the first go-round, but it needed his "whiskey voice." When he heard the playback, he commented on it himself.

Now he was giving it one last try. If he scored, we only needed to polish the mixes a little more to have a demo so strong, the reality unsettled me. It wasn't supposed to be so easy.

In the semidarkness, I saw Frankie nod. Restrained and wistful, the music crept out of the monitors. It balanced all the attack-dog numbers and, somehow, completed them. Freeing a strand of hair from the clamping headphones, Frankie closed his eyes and began to sing:

How we laughed at borderlines,
We tore down the warning signs,
The road to heaven drew us all along.
We lit the darkness with our lives,
Drank the days and . . . clutched the nights,
Then I awoke to find my friends were gone.
Some in war and some on drugs,
Some on highways, some in love,
The road to heaven leads through troubled lands.
Some survive the stormy days,
Others fall . . . along the way,
Consumed by visions, broken by God's hand . . .

On the tape, I strummed a sharp arpeggio just in front of the Les Paul's bridge, and the song lifted into the chorus:

Me, I knew when to stop. And start.
But not my brothers of the wild heart,
They had no sense of how far they could go . . .
Some died quick, while others . . . faded slow . . .

A gorgeous cry, Matty's guitar solo set up the closing verse:

I can see them young and whole,
Children playing out their roles,
The road to heaven leads some children wrong . . .

But I remain to hold them near,
I take them with me . . . through the years . . .
The road to heaven leads us on and on . . .

Matty had risen, positioning himself at the backup mike to add a high, ghostly harmony to the final chorus:

I knew how to stop. And start.
But not my brothers of the wild heart . . .
They shook their fists at lightning, and they burned . . .
Leaving me the lessons . . . no one learned . . .
They . . . never learned . . .

The song ended with a drumstick touched, lightly, to the crown of a cymbal, our coalcracker version of a Zen gong.

When he sensed that the tape was clear, Stosh said, "Fucking good, Frankie. Really fucking good."

"I don't like it," Danny Luegner said. "It doesn't showcase Frankie's voice."

Uninvited—unless by Frankie—he had slipped into the control booth during the recording. He looked more like Pan than ever, or a nasty little satyr.

"It's too . . . what's the word I want? It's one of your college words, Will, help me out. It's too *introspective*. That's what I wanted to say. You need to give Frankie a big, sweeping melody, something to show him off. A song with big emotions, with serious feelings."

I struggled to keep my temper. Everything had been going just fine.

"I wrote a ballad for Frankie. Exactly what you asked for. It just doesn't belong on this demo."

"Now, now, that's not quite true, Will," Luegner said. "Frankie sang me that other song of yours—I'm assuming it's the same one, that one about nighttime in the palace or whatever it was. You can't write songs like that. It's too dirty."

"Dirty?"

"Explicit. You can't write about women taking off their clothes and wrapping themselves in sheets and going to bed with somebody. There's no future in songs like that, no money." He shook his head mournfully. "Now, I'm not saying you're not a talented young man, Will. But songwriting's an art. Maybe you need a little time, maybe broaden your listening horizons."

Nobody defended me or the songs. The engineer stayed out of it, turning off the preamps for the night and lighting a cigarette.

"Audiences love the songs," I said. "Eclecta Records is anxious to hear our tape."

"Now that's something else I want to talk to you boys about. I'd like you to give me a fair chance, no more than that. Just a fair chance. Before you send the tape to Eclecta, I'd like to run it by my friend at Capitol."

"Who do you know at Capitol Records?" I asked him again.

"Look, Will . . . it's my job to take worries of that kind off your shoulders. That's what a manager does, he handles the business end, so artists like you and your friends here can concentrate on making music."

He put his hand on my shoulder. I didn't want to brush it off and make a scene.

"I'm not saying you shouldn't run it by Eclecta, too. But that's a small-time outfit, hits or no hits. The label's a flash in the pan. You talk Capitol, now, you're talking a big company, a *corporation*. And a big corporation means big money, fellas. Just give me first crack at landing you an offer. Then we can see what kind of deal Eclecta has in mind. Fair's fair."

"That's fair, Will," Frankie said.

"I promised Eclecta I'd send up the tape right away."

"So take it to your friend Milt Ehrlich in person," Luegner told me. "You can give it to him when you play the Fillmore East. I guarantee you I'll have it back in plenty of time. You can go onstage, knock 'em dead, then hand Milt the tape." He cocked his head and teased his chin with his fingers, the high school play gesture for a man thinking deeply. "Who knows? Maybe some other serious labels will hear you in New York? Columbia? Or Warner Brothers? Maybe you won't need me, maybe I won't have a chance to manage you boys, after all. So just give me a shot and let me show you what I can do in the meantime."

"Capitol Records doesn't have an office in Philadelphia. I checked."

"Come on now, Will. You think I live on a leash tied to William Penn's ankles? I wouldn't have survived as a manager all these years if I didn't think a lot bigger than just Philly. I don't know why you're so suspicious of me, young Mr. Cross. I wish I could reassure you some-how. But I guess Milt Ehrlich's been whispering in your ear, he's like that. All I'm asking is that you do what's right for the whole band, like we all agreed."

He turned toward Stosh and Matty. "Speaking of which, I keep my promises. I said I'd land you boys a serious club job or two, some serious-money work, and I've already got the first one lined up. And you don't have to pay me one dime in commission, this is all in good faith."

Frankie barely paid attention. He already knew.

"Ever hear of Jimmy Prince's Home of the Stars?" Luegner asked.

"No," I said. "Where is it? Camden?"

"Very funny. No, it's in Passaic. It's famous. All the top jazzmen played there, all the big singers. Mr. Principe's trying to open things up a bit, stay up with the times. He asked me to find him a rock-and-roll band that could really wow the crowd, musicians who can really play. And here's the kicker, fellas. We're talking five nights, two thousand, two hundred and fifty bucks. You hear what I just said? Where else could you boys cash in like that? You couldn't earn that kind of money playing shore clubs in August seven nights a week."

Stosh pulled out his business notebook. With the dates of our gigs.

"When is it?" he asked.

"First full week in March."

"We're back at Lancelot's Lair that week," I said.

Luegner waved away my concern. "I'll handle that for you. I've known Gus for years. He'll let you swap dates."

Stosh looked at me. "It's good money."

"Shouldn't we wait until the Fillmore gig? See what comes out of it?"

"A bird in the hand's worth two in the bush. That's what Benjamin Franklin said," Luegner told me.

"What band's he with?"

"Very funny. Come on now, Will. You may be a college boy, but I'll bet all of your friends here could use that money, even if you don't need it. I know people on Wall Street who don't make that kind of dough." He plopped down on the engineer's stool, as if my arguments had exhausted him. "All I'm asking is a fair shake. I believe in you boys, I really do. In every last one of you. And I think you should consider all of your options. Look things over carefully. Then make your decision. Look before you leap, you know what they say. Let me run your demo past my friend at Capitol, and I guarantee the tape will be back in your hands in plenty of time to keep Milt Ehrlich happy. In fact, if Frankie here wants to come down on the train and pick it up on his way to Manhattan, I'll personally put it in his hands. Guaranteed."

"Let us make some copies."

"There'll be time for that, Will. Just hold your horses. Let me show you what I can do. If you're not happy with what I deliver, we all part friends, and no hard feelings." He smiled, but there were spiders in his eyes. "At least, I hope there'd be no hard feelings."

In his world, he was faster than me, smarter, better. I always knew what I should have said, but only after he was gone.

Luegner looked at his watch. It had diamonds on the face. My father believed that only pimps and prizefighters wore watches studded with diamonds.

He sighed wearily. "Well, I've got another band to audition across town. Everybody wants Danny Luegner to be their sugar daddy. One of these days, I'm going to have to close my list. So . . . what do you want me to tell Mr. Principe? You boys want that gig?"

The others murmured their assent, nodding and shuffling about. I said nothing.

As he pulled on his overcoat, Luegner said, "One last thing. Just a formality. This one time, I'm going to book you as Frankie Star and the Innocents. A club like Jimmy Principe's needs a headline name for the marquee."

I drove home with Matty, who didn't want to talk. I fantasized about all the things I should have or could have said to Danny Luegner, including asking him if he knew his beloved Frankie Star, the next Tom Jones, was dealing heavy dope.

The rumors kept getting worse. Frankie wasn't just spreading a little weed around or shaving off dimes of hash, he was wholesaling on the better-living-through-chemistry side. The heads' grapevine back home claimed that he was fronting for the Warlocks.

I still didn't understand why Frankie would do it. But I didn't understand much else, either.

One of my wishes was about to come true.

TWENTY-ONE

The week before our gig at the Fillmore East, we played a dance at Cardinal Brennan High. We had agreed to the booking months before, for sentimental reasons. The money was a joke, but five people in and around the band had ties to the place, and its hallways had been the scene of Angela's most visible teenage sins. We had played at the school before, as the Destroyerz, and it surprised me when the priests and nuns complained less about the volume and style of our music than did the faculty and chaperones at public highs. I suppose confession needed perking up.

The heat had come on just before we arrived at the gym. Joey and Pete had lugged our gear in through the slush and we all helped set up, as much to get warm as from comradeship. Despite the grim weather, we all felt buzzed, with Angela in her friendliest mood in weeks and Laura along to show that she believed in me. Joey's new girl cracked outrageous jokes and Pete's Dutchie steady, Beth, had grown close to Red in one of the oddest friendships in local history. It didn't worry Pete, so we shrugged our shoulders.

I tried to be fair to Laura. I knew that she was fighting to claim her life, to grow strong, like a mended bone. I even grasped that her endless talk of books was a means to control the pace of daily reality. She was proud and uncertain and fragile, although her python's grip returned at night.

Determined to please me, she wore the scarf I had given her at Christmas. It overpowered her simple sweater and jeans. Her eyes seemed wildly smart that night, penetrating and pure. As she sat tucked between the other girls for warmth, her beauty rallied to startle me again. Not every male in the gathering crowd would have envied me—teenagers, not gentlemen, prefer blondes—but a mythic hero, blundering in, would have seized her.

Yet I knew that I had had enough. She had worn me out. I was sick of being on guard and wanted a girl who remembered how to laugh. I longed for an easy love, and Laura was hard. I didn't want to be anybody's crutch. And, of course, I knew that the world's supply of women was endless.

As I tuned, my fingers were cold and my ears recalcitrant. As politely as I could, I brushed off the high school kids who wanted to talk and bought two hot chocolates from the just opened refreshment table. The warm paper cups were a comfort in my hands.

I walked over to the girls, extending one of the hot chocolates before I saw that Laura already had a drink. Steam rose from a cup in her joined fingers.

She looked up from the lowest bench on the bleachers and smiled. "Angela gave me some hot apple cider."

Skeletal even in her winter coat, Angela broke the tough-girl crook of her mouth to say, "It's better for you than hot chocolate, ain't?"

"I didn't see the cider."

"I brought a thermos," Angela told me. "But that's the last of it."

I shook my head. "You never seemed like an apple cider kind of girl to me."

"What's that supposed to mean?"

"Nothing. Take it easy." I glanced at the other female faces. "Anybody want a hot chocolate?"

"I'll take it," Beth said. "I wouldn't want it should go to waste none."

We kicked off the set with "Born to Be Wild" and mixed in plenty of covers with our originals. It was the kind of gig where you just have a good time, and it was amusing to watch the kids segregate themselves into a superficially scruffy minority who clustered by the stage and longed to be hip, the dancing couples who were going to catch colds in backseats later on, and the eternal guys hanging out at the back of the gym. Given the wretched weather, the turnout was surprising. The Innocents had become a serious draw.

A young priest posted himself with the kiddie-car hippies. He shook his head wildly, not quite keeping the beat.

The cord between my guitar and my amps began shorting out. Pete just walked up onto the stage and replaced it. Nothing was going to perturb us that night, not even when Frankie did the impossible and broke a bass string. We simply ended the first set one song early so he could put on a new one.

Followed most of the way by a kid who wanted to play me a couple of songs he'd written, I found Laura wearing a beatific expression.

"That was . . . brilliant," she told me. "I never realized . . ."

I laughed. "That's a switch. You should've heard us at the Electric Factory."

"Really profound . . . it's so intense . . ."

"You all right?"

She nodded. Slowly. "I feel a little strange, actually. Sort of dizzy. Not dizzy exactly, that's not what I mean . . ."

"Are you sick?"

"No." The poor light sculpted her features and lent her mystery. "I just . . . want to hear the music. I'm okay. I just feel a little strange—"

The priest who had been rocking out in front of the stage interrupted.

"May I speak with you? For a minute?"

"Sure, Padre. What's up?" I signaled Laura that I'd be right back and strolled off with our new fan.

"You didn't attend Cardinal Brennan. Did you?"

"No, Father. Pottsville High."

He pondered that, as if calculating my penance. "May I assume that you belong to a Protestant denomination?"

"Episcopalian."

"Isn't that wonderful? The way this music brings us all together? I believe the youth revolution can be a force for peace."

"Sure."

"I mean, isn't it possible that it will be music that finally joins us all? I don't mean only Christians."

"It's just music," I told him. "In the end." It was bizarre to find myself on the other side of the argument. "The peace-and-love stuff isn't always sincere."

He frowned. "Don't you think so? Don't you think there's a universal impulse toward peace? And that music—music like yours—might awaken it? Look at how excited you make these young people."

"It's only good while it lasts. They just go home afterwards."

Uninterested in what I had to say, he extended his arms, halfway to a benediction. "We have to be open to fresh ways of reaching people, to new paths to salvation, that's the thing. We have to think in terms of all humanity."

I didn't see our music leading anyone to salvation. It startled me to recognize that I had become a cynic about the thing I loved most in the world.

"I've taken St. Thomas as my personal field of study and contemplation," he confided. "The question of whether he carried Christ's message to India. I hope to go there. I think India may have something to teach *us*."

I wasn't convinced of that, either. The priest seemed as bright and shiny as a Christmas toy.

"That's cool."

"I just feel that music can offer us a glimpse of the divine, that it carries a message of universal love. Who's to say that St. Theresa's ecstasies have no relation to the experiences of today's youth?"

I heard a double twang from the makeshift stage: Matty tuning his guitar. It was time to play again.

"Listen, Father, it's been great talking to you. But I've got to go play now."

"Just one last question. What do you make of the Mothers of Invention? As social critics?"

I broke free and hurried over to check on Laura. In case she really wasn't feeling well.

She had left her seat. Angela took my measure with narrowed eyes. Onstage, Stosh tapped his sticks over the drum kit.

"She went to the can," Angela told me. "With Red."

"She isn't feeling well."

Angela lifted her shoulders and dropped them again. *So what?*

"She seemed okay to me," the bitch said.

In the middle of the third song of the set, I saw Laura reenter the gym. Red guided her, a mother helping a child take its first steps. I decided I'd take Laura home at the next break. The band could play the last set as a trio. The high school kids wouldn't miss me.

The crisis didn't wait. During Frankie's between-song patter, a commotion ignited over on the bleachers. A girl wailed. It was Laura.

I stepped beyond the stage lights so I could see. Laura flailed her arms at everyone near her. As if to drive away every living thing.

"Go on without me." I handed my guitar to Pete, who was checking a mike connection.

An older nun and the young priest beat me to Laura. The kids were interested, too. I shouldered them all aside.

Laura had stopped shrieking. Her fit diminished to a pantomime of a tipsy ballerina. She looked at me in surprise, as if my appearance made no sense at all.

I took her, gently, by the upper arms.

"Laura, it's all right." Although I had no idea what "it" was.

Her eyes explained things. The pupils were dilated hugely.

Three steps up the bleachers, Angela grinned.

"What did you give her?" I shouted. I didn't give a damn who heard me. Let them call the cops.

Laura began to cry and shiver.

Angela's grin declined to a knowing smile. She didn't answer me.

Red tromped up the bleachers and, without breaking the motion, slapped Angela so hard across the face that it turned her chin into her shoulder.

Angela's monstrous smile refused to die.

I tried to clutch Laura to me, to get her out of there. She resisted.

"Where's her coat? Where's her goddamned coat?"

The young priest edged up. "Does she need help? Sister Elizabeth's a nurse."

The poor sap was trying to be useful, but I turned on him. "It isn't all peace and love, Padre. Check it out."

Pete's girlfriend, Beth, held out Laura's coat. Red grabbed it before I could. We nudged and tugged it onto Laura, who sobbed and shook.

"Please help me," she said. "Somebody help me. I don't know what's happening." Her voice was as soft as a child's.

I whispered to Red, "Come with me. Please. I need somebody with her."

Laura had all the symptoms of an acid trip going bad. Given her past history, I feared that she might jump from the moving car.

Red was solid. She tossed a set of keys to Beth. "Drive my car. Follow us."

Onstage, the band played on.

With Red guiding Laura toward the back door, I climbed the bleachers to Angela.

"Please," I said, leaning down toward her. "Tell me what you gave her."

Angela raised her bone-hard face. Her smile had faded and her lower lip dripped blood. She didn't wipe it clean.

"I did it for you, Will," she told me. "I did it for you."

· · ·

The roads were grim. Going down the Frackville grade, the Corvair was little better than a sled. And I was nervous. Shaken.

In the small backseat, Red cuddled Laura against her, mother and child again. Laura whimpered. Once, she said, "It's cold," in a bewildered voice. As if the existence of cold were a revelation.

"There's been some really mean blue dot going around," Red told me. "It's cut with something. That could be what she gave her. That fucking apple cider. I wondered why she wouldn't give me any."

I didn't reply. I was trying to keep the car under control.

Red began to sing into Laura's hair, so softly that I couldn't tell if it was some mick lullaby or a pop song.

"I've got to tell you something," I said reluctantly. "Laura's had . . . she's had some problems none of you know about."

"Everybody knows," Red said. "Angela told us all about it months ago. We didn't want to let on."

"Christ."

"You did your best, Will. This shouldn't have happened."

"Why did we leave the dance?" Laura asked, as if she had awakened, utterly clear of mind.

But that was one illusion among many.

"It's all right, honey," Red told her, "it was time for us to go."

"The music was . . . so beautiful. I never understood how beautiful music could be."

"There's going to be more music. In just a little while."

As we entered St. Clair, a rush of sleet hit the windshield. At a red light, I skidded into the middle of the intersection. But it was all right. Except for Red's big old boat behind me, with Beth at the wheel, mine was the only car on the street.

"I really appreciate this," I told Red.

Her eyes flashed in the rearview mirror.

"I guess you know I'm in love with her," Red said. "I mean, there's no more point in pretending."

"I didn't know."

"She's just so fucking in love with you."

"Don't cry. Please. You'll bum her out."

"I'm *not* crying. I just keep thinking I could've saved her. I know it isn't true. But I keep thinking it. Did you really love her, Will?"

"Will loves me," Laura said, enunciating as if in a speech therapy class. "He'll do anything I say. Didn't you know that?"

The stairs up to my apartment were packed with slush on top of ice. Red and I helped Laura up, with Beth watching from the sidewalk. The sleet bit.

Inside, dripping, Red asked, "You want me to stay? To help you?"

I shook my head. "Thanks. I can handle it now. Shit, I don't know if I can handle it. I just think it might be better if I'm alone with her."

"Want some uppers? To stay awake?"

"I'll manage."

She helped me remove Laura's coat. The scarf I had given her at Christmas had gone missing.

"I know where we are," Laura said.

"You're home, honey," Red told her.

Laura waved her head back and forth like a child. "This isn't my home. I know where I am." She closed her eyes and seemed about to swoon. Or dance. We got her into the soft chair by the radiator.

Crying, Red looked down at her. "I'm going to kill that goddamned bitch."

"Angela's killing herself."

"I'm going to fucking help her."

I put my arm around Red. Then we hugged each other. Mom and Pop, with the kid in intensive care.

"I love you," Laura said. It was unclear for whom she meant the words.

Breaking free, Red rubbed her knuckles across her eyes. "You were so lucky. I wonder if you'll ever know how lucky? I'd do anything for her."

She bent down and kissed Laura on the forehead.

After Red had gone, Laura looked up at me with pupils the size of dark and distant moons.

"I don't like her," she said.

Depending on the quality of the acid and the amount Angela had given her, Laura was going to be skying for up to ten more hours. I needed to stay awake, in case she started bumming out again, so she wouldn't hurt herself. I intended to make a pot of coffee, but first I knelt in front of her.

Her features were in repose, her thoughts elsewhere.

"Laura?" I said softly. "Isn't everything beautiful? Everything's so beautiful, so quiet. And it's nice and warm. You don't want to touch the radiator. Don't touch it, okay? It gets too hot. But it's beautiful to sit right here and be warm. Isn't it?"

"I want to hear music."

"I'm going to put on your favorite album. You can sit here and be nice and warm and listen to it."

"Why don't you hold still?"

I was holding still.

"Sometimes, I see two of you."

"That's just your eyes playing tricks. There's only one of me. Here." I lifted her hand to my cheek. "Just one."

"You're cold."

"We just came in from outside. Remember?"

"Where's Red?"

"She had to go. Remember?"

"She's a lesbian. She's in love with me. Isn't that sad? A girl in the clinic was in love with me, too. Women think I'm beautiful."

"You *are* beautiful."

She withdrew her hand from my cheek. "Why are there two of you? Why does your face have so much hair?"

I got to my feet and turned away. You just never knew where people would go on acid. Some could seem lucid almost the entire time, just jokey or unusually sensual. Others drifted away or plunged into dark places. People argued over the extent of the hallucinations after the fact, but the effects simply varied between individuals. For me, acid had been a treat that let me live inside whatever music was playing, but I had been able to talk my way out of a traffic stop after swallowing two tabs of the Owl. Other people really did see demons—I never did—or decided to play with knives. During my interlude as Buzzy Ritter's chosen disciple, one girl with a mild case of acne had disappeared into the bathroom and picked her face apart. Others just giggled and dug the power of the universe.

If Laura was seeing hair sprout on my face, it didn't seem to be a very good sign. I worried about the devils that might be lurking inside her head and didn't want to become a devil myself.

With my back to Laura, I put her beloved Ravel string quartet on the turntable. With the volume down low.

"This is just for you," I said. "Close your eyes and listen."

She did as she was told. I slipped into the kitchen, quietly got the coffee together, and lit the stove. It hit me that one more reason to stay awake was to keep her away from the gas.

I began to cry. Sobbing and trying to be noiseless. Fists on the corners of the stove, I leaned over the coffeepot. It was nothing specific. It was everything.

I washed my face in the kitchen sink, then turned off the flame beneath the pot and scouted the refrigerator. Eating could turn some people around when their trips were going dark. The foil pan of Sara Lee brownies seemed a good bet, if it came to that. And I always had some Oreos in the cupboard, kept in an old Charles Chips tin to save them from the mice. There was plenty of milk.

As I poured my coffee, Laura started shrieking.

"Stop it! Make it stop! Please!"

It sounded as though someone had slipped in to attack her. I ran into the room, wondering what my landlady would think.

Laura slapped at her forearms, driving away swarms of invisible insects.

"What the matter?" I took hold of her wrists. "What's wrong?"

"It's pricking me. With needles. Make it stop."

"What is?" I was baffled. "What's hurting you?"

"The music. Please. Make it *stop*."

The string quartet's second movement featured pizzicato interludes. The plucked strings had become needles to her.

I lifted the tone arm and turned off the stereo.

"All right? Is that better?"

"Tell me who you are. I need to be sure."

"It's me. Will. It's only Will."

"I know that. But you don't look like yourself. Not always. I mean . . . sometimes you do." She looked at me with fearful earnestness. "Am I going crazy?"

"No. Everything's fine. You're going to be just fine. You accidentally took some drugs. Things are just going to seem a little funny for a while."

"I want things to stop moving. Please stop moving. *Please*."

I wasn't moving. The room was still. "All right. I stopped. I made it stop. Is it okay now?"

She nodded. As a contented child might. After an interval of silence and closed eyes, she told me, "I have to go to the bathroom."

"All right."

She hesitated. "I don't remember where it is. I should know that."

I took her hand, pressed it gently, and helped her up from the chair.

"I'll show you where it is. It's just down the hall."

"It's dark."

"I'll turn on the light. See?"

"I don't want to go there."

"All right. But that's where the bathroom is."

"This is where we sleep together. Isn't it? In there? It looks so strange . . . like a little box. You really are Will, aren't you?"

"Who else would I be?"

"You don't seem like Will. Not all the time. Will's so nice to me. You're nice, too. I need to go to the bathroom now."

"It's right here."

She nodded, then crossed the threshold into the light-on-tile glare. I remembered what Angela had told me, lifetimes before, about Laura locking herself in the bathroom and swallowing everything in the medicine cabinet. And my razor blades were in there, the scissors.

"There are so many colors. I've never seen such colors."

"We have to leave the door open," I told her. "It's a new rule."

"Don't watch me."

I had no intention of watching her. I didn't even want to hear anything. Despite the vegetarian-underground notion that all bodily functions were natural and, therefore, beautiful, I remained a squeamish son of the middle class.

I headed toward the kitchen to gulp down my cold-by-now coffee. Then I stopped dead. Imagining she might slam the door and lock it.

I stationed myself in the hallway, just out of her sight.

She didn't attempt to shut the door. After a succession of normal sounds, the toilet flushed. She turned on the taps at the sink and turned them off again. But she didn't come out.

"Laura? Are you all right?"

She didn't answer.

I waited another minute, then went in.

She was on her knees, fondling the paisley print on the shower curtain.

"This is so incredible," she said. "How brilliant the person must have been, the one who thought of this. I never understood before. To make something like this, he must've been a genius. It's so . . . so intricate."

"The Persians created the design," I told her. I took her fingers and traced them over a teardrop shape. "That's called a *boteh*. It's a symbol of fertility. Like a seed."

She turned to me and opened her mouth to speak. But time stopped. She stared at me, lips parted. After a small infinity, she looked away.

"You know so much."

"I only know that because my father liked Persian rugs. He was a strange man. But a good one."

"*My* father's dead. I never tell anybody. It's a secret. He died when I was a little girl."

"Know what? I'm hungry. Are you hungry?"

"You think I'm dirty."

"No, I don't. For God's sake."

"You *do*. You told me."

I remembered. "That was stupid. I didn't mean it. We all say stupid things."

"I thought you loved me. You are Will, aren't you?"

"I'm Will. And I love you."

"You look like someone else. Your face keeps changing."

"Who? Who do I look like?"

"I don't know." She said it too quickly. She did know. But wouldn't say.

"Let's have something good to eat. Okay?"

She took my hand and placed it on her breast.

Sex could go either way on acid, as I knew from personal experience. But Laura made her desire explicit and I figured that putting her off would register as rejection, that she might obsess about the remark she'd remembered. That could have gotten bad. And the truth was I didn't want to put her off.

I tried to be gentle and reassuring, but Laura wanted more. She got the acid sweats and gave off that chemical smell the drug brought out in some people. But her intensity kept her alluring. She cried out wildly, madly, and scratched me for the first time. She didn't want to stop, and we didn't.

We had come to the end of words. Laura had gone deep into a private realm of sensation. I was a prop.

When she seemed worn out at last, I forced myself to stay awake and massage her. It only made her want more sex. Any observer would have judged that I was taking advantage of her. But she was using me.

"Oh, my God, my God, my *God*," she cried. Then she fled back into the other world.

Settling by her side, I petted her. Wondering where her soul, freed of sense, had traveled.

"So beautiful," she said. "It was so beautiful."

"Yes."

She chuckled and told me, "What he doesn't know won't hurt him."

I woke in panic. Gray light had already come to inspect our wreckage. The room reeked of our night, but Laura was gone.

Propelled by dread, I jumped from the mattress. The first thing I registered in full consciousness was that the bathroom door was shut.

I tried the handle. The lock had been turned.

I thumped on the door. Madly. Calling her name.

The bolt turned. Meekly, Laura opened the door. Her expression was pure and untroubled. Perhaps she had reached a clear-light phase. Or maybe the trip was behind her and she was just drained.

But if her facial features had nothing to say, her eyes were seas of sorrow when I met them.

"You know. Don't you?" she asked me.

She seemed all right. I thought she was. Then, two days later, on a barren February afternoon, Laura Saunders put on her winter boots and walked out the side door of her dormitory. She made it all the way to the convenience store down on the highway. Except for her boots, she was naked.

TWENTY-TWO

Angela disappeared. After the dance at Cardinal Brennan, she didn't even go home to pack a suitcase. She just took off.

I didn't think she feared the law or that she was the least bit suicidal—not in the usual way. She might have been ashamed, but I couldn't believe it. Her world had ceased to make sense in terms I could grasp. She was a mean druggie, that much was certain. Yet she was still Angela, the woman I once had desired. Furious over what she had done, I nonetheless recalled the times when we'd almost connected, two outsiders who sensed what the others didn't. From a distance, I romanticized her decline. In the spirit of the times, I saw tragedy where there was only self-indulgence.

Her attention flattered me up to the end. I was still too inexperienced to know that women in search of sympathy look to women. When they turn to men for pity, they're out for revenge.

As for Laura, I feigned compassion but felt embarrassment. And, perhaps, hatred. She had drained me. Pity would come, even empathy, in time. But first I had to know that I was safe.

No one apologized for Angela's deed, nor did anyone ask about Laura. Not even Red. Once again, Angela had made herself the center of all attention. The closest thing I got to an acknowledgment that anything had gone down was some ribbing from Stosh about how good the band sounded as a trio.

When I first learned that Angela was gone, I thought of her old girlfriend Joyce, living with the biker down in Philly. But I chose to let the rest of them figure it out, if that was the answer.

Much had changed in ways I found confusing. Not six months back, Frankie had stood outside my door in the rain, panicked by Angela's absence of a few hours. Now he didn't seem to care at all. It was Matty who was distraught.

Of course, Matty didn't say anything. But it was clear that something had gone awry. His stoic's mask cracked at odd moments and he gave in to surges of ire. At our Monday night rehearsal, a day before Laura's final exit and two days before our gig at the Fillmore East, he tore into me because my high E string was slightly flat.

"Don't you have *ears*?" he demanded. The attack had come out of the blue. "If you can't tune your guitar, I'll tune it for you."

Frankie, on the other hand, came around. Matty appeared to be right that Frankie wouldn't be content with promises, that he'd go where success beckoned. Matty's outburst aside, we all were pumped and positive about the Fillmore appearance. Everyone knew that this was the chance of all chances. Frankie talked about the gig incessantly, as if Angela had been erased from his life and thoughts. He reworked the song list for our set obsessively. And his faith in Danny Luegner seemed to be fading. Luegner had stalled about giving back our demo—I didn't believe for an instant that he had a contact at Capitol—and Frankie was, indeed, going to Philly himself to pick up the tape and carry it up to the Fillmore on the train.

Neither Angela's shenanigans nor Laura's fate detracted from our playing. At our last rehearsal, on Tuesday night, we played as if nothing but music mattered on earth and in the heavens. Perhaps we had learned, collectively, to channel our emotions into solos, chords, harmonics, and a backbeat. Maybe a psychologist could explain it. But with everything else in our lives going all to shit, we played like bareknuckled angels.

I had gotten a call from a girl down at the dorm just before I left for that final practice session. She told me what Laura had done and offered to come over to my apartment, in case I needed solace or more details. Instead of being shocked at the report, I thought of what a great song it would make.

The Big Apple was rotten, and the East Village was a wormhole. Only Joey and I had ever been to Manhattan. Before breaking with my mother over an heirloom, an aunt had taken me to a few Broadway shows. Joey and I had gone to a concert together, and back in my druggie period, I spent a week looking for peace and love, bunking in a filthy top-floor apartment with a pal of Buzzy Ritter's. In the crash pad down the hall, the litter of corpses came back to life as noon approached, and I learned to detect the sickly-sweet odor of teenage runaways dripping with the clap. One pretty girl with white-blond hair had become a sex leper after infecting dozens, but she was allowed to live in a corner of the crash pad, since she was gifted at panhandling uptown. Out on the street in the early-morning hours, I saw a boy cut down his neck with a switchblade. It sounded like ripping fabric. Buzzy's friend was trying to get it together to start a commune in Arizona, but mostly he just shoplifted food and got wasted on charitable contributions of dope. Flower power and selfless communal living existed only in set-up photographs, lying songs, and hysterical magazine articles. Maybe there really had been a Summer of Love in San Francisco, but Manhattan was all Fuck You.

Joey hired Doug Detweiler, a thug-turned-head from Auburn, to guard the van while he and Pete unloaded our equipment. But Joey was smart enough to leave his revolver at home. He really did possess a survivor's instincts.

Matty, Stosh, and I rode to the gig in Matty's Buick, figuring that it wouldn't attract many thieves. The highway was crunchy with salt and flanked with black snow. When we stopped for coffee just inside New Jersey, we took a booth that let us keep an eye on the car with our guitars and Frankie's bass inside. We really were provincials, although I had my slight advantage—enough to have warned Frankie not to try taking the subway from Penn Station, but to spring for a cab to the gig.

The clouds ran high enough to reveal the Manhattan skyline. It was the first time either Stosh or Matty had seen it. They tensed.

The city was scruffy, dense, and intimidating. Even I felt on guard as we emerged from the tunnel. Philly was kid stuff. New York was the major leagues.

"I don't know how anybody could live here," Matty said, as much to himself as to Stosh and me. I recalled Laura saying the same thing about Schuylkill County.

We were hours early but ate up part of the time figuring out where to park. Walking to the Fillmore, a raggedy-ass theater that should have been condemned, we had to run a gauntlet of panhandlers. The most creative one eyed our guitar cases and said, "Hey, I got all your albums, every one, man . . . help out a fellow musician with some spare change?"

Stosh asked him, "Which album's your favorite?"

"Aw, fuck, man. I like them all, you know?"

When we failed to give him a handout, he called after us, "You suck, you know that? You always sucked . . . your records stink . . ."

An apprentice earth mother with snot flowing over her lips tried to sell us an underground newspaper. When we declined, she offered to sell us some smack. We were relieved to spot Joey's van by the marquee.

"Downer scene," Doug the Thug told us. With his beard and old motorcycle jacket, he looked wonderfully unpleasant. "Half a dozen fuckers tried to steal shit."

"Joey inside?"

"Yeah, him and Pete. We had to wait for somebody to show up, some smart-ass Jew fuck. Hey, tell them I need to take a piss and get some coffee, okay?"

"Frankie isn't here yet, is he?" I asked.

Doug shook his head.

Backstage, it looked as if Bill Graham had economized on the cleaning budget. Old pipes dripped. The graffiti was not restricted to music theory.

Joey and Pete were glad to see us. We were reinforcements in a war of the worlds. Except for the drive, it wasn't a tough gig for them. The Fillmore East had its own sound system and we needed only our amplifiers and a few special mikes. But even Joey seemed to feel under siege, although we were practically alone in the building.

"The guy said for you to do a sound check as soon as you get here. He said it's going to get busy later."

The barely lit stage seemed huge, the hall vast. As we tuned, the sound boomed. Two ghostly figures moved at the back of the auditorium. A disembodied voice said, "Move the mike stand, not the monitor."

Matty shifted to Frankie's bass to work out the balance.

The voice came back. "You a trio?"

"No," I told my microphone. "Quartet. Two guitars, bass, and drums. Our bass player's not here yet."

"Milt Ehrlich's band, right?"

"The Innocents."

"Right. Give me a level check on number four, the one to your right."

Matty switched back to his Stratocaster and riffed a little. We started a jam, warming up, getting some life back into our fingers. The music sounded hollow without Frankie's bass punching against the drums.

"Okay, I've got you," the ghost voice said. "Wrap it up."

As we left the stage, I carried my Rickenbacker and the Les Paul, while Matty lugged his Strat and the Fender bass.

"Where the hell's Frankie?" I said.

"It's still early," Matty reassured me.

The warren of corridors, dressing rooms, and utility closets had begun to crawl with the children of the night. It wasn't a glamorous set. The other musicians arrived with rough New York skin and tough New York attitudes. The clusters of girls and women who seemed to be groupies didn't match my fantasies. To say the least. The best of them looked like Janis Joplin the morning after a nuclear blast at the brothel.

A wan, fey dude made an unmistakable pass at Stosh, who had put on a white satin shirt, cowboy cut, with mother-of-pearl buttons and fringes down the sleeves. Stosh looked horrified. Whatever attracted him, it wasn't standard downtown drags and fags.

I phoned Penn Station to make sure there were no train delays from Philly.

We still had time. Plenty, really. I hoped Danny Luegner hadn't given Frankie a song and dance about the demo tape.

A half hour before showtime, with the backstage scene growing fetid—and my heartbeat picking up—Milt Ehrlich popped in. Just as Joey caught a kid trying to take off with my Les Paul. The punk, who was physically on the verge of nonexistence, threatened Joey. Joey turned the kid so no one could see, then knuckle-punched him in the kidneys.

Milt shrugged it off. He was smiling, happy. "Hey, Will! There you are. You boys ready? Got the tape?"

"Frankie's bringing it up from Philly on the train. He's the bass player."

Milt looked at his watch. "He isn't here yet? He's cutting it close."

"He'll be here. He wouldn't blow this."

Milt's smile quit. "I hope so. I've got Mac Steinman coming down. Along with half the New York office. Don't let me down, huh?"

"We won't let you down."

He considered the situation, fussing with his mustache. "Yeah. Just don't. Okay?" He turned briefly to Matty and Stosh, who had sidled up. "Knock 'em dead, boys."

He didn't wait for me to make introductions.

I wondered if Frankie had been caught in traffic. The early-evening traffic was notorious.

The clock refused to hold still.

Pete went out to the van to give Doug a last break. He wanted to be back inside in time to catch our whole set.

Ten minutes out, Matty pulled Stosh and me together. Joey joined the huddle. I was beginning to feel sick.

"We need a plan, in case Frankie doesn't make it. We'll still open with 'Angeline.' Will, you'll have to play bass. Stosh, you know the lyrics?"

"Enough of them. I can fake it."

"I'm not a good bass player," I reminded him. "My fingers are too small."

"Stick to the basic riff. Just hit on the beat. Same thing on 'Glass Slipper.' Just keep it simple. Can you sing that one yourself?"

"Sure. But I've never done it playing bass."

"We'll switch instruments after that. I'll play bass on 'Hideaway.' You can take over on lead guitar. Stosh? You got the vocal?"

"Yeah. But my harmony part won't be there, just yours."

"That's all right." He turned to Joey. "If Frankie shows up, just get him onstage as fast as you can."

"He's not going to show," Stosh said. "The fucker's not going to show."

Matty ignored him and went back to laying out the way we'd handle the set.

The stage manager gave us an extra ten minutes. He said that no-body started on time, anyway.

When our brief reprieve was up, there was still no Frankie.

As we walked out onstage, I felt that hot, pre-tears sensation in my eyes. This was supposed to be a triumph, not a half-assed, patched-together job. It was supposed to be the greatest night of my life.

Nobody knew us, but there was a smattering of applause. Sheer habit.

The big electronic grunt as I plugged in the bass made me flinch. I stretched my fingers over the long neck, ghosting the riff that under-pinned "Angeline."

Stosh counted us off. Matty's guitar screamed in. And we were off.

But we were limping. Matty played wonderfully. Maybe he was desperate, maybe he was as sick at heart as I was. Perhaps he cared far more about becoming a big success than I realized. Stosh played off Matty's guitar instead of my bass runs. All I could do was to repeat the basic riff and hit the root notes of the chords on the chorus. The harmonies, those choirboys-with-switchblades thrilling harmonies, were missing.

It got worse when we swapped instruments. Matty could play the bass as well as Frankie, maybe better, and our rhythm section came alive. But I couldn't front a band at the Fillmore East level. I wasn't bad. I just wasn't anything much. I didn't have the voice to carry a big song, either. I could shout a blues in a bar, but I wasn't Frankie.

We did two songs without any bass, extending the middle guitar jams. Matty got the audience going with a couple of his electric-apocalypse improvisations. Stosh played a knockout drum solo. But we weren't a *band*.

There were no boos. The off-night audience didn't expect wonders. But the level of applause at the end of our set made it clear that no one was heartbroken to move on to the next act.

Backstage, Matty got several compliments on his guitar work. No one said a word to me. Until Milt Ehrlich showed up.

He didn't give me any time to speak. He just said, "You fucked me. You punk. Forget you know my number. Forget you ever heard my fucking name, because I'm going to forget yours."

He shoved his way back through the crowd.

We caravanned out of the city, but Matty drove fast and we left the equipment van behind somewhere in Jersey. We didn't say much between us. There wasn't much to say.

At Phillipsburg, Matty pulled up in front of a diner. There had been no vote on stopping.

Stosh and I ordered coffee. Matty asked for a chocolate shake and two cheeseburgers. The waitress, who was young, wanted to flirt. No one was interested.

"That worthless sonofabitch," Stosh said at last.

The waitress delivered the coffee. "Shake's coming right up," she told Matty.

Matty raised his eyes from the table. He looked past me. Toward the front door, as if Frankie might walk in. "It's my fault," he said. "I should've understood."

"What's to understand?" I asked.

Matty ignored me. He took a cigarette from the pack Stosh had dropped on the tabletop. I was stunned to see his hands unsteady as he lit it.

"Nam confused me," he told the drifting smoke. "It just mixed me up. You could count on people over there. When it really mattered. Even people who hated you didn't let you down. It made everything too easy. It spoiled me."

"So the Army spoiled you?" Stosh asked. "I like that. I should've fucking joined myself."

"It did, though. I can't explain it. I guess you had to see it for yourself. You only had to worry about a limited number of things. And that was it. You knew where people stood. The people who wanted to hurt you didn't keep it a secret. It was the only time in my life when things were easy."

The waitress delivered Matty's shake. The diner wasn't busy, just a couple of all-night truckers and one stray couple. A plate of burgers appeared on an aluminum shelf. A hand reached out from the kitchen and tapped a bell.

"Maybe you should've stayed in the Army," Stosh said. "If it was so easy." No one was in a good mood.

"No," Matty said, taking the proposition seriously. "Easy's not the point."

"Well, then, you should've become a priest. Like your old lady wanted."

"I thought about it."

Before or after Angela? I wanted to ask him. I didn't, though. I realized that I had grown afraid of him.

Joey, Pete, and Doug came in. Joey's survivor's eyes must have spotted the Buick. Or maybe it was a coincidence. There weren't a lot of diners open that late.

They stank of pot. I wished I had ridden with them.

Stosh spilled coffee on his satin shirt.

"That ain't going to come out," Doug said helpfully. The three of them took the booth next to ours.

"It wasn't that bad," Joey said. "A couple of people told me they liked it."

"Just shut up," I said. It was all right. Joey and I understood each other. Months back, Frankie had been right about that.

Halfway through his second cheeseburger, Matty said, "I expected too much."

The cold was harsh and I was anxious to get back in the car and get the heater cranking. But Matty turned toward the phone booth beneath the neon sign.

"We need to call Frankie," he said.

"Why?"

"It finishes things. You have to finish things. He's expecting us to call."

"Then to hell with him."

"No. It's important to finish things. He wants us to know what he did. He wants to know that we know it."

"We don't owe Frankie anything."

"I do. We do."

"Matty, for cripe's sake, you're talking nuts," Stosh said.

Matty shrugged and headed for the phone booth.

He never raised his voice, at least not to a level Stosh and I could hear. His face remained impassive, although we saw his lips moving and caught murmurs between passing trucks. I had expected a brief, bitter exchange, but Matty kept dropping in quarters.

Stosh and I stood shivering, glancing at each other now and then. At the sorry end of things.

Matty opened the phone booth's door. Without hanging up.

"Frankie wants to talk to you," he told me.

If any part of me expected an apology, that wasn't what was coming.

"Frankie, what the fuck?" I demanded.

After a satisfied pause, Frankie said, "I told you not to screw Angela."

TWENTY-THREE

Laura began to haunt me. I didn't expect that. Apart from a bit of posing, my initial sentiment had been good riddance.

I put off calling Joan. Rushing to her just seemed shabby. Instead, I spent weeks tearing through a succession of women who had followed the band, or who shared a class with me, or who had just brushed against me while I was otherwise occupied. I was cruel and unfair. It excited them.

My rooms still reeked of Laura. No matter who else stained the sheets and towels. I felt no love toward her. Or nothing I recognized as love. I felt an obligation. And I hated it.

Whatever I missed, I could not put a name to it. But, somehow, no one matched her. Maybe there had been magic in her secrets. Those ready girls who pushed down their jeans before pulling off their tops represented a different, lesser species. Their flesh failed to hold me.

On a trick day at the end of March of the sort whose warmth betrays you, I drove to Doylestown. Employing one of Angela's techniques, I checked the high school yearbooks at the library. Finding a picture of Laura's mother amid the faculty galleries was easy. A sensible man would have left it at that. But I hunted through earlier yearbooks and found Laura's senior picture. I traced her back through time, searching amid the candid photos and shots of the French Club and Honor Society. It startled me to find her smiling so often.

I drove to the high school where Mrs. Saunders taught, spied out the lot that held the faculty's cars, and waited. Amid a squall of teenagers homeward bound, a few girls giggled their interest. Their boyfriends regarded me as a lurking thief.

By the time Mrs. Saunders appeared, clutching folders against the wind, the world had emptied. When she turned in the wrong direction, I pursued her.

Catching up, I called, "Excuse me . . . Mrs. Saunders?"

She turned as if to face a pesky student. A quizzical expression followed. Then she darkened. All in a matter of seconds.

"I know who you are," she said.

"Please. How's Laura?"

"How dare you? How *dare* you?"

"Please, I just need to know how she is."

"If you don't leave here this minute, I'll call the police."

"Just tell me how she is. Is she all right?"

One tear left each of her eyes. The wind drove them at a diagonal. No one had ever looked at me with such hatred.

"As if you cared about her. You give a poor, sick girl drugs and pretend you care about the consequences. You belong in prison."

"I never gave her drugs. I never—"

She laughed horribly. "Am I supposed to believe *you?* And not my own daughter?" Laura's mother took one step toward me. As if on the verge of attacking. "She told me that you gave her LSD. I was a fool not to go straight to the police, a fool to promise."

"I never gave Laura any kind of drugs," I repeated. The words sounded dead. Beyond that, I could not speak.

"*Liar.*" She swept back a wind-loosened strand of hair and her tears came faster. "You'll *never* see my little girl again. Never in your life. If you ever come near her, if you ever try to find her, I'll see that you're arrested."

My folly was immeasurable. Had Laura been there, I would have slapped her for lying. It was years before I understood that she lied to save me from idiotic gallantries.

With my own eyes brimming and burning, I turned away.

Footsteps echoed mine. Then Laura's mother stopped and told my back, "Don't think you're going to have any claim on my Laura. There won't be any child, that's all been seen to."

Wind gusts slapped me as I walked to my car.

The route home passed near Quakertown. I did what any coward would have done. I stopped and called Joan.

She was already back from work. I asked if I could take her out to dinner.

The pause before she replied answered my question. But I let her say the words.

"Will . . . I can't. I'm seeing someone, it wouldn't be fair. I couldn't keep waiting and hoping anymore."

The band came apart, of course. Under Danny Luegner's spell, Frankie left for Philly. Matty, Stosh, and I honored the remainder of our contracts, with a bass player from Orwigsburg filling in. The kid hoped that the band would go on and take him along. But the Innocents were done. Just as the magic hadn't been there before Matty came home from Nam, it wasn't there without Frankie, either. Together, we had been far more than any of us could be in a different lineup. The chemistry of a great band is unique. But the compound proved unstable.

A few weeks after the Fillmore East debacle, Stosh told us that he was signing on with Luegner, who was putting together a show band to feature Frankie, complete with two girl backup singers. Stosh had been invited to be the drummer.

I felt betrayed and angry, but it didn't last. Unlike Frankie, Stosh had come out with it man to man. And I couldn't blame him for wanting to flee the county.

Frankie had dental surgery to improve his smile. Danny Luegner had fronted him the money to have it done before the show band's rehearsals started. I could only imagine how Frankie would be enmeshed.

I could not wish him well. I wanted Frankie to fail and hurt and suffer.

Stosh told us that Luegner had already booked them into clubs all across the country. After working out the act's kinks in Ft. Lauderdale, Dallas, and Scottsdale, Frankie Star and the Stargazers were headed to Reno and, ultimately, Vegas. Stosh said that Luegner chose the name because of all the moon-landing stuff that was supposed to happen that summer.

I tried to talk Matty into starting another band with me, something fresh. There was other talent around. It was worth a shot.

"I need a break," he told me. "I'm just going to do fill-ins for a while."

He took an accounting job at the Alcoa plant in Cressona. After the band's last gig, he disappeared every weekend. He was searching for Angela. He never told anyone, of course. But I knew.

I didn't want to approach Matty directly on that subject. I called Stosh and caught him at home.

"How are rehearsals? Everything cool?"

I could see his familiar shrug at the other end of the line. "Yeah. It's all right. It's a gig."

"You haven't run into Angela, have you? Down in Philly?"

"No. And you don't need nothing to do with Angela."

"I know that. I was thinking of Matty. Do you know if he's ever tracked down Joyce and that Warlock boyfriend of hers? I thought she might be with Joyce."

"She's not. I seen Joyce. She doesn't know a thing."

"So how's Red?"

"She's all right. Looking forward to getting away."

"She's going with you, then?"

"Yeah, she decided to risk it. We'll see what happens. Once we get out there. In Vegas and all."

"Well, good luck. Tell Frankie I hope he gets cancer of the throat. And the balls."

"Hey, I'll tell you something, but don't tell nobody, okay?"

"What?"

"Frankie got false front teeth now. Or whatever they call them. He looks like he should be doing toothpaste commercials."

"Maybe he will be. Take care of yourself, huh?"

"Yeah, you, too. Hey, I didn't ask. You got anything going yourself?"

"Nope."

"Something'll turn up, man."

"Say hello to Red for me."

"Yo, that reminds me. You ever hear anything about that Laura girl, the one who went batshit? Red brings her up sometimes. Fuck knows why."

"Tell Red that she knows as much as I do. Enjoy Vegas."

I tried to put my own band together. But my heart wasn't in it. Plenty of musicians wanted to get something going, but the best players I could assemble were back at the Destroyerz level. I marched through a series of rehearsals, fighting the realization that I just could not go through it all again.

I called Matty and begged him to reconsider. He was the only one left who had the magic, who might have made the months and years of playing dives and hoping for a break worthwhile again. The only place I could reach him was down at the Alcoa office. He told me that he didn't have time to talk.

I heard that he was rarely at home, that he kept a clean shirt in his car so he could return from one of his forays just before work began. But if he was obsessive, it paid off. He found Angela.

I never learned where she had been. I didn't see her myself. All I heard was that Matty had found her, that she looked like the wreck of the Hesperus, and that they were living in a rented half a double in Girardville.

I didn't dare stop by.

My mother put her house up for sale. We saw each other when she passed through Pottsville to sign some papers and decide which possessions she wanted to take along into her new life.

"I'm sorry your band didn't work out," she told me. Over a lousy club sandwich at the Necho Allen. "Have you considered applying to a better university?"

"Penn State's fine."

"It's not for serious people, Will. You know that." She still had a demure tan and looked years younger.

"How's Florida?"

"Oh, I'm not wild about it, really. But I like the place in Connecticut. I'm sure you'll see it sometime. Are you going to miss the house?"

"No."

She touched her lower lip, lightly, with her napkin. Her manners never failed her. "I'm glad to hear it. I was concerned."

"What are you going to do with the Chrysler?"

"I hadn't thought about it. Do you want it?"

"No. Thanks."

"I've told Barry Levenger you can have anything you want that belonged to your father. Anything at all."

"He was supposed to fix my license revocation."

"He probably couldn't."

"He didn't think it was important."

"Listen, Will . . . don't hold anything against him. Please. Anything from the past, I mean. He's not the worst of them. He looked out for me. And for you. Anyway, take your time. Pick out anything you want. I don't expect a house like that is going to sell the instant it goes on the market."

"Thank you. I appreciate it."

She opened her purse and clicked it shut again. After trying on a pair of expressions that didn't work, she just said, "I don't know if I should ask this or not . . . but do you still see that girl? Laura?"

"No. She's history."

A motherly smile came and went. "Well, I think that's for the best. You know I felt something wasn't quite, I don't know, not quite normal about her."

"You were right. She wasn't normal."

"Well, I'm glad you're over her. You don't see that blond woman anymore, do you? The one who was in the house?"

"No. You were right about her, too."

"Mothers have an instinct. Oh, you made me forget. What I meant to tell you about Barry Levenger. I've given him instructions. When the house is sold, you're to have ten thousand dollars. You really should have something from it."

"Thank you."

"I wish you'd put it toward your education. A better school, I mean. But that's up to you. Roger and I would help you, you know. If, for instance, you decided to go to law school."

I laughed. "I won't be going to law school."

She counted out the bills to pay the check, then calculated how many coins to strew atop them. It was always 15 percent, even in the bad years.

"Mom? I hope you'll be happy. I want you to be happy. I love you, you know. And not just because of the ten thousand bucks."

She put on her "Confucius say" face, a countenance I remembered from the good times.

"Yes, I know," she said. "It's all just so hard sometimes. Isn't it? Should I drop you at that apartment of yours?"

Danny Luegner had the gall to phone and ask if I wanted to write songs for the rock bands he managed.

Matty showed up on a sodden midspring day. He was reluctant to leave the mat just inside my door, shy of making a mess.

Words still came hard for him. He glanced around, as if he had never been in my apartment before. Then he asked, "Putting a new band together?"

I had just about given up on the idea. When I found myself back onstage at the Legion Post where the Destroyerz had struck the first chord on so many Saturday midnights, it seemed too pathetic.

"You interested? Matty, we could put a band together the minute you wanted to."

"No. I didn't mean that. I was just asking."

"Sit down, for Christ's sake."

"I'm all wet."

"You ought to carry an umbrella. Now that you've gone corporate. Take off your jacket, man."

He wore a short-sleeved shirt with a narrow tie. A plastic pocket protector held a squad of pens. His hair was still longish but trimmed up to his chin.

"Want some coffee?" I asked.

"Have any milk?"

"Brokhoff's white, or Guers chocolate?"

"Chocolate, if that's okay."

I went into the kitchenette. "Matty, you need to be playing. This is crazy. You might be the best guitarist I've ever heard."

"I'm going to play," he said quickly. "I'm just taking some time off." He accepted the glass, drank half of the contents, then wiped his mouth and chin with the back of his hand. "That's sort of what I wanted to talk to you about."

"You've lost me."

"Maybe you haven't heard? Angela's back. I'm taking care of her. She's been sick."

"Is she all right?"

"She's getting better. It takes time. She was in a hospital. For malnutrition. And other things."

"Is she off the speed?"

He nodded. "She's all done with that, she's clean. She's getting better. It's just that her system's messed up. It takes time."

"Is there something I can do to help?"

"That's what I wanted to ask you." He finished the chocolate milk, as if bolstering himself with a shot of whiskey. "She doesn't see people. I mean from the old crowd. Or anybody, really. She doesn't want to see them. She's embarrassed." He struggled, wary of jinxing life with speech. "Angela doesn't look the same. I mean, she will. But it's a slow process."

"So what do you want me to do?"

"She doesn't want to see people. Not right now. Not yet. But she'd like to see you. I thought . . . maybe you could visit her sometime? During the day, while I'm at work? It's hard for her, I think. She gets bored. The TV's not enough."

I didn't want to see Angela.

"Sure," I said. "But you're up in Girardville, right?"

He nodded again. "At the far end of town."

"The problem is they pulled my driver's license. For six months."

"For what?"

"Speeding. Ninety-five or something like that."

"You never drive fast."

"It's a long story."

"Will? Could you visit her tomorrow afternoon? I know she'd like to see you. She said so. She always thought the world of you. She still does."

"Matty, I just told you. I have no way to get there. The East Penn buses don't run up that way."

"If I picked you up? Right at lunchtime? If I leave the Alcoa at noon, I could swing by and drive you up and drop you off. I could be back in the office by one."

"That's precision swimming, man." The prospect of being trapped in Girardville, a rat-hole mining patch, with Angela for an entire afternoon filled me with dread.

"Will you do it, though? For Angela?"

I shrugged. "I've got an afternoon class. But I can cut it. Sure. If she'd really like to see me."

"I'll beep the horn. I should be here around ten after or so."

"I'll wait outside."

"You don't have to do that. It's supposed to rain again."

"I won't rust."

He rose, a huge figure in the compact room, and drew on his wet jacket.

"I'm grateful," he said. "And I'm sorry about everything else."

I waved it away. Bygones. "Hey, have you heard any rumors about Frankie getting busted? I heard he got popped with some serious dope. Chemicals."

"I didn't hear that," Matty told me. "I don't hear from Frankie."

"If it's true, though, there goes his Tom Jones act. He'll do time."

"Frankie'll manage. His old man will get him a lawyer."

"Yeah," I said. "Frankie always manages."

Matty paused to construct his next announcement. The pain of the effort showed around his mouth.

"Angela's getting a divorce. We're getting married. When she's better."

"Congratulations."

"It won't be a church wedding. It can't be. We're going to go away."

"That's great. I mean, you getting married."

"Yes. I guess it is." He was blushing.

"Matty?"

He turned from the door.

"I'll do anything I can to help. But I want you to promise me something. That you're going to play music again. I don't mean with me. Just play."

He smiled. "I'll always play music. I play now. For Angela. She likes it when I play for her." He looked at his cuff, as if he could read his watch through the fabric. "I better go. Dinner and all."

"Give Angela my best. See you tomorrow."

He hesitated for one last moment. "There's some other stuff we need to talk about. But that can wait."

TWENTY-FOUR

Matty just dropped me off. They were living in one of the smaller company houses, little more than a shanty. It still had tar-paper siding, and the front porch railing lacked a couple of spindles. My mother would not have set foot inside the door.

Matty's warnings had prepared me to find a plague victim. But Angela still looked like herself, if frail and marred and chastened. When she let me in, she moved to hug me, then stopped. But she lost control of her smile. She was missing a tooth.

The house smelled of frying.

"I made up some pierogies," she said. "When Matty told me you were coming over. You always liked Hunky food, ain't?" She smiled but managed to keep her lips close together. "Our cooking and our girls, if I remember anything."

"They seemed to go together."

She looked me over. "If I was still at the salon, I'd take you in and give you a trim."

"Maybe you'll have your own salon."

"Not on your life. You're never going to catch *me* stuck in with a pack of bitches like that again. Come on in the kitchen, eat something and get warm. You been out in the rain."

I had been. Waiting for Matty to pick me up. I followed her. The kitchen was cleaner than I expected of Angela, as if it had just been scrubbed down.

Her looks were gone, but they had been going for months. What startled me was the caution of her movements, the bent shoulders and the old-lady timidity of her hands. Before things went wrong, she had always been lively and quick, the sort of girl who, born into other circumstances, would have played lots of tennis. Now she looked as if she could use a cane.

"I fried them, since I didn't have no sour cream." She turned from the stove, summoning the ghost of her old Angela smile. "Christ, I bet you're going to correct me now. I was supposed to say, 'I didn't have *any* sour cream.' I guess I'm in the shit."

"I don't have no idea about that," I said.

She shook her head. "You can't do it. You never could sound like us, even when you tried. How's college going?"

She couldn't help herself. Her grin broke open. Revealing the gap in her teeth again. She touched her mouth. "I look like I been in a fight down at the Legion, ain't?"

"It suits you. You were always too perfect."

"Go on with you. How many of these you want?"

"How many you got?"

She was right. I loved pierogies. I ate five. Angela nibbled at one while chain-smoking cigarettes.

"You have to eat more than that," I said.

The remark was too intimate. She shriveled.

"I'm trying. I got some problems."

"You're okay, though?"

She made a muscle under her red cotton sleeve. There was nothing to see. "Yeah, I'm Superwoman."

I got up to refill my water glass from the tap.

Angela twisted, wrenchingly hard, in her chair. "Oh, Jesus, I forgot to offer you a beer." She looked down. "I forget things."

"I didn't want a beer. I would've asked."

"All we got's Yuengling, anyway. Chinese beer. Matty ain't a big drinker."

"I'll pass. But could we sit somewhere else? I don't have enough padding for this chair."

She smirked. "You always had a bony ass. Come on in the living room, I'll clean this up later."

We sat. And talked. When she went to the bathroom, I checked my watch.

Plopping back down in an old plush chair, she lit another cigarette and said, "I did some stupid things, didn't I?"

"We all did stupid things."

"But I did the stupidest ones. I'd blame the drugs, but you wouldn't believe me. You know what a bitch I was. Better than anybody."

I didn't want to talk about Laura, to relive that. I wasn't sure what might come out of my mouth, my heart.

"Matty told me you two are getting married."

She curled up her mouth, the old Angela. "I guess I got to get the divorce through first. Father Kalashko hit the ceiling when I told him. He don't really mind me living with Matty so much, but he doesn't like me divorcing Frankie." She looked down past the loose fabric of her jeans to the ancient carpet. "It should've been me and Matty all along, you know. I screwed it up. I guess I never told you that."

"As long as it's straightened out now."

"Matty was always the only one." She looked up, alarmed. "I didn't mean that against you."

"We all make some detours. I was a detour."

"Yeah, well, the truth is you were a pretty nice detour. I never told you that, I didn't want it to go to your head. I was such a bitch. I guess that's our secret now. That I liked you a lot."

"I liked you."

"You still like me, right? As a friend, I mean? Forgive and forget?"

The phone rang. Angela got up, not without effort. "That's probably Matty. Making sure you didn't kill me yet."

But it didn't seem to be Matty. As soon as the caller had been identified, Angela muffled her voice. I couldn't make out a single distinct word, but it didn't sound like a happy call. The exchange dragged on. I looked at my watch again.

She put the receiver down hard but showed a wisp of her old jauntiness as she came back into the room. She always found adversity simpler than happiness.

"Fucking Frankie," she said, tearing open a fresh pack of cigarettes.

"That about the divorce?"

"Oh, he don't give two shits about that. He got what he wanted. He wants to talk to Matty now. He says it's urgent. I wish the hell he'd leave us alone for once. I just need him to sign the goddamn papers and get lost. You want some coffee?"

"No. Thanks."

"Me neither. I was just offering." She sat back, calming down. Cigarette smoke gauzed the air between us. "We had some times, though. Didn't we?"

"Plenty more good times to come."

She whisked the future away. As if shooing a housefly. "For you there will be. I could always tell. You're the kind of person things always work out for. In the end. But look at me, look at what a mess I made of things. Frankie always said I could fuck up a wet dream."

She played back a scene or two in her head, then repeated, "We had some really good times, though. Ain't?" Her expression grew wistful, old. "Sometimes I thought it was all going to turn out different, can you believe that? That everything was going to work out. But I knew all along that Frankie would screw it up. I told you that. Remember?"

"I remember. You were right."

"I only married him because I wanted to hurt them both. I always knew that Frankie was a shit."

"Do you remember when you sat down by me last year, at the party at Joey's old place? You were a little stoned and you wanted to tell me about Matty. I can still remember exactly what you wore."

"I'm just glad I had something on. I was already nuts."

"You were the belle of the ball."

She snorted. "Yeah, that was me. Miss America."

We sounded like two geezers reminiscing from wheelchair to wheelchair in a nursing home. I had just turned twenty.

Matty was a little late. I blamed it on the rain, but I was wrong. He had stopped in Frackville to bring home a pizza for dinner.

I was ready to leave. I wished them well, but I wasn't up to any more north-of-the-mountain domesticity. And I didn't feel like eating pizza on top of pierogies.

Frankie saved me. You could say.

Before Matty could put down the pizza, Angela told him, "Frankie called. He was all screwed up, he's got some big problem. He says only you can help him." Her mouth tightened. "I told him you don't owe him nothing."

"I do, though," Matty said. "And we need him to sign the papers."

"You don't need to do anything for Frankie. For Christ's sake. I just told you he called so you don't think I'm keeping secrets."

"What did he say?"

"Not much. Just that it's urgent. I thought he was going to start bawling. He wants you to go over the house."

I spoke up. "If we left now, you could stop by on the way to Pottsville. Frankie's got a bunch of my albums I want to get back, anyway. It'd help me out." I looked at Angela. "I need to get home. College stuff."

I no longer concerned her.

"Don't you let Frankie talk you into nothing," she told Matty. "You promise me that."

"I can handle Frankie."

"Well, it took you a while the last time. Didn't it? And he's such a sneak."

She gave me a hide-the-missing-tooth smile, but it was perfunctory.

"Come back again, okay? Next time, I'll make sure I got sour cream and I'll boil the pierogies."

A wraith in human clothing, she gave me a quick hug but withheld her fallen-angel kiss. Matty and I trotted through the rain to the car.

He was silent at first.

"Angela's seems pretty good," I said. I was a dishonest man.

"It takes time," he told me. "I appreciate you coming up to see her. It was important to her." His voice was hollow, though. I assumed he was thinking about Frankie.

We turned up the highway cut toward Frackville's rear end. Matty slowed the car but kept on driving.

"I need to tell you something," he said. "And I want you to listen to me."

"What?"

"I don't care if you never want to talk to me again. But you need to listen now."

"I'm listening."

"You're not good enough, Will. You don't have it. You'll never be good enough." He took a breath that was audible over the engine noise and the rain on the roof and windshield. "You're not a musician. You're good enough to fool some people, the ones who don't know. But you'll never be happy, if you keep doing this. Because *you'd* know. It's a gift, and you don't have it. You could practice for a hundred years and it wouldn't help."

"Thanks, man."

"I'm sorry. But it's the truth. It would've been wrong not to tell you." He nodded to the steering wheel, not to me. "I'll tell you something. From the first time I saw you, you reminded me of this lieutenant we had. The good one, the one who got shot. I never knew anybody who tried so hard. All the time, he just wouldn't quit. Everybody else would give up, but he wouldn't. And it didn't make any difference in the end, because he couldn't make things be the way he wanted them to be, no matter how hard he tried."

"But you said he was a good lieutenant."

"I'm bad at explaining things. I guess that was a dumb example. Just think about what I said. You had your fun, Will. It won't get any better than it was. Don't waste any more of your life. Think about it. All right?"

"Yeah. I'll think about it, man." I wanted to weep. But not in front of Matty.

"I mean, you can write songs okay," he went on. "But that's not what you really want. You want to play, to be part of the music. And you'd never be good enough to be happy."

"You already said that."

"I'll shut up. I'm sorry."

I think he really was sorry. I believe that if he could have cut out his gift, or part of it, he would have passed it to me in that car.

At the red light, we turned toward Frankie's place, the house he had shared with Angela. I felt that I had nothing left in the world.

Frankie seemed startled to see me.

"So what's going on?" Matty asked.

Frankie hushed him. "There's a girl here, she's in the can. She doesn't need to hear none of this." He looked at me. "Him, either. It's personal."

I had never seen him so jumpy. Like he had the meth itch.

"I don't give a shit about your problems," I told him. "I just came to get my albums back."

A kid with carrot-colored hair emerged from the powder room down the hall.

"Mary Anne, go get your stuff together," Frankie said. "You're leaving."

The girl turned around again. As if she couldn't care less.

"The records are all in boxes," Frankie told me. "In there. Take whatever you want."

"I just want my own stuff. And the demo tape. You didn't pay for it. I want it."

"Send the bill to Danny. He accidentally erased it."

In that moment, I think I truly could have murdered him. Perhaps I should have. As for the tape, it had been the last memento of all we had done together, of how close we had come.

I went into the front room. The last time I had been in the house, a toppled Christmas tree had covered the floor.

Frankie kept his voice down. But I had good ears. And a grown man's voice gets louder when he cries like a scared kid.

"You got to help me," he begged Matty. "There's no one else can help me. They're going to fucking kill me, man. I mean, for real."

"Who?"

"Those bikers, man. Joyce's old man and his pals. They split from the Warlocks, they're running their own scene. I been fronting for them. There was some trouble, some mistakes."

"You owe them money?"

"No, man. I mean, not much. They just got the wrong idea about some stuff. They want all their shit back. I mean, I got it, it's all in a suitcase. With as much money as I can give them right now. They told me we'll be cool if I hand it back. But I don't believe them. Even if they don't kill me, they'll beat the shit out of me. And I just had my teeth done."

"So what am I supposed to do?" Matty asked. His voice was emotionless, noncommittal.

"They're here. I mean, down in Schuylkill Haven. In the Country Squire Motel, the one by the campus. They got a room. Number eleven. I'm supposed to take the suitcase down and give it back. But I'm afraid, man."

"And you want me to take it down?"

"Yeah. Please. They won't fuck with you, man. It's me they're after. Once they have the shit and the money, they'll leave me alone. I'm getting out of here, anyway. Please. Just take it down and hand it to them, that's all you'd have to do. You don't have to go in the room or nothing. *Please*, Matty. You're the only person I can count on, the only one I can turn to."

I walked in on them. "Don't do it," I said. "Fuck him. He's full of shit."

"Just stay out of this," Matty told me.

"Yeah, you stay the fuck out of this," Frankie said.

"Just don't do it," I said. I turned back to the boxes of albums. The LPs had been packed for storage, with mine intermingled.

After a stretch of silence bothered only by the sounds from the girl in back, Frankie said, "You took my wife. Just help me this one time and we'll be even. They won't mess with you, they know better."

"All right," Matty told him.

"Just drop her off in Haven, on the way to the motel," Frankie said. "Dump her at the corner of Dock and Sixty-one, that's close enough. She's a little bitch."

"How old is she, twelve?" I asked.

Frankie lunged for me. Matty caught him.

"Go out and get in the car," Matty ordered. He shifted his attention to the girl. "You get in the car, too."

"It's raining," she said. "I'll get wet."

"Then stay here, if you want to," Matty told her.

She really did look like a kid, like somebody Buzzy Ritter would've plucked from a street corner in the old days.

"Here, wear my jacket," I told her.

"Prince Fucking Valiant," Frankie said.

The girl and I ran through the rain. The car was unlocked. I put her in the backseat and got in up front, clutching my stack of albums.

"I don't remember seeing you around," I told her.

"I didn't see you, neither. What do you care?"

She just didn't strike me as a Schuylkill Haven girl. She didn't have that touch of a Dutchie accent the working-class kids had. And I didn't think her father was a doctor.

"You lived in Haven long?"

"Long enough."

"Where? Which street?"

"I ain't telling you. You're probably just another creep. Like that old guy, that Frankie."

"He hurt you or anything?"

"I wouldn't even let a creep like that touch me."

I couldn't figure out their relationship, how or why she'd ended up at Frankie's house. She seemed too young to be into drugs. But you never knew anymore.

"How old are you?"

"Old enough," she said. "Are we going to get going soon? He didn't even have stuff to eat in the house and I'm hungry."

Just then, Matty came down from Frankie's porch. Carrying a green vinyl suitcase. He glanced around, just once, then jogged to the car and stowed the bag in the trunk.

When he got in behind the steering wheel, I said, "This stinks."

"Frankie's been getting himself into trouble since we were kids." He shook his head. "I don't like it, either. But I need him to sign the papers for Angela."

He started the car.

"I'll go with you," I told him. "To the motel."

"No. You'd just be one more thing I had to worry about. But thanks, anyway."

"Can we go now?" the girl asked from the backseat.

Matty gave me a brief look of utter disgust with the world. He put the Buick in gear.

It was all rotten from the start. As we passed the new exit ramp they were finishing off 81, a state police cruiser pulled out and tailed us. No sooner were we trapped down in the chute of the Frackville grade than the cop turned on his bubble-gum machine.

"Sonofa*bitch*," Matty said. It was the first time I had ever heard him curse. "Sonofabitch, sonofa*bitch*."

Down the grade, a second cop car pulled out to block both lanes.

Matty didn't do anything rash. He slowed and edged the right wheels off the road, nuzzling up toward the cruiser in front of us.

For a second or two, I thought he might hit the gas and swing around the Statie's back end. But he stopped the Buick and turned off the ignition.

"Sonofabitch," he said. One last time.

His uncle wasn't screwing around this time. He came up behind us with his gun drawn. A younger cop got out of the other car, the one blocking the road. He wore a plastic cover over his Smokey the Bear hat, but Matty's uncle John strode up bareheaded.

Emulating Uncle John, the young cop drew his own revolver. Keeping his distance, unsure.

"Get out of the car," Uncle John yelled. "Everybody. Now."

We got out of the car. He was surprised to see me.

"You," he told me. I noted that his nose had acquired more character. "Get around front there and put your hands flat on the hood."

I did as I was told. The rain hammered the metal, the roadway, the new leaves on the trees. I wished I hadn't given the girl my jacket.

"You piece of shit," he said to Matty. "Open up the trunk."

Matty tossed the keys toward his uncle's feet. "You open it. You already know what's in it."

"Don't be a smart-ass. That ain't going to help you now."

Keeping his distance, with his revolver's muzzle locked on Matty, he squatted to pick up the keys.

"Don't take your eyes off him," Uncle John told the young cop. "He thinks he's Cassius Clay, or Muhammad Ali, or whatever that nigger calls himself nowadays."

He opened the trunk. Theatrically. Then he whistled. It pierced the sound of the rain.

"Officer Messner," he called to the rookie, "you're in for an education. We got a major drug haul here. And money, too. I'd say somebody's going to prison for a very long time."

He shut the trunk and came around to where the girl stood, a half-dozen feet from Matty. She was drenched and crying.

"I'll bet you're not part of all this. Are you, young lady?"

She shook her head.

"Where are you from, sweetheart? Would you tell me that?"

"Elmira, New York."

"That's a long way from here. Isn't it? You're a long way from home. In fact, that's all the way across a state line. How old are you, miss?"

"Fifteen."

"And who brought you all the way down here from Elmira, New York?"

She hesitated, but only for a moment. Then she pointed to Matty. "Him. That guy. He did it during the night. He said it was so nobody would know."

"Why don't you get back in the car now, honey? You're getting soaked. We wouldn't want you getting sick."

Uncle John turned to Matty. His smile could not have been grander. "So . . . we have a large quantity of what are obviously illegal narcotic substances. And large bills—I wonder if they're marked? Plus a fifteen-year-old girl carried across state lines for immoral purposes. I bet she's going to swear you gave her drugs, too." He inched closer. "Do you have any idea how many years they're going to put you away for? Do you have any idea how long you're going to be locked up, you worthless punk?"

Uncle John sneezed. And Matty broke his neck.

It happened in a blur. Faster than a raindrop could dissolve. The big cop didn't have time to squeeze off a single round. Roaring like a maddened bull—or a Minotaur—Matty reached out and snapped his uncle's neck. It sounded like ice cracking.

Sergeant John Tomczik fell onto his back, eyes open to the rain. When he grasped what had just gone down in front of him, the young cop fired.

He shot Matty three times. Matty never moved toward him or made any effort to evade what was coming his way. He stood there, hands at his sides, as the cop shot him in the chest and in the arm, then, as Matty fell, at the base of the neck.

Matty's outstretched arm crossed his uncle's ankle.

The girl screamed from the inside of the car. Shattered glass had cut her.

The rookie officer pointed his weapon at me.

"Don't shoot!" I said. "Please." Slowly, I raised my hands from the hood. "I'm unarmed. Don't shoot."

The window of danger passed. The cop looked away from me. To stare at what he had done. The hand holding his gun dropped to his side. His expression lost its courage, then its coherence.

"Can I check on him? To see if he's still alive? Please?"

"Oh, my God," the cop said.

The girl in the backseat kept shrieking.

I walked around the car, slowly, keeping my hands in the air and my eyes on the cop. He didn't raise his gun again. He barely moved.

I knelt beside Matty. It was all so undramatic, so nothing. There were no last words, no messages to Angela or his mother. He was dead in the right lane of the Frackville grade, with the rain already washing his blood away.

"Oh, my God," the young cop repeated.

TWENTY-FIVE

The morning of the funeral, my mother's lawyer showed up at my door before business hours.

He didn't bother with greetings, just said, "May I come in? We need to have a conversation that isn't suitable for the office."

I let him in. He looked around. As if amazed that the opium den wasn't littered with naked bodies and crawling with rats. I had never liked him, not even when he was a friend of my father's. My mother's manners had ruined me, though, and I offered him a cup of coffee.

He declined. "May I sit down?"

"Sure. Sit down." I sat down, too.

"I want you to understand that our conversation is strictly confidential. I don't intend to mention most of this to your mother, or to anyone else. Just so you understand."

"All right."

Not an especially handsome man, he had something about him—perhaps his success—that had made him attractive to women. He had a reputation at the country club.

He cleared his throat.

"Will, the police are willing to forgo any charges against you. There won't be any record of your presence at the scene of the incident."

"What charges? Jesus Christ. A state cop set up an innocent man. Then another cop shot an unarmed man. What kind of goddamned bullshit—"

"Calm down. We need to discuss this as two adults."

"Mr. Levenger . . . my friend's dead. *Dead.* He was murdered. For all intents and purposes."

"That's not how the authorities see it."

"Which authorities? Which ones exactly? The cover-up-our-asses state police? Anybody else?"

"Will, I don't think you understand the potential gravity of the charges that could be lodged against you."

"Like what?"

"Abetting trafficking in narcotics. Abetting the corruption of a minor. Accomplice to murder. And the murder of a law enforcement officer, at that."

"That's bullshit." I was up on my feet. Ready to smash things. Or break into tears. "That's complete *bullshit*. And everybody knows it. Let them charge me. Just let them. Let them put me on a witness stand."

He waited me out, then asked, "Are you finished? Can we discuss this now?"

I dropped into my chair. My eyes had grown wet. I fought it.

"Will, what's done is done. Complicating your own life isn't going to bring your friend back. Serious errors were made, I grant you that." He looked around furtively, a worried member of the underground in an old war movie. "In fact, there's been an appalling miscarriage of justice. That hasn't gone unrecognized."

"Don't *you* believe in justice? Don't any of you?"

"That's why I'm here, Will. Because I want to see justice done. To the extent still feasible. And partly because of my respect for your mother, of course. I don't want to see an injustice done to you."

"I'd win in a court of law."

"Will, you don't know that. This isn't Perry Mason."

"What is it, then?"

He looked around again. As though the Gestapo might peer in through a window.

"It's Schuylkill County, Will. Forget it."

"It isn't right."

"No. It isn't. I grant you that. But you couldn't win. No matter what happened. You can't win. Let it go."

I put on my most cynical face. But I hadn't lived long enough to make it convincing.

"Are they willing to give me back my driver's license?"

"No."

I looked past him at the gleaming day beyond an unwashed window. Levenger was good at his job. He knew when to wait. And he waited.

When I was sick enough of myself, I wiped my face and said, "This sucks."

"Yes," he said. "It sucks. I take it that means you agree to the proposition I just explained?"

I nodded. He got up to leave.

With his hand on the doorknob, he brightened. "I almost forgot. We have some good news. There's a buyer for your mother's house."

I suppose you don't care what the weather is like on the day they bury your ass. But *I* was glad of the sunlight and warmth, of the green glory days of rain had coaxed out of the landscape. The radiance of the world beyond the Catholic cemetery seemed like a belated gesture of decency toward Matty. On behalf of whatever power screws with our lives.

About fifty people showed up. Family. High school friends. Fellow musicians who stayed to the rear of the crowd. Joey and Pete. Stosh and Red. Me.

Angela wasn't there.

And Frankie didn't show, of course. His parting gift to me had been to start a rumor that I was the one who set up Matty. I don't think many people, if any, believed it. But they hedged their bets and kept their distance.

Matty's old man refused to have an honor guard from the American Legion. He showed up drunk and crying. Matty's mother proved surprisingly tough.

There wasn't much to say, beyond the official words. I recall the plastic flowers on nearby graves and the breeze flirting with the priest's cassock. I walked a few yards behind Red and Stosh as we headed back to our cars. They supported each other, arm in arm.

Angela had disappeared forever. There was an early rumor that she was living with a spade who dealt heroin down in Reading, that he was working her. But I knew what rumors were worth. After that, she was gone from the face of the earth.

As the years went by, I passed through Pottsville now and then. I heard that Frankie was dealing blackjack in Las Vegas. On my next visit, a decade later, I learned that he had come home to take over the printing business after his father died. He had married his youngest sister's best friend and they had a couple of kids.

Stosh and Red escaped for good. I ran into Stosh in 1997. Caught in the usual flight delays at O'Hare, we recognized each other immediately. He had made a decent life for himself as a session drummer in L.A. before getting into real estate. He was headed to France on vacation with his partner, Brian, a dainty young version of Matty. Brian was a digital animation artist at Disney. Stosh was enormously proud of him. The three of us had a couple of rounds in the bar.

Stosh told me that Red was doing great, after recovering from breast cancer. She was the director of a women's arts project in Santa Barbara. He suggested I look her up the next time I was out on the coast. He told me she still talked about an old girlfriend of mine.

I never learned what became of Laura Saunders, but my mother lived happily ever after. In Connecticut.

. . .

But that's getting ahead of the story.

With my stereo packed up, I was listening to pop junk on a transistor radio as I loaded my last possessions into boxes. My Pottsville life was about to go into storage, joining a few crates of my father's things. The June weather was unusually hot, and the window fan merely pushed the air around. Sweat had glued my tank top to my skin. I was tired.

Male footsteps climbed the outside stairs. My final visitor, whoever that might be.

It was Joey.

"Hey, man," he called through the screen door, "I thought you were already gone."

"Then why'd you come?"

"I thought maybe you weren't gone yet."

"Come on in. And don't worry. You missed the serious work."

The door clattered shut behind him. "When was Joey Schaeffer scared of work? Feel like smoking a little weed? For old times' sake?"

"No."

"Me, neither. I don't know what's the matter with me."

"Tell Pete I'm sorry I'll miss his wedding."

Joey sighed and dropped into one of my landlady's chairs. "I give her three hundred and sixty-five days before she weighs three hundred and sixty-five pounds. Pete's gaining weight himself, all in the gut."

"Pennsylvania Dutch cooking."

"Yeah. Shoofly pie. I never could stand it." He considered the stacked boxes, the separate odds and ends. "Want to sell your guitar?"

"I'll sell you the Rickenbacker. Two hundred."

"I meant the Les Paul."

"Not for sale."

"You taking it with you?"

"No. But it has sentimental value. If you want something to drink, there's beer in the fridge. And some orange Kool-Aid."

He got up again. "Christ, I *am* getting old. I think I'm going to go for the Kool-Aid."

"It's the heat. Fill mine back up, too."

We paused amid the ruins and drank our sugar water. "You ought to stick around," he told me. "Just for the summer. I got tickets for the thing at Woodstock. I'd rather go with you than with some chick. There'll be plenty of hippie ass to go around. They're expecting, like, ten thousand people."

"Already bought my plane ticket."

"*Quo vadis*, brother?"

I considered him. "Joey, why do you always have to play dumb with everybody but me? And with me, half the time?"

"Because it works."

"As far as 'wither,' I'll know when I get the passport stamp."

"The hero on his quest. Send me a postcard, okay?"

"I will." I sat on a box. "You know, you're the only person left I'm going to miss."

He grunted. "You won't miss me much."

"I didn't say 'much.' Just that I'd miss you. So what's next for Joseph P. Schaeffer?"

He let me see one of his intelligent smiles, the kind reserved for a very few initiates. "Funny you should put it that way, Mr. Cross. I'm selling the sound system. And the van. Got a couple of bands interested. Some kids from Schuylkill Haven want me to do sound for them, but they just don't have it. I've been spoiled. So I'm quitting while I'm ahead." He finished his Kool-Aid and made a face. "My dirty, filthy secret is that I'm thinking about going back to college. I've dicked around enough, I ought to get serious. I mean, how many parties can you throw before it stops being fun? I figure I'd rather stop while it's still fun. Except, to tell you the truth, it isn't fun now."

"It used to be the Party of the Century. Once a week."

"Yeah, well, my brother's getting out of prison. I thought I'd set a good example." He grinned. "You know where I'm coming from, man. I told you before: We're survivors, you and me. Like in that song of yours."

His grin evolved into mild and merry laughter. "Come back in twenty years, and you'll probably find Mr. Joseph P. Schaeffer behind a big desk down at the bank, just like my old man. With a potbelly and a three-piece suit."

"Why don't I have the least trouble imagining that?"

He grew pensive. "Sometimes I wish I hadn't been such an asshole while my parents were still alive. I mean, I was really the shits to them."

"Welcome to the club."

He smiled again. But it wasn't the same. "My father used to say regrets are for losers. Sentiment wasn't his bag."

"I guess you can take that to the bank."

He chuckled. "That's good. You always were a sharper customer than you let on yourself." Our eyes met. "You and me, two born cons. Everybody else thought it was for real, the poor bastards."

"It wasn't that cut-and-dried."

He lifted one shoulder in an economical shrug. "Maybe not." A siren sounded, then died away. "Guess I'd better get a move on. Before you put me to work. *Vaya con Dios*, brother." He stood and stretched. The fan buzzed. "It's been a hell of a year, though. When you think about it. We came so damned close. Before Frankie ruined it all."

"I don't want to talk about Frankie. Anyway, it's amazing we got as far as we did. As screwed up as it all was."

"It was incredible, though. For a while. You got to admit it. I mean, the music was really something. I was there, man, I heard it. It was *magic*. And what a crazy-ass bunch of people, you couldn't make them up."

"Don't romanticize it."

"Come off it, man. You had a blast." One of his Mad Joey ideas struck him, I could read it on his face. "You're good with words," he said. "You ought to write a book about the band and all."

I grimaced. "I just want to forget everything that happened and every one of those crazy sonsofbitches."

He laughed and said, "You won't."

AUTHOR'S NOTE

As she finished reading the manuscript of this novel, my wife asked, "Which sixties band did they sound like? Did you have a specific group in mind?"

The straightforward answer was that I heard the band as itself: The Innocents were the Innocents, playing songs I'd written many years before.

Yet as soon as I finished answering her, I realized that there was one band and album that did come very close to the sound of my imagined group. The first, brilliant, furious Moby Grape album, simply titled Moby Grape, is worth tracking down both for its still breathtaking quality—the wild, unleashed joy of a too-brief era in music—and as a good soundtrack for the tale of the Innocents and the women who enraptured them. Listen to "Omaha" or "Hey Grandma," to "Changes" or "Fall on You," inserting a few Jimi Hendrix guitar solos to give Matty his due, and you'll have the sound this novel sought to conjure.

Grotesquely mishandled by their record company, the members of Moby Grape never broke through to find the success they deserved. Nor did follow-up albums, with changing band rosters, regain the wonder of that first recording. Moby Grape was all about the original cast; together, its members were greater than they managed to be on their own or in other combinations (although each did fine, often fascinating work). Musically, they *belonged* together. Yet they could not endure as a human community. Perhaps that, too, sounds familiar.

—Robert Paston